I0817869

AMULETS OF POWER

Book I: A Brian Poole Mystery

Gunter Swoboda and Lorin Josephson

BONFIRE CINEMA
Film – TV - Publishing - Animation – Podcast - Theatre
Los Angeles, CA

FIRST EDITION - HARDCOVER

Published by Bonfire Cinema LLC
ISBN: 978-0-9992668-6-1

Cover & Layout Design by: Jemi Koo
Cover Design Supervisor: Sung Jae Yoon
Senior Editor: Diamond Perkins
Junior Editor: Molly Schinn
Copy Editor: Corey Lee

Bonfire C i n e m a
3705 W. Pico Blvd. Suite #35
www.BonfireCinema.com
PRINTED IN THE USA

ACKNOWLEDGEMENTS

We are immensely grateful to the exceptional team at Bonfire Publishing for their unwavering support and dedication: Miranda Spigener-Sapon, principal of the Bonfire team and our PR representative, has been crucial in promoting our work and vision through tireless advocacy and unmatched zeal—DeVonna Prinzi, whose editorial acumen and keen eye have refined this manuscript to its highest form. Our talented cover designer is Jemi Koo, who has skillfully brought this book's visual essence to life. Diamond Perkins, Molly Schinn, and Corey Lee, our meticulous editorial team, whose hard work and attention to detail have ensured the highest quality of this publication. Thank you all for your invaluable contributions. This book, a testament to your expertise and dedication, stands as a shining example of the quality we have achieved together.

Our family has been my cornerstone. Our children, whose growth into compassionate, empathetic beings fills us with pride, and our grandchildren who bring joy and wonder into our children, whose growth into compassionate, empathetic beings fills us with pride, and our grandchildren, who bring joy and wonder into our lives our life.

"Any sufficiently advanced technology is indistinguishable from magic." Arthur C. Clarke

PROLOGUE

"In the beginning, long before there was time, there was only the sea and the earth. Neither gods nor man walked upon it, nor were there other creatures to be found. Where the sea met the land, a mare stepped forth, as white as the windblown crests of the waves from which she was born. Her name was Eiocha.

On the land at the edge of the sea there grew a tree: a strong, sturdy oak. Being close to the spray of the ocean, drops of foam would kiss the branches of the oak, and small white berries would grow there. Needing nourishment, Eiocha ate the berries, which were transformed within her till she was heavy with child. When it was time, she gave birth to the god, Atho. The pains of her labour were so great that she tore the bark from the oak and hurled it into the sea, where it was transformed by the sea and became the giants of the deep."

☙ ☙

Bryn smiled as he recited the account of creation in his mind. He was a tall, muscular man, his powerful body well-honed by his constant training for battle. Dark hair, platted on the left and right, framed his handsome face. His arms, legs, and parts of his torso were painted blue with wode, summoning the magic to strengthen his powers, making him more courageous in battle. A thick gold torc embraced his heavily muscled neck, with two precious stones resting at the base of his throat.

He crouched casually in the comforting shadow of the enormous oak tree while his left shoulder rested against the rough bark. Amidst the steady rhythm of his breathing, he felt a quiet intimacy with the massive tree. Here he was, feeling, sensing the bond between him and that gigantic icon of the forest. Yet, he reflected sadly, that depth of intimacy eluded him even in the tenderest moments of making love.

Bryn relished the strength he took from his bond with the oak, which allowed him to be one with the earth, the forest, and all the living things within it. He could hear the whispers from the leaves that drifted gently on the breeze down to him. Words that came from Atho, the horned one, the green man, the man of powerful magic with whom he was allied. Words that would protect him. Words from which he sourced his virility and a life that would be long and blessed. And in his god's shade, he would be safe, hidden from others should he choose.

Yet Bryn yearned for more. A sudden pang of guilt gripped him. To want more than Atho offered was disloyal. Looking up, the massive orb of a silvery moon that dominated the sky filled him with a sense of foreboding. Why? *Could she know of his dissatisfaction?* He stopped. There was no point dwelling on this. It was not why he was here; he reminded himself. Looking out at the glittering meadow, he marveled at the silvery light emanating from the massive globe above. It illuminated the clearing like a carpet of diamonds. There was no need for his piercing blue eyes to strain through the dark of the night, as amidst all this light, Bryn could clearly see a small group of young women make their way across the grass to the edge of the forest. There, strolling amidst the lush meadow, was the real reason for his presence.

Sky-clad, the young woman was an exquisite sight in the semi-darkness of such a velvety night, Bryn mused dreamily as he watched the procession closing in on the far edge of the forest. She walked amidst others who were equally enchanting, but in truth, he had eyes only for the tall, willowy girl with bright copper-red hair walking at the rear of the group. He marvelled at the long, lithe legs that gave her an easy gait, making her appear to glide through the long grasses. As she passed through the rushes, it was as if they gently reached out to her to caress her thighs while her hands would occasionally playfully brush the tops of the sheaves.

"What can she offer you that I cannot, my brave Bryn?" The all too familiar, youthfully timbered voice that interrupted his vigil could not mask the ancient power that was as old as thought itself. A power to which Bryn knew he had become enslaved.

It wasn't a simple question, Bryn thought. He immediately looked up at Scáthach, his brow deeply furrowed by a frown. He took his time to answer her. "She is young, Scáthach, and one of my kind," he muttered eventually.

He was not interested in enlightening her any further, to tell her of the specialness he sensed in that red-haired girl. As futile as it might be, he wanted to keep his real interest in the young nymph private for as long as possible. His gaze returned to the group that was now disappearing silently into the dark shadows of the forest. When the last of the procession had finally disappeared, Bryn's eyes wandered back to the figure standing above him.

Exquisitely silhouetted by the moon, Scáthach was breathtakingly beautiful. She was right, Bryn acknowledged; what more could he truly want? Most men would give their life for one fleeting moment, one kiss, one simple caress from her. And they would think it a bargain.

Staring at her, Bryn reflected on the game they had been playing of late. From the moment it had begun it had grown in depth and vigour. This deliciously charged banter gave their sex an edge, a quality that had its own inherent danger.

When they ultimately did explode in their union, he would be left breathless and weak, while Scáthach would appear to thrive from their coupling, radiating light and heat in the afterglow of their passion.

"But you can be so much more," she declared emphatically and tilting her head invitingly to the side, "and I can give it to you, my Bryn."

Scáthach deliberately placed herself in front of Bryn, obscuring his view of the forest with her lithe body, teasing him with what she offered.

Naked, she too had parts of her body painted in the deep blue of the wode, with silver bands coiled up her arms and legs like shimmering snakes, all of which were inscribed with sacred symbols. Her shiny black hair hung loose. It cascaded down over her shoulders, a mass of long, tightly curled ringlets caressing her skin and dressing her breasts with more seductive sensuality than any garment could.

Scáthach knew that in as much as Bryn lusted for the willowy, red-haired beauty, the power she had over him was more secure than any chains that could be forged by even the most skilled master blacksmith.

Still crouched on his haunches, Bryn continued to gaze at the sinewy figure looming above him. Occasionally, a slight breeze would part her black tresses and allow a precocious dark nipple surrounded by blue to wink at him, tempting him.

The shadows hid other parts of her, but the length of her heavily oiled legs gleamed in the moonlight, beckoning him to slide his hand up the subtle curve of her exquisitely painted thigh. Following the mystic blue symbols of magic, his gaze traced the curve of her legs to their inevitable convergence. He could see that only half of her was painted with wode and that she had kept herself temptingly bare of both hair and intimate adornments.

Sensing his growing fervour, she parted her legs a little more, affording Bryn an even better view of herself.

"Come, Bryn," her lilting invitation spilled over him, evoking goosebumps that rippled across his skin, "be my lover tonight and tomorrow, I will teach you more of the arts of war."

He watched her hand slide down across her lower belly while her fingers pointed invitingly to the promised treasure. Mesmerised, Bryn breathed in the exquisite, unique scent of her musk and perfume that now drifted sensuously in the intimate space between his face and her crutch, heavy and intoxicating as any mead could be.

The combination of her shadowy, seductive figure, her tempting gestures and the rutting scent of her inflamed Bryn's senses banished any thoughts of the red-haired maid. His blood rushed eagerly to his groin. Scáthach reached out, and she instantly knew that she had struck the right chord.

A peal of laughter escaped Scáthach as her grip tightened around Bryn.

"So, my love, what more do you lust for? What can you find between my legs or the gifts of war that I can offer you?"

His answer was to reach around Scáthach's legs and draw her close enough to kiss the taunt hollow just below her navel. She responded with a long, drawn-out growl. Scáthach reached out and firmly gripped Bryn's head with both hands and pulled him even closer, the soft curls of his beard tantalising the even softer skin of her belly.

"Yes, Bryn, I know exactly what it is you want." Scáthach arched her back. She laughed and then sighed deeply as Bryn's tongue traced a path around her belly. A second later, she cried out, "Oh, you do that so well, my love!"

Bryn, on his knees and enslaved by his lust, had to admit that none of the other girls he had ever had tasted quite the way she did. The unusual mixture of her musk, the sweet perfume and the salty sweat left him without any doubt that there was no price that was too high to possess Scáthach.

Perhaps that was what made this game even more delicious. The fact that he knew that as much as he was enchanted by her, Scáthach found him equally desirable. He knew this because her body resonated to his touch like the finely tuned strings of a lyre expertly plucked by the bard.

He drew a part of her into his mouth, allowing her to gently sit between his lips whilst he gently flicked her with his tongue. She quivered and shook. Thunder rolled over them, followed by streaks of lightning, sending shudders down her length, heralding stronger storms of passion. As her moistness became wetness, she groaned, and as her wetness became a flood, her voice reached into the fabric of the universe in an ancient and unknown tongue, imploring all things eternal.

Bryn was about to pull her down beside him when she pushed him roughly down onto the grass. Catching her breath, she laughed out aloud whilst prancing to the edge of the meadow.

"Not so fast, my eager stallion. To possess me, you must swear to me that you will forsake all others." She turned and faced Bryn squarely. "Do so, and I will satisfy your every whim forever more!"

Bryn, knowing that she meant him to forsake more than other women, snarled in response to her challenge. "I can do naught else, for you had cast your spell upon me a long, long time ago. Am I not a mere mortal in the presence of a goddess whom I must obey?"

"Then mortal Bryn, I shall free you to choose." She called out to him, her promise ringing out across the meadow.

Scáthach ran further into the moonlit meadow, her raven hair flowing behind her like the clan's banner of war. In the middle of the meadow, her figure began to glow a little at first, then more intensely until she was violently lashed by leaping tongues of fire. She turned and waved her arms as she watched Bryn run towards her, the flames flashing, surging from her, reaching out towards him.

"Choose, Bryn!" Her voice rose to the rolling thunder of a sweltering summer storm. "Do so while my lust still floods the lips between my legs!"

Inflamed with desire and passion, Bryn called out across the meadow, his voice equally tempestuous. "I choose you, my Goddess Scáthach, and swear my loyalty to you for all eternity. Now, please release me from this pain of passion that burns in my groin like a furnace!"

With those words, that ominous oath, Bryn knew that he had forsaken the safety of the oak. Deafened by the rush of his desires, Bryn was unaware of the sudden silence that enveloped the meadow. No longer could he hear the whisper of the leaves or the horned man's words of magic. As Bryn reached the fiery figure of Scáthach, she reached out and enveloped him in her arms and legs, her furious ardour fuelled by his oath to her. For an instant, Bryn thought he was levitating high above the meadow when suddenly he felt their two bodies sink into the soft, damp grass and the earth beneath threatened to envelop them.

Scáthach flipped Bryn onto his back as easily as if he had been a rag doll, and in one swift motion, she straddled his hips the way she would have straddled her steed. Trying to catch his breath, he drew in more of her intoxicating musk. His head was swimming from his overloaded senses, but he surrendered to her rhythmic ride rather than stop.

An instant later, he could feel the firm grasp of her hands on his shoulders as the pace of her hunger increased, grinding him into the soft earth. As Scáthach applied more and more pressure, Bryn could feel a mixture of pain and a great surge of pleasure that relentlessly drove him to the point where he felt certain he would burst.

She released her grip, and the tingling mixture of pleasure and pain subsided, only to be replaced by the velvety wetness of her all too generous mouth and her nimble tongue teasing and tempting him to erupt.

Suddenly, like a searing bolt of lightning, his mind and body exploded. The thunderous climax snapped him into cataclysmic convulsions, rolling across him like raging surf, merging the two bodies into one.

1

As Keira reached across the chair in front of the window to re-adjust the curtains, she felt a surge of excitement wash over her. She was ready with everything in place, and it felt good. Looking around, she allowed herself to feel a sense of satisfaction with all that she saw. Her apartment might have been small, but it looked perfect with its bohemian ambience. She was particularly happy with how the colour scheme had worked with the black and red candles placed strategically around the living space and bedroom in readiness for tonight.

The furnishings, carefully chosen from some of London's best stores, had cost her a fortune, but the combination of the Victorian chairs and chaise lounge with the art deco mirrors and figurines was perfect. The whole effect, topped off by Tamara de Lempicka's *Portrait of Suzy Solidor,* was sensuous and erotic.

Smiling to herself as she moved through the rooms, Keira continued to prepare for what she hoped would be the next step towards her objective. Her current job paid well but not well enough to satisfy her desires. The trust fund was handy, but she wanted more. More money, more power and more prestige. After tonight, all that might change! No more sneaking out of the office like this afternoon. No more answering to that stupid bitch. Rhonwen was such a loser that she didn't even know that Keira always played hooky at work!

Just thinking about her boss stirred up Keira's rage. She had been playing the polite and civil colleague at the agency for two years. Still, it was becoming increasingly difficult to tolerate that saccharine-sweet smile and positive attitude. Rhonwen Tierney was just so nice, and Keira despised nice! And Brian! She would not accept that he was attracted to that pasty-faced redhead.

From the first moment she had laid eyes on him, Keira had been intensely attracted

to Brian Poole. Apart from the physical attraction, Keira had always made it her business to align herself with those in power. Still, Brian proved to be impervious to her attempts to seduce him. Puzzled, Keira had struggled to understand this. In her experience, few men could resist her dark, brooding beauty that oozed sex and sensuality.

Unaccustomed to rejection, she had carefully observed him whenever she got the opportunity. Tall, with a shock of straight black hair stylishly cut with a casual unruliness, she could sense the raw power in his body. His impeccable suits and shirts failed to hide the bulk of the well-toned muscles that rippled conspicuously underneath the fabric as he moved about.

What amazed Keira was the grace and agility that Brian displayed for a man of his stature. He could appear beside her without warning, like a shadow, startling her. This added to her attraction as Keira was never shy of relishing that visceral cocktail of danger and sex. She had heard stories in the office about him, tales about his past, which made him an even more appealing object of her desire and ambition.

And then there was Stewart! That was a complication. She still was ' sure why she had seduced him. It hadn'tt been a great plan to begin with. She had thought about getting information about Brian through Stewart but finding out they were really old friends had just killed it. Too late to backpedal, she had made sure Stewart had understood that their liaison was to remain a secret. Anyway, he was still in a position to be of advantage to her, and he had turned out to be quite diverting and definitely great in bed.

Brutally suppressing a strange little flicker of regret, Keira focused her mind on the tasks she still needed to complete. She had spent the afternoon preparing the essentials for a ritual that would, all going well, deliver to her what she wanted. Not only Brian but, as a bonus, Rhonwen's new job.

Keira had spent the past year dabbling in the occult, and this was to be her *coup de grace.* She smiled as she thought about how she would kill the old and bring about the new. She had found an antique book in her family's library that contained lore and rituals for magic, as well as lists of artefacts required to perform these arcane practices. Driven by her insatiable curiosity and lust for power, she"d studied it closely, becoming more and more invested in the idea that she could quite possibly control her fate with magic.

From the first instant of touching the ancient book just over a year ago, she had felt a strong attraction to it, wanting to keep it close to her. Over the following months, she had become convinced of the book's authenticity and its antiquity and had tried to subtly find out how it happened to be in her family's library. Her mother appeared to be ignorant about its origins as well as its contents. She had shown little interest in the subject and hadn't even noticed that Keira had taken it and hadn't mentioned it again.

Having fossicked around the net and the various libraries in London, Keira was sufficiently inspired by some very tantalising possibilities to visit a number of covens, determined to find someone to help her in her quest to learn and understand the practices described in the book. However, much to her irritation, she quickly discovered a lack of real knowledge or ambition in most groups. Content to meet and practice simple pathetic rituals and spells, most of these witches, as they called themselves, were just losers who couldn't get a date.

One coven, however, had struck her as very different. Led by a formidable and stunningly beautiful woman who called herself the High Priestess, they had met in an elegant house on one of the best streets in London. The woman had impressed Keira as someone who could be useful, but she had proved distant and watchful and had not invited Keira to meet any other members. Keira had been disappointed that the High Priestess disclosed little about herself or her coven.

At the end of the interview, and that was what Keira had decided that it was, she had the distinct impression that the priestess had virtually tried to dissuade her from joining. Intrigued and a little pissed off, Keira had decided she would do more research on her own, and when she went back, she would prove she was not someone to be dismissed. And tonight, on the full moon, she would cast a spell that would catapult her and her career into new realms of possibilities and, with a little luck, deliver Brian literally into her lap.

Smiling happily, she moved about the room, naked underneath a very sheer black silk robe that fell in softly swirling folds from the delicate jet fastening at her throat. The spell was heavily imbued with sexuality, so she had spent many hours over the last couple of evenings at the beauty salon preparing for tonight. The sensuousness of her skin, now hairless and softened, allowed her to revel in the silky texture of the fabric that brushed ever so lightly against her.

From time to time, and in rhythm to the music of a pagan heavy metal band, she would let a hand run across her small breasts and then wander across her stomach, feeling the tautness of her belly and imagining what it would be like if it was Brian's hands moving slowly and sensuously over her body. The combination of her preparations and her thoughts of Brian had an effect on her, and she felt an urgency in her desire that she would use later to make the spell work. The book had been very clear that she had to preserve the power of her climax for the right moment if she was going to reap the benefits of the incantation.

Initially surprised by the explicitness of the sexual references in a book so old, she had no problem embracing the ideas they presented to her. In fact, it made the whole thing even more appealing to her. No dead frogs or nasty pots of boiling goo. This was definitely more her style. Looking around the room, she had rearranged to accommodate an altar draped in black velvet. Standing in the middle of a black cloth with a white pentagram embroidered on it, she realised she was almost ready. The next step was to light the big black candles on either side of the ritual objects on the top of the altar.

Keira put two fingers to her lips, kissed them and then ran them across the length of both candles. She repeated this gesture of intimacy with each of her ritual objects on the altar. In the centre of the altar, a large crystal ball rested securely in the coils of a pewter dragon. Next to it lay her grimoire open at a specific page; the black and red writing on the yellow parchment, prominent even in the dim light, appeared to glow of its own accord.

An unsheathed jewel-encrusted athame, a ritual dagger, lay across the right-hand side of the table. Beside it were two large pieces of amethyst glittering in the candlelight while a thick column of frankincense clawed its way from the black pot to the ceiling, filling the apartment with the strong air reminiscent of an old church.

She ran her hand caressingly along the exposed blade and, picking it up, casually walked into the bathroom. The tiled room was faux Victorian, but the plumbing technology was all twenty-first century. She carefully placed candles and oil burners around the space, creating shimmering shadows and thickening the air. Several crystal bottles filled with aromatic oils stood beside a small ceramic bowl, and a glass of absinthe stood beside that. A small amount of steam rose gently from the hot bath she had infused with salts, herbs and oils.

Keira lifted the athame and drew a water pentagram over the bath, then, placing the ritual dagger back on the vanity, she undid the small clasp holding her robe together. It slid across her skin to the floor, and she stepped into the bath, easing herself into the warm water that embraced her body. The heady mixture of sexual tension and relaxing warmth heightened her senses further, and she drew a deep breath, enveloped by her desire.

As instructed by the grimoire, she began to focus, visualising the purpose of her coming ritual while trying to sense that she was truly prepared. When she felt ready, Keira pulled the plug, but following exactly the instructions in the Grimoire, she stayed in the bath until all the water had gone, and the bath was completely empty.

As the water swirled into the drain, she continued visualising what she wanted her spell to manifest, willing the energies that could block her incantations to drain away in the water now heading into the Earth.

Rising from the bath, she dried herself with a towel that had never been used before and had been blessed by her, using a spell from the book. Then, she began to carefully anoint each part of her body with sacred oils, reciting the incantation she had rote learnt from the book.

"Hear me, Scáthach! Blessed be my mind, that learns of your ways; blessed be my eyes, that have seen this day. Blessed be my lips that utter your name and keep your secrets. Blessed are my breasts, formed in beauty. Blessed be my knees, that shall kneel at thy Sacred Altar. Blessed be my feet that have brought me in these ways. Blessed be my womanhood and the power of my sex."

Turning towards the marble-topped vanity, she poured a generous libation to the goddess into a beautiful ceramic bowl filled with water, then picked up the glass of absinth and downed it in one go.

Keira loved the warm feeling of the faintly green liquid as it made its way down her throat. The subtle heat from the alcohol spread through her body, adding to the feeling of ease that she had from the luxurious bath with its herbs and oils. Picking up her robe, she headed for the circle in the living room, where she knelt down in front of the altar. She reached for a black bottle that stood at its base.

Pouring oil infused with potent aromatics into the palm of her hand, she slowly began to spread the liquid over her body. Beginning with her arms while swaying rhythmically on her haunches, she continued until the whole of her body shimmered with the reflections of the flames of the candles. Massaging her muscles more and more deeply, her hands found their way expertly across the slippery surface of her impeccably smooth skin. All the while, the rhythm of the music encouraged her hands to keep pace.

With each passing second, Keira's desire became almost too much to bear. As she allowed her hands to move closer and closer to the heat between her legs, her nipples stood hard and erect, reinforced by the little gold rings against which her fingers would occasionally flick. She could feel them trying to pucker more, but there was only so much tension they could attain.

Soon, she would be able to release the tension and feel the release she had longed for. As the music filled her with an even deeper yearning, she began the final aspect of the ritual, moaning with pleasure as she moved closer and closer to a climactic peak. Suddenly, she felt that familiar pitch that told her that her moment was close to hand.

Keira opened her mouth, and her voice boomed into the room with power clearly not hers. "Oh, Great Goddess Scáthach, Goddess of Magic, hear me! I beseech you to descend into me, Keira, your loyal vessel and follower. Bless me and my Rite with all your power."

Keira had barely finished the last words of the invocation when her body exploded with the rapid convulsions and tremors of her orgasm, the waves of which kept coming and coming, seemingly never to end. Although she was by most standards somewhat of a sexual athlete with more than the usual appetite, she was caught completely off guard by the intensity of this experience.

As her body continued to tremble and shudder in the throws of orgasmic peaks and troughs, she collapsed backwards, unable to support her weight. Wave after wave continued to wash through her body, reaching deep into the very core of her being.

Finally, in what seemed to be a never-ending paroxysm of breathless delight, Keira sensed the ebbing phase of her orgasm. She struggled to focus on regulating her breathing, which laboured in and out of her lungs, trying to draw in much-needed air. To breathe was her first intentional thought since beginning the invocation.

Slowly, Keira regained her strength. When she first tried to stand up, her legs refused to support her, and the best she could muster was to rest on her knees. Then, gradually, she noticed a surging power from deep within her that vibrated with a harmonic shiver that left her mind and body tingling.

Sitting naked and drenched in sweat on the cloth within the Circle, Keira slowly became aware that her senses were suddenly more acute than before. Not only could she hear the small drops of rain pounding on the window pane that had been imperceptible to her earlier, but now she could tune into sounds by sheer will, picking and choosing what she wanted to hear.

Her sense of smell was now so finely tuned that the deep, pungent aromatics in the room were almost too much for her to bear. Suddenly her own musky scent rose up from between her damp legs, threatening to overpower her, attempting to lure her to another bout of organismic delight.

This dramatic, unforeseen change had Keira burst out laughing, a laugh that was usually the result of some intoxicating drug. The rush of power excited and puzzled her, and that ultimately could prove more intoxicating than any drug she had ever tried. But her own senses and what she had just experienced forced her to sit there and assess herself.

"Had the ritual and spell really worked?" she wondered. "Or could this be just some sort of flashback to an evening of pills?" Yet she immediately knew that this experience was different.

She reached up and carefully ran her fingers through her hair. Each and every follicle felt alive and tingled with a raw spark. Once more, she tried to slowly get to her feet, feeling constant surges of energy running through her muscles. Walking to the bathroom, she felt her legs like lithe springs tempting her to leap the distance.

Once in the semi-dark of the bathroom, she felt her eyes instantly adjust, allowing her to make out things with unusual clarity. She had seen documentaries on night vision goggles, but this was much better. *"I must take a look at myself."* She flicked the lights on and immediately had to dim them as the sudden luminous flare was almost painful. As Keira's eyes adjusted, she looked into the mirror, but the image that reflected back to her resembled her only up to a point. Her bare, tanned skin had darkened a few more shades, and her hair, normally dark with soft waves, was now thick and curled.

She stepped back, shocked, then leaning forward into the mirror, took a closer look. Her face was slightly more angular than before, and her shoulders now appeared to be broader. Her breasts, straining against her skin, stood proudly out from her chest while her nipples were surrounded by dark areola. As Keira let her eyes wander down her body, she marvelled at the subtle but definite physical changes she appeared to have undergone during the ritual. She now felt a mixture of curiosity and fear. "*Shit, what did I do?"* she wondered.

Trembling, Keira stepped back. The figure reflected back in the mirror was indisputably her, but with a primitive, earthy edge that visibly radiated an unearthly power. In that instant, her own reflection frightened Keira, and if there was one thing she was not, it was easily frightened.

2

Satisfied that she was in no imminent danger of being annihilated by the chaotic stream of cars ploughing their way through the torrential rain, Rhonwen launched herself bravely from the precarious exposure of the bus stop towards the beckoning safety of her apartment building. Nimbly avoiding the cascades of water flung to the side as tyres slid over the flooded bitumen, she swiftly navigated across the wide road. Although she was able to avoid colliding with any of the many cars blocking her path, she could do nothing to avoid getting soaked by the relentless pounding rain.

Barely squeezing between two parked cars, it took Rhonwen only a couple of long strides to reach the first of five steps leading to the heavy wooden entrance door tucked into a recess in the front of the old Victorian building. Squeezing into the tight space between the wall and the door, she gained a little shelter while she impatiently flipped back the brown leather cover of her mannish bag and fumbled for her keys.

"Bugger!"

Irritated that her keys didn't just automatically slip into her hand, she forcefully wiped her face with the back of her sleeve and peered back into the dark abyss of the satchel. One more time, she thrust her hand into the bag, pushing her wallet, coins, a hairbrush, and all the odds and ends she had accumulated aside. With a sudden metallic click, her fingers wrapped around a bundle of keys that she quickly pulled from the bag.

"Finally!" She sniffed, quickly separating a large old-fashioned key from the rest; she inserted it into the lock. She pushed the heavy door open, letting herself into the building's foyer and almost collided with her neighbour Lydia.

"Hello, Rhonwen, you look drenched!".

"I feel like I swam home. Isn't the weather awful?"

"Absolutely! But I won't hold you up chatting. You're dripping everywhere."

Rhonwen looked down at the growing puddle at her feet. "Oops! So sorry! I'll see you later then."

Smiling kindly, the older woman started to turn towards the half-open door of her apartment, then quickly looked over her shoulder. "By the way, good luck tomorrow. I do not doubt that you deserve this promotion. You just remember to believe in yourself. I certainly do!

"Oh, thank you, Lydia". Rhonwen flashed her a grateful smile and then headed up the stairs.

By the time Rhonwen had reached the front door to her apartment, she had left a wet trail along the stairs and the corridor. A pang of guilt made her wonder if she should get a mop and return and erase the telltale puddles. But she quickly banished the thought as she unlocked the door to her apartment. It would dry, and she was tired.

She barely had time to close the door when Sooty, her cat, rushed and crowded around her legs, purring loudly for attention.

"Hello, gorgeous."

Ignoring her soaked clothing, she dropped her handbag on the floor and quickly bent down to pick up the cat and give him an affectionate squeeze. Making her way up the hall to the bathroom, she kept rubbing her face into his lush fur, and she felt herself relax.

"Come on, let me get changed, little one." Rhonwen quickly slipped out of her wet raincoat and hung it on a hanger in the adjoining small laundry space. Kicking off her shoes, she started peeling off the wet outer layers of what had been a very crisp and elegant business suit when she had dressed that morning. Having hung her jacket and skirt up to dry, she wandered across the hall to her bedroom with a persistent Sooty meowing loudly as he tried to wind around her legs.

Stretching her shoulders to release the day's tensions, she went over to the window to close the blinds and then rummaged through the clothes on the chair for her comfy tracksuit. Deciding to take a bath, she threw it on the bed. Looking down fondly at Sooty, she smiled and informed him of her plans. "I'll just soak away the day for a while before dinner."

Undoing the small pearl buttons on the wet, white shirt, she walked back to the bathroom and, having carefully hung it up on the hook to dry, she sat on the edge of the bath and reached down to turn the taps on. Standing up, she grabbed a towel and quickly and vigorously towel-dried her long mane of fiery red hair. Looking up, she flicked it off her face and turned towards the wide mirror above the vanity.

Unhooking her bra with her right hand, she released a pair of voluptuous, white-marbled breasts that were crowned by a set of puffy, pale pink nipples. As the bra dropped to the tiled floor of the bathroom, she slipped out her cotton briefs and, straightening up, she scrutinised herself closely in the mirror.

Her face, even featured with a small pert freckled nose and full dark pink lips, was devoid of any make-up. Rhonwen had never become comfortable with the idea of using makeup. She had tried it once when she was a teenager. Her best friend Sarah had persuaded her that it was no big deal, only to be told by her mother that if she intended to look like a hussy, she should find somewhere else to live and not subject the family to shame.

Yet, her choice to forego makeup was rooted in more than old habits. She had long moved past seeking approval, particularly her mother's. Over the years, she had embraced her natural appearance, finding confidence in her authenticity. Not wearing makeup also meant reclaiming both her time and money—resources she preferred to invest elsewhere.

Rhonwen pulled a face at her reflection. Many years of believing she was plain acted as an efficient filter, preventing her from seeing what everyone else saw. An attractive redhead with a voluptuous body, long slender legs and the most exquisite alabaster skin, crisscrossed by the hint of pink and blue veins. Her face, softly angular, had a classical beauty that was most frequently seen on the statues and paintings of the antiquities. What she did lack, however, was the grace and bearing of someone who felt good about themselves.

Rhonwen turned sharply away from her reflection in the mirror and reached down to turn the water off. Wrapping herself in a towel to ward off the chill of the evening, she went into the lounge room to turn on the heater and TV before returning to the bathroom. Taking a small container from the vanity, she sprinkled a liberal amount of bath salts into the water to dissolve into white swirls that swiftly spread through the bath.

Satisfied, Rhonwen cautiously eased herself into the soft, warm water. As it enveloped her, she let out a contented sigh, letting her whole body relax in the water, while Sooty jumped onto the side of the bath and sat carefully at the end of the tub next to her head.

She smiled. "Hello, Sooty. So you've come to watch over me, then, have you?"

Sooty squinted as if to answer her, then quickly rubbed his cheek forcefully against her face. "Careful, you"ll push me under, you big brute!" The heat of the water started to work on the tension in her body, and Rhonwen felt herself starting to drift into a relaxed, dreamy state, floating in the perfume of the bath salts and steam. Closing her eyes, she had just started to drift off when abruptly, thoughts about her day and work crowded into her mind, and a wave of anxiety washed over her.

Tomorrow was the big day. The interview for a job she wasn't sure she even wanted. She liked her current position working with Brian. These last four years with the company had been the best of her working life. The work was important, the pay and perks were great, and the agency's covert links to MI5 gave it prestige. Now Brian wanted her to take over a new research department collecting and analysing incoming intelligence and working on sensitive assignments. It was a great opportunity, and she knew she could do it. After all, she didn't want to be a PA all her life, but it would mean leaving Brian.

Suddenly agitated, Rhonwen restlessly started to wriggle around, her sense of peace shattered by her thoughts. *That's it, of course, your silly crush!* But it was too late. Pulling the plug and jumping out of the bath failed to stop the warmth stirring between her legs and images of dark hair and powerful shoulders from invading her mind. Everything about him, from how he walked with that careful, graceful animal quality to the penetrating gaze of his blue eyes, captivated her.

Turning on the shower, she grabbed the soap and vigorously started to wash, irritated with herself for giving in to her stupid fantasies about someone who was way beyond her league. She almost broke the tap in her anger as she turned off the water. *Get a grip, you romantic fool!* This is why she had gone ahead and applied for the new job. She needed to separate herself from Brian before she made a complete idiot of herself. What if he caught on? Remembering the heat in her cheeks when he had brushed lightly against her the other day made her squirm. Grabbing a towel, she dried herself as quickly as she could.

The sound of the TV intruded into her thoughts as Sooty became more insistent on her attention. *"Come on, Sooty, let me get dressed, and I'll feed us both."* With that, Rhonwen's natural bent to pragmatism took over. She firmly locked up her desire and fantasy and set about organising herself for the evening, deciding on an early night so she would be fresh for the interview in the morning.

3

"8.30? What the hell happened to my day?"

Talking to himself had become a quirky little habit in recent times, and when his closest friend Stewart pointed this out, it had led to a spirited exchange about Brian's advancing age and lack of a companion. Ignoring Brian's ominous frown at the time, Stewart persisted in badgering him with the idea that he needed a woman in his life, and it was only when he had pointed out that Stewart was also single that Stewart had capitulated. Both men understood the fact that he was probably right.

Brian had been leaning against the wall, gazing through the office window at the rain as it washed down around the London skyline, thinking about the next day. Stewart had figured in those thoughts quite a lot. *What was he thinking? Or rather, what part of his anatomy was he thinking with?*

Walking back to his desk, he tidied up the documents scattered across its surface. He had been happy with the selection of candidates except for the one whose file now rested on top of the pile. When he had first found it on the bottom of the stack, he had been a little bemused and angry. He immediately realised how it had got there. Stewart obviously hadn't been able to resist the temptation of a little office seduction.

Oh well, Keira must have fulfilled the criteria, or she wouldn't have made it through the HR cull, but she was the last person he wanted in the job. Not only her lack of experience but also her temperament was all wrong. As far as he was concerned, the job was Rhonwen's and the interviews tomorrow were just window dressing.

He had worked with Rhonwen long enough to appreciate her knowledge and skills in all sorts of circumstances. As far as he was concerned, she was the best choice for the position. During preliminary discussions about the new department, he had made it clear that he was confident that she would meet the company's expectations. He knew that several of the directors agreed with him. He felt confident in Rhonwen's ability, but strangely, he had sensed that Rhonwen herself had some reservations. But then again, he often felt he didn't have the full picture of her. She was smart and discrete, totally appropriate in her approach and manner, with her understated elegance and clean, professional look. But underneath the surface, he felt she was more complex than she appeared.

Brian had known enough women in his time to be able to see through the clothes. Not as skinny as most of the girls of today, he found her quite alluring, especially her deep green eyes, set like two precious emeralds against the alabaster canvas of her skin. He pondered briefly on the shape of her breasts and then smiled when he thought of the line of her legs and what he would find between them. He was beginning to lose himself in his own lusty fantasy. *"Not so different from Stewart, really, are you?"*

He smiled ruefully at himself as he put away his documents and closed down his computer. Brian did not doubt that Keira's name on the interview roster was because she had traded sex for a shot at the job, and he had to admit he was more than a bit irritated with Stew over this.

He remembered the first day she had sauntered into the office, carefully attired in a sort of neo-gothic chic, almost too much but somehow still passable. He had watched her sizing up the office staff and how she had immediately focussed her attention on him.

Ambitious and possibly dangerous, Brian had thought to himself at the time. *Keep your guard up with this one, my boy, he* had told Stewart, who simply shrugged his shoulders and laughed. "What was the worst that could happen?" he had asked Brian while he winked mischievously.

Brian and Stewart went back a long time. They had met on their first day at Eton when the two bumped heads reaching for a small coin someone had dropped on the impeccably kept lawn of the Churchyard. They locked eyes instantly, sizing each other up when Stewart burst out laughing. "I'm Stewart Eggleston. Whom might you be?" The bond was forged there that day, and the two boys had become inseparable, embarking on a journey that took them through school, military training and active service, and now more recently, into the Agency.

Right, enough of this. If I keep up this daydreaming, I'll still be here at 9.30. Time to get some food.

He picked up his mobile and hit a key. "Chin? ... Yes, it's me, Brian. ... I'll be by in 15 minutes. Yes, the usual… See you then." He then hit a second key. "Gerry, are you free for a ride home? Great, see you in five."

Grabbing his coat from the closet, he walked out of his office, the door slamming shut and the automatic lock sealing the room from unwanted visitors. Strolling to the lift, he stopped next to Michael Jones, the director of operations, who was also on his way home.

"Ah, Brian. All set for tomorrow?" Michael paused and leaned across to push the button again. "Should be just a formality, really, shouldn't it?" He quickly glanced at Brian, trying to gauge his reaction.

Brian smiled reassuringly. "I Haven't seen anyone's application that comes close to Rhonwen's. You"ll see; she"ll do us proud." Brian didn't miss Michael's slight frown. "I know You're right. I had Walcott from HR on the phone again, wanting to make sure everything was kosher. He is a suspicious man, you know." Brian nodded. "He's only doing his job, Michael."

Suddenly a loud ding announced the elevator's arrival, and the silver metal doors slid open. The two men stepped inside and rode the lift silently to the ground floor. Stepping into the vast, bustling foyer of the office building, they said goodbye as Michael headed quickly towards his waiting wife, parked immediately outside the front door. Brian stepped into the driving rain, spotting Gerry's cab pulled up across the road. Pulling his raincoat around him, he hurried over and jumped into the back.

"Straight home, Gov?"

Brian smiled warmly into the eyes, looking at him through the rear vision mirror. "Chin's first, please, Gerry."

Sitting back in the seat, he stared at the rain, aware that Gerry had quickly sensed his mood and was happy to drive in silence. That was the good thing about surrounding yourself with mates, he thought to himself. Gerry, like Stewart, was a long-time friend, and all three of them had served together in Kosovo.

Ten minutes later, to the sounds of irritated drivers honking their horns while trying to wind their way around a stationary cab, Gerry swerved into a vacated parking spot outside a Chinese restaurant. Brian quickly jumped from the vehicle and ran into the garishly lit building. A minute later, he was back in the cab holding a small brown bag. Gerry smiled and drew in a long breath, catching the unmistakable aroma of Mongolian lamb and the undertone of fried rice.

"Nothing, but a creature of habit, you are, Gov." Gerry laughed as he pulled away from the curb. "You've ordered that same meal for at least the last six months".

A few minutes later, Gerry pulled out of the traffic to let Brian out at his front door.

"There you go, Gov. Have a good night."

"Thanks, Gerry. You, too."

With a few quick strides, he was up the stairs and let himself into the foyer of the Georgian Terrace he called home. Divided into three spacious apartments, his took up the entire top floor. Brian took the stairs two at a time and was quickly through his front door into the hallway. Its crisp, modern white walls and black tiled floor contrasted starkly with the antique hall table, where he dropped his keys. Automatically waiting for the lock on the front door to click closed, he paused before making his way into the kitchen.

Having left his dinner on the bench, Brian returned to the hall and opened a panel in the wall connected to the rear of the walk-in wardrobe in his bedroom. He was suddenly starving. Quickly hanging up his coat, he pulled at his tie, releasing its grip on his throat and started to undo his shirt. Having efficiently stripped down to his jocks, he caught sight of himself in the mirror. Yes, there were dark circles under his eyes, but all in all, he was happy with what he saw. Despite his upper torso sporting a number of scars of various lengths, he was still in good condition.

Dragging a tee shirt over his head, he went back to the kitchen to retrieve his food and pour himself a large glass of red wine. Putting his dinner into a bowl, he headed into the living room and looked for the remote. Finding it on the floor where he had recklessly abandoned it the evening before, Brian flicked on the telly and settled on the leather sofa facing a huge flat-screen TV.

Leaning over the bowl and sniffing the aroma spreading upwards, Brian took little notice of what programme was on as he demolished his dinner with single-minded determination and speed. Eating fast was a legacy from his service days when sometimes you only had a few minutes to down whatever food you had.

Cleaning the last morsels of food from the bowl, he reached for the large glass of wine and relaxed back into the sofa, staring vacantly at the screen. He rarely watched it, using it mainly for white noise while he let his thoughts wander. Tonight was no exception, other than the fact that he felt unusually fatigued and oddly uneasy. None of the programmes captured his attention, and he found himself drifting off. Rousing himself, he decided to call it a night and took his dishes to the kitchen and halfheartedly rinsed them off. Having quickly brushed his teeth, he stripped off and slid between the sheets; he sighed deeply and stretched his body out, grateful that none of his old wounds were plaguing him.

4

Brian sat bolt upright in bed, his breathing rapid and shallow. His face was soaked with beads of sweat that turned into rivulets while a musky, earthy smell lingered in his nostrils. His upper body, too, felt damp. The lingering odour reminded him of the times in his past when he had been out in the dewy pre-dawn air.

Still a little confused and uncertain of what was a remnant of a dream and what was reality, he ran his hand down his body only to feel a cloying wetness on the sheets closer to his groin. He remembered that feeling from his early teens but he hadn't had a wet dream since becoming sexually active. Whipping the sheets back, he swung his legs over the side of the bed.

Annoyed, he pulled the wet sheets off the mattress while wiping the sticky mess off his belly. He made straight for the bathroom, where he washed himself with cold water and then, with a fresh towel from the vanity, he dried himself vigorously as if it would bring him back to his senses.

He stared for a long time into the mirror above the white washbasin, where his sweat-soaked, ruffled hair and flushed face stared back at him. It was a familiar reflection and one that was usually accompanied by the presence of an attractive woman in his bed. However, the scratches across his chest and abdomen were not familiar, and it looked like a ferocious animal had mauled him.

Puzzled, he looked closer at the wounds and shook his head in disbelief. *Did he do this to himself while having a wet dream about Keira?* Brian couldn't help but laugh out loud. *The shrink's going to love this when he hears it*, he thought to himself. He wondered what his subconscious was trying to tell him.

Walking into the kitchen, he opened the fridge and reached for the milk, but abruptly changing his mind, he pulled a bottle of orange juice from the shelf. Unscrewing the lid, he took a huge gulp, swishing it around his mouth, enjoying the slightly tart and tangy sensation.

Standing there for a moment, reflecting on the content of the dream and its almost surreal vividness, Brian was surprised that he could still smell, feel, and taste his nocturnal experience. How could a dream be so real? He looked at the clock, his sense of unease from the previous evening returning. Seeing that it was already 5:30 and seeking to distract himself, he decided to get on with the day rather than go back to bed.

Heading back into the bathroom, he turned the water on and jumped into the shower using the sharp pins of water beating across his back and sluicing down his legs to clear his mind. He focussed his attention on his schedule for the day, which included the interviews for the new position, then a meeting with the directors and one of the Ministry secretaries, and finally, a stern chat with Stewart.

Having dried off, he reached into his chest of drawers to retrieve a pair of boxers, and his attention was caught by something making a clunking sound. Curious, he rummaged around until his fingers suddenly met a largish oval object, which he pulled out into the light. It was the gold chain and pendant that an old gypsy woman had given to him years ago when he was in Kosovo. How curious to find this now. He hadn't thought about those days for a very long time. It had all been so strange, holed up in that bombed-out house, surrounded by an undetermined number of Albanian separatists. He, Stewart and Gerry cut off from their unit.

Memories flooded in. The persistent mortar and small arms fire that kept them pinned down. Searching the ruins, the three discovered the old crone hiding in the only remaining room. She screamed at them angrily as she tried to stem the flow of blood running down her arm from what appeared to be a very nasty laceration. Initially, she attempted to attack them with the broken leg of a chair. Then, catching sight of their uniforms, she suddenly capitulated and allowed Gerry to look at her arm and eventually dress the wound.

The really strange thing was the way she kept staring at him. As they had waited for the shelling to stop, she had constantly watched him, her dark eyes intense and calculating. Finally, she muttered something, gesturing for him to go to her side. He had asked Gerry to translate, but she used a dialect Gerry didn't understand. Brian distinctly remembered feeling very edgy and uneasy in the same way that he was feeling now.

The next morning, their unit found them after securing the surrounding countryside. While loading the old woman into the armoured personnel carrier, she shouted loudly at the soldiers who tried to help her with the bag she was clutching to her side. One of the locals who was attached to their unit had looked at Brian very oddly and then explained that the old woman was demanding that he speak with her, when Brian had approached the stretcher, she grabbed his arm and looked up into his eyes.

"She says that you have been sent to her by fate, " the young man translated. "That you must be true, or all will be lost."

Brian had gently rested his hand on her shoulder to reassure her, and he had been rewarded with a toothy grin and a gnarled hand reaching for his sleeve. Pressing something into his hand, the old woman kept repeating a phrase over and over. Strangely, he could remember it really clearly now.

"*Parruka tutu ta atch misto.*"

As the old lady was loaded into the APV, he turned to his translator to ask what she had said and looked down at what she had put in his hand. He had been astonished to see a large pendant on a thick gold chain. Turning back, thinking of refusing such an unnecessary gift, he found her looking at him and making a sign with her good arm, like some blessing. She had shaken her head emphatically as if she knew he had wanted to return the pendant to her. Hesitating, the door of the APV closed, and the truck pulled away before he could act.

Standing in his bedroom, he smiled at the memory of that one day in the mountains. He had tried to return the pendant, but the private quickly pointed out that it would insult the old woman to return her gift, and he was best off keeping it. He hadn't really thought about it again.

He looked at the chain with its heavy pendant for a brief second, planning to put it back in his drawer, but then, without another thought, fastened it around his neck. Looking at himself in the mirror, Brian could see how it snuggly rested on his chest as if it belonged there. He felt a kind of warmth around the skin where it lay, and for some peculiar reason, he felt calmed by its presence. He started to think that this was just too curious and strange, especially after such a weird dream, and then that thought just seemed to slide away as he continued to get dressed.

❧ ❧

Cursing herself as she hung over the handbasin, washing her face with cold water and rinsing her mouth out, Rhonwen felt another wave of nausea wash over her.

"*Surely this can't just be anxiety? I Haven't had a panic attack since I was a teenager.*" It was still very early, and she had plenty of time before she really needed to start getting ready for work, but as she stood there gazing at her reflection, she felt quite hesitant to go back to bed. She desperately wanted to avoid the risk of re-experiencing that awful dream. But on the other hand, she really needed some more sleep, or she could completely stuff up at the interview.

Finally, allowing the more sensible side of her to win, she headed back to the bedroom. Sooty hovered around her feet, complaining loudly and almost tripping her up as he suddenly halted in the doorway. His hair stood on end, and his tail, huge and spiky, twitched angrily through the air. As she reached down to try and calm him, he hissed at her empty bedroom and backed away from her.

"What the hell is the matter with you?"

But Sooty was still backing away, staring into her dimly lit bedroom, completely spooked by something. Rhonwen flicked on the light switch to look into the room but couldn't see any reason for Sooty to carry on this way.

"You would think it was you having the nightmares!"

Thinking about the dream that had woken her, she shivered. Remembering the images of terrifying masks, garishly painted and sporting horns and feathers, and the feel of a multitude of hands all over her body, she almost panicked again. Naked bodies with faces painted in blue and a sense of incredible fear at the sound of some chanting came back clearly, and she suddenly remembered that she wasn't the only one there in that awful place. Brian was one of the men with blue paint, and she was sure Keira was one of the naked women.

"Get a grip!" Rhonwen's rational side asserted itself as she quickly consigned the dream to a mixture of her anxieties about the interview, her stupid crush on Brian and her sense of unease around Keira. *"That's what all this is"* she thought to herself as she turned off the light and went back to bed. Pulling up the quilt against the chill in the room, she was surprised to see that Sooty had stayed in the hall. Normally, Sooty would be hot on her heels, claiming his part of the bed, but he hovered by the door, miaowing loudly and moving nervously from time to time.

"Well, stay there then!" Rhonwen called out nervously, "I'm going back to sleep."

Despite the window being closed, she continued to feel a chill breeze drifting about the room. Finally, too exhausted to notice the changes around her, she drifted off to sleep only to find herself back in the dream, participant and witness to something that gave her a sense of foreboding. Within her, Rhonwen could feel the rage building up. Rage and fear were threatening to overwhelm her just as she was brought brutally back to reality by the shrill sound of her alarm clock.

Sitting bolt upright in her bed, she tried to orient herself towards the breaking morning light as it squeezed through the cracks in the blinds. She reached across and pushed the button that silenced the alarm, and for an instant, the hush was soothing. But as she swung her legs over the side of the bed, she was swamped by fear rising up through her body and clawing at her throat. And then the rage took hold and completely consumed her.

Gavin had spent a restless night in his comfortable apartment above the shop. Spacious and elegant, the apartment's interior was significantly larger than the exterior of the building would suggest. It was not a clever architectural design feature but rather a careful manipulation of space around a particular focal point. It was, in essence, magic. And it was magic that was the cause of his unease.

It had started the previous day when he was distracted by a persistent nagging, like a rat gnawing at wood, that something was afoot. But he hadn't been able to put his finger on why this magic was bothering him. Finally, towards midnight, it peaked as if the universe had been shaken from a long slumber by a rupture, tearing through its naturally chaotic fabric, and he realised that someone was meddling. This was not the work of a trained practitioner.

It had been an ominous feeling that had reminded him of a child playing with a knife, a child that had no real understanding of the danger of what it was doing and, more importantly, absolutely no appreciation of the consequences of its actions. *Yes,* Gavin decided, *after all this time, that someone was at it again, unwittingly meddling with something that they didn't understand.* Ignorance was always a problem; unfortunately, it was often accompanied by a distinct lack of caution. Cynically he reminded himself that he had been around long enough to watch humanity lurch from one disaster to another, somehow surviving whatever crisis loomed before them. They didn't really need him. For the last few hundred years, he had lived happily amongst them without needing to watch what they were up to. The retreat of magic from the minds of humans meant his burden had been lifted.

But now, something dangerous was disturbing his peace. Although not skilful, whatever was taking place in the arcane world stunk of real talent. And whoever this was, they were untutored. The feel of the magic was uncontrolled. Walking over to an octagonal-shaped table draped in a deep blue cloth, Gavin passed his hand over the bowl of clear water in the middle of a circle.

Ancient symbols and writings stood out prominently in a brilliant white, contrasting with the cloth so that they seemed to stand out by themselves and move as the light from the candles danced and created shadows across the walls of the alcove. The water clouded over for an instant, but as Gavin's hand crossed the right edge of the vessel, it cleared again. "What do you want from me?" He exclaimed in frustration.

Walking to the bookshelves, he ran his fingers along the rows of leather-bound volumes of ancient and more recent texts. The block to seeing who was dabbling in the arcane world would perhaps be dispersed with the right incantation, but it had been aeons since he had been called to use his talents.

Foolishly he had let go of the regular routines from his youth, wherein he would practice and study for a certain period of each day. Complacency had crept into his existence over the last few centuries as the world had embraced the mundane and forgotten the sacred.

"Ah, here we go." He pulled a volume from the shelf and carried it to the table. Placing it carefully on the flat surface, he gently opened it, and studying the ancient parchment in front of him for a moment, he moved his hand across the bowl again. This time the grey-white cloud did not immediately disappear but spread across the surface of the water, and an image manifested, revealing the face of a young woman. "Who are you?" Gavin asked. "And more importantly, where are you?"

He had barely finished the question when the image in the bowl disappeared. "Damn it!" Peering into the clear water, he frowned with frustration. He had no idea whose face he had seen in that brief moment, but he knew that he would not be able to solve this puzzle simply by staring at it.

Realising that it was now very early in the morning, he headed to bed. Still, within minutes of reclining and closing his eyes, his mind was inundated with a kaleidoscope of images. Faces, landscapes and symbols all jumbled together in a frenzy that made it impossible for him to sleep. He could almost taste it—something familiar, something sinister. Getting out of bed, he walked across the room to the window and, pulling the blind back, looked out across the narrow lane. Water pearled and ran down the window, leaving thin wormlike trails on the glass. Occasionally the wind gusted, smashing the rain noisily against the window while obliterating the tracks of water only to create new ones.

As he stood watching this growing force of nature take the city, reminding it of her power, a feeling of dread grew within him. He felt his heart race and his breath grow short while small beads of sweat glistened on his forehead. Across the millennia, he had faced many battles and won. Suddenly nauseated, he rushed to the bathroom, where he barely made it to the basin before he threw up. Looking down into his vomit of the splattered remnants of grass and blood pooling in the pristine white ceramic, a memory tugged at the edge of his consciousness. Purged, he felt an immediate sense of relief, physically and metaphysically, but now his sense of foreboding increased as a familiarity teased at his memory. Blood and grass! What had been called into being this night? Something from the far past that should stay there, no doubt.

Filling a glass from the vanity with cold water, he had rinsed his mouth out, ridding himself of the bitter, salty taste of blood and bile. Accepting that sleep would not visit him this night, he returned to the living room and settled into a chair to await the dawn.

5

By midday, Brian was sitting at his desk, trying to figure out how the morning had turned into a complete disaster. *What was going on?* Nothing had gone the way that he had planned. It was just crazy, and he had difficulty getting his thoughts to make sense of it.

First, there was Rhonwen. She had arrived for her interview confused, distracted and completely unlike her normal self. He had tried to be supportive, asking her if she was unwell, only to find his usually competent assistant vague. And then, having apologised in a hesitant sort of way, saying she did n't know what was wrong, she had quite suddenly changed back into herself, straightened up and said, "I'm OK."

Brian had offered to reschedule if she was unwell and, for a moment, had thought that Rhonwen would take him up on the opportunity, but she had looked at him sharply and replied in a brusque voice. "No. Let's get on with it!" Asking her if she was sure, he had hardly gotten two words out before she cut him off rudely, telling him she just wanted to "get on with it".

The sudden silence in the board room had emphasised everyone's awkwardness. Having finally broken the uneasy silence, they began the interview. Brian had been stunned by Rhonwen's inability to reply coherently to the questions. He was even more appalled by her irritability and rudeness.

At the end of the interview, everyone had been visibly relieved as they watched her leave, and Michael Jones had looked across the table towards Brian with an alarmed frown on his face. Brian had been so stunned by the total incongruity of what he had just witnessed that he couldn't even begin to think of a response.

But it was the last interview, Keira's, that had floored him. In sharp contrast to Rhonwen, she had quite literally lit up the room. She was dressed in an elegant grey, striped business suit and a beautiful white blouse, and·there was no sign of her usual slightly gothic style. Her makeup was flawless with a modern female executive's subtle tones and shades, and her hair was tamed in a simple style.

Well, she certainly looks the part, Brian had thought as he watched Keira stride across the boardroom floor with the grace and elegance of a cat.

He had been just as captivated by Keira's presence as the others in the room, and he had realised that there was something distinctly different about her appearance apart from her clothes. Her skin was darker than it had been yesterday, and she exuded strength and power he had not noticed about her before. Her frame seemed squarer somehow, and she had the spring of a seasoned athlete in her step.

When she"d reached the edge of the boardroom table and stopped, she had beamed a stunning smile at the interview panel, greeting them with confidence and finesse. Michael Jones had not been the only one to shift in his chair; his attention focused as he leant forward. Amused by Michael's eagerness, Brian had thought that the director could, in this instance, be almost accused of being at risk of drooling, something he had never seen in the man before.

Realising that he, too, was leaning forward, Brian had sat back suddenly, aware of the hypnotic effect Keira appeared to be having on all of them, including himself. Added to this, to his consternation, he had found himself watching Keira from the uneasy perspective of having had a wild sexual skirmish with her during the night, albeit in a dream. Remembering it had made things even worse as he had been all too aware of a tightness in his groin.

As if reading his mind, Keira had looked straight across at him, and he had felt his face flushed like a gawky teenager. All she had said was "Good morning Brian", but it seemed laden with meaning. He'd struggled to keep the tone of his voice casual as he had greeted her, hiding the slight tremor that came with the feeling of being caught out doing something naughty as if he was still a child.

Having been oblivious to the charged nuances of the interchange between Keira and Brian, Michael had just smiled approvingly at Keira. His enthusiasm then set the scene for the remainder of the interview in which Keira performed in a totally professional manner, displaying a knowledge of their industry and a keen intelligence that had left Brian stunned.

Now leaning back in his chair and staring out at the skyline from his office, Brian was obsessively going over and over the morning's events. The board's decision was unanimous, but how could it have been otherwise? It didn't matter that he and Michael knew that there had been something radically wrong with Rhonwen today. Keira was definitely the best candidate on the day, and now it was his job to deliver the news to them both.

A sharp knock on the door startled him out of his reverie, interrupting his pointless ruminations. He heard the growl in his voice as he called for whomever it was to come in. Stewart sauntered into the room, and Brian immediately recognised the nonchalant demeanour his friend affected as a cover for nervousness. Clearing his throat slightly, Stewart asked casually,

"How"d it go this morning?"

"You put Keira up for the job?" Brian asked quietly.

Stewart didn't hesitate as he answered in the affirmative, looking straight into his eyes, obviously prepared to be upfront despite knowing Brian would be irritated.

"Then you"ll be pleased to know she's got the job."

Brian kept his voice matter of fact, watching Stew's reaction and noting his legitimate shock at the news.

"What? But that job was tailor-made for Rhonwen. I don't understand."

"Neither do I. Rhonwen was irritable and surly and answered our questions with hostility that was just plain rude! It was like she was a completely different person.

Stewart sat down heavily on one of the chairs. "Rhonwen, surly? I didn't think she knew what it is like to be bad-tempered."

"Well," Brian shook his head. "She does now."

Stewart sat quietly before speaking again. His voice was serious. "You know, I didn't think for one minute that Keira would get the job. Yes, she met the criteria, but only just. She doesn't have the depth of experience that Rhonwen has. " He paused and frowned as he continued.

"Before you get too pissed off with me, I did make it clear to her that other than putting her application through to HR, the rest would be all fair and square and above board."

"It's all right, Stewart. I know." Brian walked to the window and looked out. "Have you seen Keira today?"

"No, actually, I Haven't." He paused. "Why?"

"She looked quite different. The little Goth Girl was gone, and Miss Wall Street had well and truly emerged." Brian stopped and turned around to look at Stewart. "Did you coach her at all? I need to know."

Brian's tone left no ambiguity, and he knew that Stewart would be honest with him. "Absolutely not. Anyway, it doesn't matter how she looks. It's whether she can do the job. It's odd, though, that Rhonwen fluffed the interview. I didn't expect that."

"After today, I'm starting to think anything is possible". Brian replied. "Stew, Keira not only looked different, but she was also different. The voice, her poise, what she knew. Frankly, I didn't know that she had it in her".

Going back to the desk, he sat down feeling flat and apprehensive. "I have to tell them both the outcome. Keira will be on the usual three-month probation before being permanently appointed, so I guess we'll have an opportunity to monitor the situation. But right now, I need to go and find Rhonwen". The whole idea of speaking with her made him want to run, but taking a deep breath, he looked up at Stewart and continued. "I'll catch up with you later."

Stewart got to his feet and moved towards the door, then turning around, he looked at him, his expression serious; "How do you think she will take it"?

"Badly."

ꕥ ꕥ

After literally bursting from the boardroom Rhonwen had crashed into one of the junior clerks snarling at him to get the fuck out of her way. Instantly feeling dreadful and full of remorse, she apologised to Marty, who just stood there with a look of complete bewilderment.

Fleeing around the corner of the hall, she found an empty meeting room, and after turning the lock, she collapsed into one of the chairs, weeping hysterically. It had taken a long time for her to settle, and after wiping her eyes, she had sat at the window watching the clouds while she tried to organise her thoughts. She was completely confused by what had happened and felt like she would spin out of control again. Gripping her arms, her nails digging in to keep her from screaming as competing feelings of rage and despair lashed her, she had ridden out the storm of her emotions.

Finally, after what seemed like hours, she felt a little calmer. Needing to wash her face before going back to her office, she left the small room and bravely stepped back into the corridor. Relieved that no one was in the hall, she quickly ducked into the Lady's washroom, rushed to the basin, turned the faucet on, and thoroughly doused her face with the cold water. Straightening up, she caught a glimpse of her face and almost burst out crying again but out of the blue, another wave of anger burst through.

Fuck them, she thought. *They are not going to get the better of me.* She peered closely at her reflection and found a pair of very sad and puffy eyes staring back at her. The dark circles, and the pallor of her skin evidence that besides the emotional rollercoaster she seemed to have no control over, she was also utterly exhausted.

There was a sudden knock on the door. Rhonwen froze, staring at herself in the mirror. "Think," she muttered to herself. *It couldn't be one of the women; they would have just walked in unannounced. It must be one of the men, but who?*

"Rhonwen?" She instantly recognised Brian's baritone voice. It was peculiarly less commanding than usual, almost timid. A part of her recognised that Brian was afraid of her, but her primary reaction was rage mixed with humiliation. That he should be a witness to her complete meltdown was more than she could stand.

"It's Brian, Rhonwen. Please, I need to talk to you. Are you all right?"

That would be right, she thought; I'm *going to get told I didn't get the job in the toilet.* Another wave of rage threatened to take control of her, and she fought to control the urge to scream at him. Breathing deeply, she deliberately lowered and softened her voice.

"Just a minute, Brian".

"No problem. Just take your time; I'll wait."

Rhonwen quickly dried her face and then called out.

"Come in!"

The door slowly opened, and Brian's shock of black hair appeared, followed by the rest of his head. The deep furrows on his forehead signalled his concern. He gingerly stepped into the Lady's washroom and furtively looked about.

"We are alone, aren'twe?" He asked.

"It's all right, Brian. It's just you and me." A part of her recognised that being alone with Brian under different circumstances would have been thrilling, but all she felt at this moment was a massive desire for him to go away. Taking a breath, the best she could do was muster a feeble smile.

"Well, that's good then." Brian paused and eased himself further into the room. He stepped around the tiled corner next to the hand dryer and, trying to look casual, lent against the wall. The proximity to the dryer triggered the start mechanism, and the washroom was suddenly filled with the rushing sound of blowing air. Brian jumped back as if stung by some ferocious insect, his nostrils flaring with irritation, before he gathered himself together, standing in front of her, his gaze sweeping the room.

"Sorry!" Brian said in a firmer voice. "Could we go somewhere else to talk? I really do not want to have this conversation here."

Her warring emotions shifted again; Rhonwen almost felt sorry for him as she answered. "There is an empty meeting room across the hall. We can go there."

They quickly left with Rhonwen leading the way to the room she had spent the last hour and a half hiding in. Once she heard the door shut, she turned to face him, determined to regain control; she took a deep breath and said, "It's OK. I know I stuffed up."

She saw him watching her carefully as if she might break, and in a way, she felt she actually might. The last thing she wanted to do was talk about it. The rage was teasing her mind, and despite it being unfair, she felt it was somehow his fault. He was gentle as he asked her what had happened, and somehow, instead of being reassuring, his concern was making it worse. She only just managed to contain her emotions as she replied.

"I really don't know. I didn't sleep well last night. I had these horrible nightmares." She stopped and looked at Brian. *I can't tell him about any of this stuff. He is just going to think I am mad!* Putting on her best professional voice, she continued.

"But none of that really matters, does it?"

She noticed that Brian looked at her oddly and seemed to shiver. He seemed distracted as if her admission was somehow important. He muttered something about not sleeping well either and shook his head in a preoccupied way that she found completely inappropriate. Perversely, despite her reluctance to talk to him, she was irritated that he had lost focus.

This was about her. It was her job, and for some bloody incomprehensible reason, she had made a complete fool of herself. The shame and humiliation suddenly swept over her, and she felt like she was going to burst into tears again. Then, almost within the same moment, the anger rose again, like an angry snake ready to strike whoever was there. She only just managed to tame it before she opened her mouth.

Hanging onto the side of the table she was standing next to, she took another deep breath and then asked the question hanging between them.

"So, Brian, who did get the job?"

She saw the dread in his eyes, which confused her. She was trying to fathom what would cause this as she listened to him. Her pulse was hammering away inside her head, and she couldn't think. His voice seemed to be far away as he went on.

"Rhonwen, I want you to know that I did my best pleading your case, but ultimately, I had to bow to the panel's judgement."

He paused as if waiting for something, for her to say something. It was as if he was afraid she would lose it, but why would she? She heard her own voice, tight and almost snarling, as she demanded that he tell her who got the job.

"They gave the position to Keira Blair." He replied. Quickly adding, as if it would make it more palatable.

"You need to understand that it is on a three-month trial basis, and there will be a stringent review at the end of that period."

Keira! Rhonwen couldn't believe what she had heard. She hadn't known Keira had applied. As it sunk in, the fragile grip she had on her rage evaporated. She could feel the blood draining from her face, and she knew she was tightening her jaw, clamping down hard on what she wanted to say. She felt like screaming and knew that if she didn't release that scream to free it from the pit of her guts, she would never breathe again.

Brian reached out with both hands, obviously trying to offer her comfort. It was a caring gesture, but it made her want to hit him. Unable to contain her rage, she erupted with seething fury and violently brushed his arms away.

"Get away from me, Brian!" she hissed at him. "Just get the fuck away from me!"

As Brian stepped back in shock, she took the opportunity to get past him to the door. Throwing it open, she ran out of that room, along the empty hall, and out the fire door. She was on the road before she stopped.

6

Stewart walked across the grey-carpeted floor to his office. His conversation with Brian had left him feeling a little nervous. He knew his relationship with Keira would be frowned on by HR. They had always made it very clear that they disliked office affairs, as they did anything that could compromise security and the efficient running of the organisation.

Thinking back on his conversation with Brian, he realised that he had been surprised at the subtle tone of admiration for Keira he had heard in his voice. Brian had always kept a cool reserve and distance from Keira. He had even gone as far as warning Stewart to keep his distance. No matter how hard Keira had tried to win Brian over, he had resisted firmly, keeping the relationship on a courteous and professional level and never anything more.

Initially, Stewart had watched Keira with amused objectivity, knowing that her attempted flirtations were a waste of time. When he suggested that to her, she responded that trying was still fun; none of this had stopped Stewart from pursuing his own game with Keira. They had danced around each other for months, and eventually, having given up on Brian, Keira had started to take him seriously. He had truly enjoyed the chase and her capitulation. She called them bed buddies; he called them friends with benefits.

Still musing about the implications of this morning's interviews, he heard a commotion outside the hall. Looking out, he caught a glimpse of Rhonwen disappearing through the fire door into the stairwell. Seconds later, Brian emerged and, hurrying to the lift, pressed the button several times. Stewart had enough time to see that Brian was flustered before the sound of a chime signalled the arrival of the elevator, and Brian quickly jumped in, disappearing behind the closing doors.

As Stewart turned back into his office, pushing the door closed behind him, he glanced down to see a dainty foot dressed in a python pump heralding a visitor. He didn't need to see who it was. Christian Louboutin was one of Keira's favourite shoe designers. No one else in the office wore them. He hesitated for a second, uncertain of wanting to see Keira right this moment, but there was no choice in the matter as she forcefully pushed the door open enough for her to slide in.

"What's the matter, Stewie? Not pleased to see me?"

Her seductive drawl was accompanied by her forefinger carefully tracing the line of his jaw and finishing with an ever-so-subtle flick of her nail against his chin.

"Ouch!" Stewart exclaimed mockingly while firmly grasping her hand in his. He stopped to scrutinise the figure standing in front of him. Brian was right. Apart from the classic executive chic she had slipped into, there was something very different about Keira today.

"You're quite right, Stewart." She slid her hand from his and turned away from him to walk a few steps into the open space of the office, where she did a quick twirl. It was as if she had read his mind. She stopped and placed both hands provocatively on her slightly tilted hips. "I'm not the same girl you've had before."

Stewart didn't answer her. He had gone into a well-trained and rehearsed place in his mind, from which he assessed anything that bothered him. It was a skill he had been drilled in, and one that he very rarely revealed to anyone. He preferred to maintain an affable and simple persona to most people he met. He liked playing the charming seducer and party animal. It was also a good foil to Brian's dark and mysterious intensity, an archetype that drew instant attention from most women.

He noted that her skin was darker and her jaw more squarely set. Her hair which normally fell in smooth broad waves down to her shoulders seemed more tightly curled with a stronger glossy sheen. Her make-up was much more subtle yet still emphasised her sparkling eyes.

He let his gaze wander down the length of her. She had broader shoulders, and her waist was more tucked, although he figured it might be the result of her exquisitely tailored suit.

Her breasts appeared more elevated, and although she displayed no cleavage, they maintained an air of provocation. The skirt of her suit fell elegantly along the curve of her thighs, giving them the appearance of being neatly covered yet at the same time enticingly displayed.

"When You're done undressing me," Keira suggested, winking at him. "let me know if you like what you see."

Stewart snapped back into character and winked back. "Am I a blind man? Of course, I like what I see. Anyway, You're the last person that needs to fish for compliments."

He stepped a little closer to her and casually drew her into his arms. Hints of bergamot, musk and ylang-ylang enveloped him. He loved Keira's unusual perfume tastes, but what he noticed most was that underneath her exotic perfume was her own unmistakable scent of sex that appeared to rise up, independent of the others. *You horny little thing*, he thought.

Keira ran her hand across his chest and then, casually adjusting his tie, pouted. "So, darling, will you help me celebrate tonight?"

"Celebrate?" He feigned ignorance.

Keira stepped back from Stewart and cocked her head. "Of course!"

She paused, stepped behind Stewart's desk, and gracefully sat in his Chesterfield. Leaning back as she lifted her legs up to put them on the corner of the desk, her skirt rode up, revealing the lace tops of her stockings and the black of a garter belt. She watched Stewart carefully while at the same time casually running her hand up her leg.

"Brian's told you, then?" he asked.

"No, but you just did." She smiled. It was a knowing smile, and Stewart had to admire her. Perhaps they had all underestimated Keira.

"Shouldn't you wait till it's official?" He walked over to the edge of the desk, where he placed an inquisitive finger on the top of her stockinged foot, drawing little circles on it.

"Why? We both know. What else matters?" She slowly slid her left foot off the corner of the desk while hitching her skirt higher, revealing her upper thighs. The newly revealed triangle of lace instantly drew Stewart's attention.

Keira smiled archly as she slowly ran her hand up the inside of her leg. Undecided whether he would play along with her game, Stewart stepped in between her legs and casually leaned over her. He was about to kiss her when there was a loud knock on the door.

He instantly straightened up and moved to the side of the desk, pulling Keira's right leg off the corner and forcing her to close her legs to maintain her balance and modesty.

"Yes?!"

The door opened, and Sylvia, Michael Jones" assistant, looked into the office. She hesitated a little, critically surveying the scene in front of her. She continued as she could see nothing out of the ordinary except Keira sitting in Stewart's chair behind his desk.

"Mr Jones and Mr Poole would like to see you, Ms. Blair."

Keira immediately sat up and, in her best office manner, said, "Thank you, Sylvia. Let them know that I'll be there in a minute." She smiled. "It wouldn't do to keep them waiting, would it?"

"I'll let them know, Ms. Blair," Sylvia said matter-of-factly. She left efficiently, pulling the door closed on her way out.

"You"d better be off then," said Stewart.

Keira looked at him, a sweet, inviting look in her eyes. "Will I see you tonight, then?" she whispered.

"How can I resist such a tempting offer?" He kissed her on the forehead and, gently but firmly, pushed her towards the door. "Off you go, and I'll see you at the Crow at six. OK?"

As the door clicked shut behind Keira, Stewart sat behind his desk and stared out the window, trying to make sense of the last few moments. Apart from the physical differences he saw in Keira, he was trying to understand what was different about her. She had always been cocky; narcissistic, it said in her psych report, so that wasn't it. He had liked that in her as it made her sexually provocative and edgy - a pleasant distraction from the less adventurous girls he had encountered. She truly was up to anything, and this was what was now more enhanced.

It suddenly occurred to Stewart that Keira was not the only one that had changed overnight. Rhonwen was also decidedly different and had exhibited characteristics totally at odds with what he had come to expect from her. If anyone had suggested that she even had those traits twenty-four hours ago, he would have laughed at them. Similarly, Brian was distracted and preoccupied in a way he rarely saw him.

Stewart smiled to himself. Brian should really acknowledge his attraction to Rhonwen and be done with it. Policy be damned, there definitely was a chemistry between the two, but whenever Stewart brought it up, Brian would have none of it. *So what*, he had said to Stewart on the occasion it had come up in conversation over a pint or two. *I'm her boss, and that's that.*

Stewart's rumination's were suddenly interrupted by the ring of his mobile. As the Pacemaker's signature tune rang through the office, Stewart put the call on speaker.

"Gerry, my friend, what can I do you for?" he asked amicably.

"Brian rang. He had me chase a cab "cross London with one of his girls in it. Said she was out of sorts, and he was worried "bout her."

"Ah, yes, Rhonwen. Quite right, things have been a bit messy here today, Gerry. So what have you got?"

"The driver let her out in Kensington. He said she was very upset. That's all. She disappeared into Holland Park, so there was no way to see where she went."

"OK, Gerry. I'll let Brian know." Stewart was about to hang up when Gerry pulled him up.

"Gov, you want to tell me what goin" on?"

"Wish I could, my friend. So far, all we have is that one of Brian's staff missed out on a job, and she's not happy."

"So do you think I will be needed later?" Gerry asked.

"No, I don't think so." Stewart replied.

"OK. Keep me posted."

"Will do. I'll talk to you later." As Stewart tapped the phone's screen, he was puzzled. *Why would Rhonwen take off like that?* This was another facet of her that was very strange. He would never have thought of her as impulsive or emotional.

Frustrated, he decided that it was time to stop these mental meanderings. They were leading nowhere other than raising his ire. He disliked it immensely when he wasn't able to figure things out. He touched the screen on his phone. Brian's voicemail answered, asking the caller politely to leave a message.

"Brian, Gerry said she got out of the cab in Kensington. Get back to me when you can." He paused for a moment. "I'm sure she"ll be all right. She needs to blow off some steam. We need to speak."

7

Rhonwen was furious with herself. In one short day, she had managed to stuff up a job interview, alienate her boss, and completely lose any sense of professionalism. She decided quite morosely that her life couldn't get any worse. What did Brian think of her? Tears slid down her face, and she turned as far from the driver's line of sight as she could.

As she stared out the window, watching the rest of London go steadily about their business, she gradually calmed and settled into the seat. Her intense emotionality had completely sideswiped her. She couldn't figure out why she had become so anxious, and what was even more perplexing was how she had lost control. Even at her worst, as a sixteen-year-old, she had never lost control. She had always been grateful that she did it quietly when she panicked. But not today! *Why?*

She allowed herself to become distracted by the hypnotic flow of the traffic and the rain. Still, as the drops of water skittered across the window, she gradually became aware of the time, realising it was early afternoon. The thought of going back to the office made its way into her mind, but she dismissed this immediately before the panic could take hold of her again.

Reaching out for her handbag to find a tissue and wipe the tears from her face, she found an empty space and instantly became aware

that, in her distress, she had fled the office without it. Panic threatened again, but she ruthlessly rammed it back down.
"Driver?"

The cabbie, who had been worriedly keeping his eye on Rhonwen through the rear vision mirror, cocked his head towards the back and replied.

"Yes, Miss?"

"I'm terribly embarrassed about this, but I, aha, well, I left the office in a hurry, and I seem to have forgotten my purse."

The cabbie came straight to the point. "So, you can't pay the fare."

Tears started to spill out of the corners of her eyes again, "I'll have to get out here and pay you later..." her voice drifted off as she looked helplessly at the cabbie, half expecting an angry outburst from him as he pulled over. She cautiously looked up, trying to wipe the tears from her eyes with her hand, and found that, unexpectedly, there was a concerned look on the driver's face.

"Don't worry about the fare, Miss. Are you sure I can't take you home or to a friend?"

Rhonwen looked out the window and found they had pulled up next to Holland Park. "No, it's fine here. The rain has stopped, and a little fresh air and a bit of a walk might just be what I need."

After the day's events, Rhonwen was still easily flustered, so she checked again with the driver about how to organise payment, trying to assure him that she wasn't a cheat.

"Are you sure? Give me a piece of paper, and I'll give you my details."

"It's all right, Miss." He quickly wrote down the amount of the fare on one of his business cards and, reaching across the seat, handed it to her. "Take this. You can call the company and organise the payment over the phone."

Touched by the cabbie's understanding, Rhonwen almost started crying again, but she managed to hold it in check and quickly got out of the cab. Leaning down, she started to thank him for his kindness, but before she could finish, he just shook his head and protested, "It's nothing, Miss. You just take care of yourself, now."

With those words, he took off, the cab disappearing from Rhonwen's sight in the thick of London's traffic. Standing there, she felt completely alone for a moment, but looking across the park, she gathered herself together again. Fresh air and a change of scenery would give her time to get some perspective on this morning's fiasco, so she crossed the road and made her way along Holland Walk.

As she walked along the length of the park, she thought about the last twenty-four hours in an attempt to make some sense of it. She absent-mindedly turned a corner, and just as it started to rain again, she noticed a small antique shop tucked into the face of an Edwardian terrace. Familiar with the area, Rhonwen mused that she couldn't remember ever having seen this one.

On impulse, she crossed the road, thinking to take shelter from what was becoming a downpour, and pushed open the door. A little bell attached to the frame announced her arrival. Startled, she stopped for a moment, waiting to see if someone would appear, but to her relief, there was no sign of anyone. The last thing she needed was a pushy salesperson. As she stepped into the showroom, she felt herself relax.

The shop's interior was a chaotic collection of furniture, fittings and odds and ends from various times and places of long ago. The smells of old wood, oils, and a hint of lavender permeated the confined space, adding to the atmosphere of antiquity and lending itself more to a museum than a shop.

It was the lavender that really drew Rhonwen further inside the shop. She felt soothed by its familiar presence, and she relaxed as she walked about the clutter of chests, cupboards, drawers and desks, forgetting her grief and anger as if it was a coat she had left at the front door.

One desk in particular, a combination of ebony and rosewood with ivory inlays, caught her eye. It was a stunningly beautiful piece. If it was authentic, it was most likely from the Napoleonic era. The upper section consisted of a decorative gallery, and the lower section had a slanted writing table that opened to a small fitted interior. The whole thing was supported by reeded tapered legs.

Running her fingers over the top edge of the gallery, it felt a little rough, so she stopped and stepped to the side of the desk to take a closer look. As she bent down, she suddenly spied a mirror against the wall to the side of the desk. It was almost completely obscured by the host of other bric-a-brac cluttering the space around it.

It was large—an English gilt oval portrait mirror, profusely decorated in the Adam style. At the top of the mirror, instead of the traditional urn, it had some crystal or gemstone embedded into the gilded wood. The decoration was clearly unlike the rest of the frame, and Rhonwen thought it a curious deviation from the style.

How odd, she thought as she leaned over to touch the piece. A tingling suddenly ran through her fingers like an electric charge. Shocked, she immediately withdrew her hand and stepped back. Intrigued, she quickly recovered and bent back down to inspect it more closely. She felt surprisingly drawn to the large stone.

Rhonwen carefully scrutinised the piece before touching it again. This time, nothing happened. Examining it more closely, she decided that it must have been a piece of jewellery fitted to the mirror and that it probably had not been part of the original design. It looked oddly out of place, yet at the same time, it appeared to fit perfectly at the top of the mirror as if it were there to complete the balance of the frame.

She took another step back, and in her mind, she could clearly see the mirror above the fireplace in her lounge room. *Yes, it's perfect. This is it!* A sense of excitement rose in her as Rhonwen continued to imagine the mirror decorating that empty space on her wall. Her longing to possess it became stronger, and she leaned forward again, gingerly touching the mirror—the feeling of wanting it growing as she ran her hand along the frame.

"It is beautiful, is it not?"

Startled, Rhonwen almost kicked the mirror over as she jumped back and spun around to find herself looking into a pair of sparkling blue eyes.

"I'm sorry, my dear. I had no intention of frightening you. Can I help you with anything?"

The man Rhonwen was looking at was exquisitely handsome. He was lean and very tall and dressed elegantly in a pair of tan trousers with a plain white linen shirt that billowed around him, its sleeves rolled up to the middle of strong, tanned forearms. He exuded a serenity that appeared to envelop Rhonwen like a mantle. She drew in her breath and felt her chest getting a little tight, but the man's warm and kind smile reassured her.

"No, no! It is me who should apologise for overreacting and jumping out of my skin. I'm sure you didn't mean anything." She stopped and sighed.

"It's just... I Haven't had a very good day. However, I think it's just taken a turn for the better." She smiled and looked at the mirror as she continued, "It's lovely. Can I ask how much it is?"

The man leant casually against another desk and folded his arms across his broad chest. He tilted his head to one side and sized Rhonwen up. "Well, it's marked down to a thousand pounds."

Disappointment flooded Rhonwen. She had expected the mirror to be expensive, but this was way out of her price range. She looked at the mirror again, her hands reaching out, touching it, caressing it in a salutary gesture of parting.

"Unfortunately, that is quite a lot more than I can afford," she muttered.

She thought for a moment that the man may want to haggle, but Rhonwen decided that she had no intention of bargaining with him. She knew she wasn't good at it. She sighed again, her hand still resting on the mirror, the picture of it above the fireplace vividly in her mind. But, as she stood there, a kernel of rebellion stirred within her heart. Her decision had been instant, based on her usual frugal approach to spending on herself. But she really wanted the mirror. She was a little surprised by the strength of her desire, but somehow that didn't seem important. She did, in fact, have the money.

The thought that she was being impulsive occurred briefly, but then it seemed to slide away as she started to rationalise. *She earned good money, which mostly ended up in investment accounts. Plus she had her inheritance from Aunt Sophie, and, anyway, this was an investment. After all, her accountant had advised her to buy art and antiques for long-term security.*

"A thousand pounds." Rhonwen let the words roll off her tongue.

"That's right." The man said in that nonchalant manner.

Suddenly remembering that she didn't have her purse, Rhonwen sighed deeply and shook her head. "As much as I like it, I don't have my bag with me, and I couldn'tt ask you to hold it for me."

"No problem. I can fill out the invoice, and you can give me your credit card details when we deliver it. It's far too heavy for you to take home on your own anyway."

As much as Rhonwen looked for obstacles to the purchase out of sheer habit, logically, there appeared to be none. It seemed that it was now entirely up to her whether she would relent and give in to that overwhelming desire to have the mirror in her possession. Surely she deserved the mirror. Being frivolous just this once was not going to break her, and it would definitely help make up for the day's disaster. Rhonwen took a deep breath and, feeling like she was stepping off some imaginary ledge into an abyss, looked the man squarely in the face.

"What the hell? I want it."

"Then, my dear, you shall have it and not regret it." The man held his hand out. Rhonwen smiled nervously and looked down. She hesitated for a second and then, with a newfound determination, firmly shook the man's hand. An odd sort of electricity seemed to flow between the two, and for a second, Rhonwen felt bathed in warmth. Then it stopped as suddenly as it began.

She caught her breath and said resolutely. "That's done then! By the way, my name is Rhonwen Tierney."

"Pleased to meet you, Rhonwen." He said with a broad smile. "And you can call me Gavin." For the first time, she heard the trace of a Scottish drawl in his speech.

8

Gavin knew who had come to visit him, although they had not yet met in this incarnation. There had been many such meetings over the centuries. As with all the bloodlines, hers went back in time to where there were no legends, when gods walked amongst mortals, before the time of the *Tuatha Dé Danann*. It had been the time of the first quickening when some had become immortal.

As he'd watched her potter through the shop, Gavin sensed that she, unlike her predecessors, was completely unaware of her bloodline's history or of the powers that lay dormant in her genetic makeup.

Reaching out with his mind, he was instantly aware of the turmoil within her. It was acute and raw, but she was managing to contain it. She had obviously experienced some trauma in the last few hours. He couldn'tt sense any underlying emotional vibrations that would signal that she had talent. He thought there might be something, a whisper of the right harmonic pitch, but her energy was very confusing. The Amulet had recognised her. He had felt that very strongly.

Gavin knew that whatever had brought Rhonwen to him and his shop, she was now unable to turn back. Finding the mirror, her attraction to it, signalled that her destiny was now entwined with his. What he wanted, what she wanted, no longer mattered. Her genetic template had led her over this threshold, and his responsibility was to nurture and mentor her through what would inevitably unfold.

Watching her inner conflict over the cost of the mirror and her intense desire to own it had been interesting. The mirror had chosen her, and she had been unable to resist. This encounter between an heir and her inheritance always stirred up the magical forces, but never on the scale he experienced last night. This was not the answer to what that had been about, but Rhonwen's sudden appearance in his shop today had to be connected somehow.

Putting his disquiet aside, he played out his part of a shopkeeper, neither persuading nor dissuading her from her decision to purchase what was, in reality, her own possession. Sophie had told him when she had given him the mirror for safekeeping that she thought Rhonwen would be the one who would claim it. If he was honest with himself, his promise to Sophie was the only reason he was still in London.

And here was Rhonwen, completely ignorant of what she was involving herself with as he guided her to the desk at the back of the shop to do the paperwork. After settling her into a chair, he completed the invoicing and documentation, organising a delivery time for the next day. Having seen her to the door, he had wrapped the mirror and stacked it in the alcove at the back, ready for delivery. For some reason, he felt impelled to set wards on it. A part of him wanted to dismiss the urge, but he knew better than to ignore such an impulse.

He had only just returned to his desk when he became aware of a tall, willowy woman dressed entirely in black entering the shop. He instantly warded himself. Closing the order book that had been open in front of him, he slipped it out of sight amongst some other papers. He smiled as he watched her glide around the objects and furniture towards him, as always beautiful and always dangerous.

"Morgan," he said, deliberately making his voice low and welcoming. "To what do I owe the pleasure?"

"Do not play games with me, Gavin. You know why I'm here. You felt it. Something has disturbed the usual harmony". She stepped closer to him and ran her finger along his chin. "Tell me, my fey, who was she?"

As Morgan tried to draw him in with her seductive tones, Gavin gently but firmly removed her hand from his face. "Now, who's playing games, Morgan." He smiled at her. "How many centuries have you tried and failed in this with me? Besides, I couldn't rob you of the pleasure of finding out for yourself, could I?"

Gavin watched Morgan as she casually settled herself into the chair recently vacated by Rhonwen. She took her time arranging herself, her hawklike gaze scanning the top of his desk. Looking up at him, still standing on the other side of the desk, she laughed, the throaty sound echoing through the shop. "You and I, Gavin, could be such great allies."

Gavin thought he could detect an almost imperceptible tone of longing in her voice. However, he quickly dismissed any notion that this could, in fact, be possible. On more than one occasion, he had seen what happened to Morgan's allies once they had served their purpose. Aside from that rather powerful disincentive, they had always followed very divergent and irreconcilable paths. Realising she wasn't going anywhere soon, he seated himself opposite her.

The fact that she was here questioning him about the disturbances last night was worrying. It had been on his mind that it was something she was involved in.

"Morgan are you telling me that you had nothing to do with last night?" He challenged, allowing his voice to carry a tone of disbelief.

Morgan didn't answer immediately. Gavin continued. "It's not one of your little acolytes, is it?"

Morgan's reaction was quick and sharp. "Do not try to trivialise me, Gavin!" She paused. "Or what I do."

She tapped her foot irritably, then continued with an icy edge in her voice.

"None of them are that strong, you know that."

"Are you sure?"

Gavin watched her closely, trying to discern if she had been as surprised by last night as he had. She could be lying, or this could be some elaborate manipulation. She was well known for her intricate plots. No, he thought, whatever happened last night was neither controlled nor elegant, and Morgan was a consummate practitioner of the arts. Never sloppy.

Morgan watched him as carefully as he watched her and then finally broke the silence as if coming to a decision. She spoke softly but very clearly.

"You and I both know that the disturbance was serious. It tasted like something ancient. Something truly malevolent, and we may need to join forces here."

Surprised by Morgan's assessment of the level of danger, Gavin sat back and thought carefully about how to reply. He felt his ambivalence about her intruding into his evaluation of her suggestion. Deciding to test her, he replied. "That, my dear Morgan, is highly unlikely".

She smiled, but the gesture lacked warmth and somehow reminded Gavin of a predator's snarl.

"Really, Gavin?" She tilted her head, and the raven hair cascaded across her shoulder, slightly obscuring her face.

Gavin couldn't help feeling that she knew something he didn't. *But what?* He thought. What if she was right and last night was a portent of a serious threat? His train of thought was interrupted by her suddenly rising from the chair. She leant across the desk, her face so close to his he felt her breath as she spoke.

"There's no point guessing, is there? Think about it, Gavin. You and I!"

She winked mischievously at him, straightening up, adjusting her dress, and gathering her purse; she turned towards the door as she said. "Come, let go, and all will pass as it must."

Moving quickly, Gavin was on his feet, making his way around the desk towards the door to let her out. So far, this had been one of their easier meetings, and he was keen for it to end before it deteriorated. But she suddenly turned and stopped before him, her breasts touching his chest ever so lightly while she leaned into him, her hair softly brushing his face. He could smell the subtle intoxicating tones of her perfume.

He watched her closely but did not move away or allow her to sense his disquiet. Her lips brushed his cheek lightly at first but then more firmly as her tongue lingered.

"Where is your army, Gavin?" she purred. "Where are your acolytes? Do you still have any, or do you now shun the rush of power that they bring you?"

Her voice, deep and smokey, resonated, not just in his ear but throughout his body. For a second, Gavin thought he could feel a slightly chilly breeze, but then there was only an ominous silence. Morgan stepped back, and with a predatory smile, she turned away and was gone, the door clicking shut behind her.

As soon as he looked towards the desk, he realised what she had done. The invoice book was now on top of the pile of papers instead of underneath them.

"I am a fucking idiot!" Gavin exclaimed loudly. How could he have been so stupid as to let his guard down and let her get the better of him? For that, there was no excuse! Yet, there had been no real need for constant vigilance for a long time. He sighed, suspecting that those days were gone, and reached for the phone. "Erik, we have a problem." He paused for a moment. "No, it's much more serious than that."

9

Staring moodily out of the window, Brian was oblivious to the irritating sound in his office. Flicking his pen against the paperweight on his desk, he tried to process the day but was too distracted. He had asked Gerry to monitor Rhonwen's place and let him know when she arrived home. That had been hours ago, and he was getting increasingly impatient and, to be honest, a little worried. Where on earth could she be?

The sudden interruption of his mobile startled him, and he almost dropped it as he snatched at it. "Yes, Gerry!" He paused. "OK, then."

Breathing a sigh of relief, he mentally ticked that off his ever-increasing list of things to worry about today. He had Rhonwen's bag, so he had an excuse to contact her and organise for her to either come back to the office or for him to drop it off to her. He felt uncomfortable with the tension between them and knew he needed to resolve it, but for now, he needed to direct his thoughts to other matters.

He had hated having to join Michael to tell Keira she had been the successful candidate for the job. Luckily Michael had taken the lead and been very clear that it was a probationary appointment and that she would be closely monitored. But Keira had taken all of that in her stride. She showed no surprise, only informing them they would not regret their decision.

And then she looked straight at Brian and made a heavily laden comment about knowing that he would keep a close eye on her. By then, he had decided that nothing Keira said would surprise him. She was right; he would be keeping a very close eye on her.

The problem was that she seemed to shimmer every time he looked at her. The usual sexual tension he had ignored for the last couple of years was now so dense he could almost see it. Brian had noticed that even Michael was uncomfortably aware of it and found it distracting. To his credit, Michael had remained completely professional. After assuring her that he was certain she would do her utmost to apply herself to the challenge, he had made a strategic withdrawal back to his office.

Feeling uneasy at the thought of being alone with Keira would have been enough reason to beat a hasty retreat, but there had been an even more pressing need for him to get out of that boardroom. The pendant that he had almost forgotten about had started burning his chest. Almost slamming the door against the wall as he had rushed through it, he had practically run down the hall to his office. Once there, making sure the door was locked, He'd almost torn the button off his shirt as he wrestled to open the collar.

Removing his tie, He'd undone the first four buttons on his shirt and, pulling it open, looked at himself in the mirror behind the door. Staring at the pendant hanging from his neck and nestled against his chest, he was amazed to find it glowing a subtle red and orange. At the same time, his skin underneath tingled with some electric current, intense enough to be uncomfortable. He had immediately closed his hand around the piece thinking to yank it off, but He'd stopped, letting the gem rest in his hand. He suddenly knew he shouldn't remove it.

Puzzled, Brian had stood by the mirror staring at his reflection as the tingling in the skin of his chest subsided and the glow of the stone dimmed. Strangely, he had liked the feel of it in his hand. As he had looked closely at the pendant and his chest, he could now see nothing out of the ordinary: no mark or discolouration and no heat in the pendant. Now, thinking back, he wondered if it had all been a figment of his overstimulated imagination. *But,* he thought, *I know what I saw and felt.*

A sudden knock at the door wrenched him from his thoughts. "What?" The question rang out, sharp with an edge of aggravation. The door handle rattling reminded him it was locked. Hearing Stewart announce himself, he flicked the lock off and, staying out of sight of the hall, pulled the door open just enough to let his friend slide through. Stewart's gaze slid quickly from his face to his chest. "What the ..," Stewart started, but Brian had ushered him into the room and closed the door before he could say anything more.

"Are you OK?" Stewart asked in a hesitant voice. Very aware that he had forgotten to do up his shirt, Brian thought about it for a minute before answering truthfully. "You know, I'm not really sure."

"I didn't know you were into wearing bling." Stewart quipped, obviously hoping that a bit of humour might help.

"It's that pendant the old Gypsy woman gave me in Kosovo." Brian tapped it gently. "I could swear that it reacts to me in some way."

It was Stewart's turn to frown. "What do you mean *reacts*?" He responded.

"It's odd. This thing has been untouched at the bottom of my underwear drawer for ages. Then, this morning, when I reached in to get a pair of shorts, it just fell into my hand."

Stewart cocked his eyebrow, his expression wary as if he wasn't sure how to respond. Knowing that Stewart didn't know what had happened during the night, Brian hesitated. How close was he to Keira? Would he laugh it off, or would he get the shits? Making up his mind, he told Stewart to ensure the door was locked and sit down. As Stewart lowered himself into a chair close to the desk, Brian took a deep breath and launched into what he felt was a very embarrassing admission.

"Stewart, I don't want you to take this the wrong way, but I had this strange dream ... about Keira."

"What do you mean strange?" Stewart asked in a puzzled voice.

Brian shook his head. "Well, it was an exceptionally sexual dream. A nocturnal emission, sweating, the works."

Stewart frowned. "I still don't get it. So you had a wet dream about Keira, so what? You know I'm not the jealous type. Anyway, what has that got to do with the pendant thingy?"

"It's not just the sex part of it". Brian said as he stood up and undid his shirt further to reveal the scratches and marks all over his torso. "How does this happen in a dream?"

The look on Stewart's face would have made him laugh at any other time, but now it just made him feel even more confused. Looking at his best friend of nearly thirty years, he didn't know where to begin.

"You are telling me that you had a sudden urge to wear that pendant after dreaming of having sex with Keira and that you were physically assaulted during that dream?" Stewart responded in a more serious voice.

"Damn it! I know it sounds mad. It sounds mad to me too. That's the whole point." He snapped.

Seeing Stewart frown, he quickly continued. "Sorry, I'm not angry with you. I'm simply frustrated with not understanding what is happening here. Its everything. The dream, the strange way this pendant leapt into my hand this morning, and the compulsion I felt to put it on."

Stewart looked intently at Brian as he replied. "I agree with you, altogether it's been a very odd day". Brian leapt at the opening, and suddenly it all spilled out.

"You see. That's just it. The last twenty-four hours have been more than odd. Think about it, Stewart."

Brian paused and held up his hand as if counting something down. "Initially, everything is on track for Rhonwen to slip into the new job after an interview that is essentially a mere formality. Then last night, I had an adolescent midnight to-dawn rampage and, in the morning, the inexplicable desire to wear a gypsy pendant. Today Rhonwen arrives in a mood that is, to say the least, completely out of character for her. And she mentioned that she had nightmares last night and didn't sleep. That is, of course, when she was prepared to talk to me. Then there's Keira. A completely unlikely candidate who not only seizes the moment, she presents herself in a completely different manner to normal, and quite frankly, it's more than just looking different."

Brian stopped and drew a breath. "Oh, and to add to it ten minutes ago, this thing feels like it's about to burst into flames."
Stewart's forehead rippled into lines as he frowned. "What do you mean, it got hot? As in burning?"
"Yes. Oh, I know I could have imagined it about the pendant; you must have noticed how different Keira and Rhonwen were today?"
"Well, yes, actually". Stewart replied thoughtfully. Did you know Rhonwen told Marty to "Fuck Off"? I would never have believed it before today, but she was absolutely not the Rhonwen who normally works here. None of it makes sense, but you're right. Both of those girls are different, and I agree about Keira too. She" 's changed somehow, and I don't know any beauty parlour that can do that overnight."
Brian looked at his friend with concern. “You’re going out with Keira tonight, aren’t you? I'm not judging. It’s just that you might want to be a little careful."
Stewart looked thoughtful as he answered. “It's just a little drink to celebrate. Nothing serious, just a bit of fun. Look, if you want, I could brush her off and have a drink instead. You sound like you need it."
Brian was very tempted to say yes. Drumming his fingers on the desk, he finally sighed. "No. It"'s OK, Stew; I have Rhonwen" 's stuff here. I need to call and organise to get it to her. I don't think she is coming back here for it. At least not today. The thought of dealing with her chaotic emotions was a little daunting, and he was certainly in no mood to be good company, but he felt he needed to make sure she was OK.
"You go ahead, Stewart, but just watch yourself. That girl is trouble."

10

Buoyed by her impulsive acquisition of the mirror, Rhonwen went home. She had felt a little better since visiting the obscure antique store, although she was sure that she would lose her newly regained composure as soon as she had to deal with work again.

In the meantime, since she had been extravagant and self-indulgent, she was determined to enjoy her expensive purchase. Quickly glancing around to make sure no one was observing her, she retrieved the spare keys to the building and her own flat from their hiding spot in the small garden at the back of the building. She had let herself into the foyer and was unlocking the door to her flat she suddenly saw Lydia coming up the stairs.

"Hello, Rhonwen! You're home early."

Rhonwen became aware of the tentative concern in Lydia's expression, and her hard-won calm crumbled into tears. Lydia was at her side, putting her arm around her almost before she could open the door."Let's get inside, and I'll put the kettle on," was all Rhonwen heard as she sobbed, shuffling along the hall into her lounge room.

She could hear Lydia in the kitchen. "I know exactly what you need. A good cup of tea. You sit here, and I'll get it ready. Now, I won't be long, Rhonwen dear."

"I'll be fine, you know, Lydia. It's just that..." she suddenly hesitated, unsure how to explain the events of the day. Another sob escaped her as she tried to fight her tears back. "I'm such an idiot."

Lydia immediately interrupted her. "No, You're not. Take some deep breaths, and you can tell me what happened in a minute."

Returning to the living room, Lydia set the tray on the coffee table and sat down beside her. Rhonwen was grateful that the other woman remained silent as she poured the tea. Although she was much older than Rhonwen, she had been a true friend, and Rhonwen started to calm, breathing deeply and deliberately relaxing the tension out of her shoulders.

Lydia had lived in the apartment block long before Rhonwen arrived. She had been a close friend of Aunt Sophie's and had been kind to her from the moment she"d taken over the flat. Rhonwen had felt instantly comfortable with Lydia when she moved into the apartment block and was pleased to have the comforting presence of a maturer woman. Given that her relationship with her own mother had never been very good, a situation compounded by her mother's religious zeal, Rhonwen had yearned to be nurtured. So when Lydia asked her what had happened, she felt no embarrassment about telling her, but she did feel some confusion about what to tell her.

Rhonwen sat there for a moment, thinking the day through, trying to understand what had happened. "You know, it's all a little odd." She hesitated for a second.

"Go on, Rhonwen," prompted Lydia.

"Well, to start with, I had an absolutely shocking night. I was so anxious that I spent most of it in the bathroom, throwing up. But it was different from how I usually feel when I am anxious. But that could have been because of the nightmares. Anyway, I was a complete mess this morning, and it wasn't just the tiredness and anxiety; I was really angry all morning. Not just because I didn't get the job but before I even got to work!

Rhonwen sensed that Lydia was confused and realised she was babbling. She knew Lydia was trying to be helpful when she replied that it was pretty normal to be nervous before an interview, but she couldn't accept that as the answer.

"I know. Believe me, I know." Rhonwen replied. "But this felt different. I was in an absolute rage and couldn't keep it in. I was rude, and I even told one of the clerks to fuck off. But the worst thing was my brain refused to work, and I completely stuffed up the interview."

"Oh, sweetheart, I am so sorry".

Suddenly Lydia's sympathy was too much, and Rhonwen burst into tears again. "You don't understand. It's even worse. Keira got the job!"

Lydia looked surprised. "What? But isn't she junior to you? How did she get the job?"

Rhonwen shook her head. "I don't know, but she did." She sat there, thinking about Keira, and a sudden wave of rage filled her mind. Looking directly at Lydia, she snarled. "Yes, I do. She fucked her way in! That tart is so cunning. You should have seen her dressed perfectly in a suit instead of her usual slutty look! I didn't even know she had applied, but looking back at how she strutted around the office, it was like she already knew she"d won.

Lydia was clearly shocked by Rhonwen's strong language and the anger in her voice. Seeing the look on her face, Rhonwen felt herself flush with humiliation. "You see! I don't understand what's happening to me. I am not myself. I am so sorry, Lydia." Her voice trailed off, and she started sobbing again.

Lydia stayed with her for nearly an hour, and Rhonwen was exhausted and wrung out. When the phone rang, Lydia jumped up. "You stay there; I'll get it."

"Thank you, Lydia."

She quickly returned. "It's your boss, Brian. He's got your handbag and coat and wants to know if he can drop them off to you."

Rhonwen's sense of calm almost disintegrated then and there, but, taking a deep breath, she straightened her shoulders and got up off the lounge, saying. "I don't really need them tonight, but I had better speak with him myself." She returned a few minutes later, looking a little put out. "He agreed not to come around tonight, but he insisted on bringing my things over tomorrow afternoon."

Looking at the clock on the mantlepiece, Rhonwen suddenly felt guilty about taking up so much of Lydia's time. She took a deep breath and walked over to the older woman, who was stacking the tea cups and saucers on a tray. Bending down to help her, she quietly thanked her for her support. "I am going to have a shower. I appreciate your help. I'll be OK." She said to her friend as she said goodbye at the apartment door, thinking that if she said it firmly enough, it might come true.

It was several hours later that Rhonwen almost jumped out of her skin at the sound of the security doorbell. Rhonwen had buried herself in a novel after her shower, and she now felt a flash of irritation at the idea that it might be Brian, ignoring her refusal to see him tonight. Tempted to hide and not answer, she looked out the window and realised it was late afternoon. *The Mirror!* She had organised with Gavin for it to be delivered today.

She quickly raced to the intercom in the hall and found that it was Gavin himself downstairs. She let them in and then opened her own door, sliding the stopper in to prop it open. She could hear the voices of two men coming up the stairwell, one of which had a familiar timbre and drawl. As they came into view, she saw they were carrying the package carefully between them.

Just as they arrived on the landing, she heard Lydia call to her from the next landing. "Everything all right, Rhonwen?" Craning her head over the stairs to look up, she grinned. "Lydia, I have been very naughty. I bought myself something beautiful, and it's just being delivered."

Turning back to the men who were now right beside her, she was greeted by Gavin. "Hello there, Miss Tierney!"

"Hello, Mr.?" She stopped, suddenly realising that she did not know his surname.

"Gavin will be fine," he said with a wink. "I'd like you to meet a friend of mine, Erik."

Gavin nodded towards a tall, solidly built man with long, flowing blond hair and a glowing blond beard tightly cropped around his face. He grinned and then said hello in a voice that carried a hint of a Scandinavian accent. Rhonwen immediately took to him, and feeling embarrassed that she might be a little obvious, she quickly invited them through the door.

"Come into the living room." She said excitedly, then stepped to the fireplace and pointed to the bare space above it. "There! That's where I want it."

She took a step back for the men, who now placed the large wrapped object against the fireplace, when she suddenly saw that there was no hook available to suspend the mirror from. Gavin and Erik looked up at the empty space, and Erik spoke up, his English laced with a Norse accent. "No problem, Miss. I've got some tools in the car. I'll run down and fetch them. Won't be long now."

Before Rhonwen could reply, he took off down the hall with an agility that belied his solid frame.

"I'll have to pay you for your time, Gavin." She said in an apologetic tone.

"No need, Miss Tierney, it's all part of the service."

Suddenly, Erik was back in the room, and the speed with which he returned surprised Rhonwen. "That was quick!"

He grinned broadly. "I like to keep fit, Miss, ja."

As she watched him unpack an electric drill and several hooks, she noticed he was not even out of breath. Then she looked at the size of his arms and mused that he truly was a very fit man indeed.

"Well, thank you for doing this, Erik; I don't know how I would have managed."

Although she tried to sound matter of fact, Rhonwen felt coy and could feel a blush creeping up over her face. It was the same as it always was in just about any situation with unknown men; she would have preferred to retreat to some safe corner of the room.

Erik beamed at Rhonwen. "I am sure a lovely woman such as yourself can more than take care of herself."

Gavin laughed at his friend's blatant flirting while Rhonwen blushed even more deeply, suddenly picking up on the not-so-subtle tone of the conversation.

"I'm sorry, I didn't mean, " her voice trailed off

Lydia appeared at the door of the lounge room. She had a strange look that puzzled Rhonwen, but she was too self-conscious to try to interpret her friend's expression and took the opportunity to retreat to the other side of the room.

Erik measured the wall and installed several strong brass hooks from which to suspend the mirror, which Gavin had finished unwrapping. Lydia suddenly gasped as she saw the piece emerging from the thick brown paper and bubble wrap. Rhonwen was puzzled by a look in Lydia's eyes as she peered at the mirror. She seemed calculating somehow, but Rhonwen dismissed it, too caught up in the moment as the older woman exclaimed. "Oh my, that is simply beautiful, Rhonwen."

"Isn't it?" She stopped and then demurely confessed. "It was frightfully expensive, you know."

Lydia came across the room and put an arm around her, and, smiling brightly, said. "Never mind that, dear. You know you deserve it."

As the two women stood back admiring the mirror, Gavin and Erik busied themselves, hanging it onto the newly fitted hooks. For a second, Rhonwen thought she saw the piece on the top of the mirror radiate with a faint orange glow, but when she stepped closer to inspect it, there appeared nothing unusual about the strange decorative piece or the rest of the mirror.

She stepped back and almost tripped over Sooty, who appeared very excited with all the commotion and seemed to have taken a liking to Gavin and Erik, slipping in and out of their legs, purring loudly and then making his way around to Rhonwen and Lydia.

Rhonwen quickly bent down and whisked him into her arms. "You silly cat! I almost fell over you."

Finished with the task of hanging Rhonwen's new acquisition, Gavin and Erik were paying Sooty the necessary attention, and the black feline was purring loudly. "That's odd." Rhonwen said, surprised at the cat's friendly demeanour. "Sooty doesn't usually take to strangers. In fact, he can be downright mean to people he doesn't know."

Gavin, busy scratching Sooty's chin, nodded slowly, speaking to the cat. "But we're not strangers, are we?"

Rhonwen thought it a curious remark but was distracted by her sudden realisation that she would need to get her spare chequebook from her bedroom since she didn't have her handbag. Quickly returning, she started writing out the details.

"Do I make this out to you personally or the shop?" she asked Gavin. He told her to make it out to the shop and handed her an invoice before turning to help Erik pack up the wrapping and tools. Rhonwen noticed that the delivery charge was very reasonable, and looking up, she asked Gavin about the cost of hanging the mirror.

"That is just part of the service."

She was about to protest, and then, for some reason, the idea slid away from her mind, and she completed the cheque, handing it to Gavin without further argument. He reached out, and they shook hands. "Thank you for your business, Miss Tierney." Then, pausing, he looked deep into her eyes. "If ever I can be of any assistance to you in any manner at all, please call me."

Bending down to scratch Sooty's head, he murmured. "You remember that as well."

The cat purred in response as if he understood what was asked of him. The sudden sombreness was interrupted by Erik's cheery voice. "I, too, am equally available, Miss. Especially on those long, cold winter nights."

Gavin laughed and pushed Erik towards the door of the apartment. "You"ll have to excuse my forward friend here". Erik turned and looked at Rhonwen. "I am always available for flame-haired beauties such as yourself".

Rhonwen, unused to being flirted with, didn't know what to say or where to turn. Looking at him, she was drawn to his beautiful grey eyes, and suddenly, she felt very calm. She managed to thank the men and see them out to the landing. When she returned, she found Lydia standing in front of the mirror with a look of wonder on her face and a look in her eyes that Rhonwen didn't recognise.

She started when she realised that Rhonwen was watching her. The strange look disappeared as she smiled brightly and motioned towards the mirror with her hand. "How on earth did you find it? It is absolutely wonderful!"

11

As Stewart and Keira stepped out of the warm pub into the cold night, he watched her embrace the freezing winds sweeping around her. He was surprised that rather than seeking shelter from the gusts, she appeared to relish them. Then, with the elegance of a dancer, she slipped out of her coat and tossed it to Stewart. He plucked it from the air and threw it casually over his shoulder, watching her throw her arms high and spin around on the tips of her toes.

"Don't you just love the chill in the air?" She asked as she flung her head back, revealing her beautiful white throat.

"I have to say," Stewart replied, putting his arms around her and drawing her close. I much prefer warmth." He winked sheepishly, "especially the warmth of your thighs."

Keira laughed, bringing her own arms down around him. For a moment, he thought she seemed softer and not as edgy. She kissed him, and he felt her tongue linger; then, out of the blue, she bit him on the bottom lip.

"Ouch!" Surprised, Stewart reached up and wiped his lip. A small smear of blood covered the back of his hand. "What the ..."

Keira interrupted, reaching up and pulling his face back down to hers and kissing him once more, gently this time. She sucked on his lip and drew a small amount of blood into her mouth. "You taste so nice."

Stewart thought her casual observation sounded as if she was talking about a midnight snack. He could feel the skin on his arms pucker into two tight little bumps. Watching her carefully, he saw the usual mercurial Keira looking back at him, but there was still something he couldn't put his finger on that was different.

"And, perhaps you can taste me later at my place." Keira cocked her head and winked at Stewart.

Keira's invitation took Stewart completely by surprise. In the time they were bed buddies, as Keira liked to refer to them, they always stayed at his place. On the few occasions where he had suggested that they go to her apartment for a change, she had played coy, finding one reason or another why they should go to his. For Stewart, this had added to her intrigue, and from time to time, he had teased Keira about it, suggesting that she was either secretly married or still lived at home, a rich daddy's girl unable to look after herself. Keira would play along with Stewart but would never change the venue until now.

In the back of his mind, Stewart reflected on his conversation with Brian earlier that evening. His friend was right. There were odd things afoot. For an instant, he had the strange feeling that there was something big, very big, about to happen. Stepping back and watching Keira's almost childlike antics in the cold, he smiled. They were, comparatively speaking, in safe corporate jobs far removed from the dangers of military actions and covert missions. *So what big event were they likely to be involved in?* He thought.

Suddenly Keira jumped out into the street, where she hailed a cab. With a squeal of tyres, the driver pulled over, and Keira, having run back to Stewart, now pulled him into the vehicle, where the two settled into the back seat. She called out the address, and the driver sped into the traffic.

When Stewart stepped into Keira's apartment, he was immediately drawn to the decor. His own hedonistic streak instantly related to Keira's lush tastes. "Welcome to my parlour, said the spider to the fly." Keira whispered into Stewart's ear.

He ignored the loaded reference and took an admiring look around the room. Spying the Lempicka, Stewart went over to have a closer look, noting the wonderful bordello-like feel that the green and burgundy colour scheme created. "This place is fantastic, Keira." He said, running his hand along the gilt frame of the painting, realising that it was real and not a print. He then strolled casually around the room, inspecting the bits and pieces that gave the space such character.

"Why thank you, kind Sir."

Stewart was truly intrigued by what he saw. He knew that she was a Goth or at least a little rich girl playing at it, but the work that had gone into the apartment was significant. Each piece was carefully selected and placed to create the required ambience.

Keira had disappeared into the kitchen and now came back with two Champagne glasses. As she passed one of the glasses to Stewart, she casually observed, "Did you know that the first glasses of this type were fashioned on Madame de Pompadour's breasts."

"It was my impression that Marie Antoinette's breasts did the honours." Stewart replied.

The two often played a game of one-upman ship with respect to what they knew. In one of Brian's frustrated moments with Keira, Stewart had pointed out to him that she was quite knowledgeable and that he should give her a bit of a break rather than constantly criticising her. He inspected his glass more carefully, holding it up and turning it against the muted light emanating from an art deco lamp in the shape of a naked woman holding up a torch.

"I suspect it would fit perfectly against your own." Stewart smiled at Keira.

"Perhaps," she conceded. "You can always check for yourself."

Stewart sensed that the Champagne was a cue to congratulate Keira on the new job, and given how the evening had progressed so far, he was not inclined to disappoint her. He walked across to her and raised his glass.

"To the new kid on the management block. All the best, my sweet; I'm sure it will all work out."

"Thanks, Stew." Keira took a sip, lent across to Stewart, and kissed him on the cheek.

"You are sweet." She put her glass down and poked him gently in the chest. "Now, you be a good boy while I slip into something less comfortable."

"Don't you mean more comfortable?" he replied with a wink.

"I meant what I said," was her curt reply, and she disappeared into her bedroom.

Left on his own, Stewart's curiosity drew him to a covered table against one of the walls of the living room. He walked over to it and, lifting the draped cloth by one of its corners, cautiously peered underneath. Somehow he wasn't too surprised to see a collection of occult paraphernalia covering the table. He smiled and dropped the corner of the cloth back into place.

Sipping his champagne, he wandered over to the bookshelf, interested in what he might find there. A fair number of the books were on the occult, which seemed to be a pretty comprehensive selection. There was a large space among them that suggested something that was usually kept on the shelf was elsewhere. He was aware of himself automatically filing this observation, as he would if he was working, but before he could reflect on why he did this, he was startled by Keira's voice.

"Are you going to keep me waiting forever?"

"Of course not, Keira, my sweet!" Stewart called out.

When he got to Keira's bedroom door, he stopped short. The mood of the room was far from the girly seductiveness that Keira had displayed earlier. The decor and Keira's demeanour emanated a dark gothic atmosphere that reminded Stewart of a temple or place of worship.

The interior of the bedroom was draped in red and black, with candles lit everywhere. They cast flickering shadows against the walls. The four-poster bed had curtains drawn back and tied, and the red satin sheet glistened seductively to him.

Keira stood at the end of the bed, much of her obscured by the shadows in the room and the indirect light of the candles, a vision of feminine power that mesmerised Stewart. For an instant, he had to remind himself to breathe; he was so caught up in her beauty.

Her raven hair seemed to stand out from her head in tight curls, and her face was set in a stern yet alluring mask. Her blood-red lips were slightly apart, with the tip of her tongue resting between them, while her eyes flashed challengingly at Stewart.

Around her neck was a gold torque, at each end a bright-red stone that flashed brilliantly in the raw candlelight. Below her bare breasts, her body was braced in a black and red corset that tightly tucked in her waist and flared out over her hips where her right hand rested provocatively, while her left hand lingered at the top of her thigh where her long leather boots ended. A small silver tassel hung off the lower edge of the corset. It directed his attention to her glistening pubic hair and the little piece of jewellery dangling provocatively between her parted legs.

Stewart could feel a surge of passion through his body and mind, inflaming him with a searing heat. He felt her raw sexual energy capturing him, leaving him imprisoned in a sensual mist. At that moment, Stewart felt that little else mattered but Keira. As his eyes wandered over her body, Keira's blackened nipples noticeably puckered and extended provocatively towards him, an inescapable invitation.

Stewart suddenly realised that their breathing had synchronised to an erotic rhythm, underscoring their lust for each other, while the space between them seemed to sizzle with an electric charge. He hadn't noticed until now that, in addition to the candlelight, the room was filled with the sound of a primitive chant that was barely audible yet quite distinct. In that instant of awareness, it appeared to become louder, and amidst it Keira's voice reached out to him.

"Will you come to me, Stewart, or shall I fetch you and force you to do my bidding?"

Despite the assault on his senses, Stewart maintained some objectivity. A small part of him recognised that although it was undoubtedly Keira's voice, it had a timbre to it that was completely unfamiliar to him, resonating with a subtle lilt to her speech that was not normally there. What remained of his reason questioned what was going on, only to be ultimately overridden by the rise of his lust that quelled any logical thought. He wanted only to surrender to the overwhelming desire to fuck her.

His subconscious tuned automatically into the mood, and he joined the game; dropping the timbre of his voice, he replied theatrically.

"I, Stewart, will not do your bidding but will reach out and ravish you as the prize that has been sent to me!"

Her response was to snarl at him.

"Your prize I am not, for first you must beat me, and if you cannot, then I, Scáthach, shall demand your surrender, and you shall do my bidding evermore."

Suddenly, with the speed of a predatory cat, Keira launched herself against him, and the force of her assault threw both onto the floor. Stewart felt his chest almost collapse, painfully driving the air from his lungs as she straddled his torso. She immediately leaned down and forcefully pressed her mouth against his lips, her tongue ravenously exploring his, then moving across his face while biting and scratching his chest. Intermingled with her perfume, he could smell it so unmistakably raw and sexual that it drove his passion higher.

Stewart was taken completely by surprise by her and was at a loss for what to do. His frenzied mind wanted to retaliate and make her submit to his will and passion, while the other part of him wanted to calm her down, challenged by her deep-seated animalism.

One of her bites, hard into his neck, resolved the issue for him, and years of training and combat experience took over, releasing him from any civilised restraint. A surge of power followed, the sudden release of adrenaline, and he grabbed her arms. With the well-honed movements of a warrior, he lifted her off his chest and flung her beside him while at the same time landing on top of her.

A deep groan escaped Keira, and he thought for an instant that he must have really hurt her, but he immediately realised that she was gathering her strength. He suddenly felt her pelvis arch into his groin, and it took all of his experience to avoid being thrown off against the wall beside him.

Sitting over the top of her, Stewart saw her eyes flash with passionate fire and her breasts heave and strain against his weight. The sight of her hard, black-painted nipples conquered any remaining reason, and he grabbed her wrists while pinning her arms onto the floor beside her head. Having restrained her, he leant over and kissed her passionately on the mouth.

Then, he felt her shift from her original combative mood to a more passionate one, and she began to tear at his clothes. Together, they undressed him, discarding the clothing across the room while kissing and caressing each other's bodies.

Now naked, Stewart broke free from Keira's embrace and jumped to his feet. He bent down and, in one fluid motion, scooped her into his arms, turned, and threw her onto the bed, where he snapped the ties on the corset, freeing her glistening body.

Keira groaned, partly from being liberated from the constraints of the garment but mostly because of Stewart's exploring hand slipping between her legs, finding its way into her longing body. He grinned at her. "I have vanquished you, and now I will ravish you as promised."

"Do with me as you want, for you have bested me!" Her voice rumbled in her chest while her own hand reached for Stewart, drawing him into her embrace.

Suddenly, as Stewart plunged into her, Keira arched back, her head snapping into the satin pillow while her eyes rolled back, the whites of her eyes eerily staring at her lover.

12

After their frantic lovemaking, Keira appeared totally spent and immediately fell asleep in his arms, snuggled in close, her head resting gently on his chest. All of this had confused him even more. *How could she go from being almost demonic to then changing into what he felt was an uncharacteristic childlike softness?*

He had laid there, ill at ease, trying to process what had happened. Deciding that he wanted to be in his own place, surrounded by familiar things, he gently moved Keira, careful not to wake her. As he crawled around the floor gathering his clothing, his hand came across something hard under the bed. Pulling it out into the dim light from the last of the candles, he found that it was a book. He immediately remembered the gap in the shelves in the other room.

Quietly blowing out the candles, he took his clothes and the book to the lounge and looked closely at a very old leather-bound book after dressing. The cover was heavy, expertly embossed with gold symbols and carved wooden corners. And it was locked, which had added to its mystique.

Now running his hand over the front of the book, he noticed the outline of a raised piece of leather that appeared out of place. It had loosened along one of the edges, and the small gold clip that anchored it to the cover of the book was half open. Giving into his curiosity, he carefully opened the clip and lifted the leather flap.

Shocked, he recoiled, almost dropping the book. Inhaling sharply, he saw a jewel embedded in the wood and leather pocket underneath. It was exactly the same as the one Brian had been given by the gypsy woman all those years ago. The one he was now wearing around his neck! He stared at it for a few minutes, then quickly concealing it again, slipped back into Keira's bedroom and slid it back under the bed.

Initially hoping to flag down a cab, Stewart found the street deserted and, feeling restless, decided instead to set out and start walking home. He needed to think, and the cold air would clear the last of the champagne from his head. A half-hour of brisk walking saw him letting himself into his apartment, where, exhausted, he threw himself onto the couch.

Lying there in the dark, Stewart became aware that he ached all over. Looking down at his shirt, he could see the vague outlines of some stains, so he reached across and flicked the lamp on the table beside the couch. The stain was a dark red, and he immediately knew that the scratches Keira had inflicted had continued to bleed.

Annoyed at the prospect of ruining his shirt, he jumped up and headed into the bathroom, unbuttoning it to inspect the injuries from the night's events. Although not deep, the raking marks on his chest and back had bled profusely, far more than superficial cuts would normally. Having seen enough wounds over his years in combat, Stewart was puzzled how such superficial scratches could persist in bleeding.

He opened the cabinet above the sink and took some cotton pads and antiseptic. Gently cleaning the marks, he applied some ointment to his chest, a slight stinging the only discomfort. Peering at his reflection, he saw himself as he always looked. There was no sign that he had changed, yet he felt that something dark and deeply disturbing had somehow marked him.

Unable to sleep, he went into the small study attached to his bedroom. Sitting down at his desk, he pulled a notepad from the drawer and in minutes, the page was covered with a series of small circles and lines. Stewart had a long-standing habit of mind mapping whenever he needed to make sense of something that was confusing or puzzling him. He had a deep trust in his approach, although to most onlookers, it often appeared chaotic and nonsensical.

When he had finished, he sat back, his forehead furrowed by deep lines. *Well, that was about as useful as tits on a bull.* Stewart had heard the expression from an Australian soldier a long time ago, and he felt that, in this instance, he couldn't think of anything better to describe the futility of the exercise. At this moment, he had a simple set of what appeared to be random facts.

Fact: Rhonwen had not only acted strangely in the last twenty-four hours, she had been like a completely different person. Fact: Brian had started wearing an old jewel given to him by an old gypsy with no explanation other than it felt right. Fact: He found an identical jewel in Keira's apartment, embedded in an antique witchcraft volume. Fact: Keira has a table full of occult bric-a-brac that she keeps hidden from view. Fact: Keira has looked physically different over the last twenty-four hours and just now had been sexually different.

Stewart sat there for a long time, staring at the heading "Conclusion" printed boldly on the otherwise blank page.

So, this has something to do with witchcraft? he thought. *That's impossible!*

Despite instantly trying to dismiss the absurd idea, it somehow refused to be eliminated from his otherwise logical equation. On reflection, though, he had to admit that he felt distinctly out of sorts in Keira's apartment, as if he had been hypnotised into some trance state.

Another explanation that came to him was that she could have drugged him. Keira had some interesting and peculiar friends who seemed to move in strange circles where pretty well anything could be obtained if you had the inclination and the money. It was, therefore, not out of the realm of possibility that he had been subjected to some new experimental pharmaceutical.

He was very well aware that Keira herself was quite liberal in her views and attitudes towards drugs as well as in her behaviour. He had always kept this knowledge from anyone in the office, especially Brian, who would dismiss her if he found out. It was also a fact that Keira had never shown positive in the random drug tests the firm carried out from time to time. He had, therefore, felt that she was trustworthy enough.

Despite all of that, Stewart had always felt a little guilty about keeping this information from Brian. He had rationalised it to himself by thinking of himself as keeping an eye on her, even though that was more in his own interest rather than that of the firms. He suddenly stopped. *"You're losing it, Stew," he thought.* A small chuckle escaped him when he thought the next idea he would arrive at was that aliens had abducted him.

Leaning forward, he wrote, Question: Had he lost complete perspective on the whole thing? Sitting back, he pondered that for a while before deciding that the time had come to disclose everything to Brian. His instinct told him they would need both brains to solve this puzzle.

13

When Keira awoke on Saturday morning, she felt like she had been struck by a heavy object. Half asleep, she reached across the satin sheets, their chill indicating that Stewart must have left her some time ago. She sighed, conscious of the emptiness that surrounded her and that echoed within her. It agitated her, and she felt the growing need to fill it with something or someone. Nagging at the corner of her mind was a sense of discomfort about this unease with her own company. Normally, she preferred to wake alone, without the demands of another to interfere with her routines.

Irritated by this strange feeling, she sat up and looked across into the small mirror on the vanity. Her eyes were bloodshot, and her hair was a chaotic mess that stood up every which way. She swung her legs across the edge of the bed. She felt stiff and bruised rather than the powerfully fluid movements of the night before. The mirror revealed that she sported several serious bruises along her arms. She assumed that there would be a few more on the rest of her.

Placing her feet firmly on the ground beside the bed, Keira stretched her sore frame, trying to undo the tension in her muscles. "Shit!" The pain was intense. *What the fuck?* she thought to herself.

As she headed to the shower, she was keenly aware that whatever power she had felt in the last 48 hours appeared to have vanished. She felt physically clumsy and awkward; her whole body ached, and she had a screaming headache. Emotionally she was fragile as well. Close to tears, Keira suddenly felt angry. Confused, she tried to clear her head, and for a moment, she wondered what Stewart had done to her last night.

As she stepped into the shower, she thought about it and realised that feeling so good yesterday and so bad today was unnatural. And she knew Stewart wasn't to blame. This was somehow her own doing. She had asked him back to her place, and although her recollection of last night's events was a little sketchy, she challenged him, and he certainly stepped up to the plate. Keira leaned against the wall, letting the hot water run the length of her body, soothing her aching muscles while still trying to put the pieces together. Bits of memory slid around her consciousness, and she found it difficult to put the fragments together. She remembered that it was wild, but something else was nagging at her.

As she dried herself, the bruises and scratches disturbed her. She wasn't sure she liked what had happened last night. And she didn't really know what had happened anyway. Maybe this was because of the spell. The ritual she had followed had worked. She had got the job, and Rhonwen had fled the office, making a fool of herself. She had achieved part of what she wanted. But then again, it hadn't been Brian with her last night.

No, something else was going on, and she sensed that it had to do with the magic. A stranger to asking anyone for help, Keira realised that she would need to speak to someone experienced in magic. If she were to profit from her foray into the arcane arts, she would need to allow some guidance. Morgan, the charismatic high priestess of the last coven she had attended, had impressed her as someone who might know something about real magic. She had dismissed the other covens she had found as consisting essentially of a few try-hards and sycophants.

Morgan, however, was different, very different. Haughty and mysterious, she exuded power. Whether she was the real deal was difficult to judge, but Keira had felt that there was more to Morgan than she had let on. Shaking her head to release the waves in her hair before she dried it, Keira couldn't help wondering if it was her own wishful thinking. Despite her experiences over the last few days, she still teetered on the edge of being a true believer.

Generally comforted by her own sense of superiority, Keira pondered her newfound weakness. Her mother would certainly not approve. Not that Keira would tell her anything of what she had been up to, even though there would be the usual interrogation at their monthly lunch. Making up her mind to call Morgan, she returned to the bedroom to find her phone.

"Morgan? Yes, it's Keira Blair. I was hoping that I could speak with you. No, I'm all right; well, not really. No, nothing serious. At least, I don't think so. Yes, I would like to meet with you." Your place in an hour? Great. I'll see you there."

Relieved at Morgan's understanding reception, Keira hung up. She dressed quickly, taking pains to present a sophisticated and expensive image, not only to bolster her own mood but because she sensed it was expected. Morgan had impressed her as someone who would disapprove of a sloppy appearance. Going to the kitchen, she found a couple of painkillers to help with her splitting head, and deciding to get coffee on the way, Keira headed out the door.

Keira was awestruck by the books and antiques arranged within the huge space when she stepped into Morgan's library. Previously they had met in one of the reception rooms on the ground level, so this was Keira's first glimpse of the depth of luxury and wealth at Morgan's command. The walls were covered with shelves that ran from the floor to the ceiling and had been constructed from rare and exquisitely crafted timbers. Several glass-topped display cases occupied the more central spaces and appeared to Keira to contain rare books and artefacts.

In front of an enormous bay window stood a beautiful library table made of burr oak with a bull nose edge. At each of the four corners of the table were carved floral designs. The entire edge of the table, which stood on four well-turned legs on heavy brass castors, was carved in an oak leaf pattern, while the writing surface was made from a deep red leather with guilt edges embossed with oak leaves. One of the corners of the large table was occupied by an antique banker's lamp, hovering over a pile of what looked like parchments.

The setting of the room and its splendid contents had so captivated Keira that she barely noticed the conversation between Morgan and the man who had introduced himself to her as Morgan's son. As the door shut behind him, Morgan's voice drew Keira's attention away from the statue she examined. Turning around, she found her hostess sitting regally in a beautifully upholstered Queen Ann armchair. She smiled at Keira and said in a warm and welcoming voice. "How lovely to see you again, my dear." Then, pointing to a chair towards the side of the desk, close to where she was sitting, she continued, "Come, take a seat, and we can take our time to discuss what it is you came for."

Keira walked over to the chair and quietly sat down. She felt as if she had stepped back in time and arrived in the headmistress's office, having been caught breaking one of the many rules that governed a schoolgirl's life. "Thank you for seeing me, Miss ..." Keira stopped suddenly, realising that she did not know the woman's surname.

"Call me Morgan, dear. There's really no need to be formal, is there?"

The door opened before Keira could thank her, and an older woman entered carrying a tray. As she put it down on the table, Keira recognised the costliness of the china and silverware. It matched the rest of the house, and its familiarity helped somehow to make her feel a little more settled. Noting the pile of scones, her stomach rumbled, and Keira realised she hadn't eaten since sometime yesterday.

As Keira watched, the woman curtsied and left the library. The incongruity of Morgans's informality with her and the old-world deference of her staff struck Keira as a little strange. However, she didn't have time to think further about it as Morgan had risen from her chair and was now serving the tea, passing her a cup and plate.

"We will have our tea first, I think". Morgan smiled warmly as she spoke, then took her own tea and returned to her chair. She was charming as they chatted about her collection of rare books, and Keira relaxed. She had polished off a couple of the scones and felt more comfortable when Morgan, putting her own tea cup down, looked directly at her.

"Now, how can I be of assistance, my dear?"

Rarely at a loss for words, Keira struggled momentarily to think of where she should begin her story.

"Do you remember telling me not to be hasty and go away and think about why I wanted to join a coven?"

Morgan nodded. "Of course, dear. Why would I forget?"

Despite feeling more relaxed, Keira remained alert and watchful. She wondered whether Morgan's subtle compliment was genuine or if the woman was trying to disarm her. "Well, I did as you suggested." Keira paused.

"Go on." Morgan encouraged her.

"Ahem, what I didn't tell you is that I had already been practising certain rituals and incantations." She stopped momentarily, thinking Morgan had shifted slightly in her chair.

"And the problem is exactly what?"

The almost imperceptible edge to Morgan's voice did not escape Keira, whose radar for danger had been well-honed at the exclusive private schools she had attended. However, despite her vigilance, she decided to put her caution aside to a degree. She answered carefully, certain that if anyone could shed some light on what was happening to her, it was the woman sitting before her.

"I recently performed a ritual incantation and since then have noticed certain changes about me that are, to say the least, a little weird."

"Isn't that what we are looking for, Keira, the unusual and strange?" Morgan smiled as if inviting Keira into a conspiracy. "I suspect the very last thing you are striving for is mediocrity."

Keira didn't answer immediately, reflecting carefully on Morgan's observation of her. When she did reply, her voice was soft. "You're right. That's not what I want. However, I want to understand what happened, and I thought you may be able to explain it to me."

Keira stopped speaking for a moment and looked intently at Morgan. "I was hoping that you would teach and guide me."

Morgan got up, her black dress swishing against the white silk cover of the chair. She very casually strolled around the desk to where Keira was sitting. Smiling reassuringly, she moved around to stand behind her; she placed her hands on Keira's shoulders. It was a light and gentle touch as if to reassure Keira that everything was all right, and despite herself, Keira felt herself relax back into the chair.

"Well, my dear, if I am going to help you, you must be open and honest with me."

Morgan's hands continued to linger for an instant, and then one of her fingers ran along the top of her shoulder to the nape of her neck, where it stopped. "Tell me everything, Keira."

Morgan's voice seemed to penetrate Keira's mind, and she completely let go of her doubt as an unaccustomed warmth engulfed her, dispelling any of her previous reservations.

14

Morgan had watched from across the road as Gavin and Erik carried a heavy, well-wrapped object into the apartment building. They might have seen her had she not chosen to observe the goings-on through the eyes of a massive Rottweiler looking out of the back window of a car. Gavin appeared very alert, and his Viking friend had been equally watchful. It had been a while since she had occupied an animal's body, and she had enjoyed the rippling muscles and keen senses that came with the experience. For someone of her skill and calibre, it was a simple thing to do and required little or no energy to either invoke or to maintain; however, in these times, there were few, if any, who had the gift or the necessary skills in the arcane arts to do this.

She watched the two men, thinking about Gavin's feeble attempt at hiding the Tierney girl's details. He had not always been so easy to best. In the old days, Gavin would have seen through her and done a better job of hiding what he didn't want her to know. Aware that he must be furious with himself, Morgan had savoured that little victory.

Having taken a good look at the building and its surrounds so that she could scry it out later, she had gently withdrawn her consciousness from the animal hosting her. Then, she settled back into her body, safely seated in her car a block away. She had found herself intensely curious and irritated by something nagging at the edges of her mind. Not having any idea what it was that Gavin had given Rhonwen Tierney was irritating. After the disturbance on Thursday night, she knew that someone was coming into their power. It could be the Tierney girl, but she just had a feeling there was something more important going on here.

Now still preoccupied by the puzzle of the disturbances of the last few days and having found little information so far, Morgan had been surprised by the call from Keira. After speaking with her over the phone she had felt something click into place. Yes, this girl was somehow involved in what was going on. She"d remembered the young woman who had sought to join the coven a few months previously. Morgan had been unsure of the girl's motives for wanting to join, and although she appeared to have the right potential, Morgan had put her off, suggesting to Keira that she should think carefully about her next step.

Almost exactly an hour after her call, Keira had arrived and been ushered into the library by her stepson, Jean. She had sent him off to ask Clara to make some morning tea for them and then turning to greet Keira her alarm bells went off immediately. When Keira had walked into the room, Morgan recognised a distinct difference in her aura. The unusual harmonic resonance emanating from the young woman was somehow familiar, but she couldn't quite put her finger on it. *So that's what happened the other night."*

Aware of Keira's caution, she had taken pains to disarm her and make her feel comfortable. Rather than getting straight to the reason for Keira's visit, Morgan took her time, not wanting to rush the girl. Whatever Keira had done obviously had implications that she didn't understand, but now Morgan was getting impatient with her reticence. Morgan's instincts were always right, and just now, they were cautioning her to wait. Alienating this girl would not serve any purpose at all.

She knew that Keira was being especially careful about how much she said and what she alluded to, and to some degree, Morgan could understand that. The two didn't really know each other, and disclosing anything to do with Wicca or the arts would, in most circles, get some very odd reactions. But the girl was here for exactly that reason, to discuss the craft, and yet she was still reluctant to offer details of what she did and what had happened to her.

Finally, she decided to take matters into her own hands. Using her voice to lull Keira into a more relaxed state, she moved quietly to where she sat and made the connection. The moment she touched Keira, she felt an intense sense of apprehension.

15

Stewart had waited until a reasonable hour to contact Brian and had not been all that surprised to find his friend at the office despite it being Saturday. The fact that the office door was locked was, however, unexpected. Curious, Stewart knocked and called out that it was him.

"Come in!"

A buzzing sound accompanied the click of the security lock, and Stewart pushed on the heavy door. "How come you locked the door?" He was still feeling unusually wary and hearing the note of irritation in his own voice, Stewart was just about to apologise for his peevishness when he realised Brian was not alone.

"Stewart, this is Professor Hayden Cooper. He is an archeologist I know who specialises in ancient Celtic artefacts and icons."

Stewart had always considered Professors old men with grey beards and glasses. Hayden Cooper's appearance, however, completely demolished Stewart's preconceptions. Here was an elegant man in his late twenties or early thirties, dressed in a stylish set of dark tan trousers and a black T-shirt under a corduroy jacket. His face, clean-shaven and lightly tanned, had an open mobile expression that appeared to invite conversation.

On the chair beside the young man lay a trench coat and a long striped scarf reminiscent of Oxford or Cambridge.

Hayden unfolded himself from his occupied chair and turned, offering Stewart his hand. "Nice to meet you, Professor Cooper."

"Call me Hayden; I'm uncomfortable with the Professor thing."

"He would have done that anyway, Hayden," Brian interjected. "Stewart doesn't stand for formalities. Given half the chance, He'd probably call the Queen Lizzie if he were to ever meet her."

Hayden laughed. "A man after my own heart."

Brian lent forward and placed the pendant that had, until recently, lived unobtrusively in his sock drawer on the desk. "This is the pendant I told you about over the phone. I am very curious about its origin."

Returning to the desk, Hayden picked up a jeweller's loupe and peered at the pendant. "This is an interesting piece. When you described it over the phone, I did some research."

He flipped open the laptop he had brought and invited them both to come over and look at the screen. Scrolling down the page, he stopped at a drawing of a pendant that looked just like Brian's.

Turning an excited face back to both the men behind him, he continued, "It looks the same! If it is what it looks like, then it's part of a set. According to some myths, this could be one of five amulets that, when placed together, form a conduit into the magical dimension and thus imbues the owner of the pieces with enormous power." He paused for a moment. "From memory, I thought they had disappeared sometime in the Middle Ages, and I have no idea how this one got to Eastern Europe. It doesn't belong there at all!"

Stewart listened intently while wondering how much Brian had already told him. "So what else can you tell us about it?" Stewart wanted to know."

Hayden retrieved a large magnifying glass from his satchel and inspected the pendant carefully.

"Well, some of the setting is definitely late twelfth or thirteenth century, but the inner part that encircles the gem is much older. There's an inscription in old Norse, maybe from around the fifth or sixth century." He stopped to scratch his forehead. "Unfortunately, I can't tell you much about the origin of the stone other than it looks like it could be a diamond. Gems aren'tmy expertise, but the

Amulets are supposed to be valuable in what we call the Mundane world so that would fit."

Stewart was surprised. "But this doesn't look like any diamond I've ever seen."

Hayden smiled at Stewart's observation. "That's because You're used to seeing expertly facet-cut stones on women's fingers."

Brian scratched his head in a way that Stewart recognised meant he was calculating something. "So apart from its historical value, this is worth a lot of money." Hayden nodded. "In my view, if this is authentic, then this piece alone is invaluable. It could be an extraordinary historical find, and if the other four matching amulets were to be discovered as well and verified, it would be up there with the Saxon Hoard as one of the most significant finds of the last hundred years. It's just so unexpected that it was found in Europe. The five amulets are supposed to be linked to the British Isles exclusively. This is really very exciting and needs to be investigated."

The young academic sat back in his chair and silently contemplated the other two men, both of whom were more than stunned by Hayden's revelations. Stewart was the first to break the silence in the room. "Going to retire are we, Brian?"

The three chuckled at Stewart's light-hearted quip but then settled down to a more serious note.

"Is it possible that a stone of this kind can glow of its own accord?" Brian wanted to know.

Hayden didn't answer immediately, pausing to consider his answer. "If you mean can it reflect light so that it appears to glow, then the answer is yes."

Brian shook his head. "No, no. I mean, can it actually glow of its own accord?"

Stewart knew where Brian was going with this, yet decided to sit back and wait to see what reaction that question got before putting his own thoughts out there. The professor shook his head. "I'm not a physicist, but that seems completely improbable to me." He paused and then said. "Although if you believe the mythologies and legends, gemstones have always been associated with certain magical properties. Usually for protection in battle or against demons or the dark forces."

Hayden looked across at Brian, who appeared unable to take his eyes off the amulet as if expecting it to speak to him. "Apart from its obvious monetary value, this piece is a very valuable archeological find, and I would love to have the opportunity to study it further. What are you planning to do with it?"

Brian seemed startled by the idea that he should part with it. Watching him tense up, Stewart decided to keep things light-hearted. "Why don't you just keep wearing the amulet for now? It couldn't get a better bodyguard than you, could it?"

"It's as good a thought as any, I guess." Brian agreed, his relief obvious as he turned to Hayden.

"Thank you very much for the information, Hayden, and for coming around on such short notice. I would appreciate any further information you can find about this amulet, but for now, I think I will keep it in my possession."

Hayden got up, looking more than a little disappointed and, collecting his things, went to shake Brian's and Stewart's hands. "It is your call to make for now, Brian. But if this is authentic, there are protocols." He said in a serious voice that belied his friendly smile. "It was a pleasure to meet you both. It certainly made for a most interesting morning. For my part, it definitely calls for more research, and I will most certainly get back to you with anything that I find out. Similarly, I would appreciate it if you could let me know if you come across anything that would tell us how this piece came to be in Eastern Europe."

Stewart and Brian nodded. "Absolutely." Brian said. "You know, it would probably be safer if this was not mentioned to anyone else for now, given the value of the stone itself. I would prefer not to have to fight off some jewel thief while we all follow whatever leads we can find about this and the other pieces."

"I appreciate that, so I will be discrete and do all my own legwork on this one. I'll call if I find anything useful, and I look forward to hearing from you if you find out about any of the others." Hayden replied and headed for the door. Brian and Stewart watched silently as the heavy office door shut behind the young academic.

The instant the lock clicked into place, Stewart turned excitedly to Brian. "Guess what, my friend? I know where there's another one of these stones."

Brian's eyes popped almost out of his head. "You've found a second amulet?"

"I think so. Keira has an exact duplicate of that amulet embedded as an ornament in an antique book of magic. I can't be sure if it was the real deal or just a fake as I only got a quick look at it."

For an instant, Brian and Stewart sat there in silence.

Brian frowned. "A book on magic?"

"Yes. And not only that but well, that's what I wanted to sort of talk to you about this morning."

"Go on."

"It's gotten somewhat complicated. This was the first time I had actually been to Keira's place. She is usually pretty cagey about it, but, well, last night everything got a bit spooky."

Brian lent forward over his desk and looked closely at his friend. "What do you mean by “spooky”?"

"That hunch of yours, that all of this, Keira, Rhonwen and the amulet is damn odd, is absolutely on the mark. Look at this!" Stewart unbuttoned his shirt and dropped it off his shoulders, exposing the various scratches and emerging bruises, knowing that they mirrored those marking Brian's body after his dream about Keira.

Seeing Stewart's injuries, Brian cocked his head, recognition flaring in his eyes. Brian sucked his breath in. "This is Keira's handiwork?"

Stewart nodded. "Absolutely. The whole night was insane. She was not only different in one way, she was all over the place. First, she invited me back to her apartment, where I had never been welcome before. So, while she's busy, I look around and find a table full of occult stuff stashed in the corner of the lounge room. OK, I can sort of understand that. It's not so far from what I might expect. But she changed into some fury and launched herself at me like a predator, hence the wounds. I mean, don't get me wrong, the sex was fantastic, but it was also a bit scary."

"So the whole ferocious sex fiend thing isn't normal, Keira?" Brian asked, a hint of curiosity in his voice.

"No, that's just the point, and it doesn't end there. Afterwards, she changes again. This time she goes all soft and vulnerable and almost begs me to stay the night. We never spend the night together!" He paused for a minute. "Brian, whomever I had sex with last night may have looked like Keira, but you can be damned sure that it wasn't her. Even her voice had changed. In fact, it sounded as if there were two voices at work."

Stewart got up and walked over to the window. He stared out for a while and then turned around. "This is getting more and more bizarre, my friend, and I still don't have any logical explanation for any of it."

Brian was silent for a few minutes, then asked;

"Do you think Keira is a security risk?"

Stewart wasn't surprised. Brian had become the soldier again, but he was puzzled about how to reply. "I don't know. I don't know what risk she would pose or how we could begin to work that out. So far, she's just acting very weird and out of character. But the reason why she is doing that? Who knows." He paused. "Do you want to take it to the boss?"

Brian shook his head immediately. "And say what? We think Keira is a sex-crazed witch who might be possessed and a security risk. Oh, by the way, she packs a great punch for a girl!?"

Stewart smiled at Brian's summary and then frowned. "Hmm, when you put it like that, it does sound just too bizarre. But what about the amulet? The book it was attached to looked ancient, but I didn't get a chance to get a really good look."

"That poses an interesting dilemma in itself," Brian said, his voice drifting off, "which is how do we get our hands on it so we can check out if the amulet is real."

Stewart's reaction was immediate. "Oh no, you don't!"

"Let's not be too hasty." Brian tried to cajole his friend. "Stewart, the next time You're in her apartment, you could just ..."

Brian didn't finish the sentence before Stewart cut him off.

"And say what? I just so happened to be snooping around your flat and found this precious object we would like to examine?" Stewart drew a deep breath. "I don't think that will go down too well with Keira."

"OK, Stewart, then what we need is a viable alternative. We certainly can't use our usual Operatives for this job."

16

Had Morgan paid a little closer attention the previous evening, she would have noticed that further down the road, a youngish-looking man was taking a similarly keen interest in Rhonwen's apartment building and, like her, was trying to stay out of sight. However, unlike Morgan, he relied on stealth, not magic.

Tall and slender, the man had an angular face, a prominent nose, and a square chin. His flaxen straight hair hung across his forehead, masking a frown. As Shakespeare described it, he had that *"lean and hungry look"* which appeared to miss very little.

Now, sitting in a cafe just down the road where he had a good view of the front door, he felt the usual rage when he thought about how his cousin had ended up with the apartment that was rightfully his. But now he was going to teach that insignificant little bitch a lesson. She was bound to go out sometime this morning, and all he had to do was wait for his opportunity.

Sitting in the corner of the window, sipping his coffee and waiting for Rhonwen to leave, he found himself thinking back on all the injustices in his life. The bitterness he felt was deep and longstanding, having started with his father's death. He had only been five when he had been left alone with a mother who had passionately wanted a daughter. She had constantly punished him for his so-called shortcomings. His maleness.

Then there was his expulsion from school after being found cheating on an exam, like he was the only one! Next was his lack of success with girls who would always, after a short time, be just like his mother and abandon him. And then, to add insult to injury, came the loss of his Aunt Sophie's apartment to some distant cousin. He could feel his anger rising up and filling him with hatred, but he knew better than to let it take over.

After all, he had turned it all around. It had been his plan to head to the Continent that had given him his success. Over the last three years, he had done very well there with no one to hinder him. He had set up around the resorts in the South of France that the rich Americans favoured, and in a short space of time, He'd established a reputation for being able to arrange most things. Especially if they were illegal, Declan would see to it for girls, boys, drugs, whatever his clients wanted, for a price.

The business had boomed, and as the status of his clientele improved, so did his fee. Consequently, he became more and more selective and less available, although this did little to harm his reputation. Far from it, everyone took it as a sign that he was good at what he did and in demand. He developed a persona that allowed his clients to think they were safely flirting with the notorious Marseilles underground.

They were totally unaware that Declan operated independently and had no agreement with any of the criminal elements in charge of the city. He didn't need the Borsalino. He had a nose for profit and knew how to manipulate the system. This, of course, had been a very risky way of conducting business. There was always the possibility that he could have interfered with someone's plans, and then he would have disappeared. But he had a nose for danger and had managed to elude notice and most other hazards for quite a while. Enough times at least, to stash away a considerable sum of untraceable cash.

Sitting there, he wondered if his luck might have run out. It was now just over a month since he had accepted an invitation to a wealthy entrepreneur's coastal retreat, and everything had changed. After the perfunctory pleasantries, the man, who had declined to give Declan his name, asked the young Englishman about business and quite bluntly wondered how long he anticipated staying alive in Marseilles. Shocked by this unexpected bluntness, Declan had been uncertain how to reply, so he had politely asked if the man had heard anything he should know about.

The reply had been just as vague and puzzling, inferring that it was logical to assume that his demise through misadventure was simply a matter of time. Declan remembered the hairs standing up on the back of his neck as the guy sat back and quietly lit a large cigar. He had just stared at Declan for what seemed like ages when he leant forward with a predatory smile and said, "What do you know about antiquities?"

It had been so unexpected that Declan had answered truthfully that he knew very little despite his family having a considerable collection. Then without any further explanation, the man had beckoned him to follow as he led the way into a large study across the hall. Declan trailed behind, contemplating making a run for it, until he noticed the rather large shadow of a henchman in the front door's glass. Realising he had no choice, he was led to the window and a large desk. On top were a couple of old-looking books, one opened at a page that showed an etching of a rather fetching woman standing in front of a mirror.

It took Declan only a few seconds to realise that he knew that picture. It had belonged to his great-grandmother, and he had always liked it. He didn't know why, but he had particularly liked the look of the mirror in the background. The man smiled at Declan. "Do you now see why you are here?"

Declan, maintaining an excellent poker face, but feeling completely at a loss as to what this guy wanted, had deliberately kept his reply casual. "You are interested in antiques."

The man chuckled. "Ah, if it were that simple, Mr Tierney."

Declan had almost lost it then. He didn't use his real name in France. The fact that this guy knew who he was represented a serious problem, and he had only managed to keep a straight face and not react as he waited for the next move. His host picked up another book from the other side of the large desk and opened it, inviting Declan to look at the page he had marked. This book appeared to be some scholarly work, and the picture before him was a drawing of some sort of stone, oval in shape and quite large by the look of the measurements. Quickly reading the description beneath the picture, he was informed that this was an ancient Amulet thought to be used in magic rituals in the past.

Declan was puzzled. The stone seemed familiar. On the opposite page was another illustration, these one of five shadowy figures, each holding a stone aloft. The stones were glowing, and traces of white light connected them to each other. He was trying to figure out the connection between this and his great-grandmother when his host spoke again, this time his mouth so close to Declan's ear that he felt his hot breath. "Do you see?"

Declan had turned back to the first picture and suddenly realised what he had missed before. The mirror had a stone in it, just like the stones in the other illustration. Looking up, He'd responded. "There's one of those stones in the top of the mirror".

The man had smiled and said quietly, "I appreciate your keen sense of the obvious, Mr Tierney. I also know that you are aware that the mirror with the stone in it belonged to your family. So let's stop playing games."

Having done his own research over the intervening weeks, Declan now knew that he had been speaking with Jean Bran. And that he was as dangerous as he had seemed at the time. He was aware that this meeting was a turning point in his life. There was no room to manoeuvre. He either went along with the proposed job, or he would probably disappear. The ever-present burly guard at the door was a dead giveaway. He remembered the conversation exactly. Keeping his voice steady and his smile as affable as he could manage, He'd replied.

"You are obviously interested in my family's mirror, or at least the jewel in it. Am I right to suppose that all of the jewels are of interest to you?"

"I can see you have begun to understand why I called you here, Declan. May I call you Declan? After all, I am offering you a commission, a very big commission to do a little job for me, so why stand on formality."

Declan seeing the possibility of a way out, had quickly informed Jean that he had no idea what had happened to the mirror. But he was quickly disabused of any notion that he might get out of this by Jean's reply.

"I happen to know that your Aunt Sophie owned that Mirror and left all of her possessions to your cousin Rhonwen, who now lives in your Aunt's London apartment. I want you to get it for me."

Declan had been stunned. He had had no idea that his Aunt had the mirror, but then again, she had never invited him to her place. The thought that this job might give him a chance to create havoc in Rhonwen's life had appealed to him. It seemed like a way of making a positive out of the whole thing. But certainly not enough of a positive. He hadn't known then that he would also be offered a very good financial incentive.

Jean had told him he would offer Declan two hundred and fifty thousand pounds to retrieve the stone from his cousin's flat. However, if he was successful in this task, Jean was also offering him the opportunity to, as he put it, "aid me in locating and securing the other matching stones." He offered a further two hundred and fifty thousand for each. Counting the one in Rhonwen's possession, Jean had told him that three others were yet to be found. This would give him a total of one million pounds.

Declan had already decided to accept the job. His time in Marseilles had always been limited, so given that he did not doubt that refusing the offer would lead to his immediate death, he had been very clear in his mind that he had no choice. The money, however, was extraordinary and a little worrying. He decided it was necessary to be candid about the fact that he didn't have the contacts or skills he thought would be necessary for this job. He knew better than to pretend he could pull this off easily. However, his host had been very clear that he had chosen Declan for very carefully considered reasons that he was obviously not going to disclose. He had insisted that he had every confidence that Declan was *"the right man for the job"*.

Declan had found this cryptic response somewhat unsatisfactory, yet strangely the feeling had passed quickly, and it seemed reasonable to accept what he was hearing without further questioning. However, his survival instincts were still very much online. Declan had decided he needed to clarify his position, so he asked if this was one of those offers that couldn't be refused. Jean Bran's answer was still at the very forefront of his mind. With a rather reptilian smile, Jean had said, "Not at all. However, as you can appreciate, all choices come with consequences, and one should always be willing to carefully factor those into the equation."

Then the bargaining began. Worried that if he was to be paid when the task was completed, there was no guarantee he would ever see any of the money, Declan asked about the details. What if he found only a couple of the stones? Or worse, no more than the one they already knew about? What then? Would he be paid as he recovered each of the stones? Jean had looked back at him keenly and appeared to think carefully for a moment before answering. He had responded that there was some merit in what Declan had said but countered with an offer of one hundred and fifty thousand pounds for each stone, paid as he found them. But if Declan found all four, he would receive the balance of the original one million pounds offered.

Once they had agreed to terms, Declan was introduced to Max and informed that he would be his contact person. He had been escorted out of the house, and later that day, having done some digging, he found that the house was supposed to be empty while its owner was away. He had been back here in London before he could confirm Jean's identity.

As he watched the busy street outside, he turned it all over in his mind. Max had informed him that he would let him know when he wanted him to act and that he had to be ready to do so immediately. So he had now been cooling his heels for weeks. But it had given him time to organise himself and to do his own research. It had been more difficult than he had thought to find out the identity of his new employer. He was still trying to determine the extent of Jean's interests, given that he covered his tracks with exceptional skill.

Declan had put everything in place. He felt quite confident that he could vanish from sight if he needed to disappear. A million pounds was very tempting, and he was intrigued by the new work's possibilities, but he was a realist and a survivor. He was not about to get himself killed.

17

Morgan watched Keira dozing on the day bed where she had left her. She had learnt a great deal from the young woman. Most importantly, she had found a space in the young one's mind that she had not been able to penetrate. Blocked by a dark impenetrable wall, Morgan stood before a locked door to which she did not have the key. No matter how hard she pried, she could not find her way in.

A power greater than hers had taken possession of that corner of Keira's mind, and she recognised the taint of it. "*Scáthach That was what the disturbance had been the other night. That bitch was trying to come back, but how? The spell Keira had used shouldn't have been enough to open up the portal*".

She had been forced to change her approach the moment she had become aware of the remnants of Scáthach's presence. Feeling somewhat frustrated, she had spent the last few minutes removing any trace of her intrusion into Keira's mind. The Grimoire was important. The images in the girl's mind were of an extremely old copy she had taken from her family's home to her London apartment. Keira's memories all pointed to her family being unaware of its value.

Keira wasn't going to be able to give her any more answers. There were plenty of interesting threads to follow, but first, she needed to solve the riddle of the Grimoire. She would know whose it was when she got her hands on it. Looking at the lovely afternoon, Morgan decided a drive would clear her head.

"Jean," she silently summoned her foster son and protégé, and, moments later, a man in his early thirties entered the room and made his way over to where Morgan still sat on the edge of the divan contemplating Keira.

"A new acolyte, Mother?" He smiled sardonically.

Morgan smiled back. "This one is a little different to the others, Jean." Her smile suddenly vanished. "With this one, you will abide by some rules."

"Rules?" Jean interjected. He despised rules.

"Yes, rules." Morgan's voice had gone as sharp as a duelling blade. "She is completely under my protection, and you are not," she hesitated, searching for an appropriate word or phrase, "to play with her."

Jean feigned disappointment. "But, Mother..."

"No buts, Jean, and I mean it. I will be out for a while, and I need you to keep an eye on her until I return." Morgan's demeanour shifted back as instantly as it had just moments before. Grinning suddenly, she declared, "I think I'll take the Ferrari."

Having made her decision, Morgan grabbed her handbag from her study and headed down to the garage. She was looking forward to getting out. The last thing she had expected was to deal with the warrior goddess again, and she needed time to clear her head. Arriving at Keira's apartment, she used Keira's own key to let herself in. Roaming the rooms, she wasn't sure if she liked the bordello look. She had just finished looking over the shelves in the living room when she heard a noise at the apartment door. Irritated by the interruption, she had waited out of sight in the living room.

The person entered the hallway and quietly closed the door, and she sensed stealth in how he moved. Ah! A man who was not supposed to be there. She glided silently out into the hall to confront him. He was obviously shocked by her sudden appearance and took a step back, but quickly reclaimed his wits and arranged his face into a confident smile as he spoke.

"Well, hello! You caught me by surprise!"

Morgan casually looked him over. *Hmm, how handsome is this stranger? She* thought, amused. Then she remembered the man as someone in Keira's memory. A colleague from work and someone she beds. For an instant, she was tempted to use magic to erase any trace of their meeting, but she was curious and decided that it would be more amusing to find out more about him and how he fitted into the picture of Keira's life.

It was as if Stewart was reading her mind. "I'm Stewart," he reached out his hand, "and who do I have the pleasure of meeting in Keira's apartment?"

Although his voice was cheery and light, it had an unmistakable edge, so Morgan smiled as disarmingly as only she could. "I'm Morgan, a friend of Keira's and," she paused and took Stewart's hand in hers, "having heard so much about you, I feel that I already know you."

"Then we're almost friends, aren'twe?" The young man replied. He was obviously suspicious, but instead of confronting her, he turned on the charm.

"If you"ll excuse me, I just need to get something from the bedroom." He winked and beamed sheepishly at Morgan, who became even more intrigued by this man.

"No problem. I had just dropped in to get some earrings Keira said I could borrow." She coquettishly flicked her hair back and smiled. "You know what girls are like?"

"Of course." Stewart nodded conspiratorially and then disappeared into the bedroom.

"So, are you meeting up with Keira, then?" He called out from behind the half-closed door.

"Yes, as a matter of fact, I am," Morgan replied casually, "Do you want me to give her a message?"

"No, that won't be necessary."

Morgan knew he was no more an invited guest than she was. She wondered if this mortal would lose his obviously well-trained cool. "It's not a problem, you know." She said in a sweet and helpful-sounding voice.

He was good. He suddenly appeared back in the doorway, his lean, athletic frame blocking the light from the bedroom window. He held out his hand, his blue eyes sparkling with an icy edge that was reflected in his voice. "I'll put the spare key back, shall I?"

The air between the two was as dense as treacle, and a knowing silence hung between them as they stood in the doorway. For Morgan's part, she admired this man's strength of character and astuteness in sizing her up. He may not know who he was dealing with, but she knew that he had quickly decided that she was not at all she appeared to be.

Morgan smiled at Stewart and stretched out her closed hand to him. She slowly turned her fist over and opened it. Her eyes never left his face, and she had to suppress her desire to burst out laughing when she saw his reaction to the small house key in her hand. He recovered quickly, smiling tightly, took the key and suggested that since they were both ready to leave, he would escort her downstairs.

She was about to empty Stewart's mind of the encounter and send him on his way, but something stayed in her hand. Something teased at the back of her mind, something old and familiar that unsettled her and she had decided to be cautious. The Grimoire could wait. She could come back next week while they were both at work when she would have more time. Amused by his bravado, she let him lead the way, wondering what he would think if he ever tried to use the key, as it would simply disintegrate in the lock.

Driving home, she thought about how she would approach Keira. She needed more information about Keira's family, and she had already discovered that she wasn't going to find it in Keira's memories, so there was no point holding her. Anyway, she would be missed. No, for now, she would have to reassure the girl and bind her into an alliance. Using a seduction spell would have been fun; after all the girl was very attractive. But the presence of Scáthach made that a bit too risky. Even she was vulnerable during the throes of an orgasm.

She found Keira on the chaise lounge where she had left her, with Jean sitting across the room at the desk doing something on his laptop. There was no sign that he had disregarded her instructions. Keira looked untouched and peaceful.

"Thank you, Jean. Could you organise a taxi for Keira while I bring her back?"

"Of course, Mother."

As Jean closed up his computer and left the room, Morgan gently moved Keira into a sitting position using the cushions to support her and laying her hand lightly on her forehead; she said a silent incantation. To a casual observer, Keira seemed to rouse from a deep slumber. She breathed deeply and slowly and, opening her eyes, blinked at the intrusion of daylight from the windows opposite where she was sitting.

"Hello, my dear. Are you feeling all right now?"

18

Keira felt as if she had been transported into someone else's dream. A voice, melodic yet resonant and powerful, had urged her to relax and succumb to her deepest desires. There were no words that she could hear; only their echoes reverberated through her mind, the lingering warmth, the sense of total contentment.

She languidly scanned the vast room towards the French windows through which the afternoon sun streamed. A woman stood silhouetted in the light; her elegant profile turned towards the garden outside. Suddenly, Keira was suffused with lust, her groin tingling with a potent heat that distracted and confused her. Her eyes riveted on the woman in front of her, Keira tried to gather her thoughts and pushing past the fogginess that seemed to have enveloped her mind, she suddenly realised that she was looking at Morgan.

At the same time, she became aware that she was lying on some day bed, which for some reason, seemed odd. Slowly her memory cleared a bit further. *Yes, there it was,* she thought. Something had happened; this lust wasn't her. It made no sense! She could feel the wetness of completion, yet she was hungering for Morgan. She didn't do women. So who? Who had she just had sex with?

A wave of nausea passed over her, and she watched herself. She looked down at Stewart and some predatory thing that looked a bit like her. She knew this was her, transformed, intent on sexually devouring those she lusted for. She knew that she derived not only pleasure but power. But what power? At this point, the vision faded like a thinning trail lost in the sand eroded by the wind.

There were simply no further fragments; nothing more was to be found. Keira sighed, a lassitude robbing her of any desire to explore her mind further. Her nausea faded; she sensed rather than saw Morgan turn towards her. She felt another enormous surge of lust.

"Hello, my dear." Morgan walked casually towards the bed and, sitting next to her, gently brushed a lock of hair from Keira's face. Keira felt compelled to lift her arms towards Morgan, wanting to draw her into an embrace. But Morgan gently laid them back by her side and said.

"Hush, my sweet. This is not the time."

Keira was about to protest but suddenly realised that she was held by some invisible force and was able to move only within a small space, and when she opened her mouth to speak, she was unable to make any sound. About to panic, her eyes locked onto Morgans, and she instantly settled back into her earlier languid state. Lying back into the silken pillows, she only felt slightly curious about her indifference to her captivity.

Keira groped for a sense of awareness as she woke. She felt refreshed and calm but puzzled about how she came to be in a lounge when her last memory was of being in a chair. Looking directly into Morgan's lovely eyes, her immediate reaction was one of pleasure and safety. "What happened? Did I faint or something?"

Morgan smiled reassuringly at her and, taking her hand, unobtrusively traced a pattern on Keira's palm as she explained that Keira had indeed fainted.

"You must have been very tired after what you have been through, and I have to say it all seems very strange. I have some ideas of where I might be able to find out what went wrong with your spell, but I am sorry to say I can't give you any real answers right now."

"How long was I unconscious?" Keira asked as she sat there contentedly, allowing Morgan to hold her hand, her mind only just registering the strange movement of Morgan's fingers on her palm.

"Oh, I let you have a little sleep, so it's been a couple of hours, but you look quite refreshed now, so it was probably good for you, don't you think?"

Keira couldn't think of any reason why she would object to being looked after, and yet she felt a sense of wariness. Deciding to play along with Morgan, she smiled sweetly and removed her hand from the woman's grasp, feigning a need to straighten her hair. Thinking about what Morgan had said about the spell reminded Keira of the reason for her being there in the first place. She felt a wave of anxiety wash over her. Fully alert now, she moved to the edge of the lounge, signalling her desire to stand up. As she did so, she collected her thoughts and, looking up at Morgan, who was considerably taller than her, she put on the best social face and asked, “So you think I somehow mucked up the spell?"

"Well, my dear, there seems to have been some unintended consequences. But I am sure I can help you get to the bottom of it, and together we can reverse that part of the spell without undoing all of it."

Keira couldn't disregard the nagging feeling that more had gone on during the afternoon. For some reason, she wasn't convinced she had just had a nap. To begin with, she had no memory of having actually told Morgan anything about the spell or about what had happened with Stewart! She did, however, have a vague memory of Morgan speaking with her from somewhere behind her and the feel of heaviness in her shoulders. As she focused more, she became aware of other hands, of pleasure. Sensations rather than memories.

Thinking about this, she felt an urgency to leave. She needed to go home. Gathering her bag and locating her shoes, she started getting ready. "So what is our next step? Should I be doing anything?" she asked as she moved towards the door of the library.

Morgan smiled warmly at her and escorted her out into the hall. "How about I give you a call when I have managed to find out anything useful? Probably in a couple of days. In the meantime, it would probably be a good idea if you don't do any more magic of any sort."

Keira happily agreed. Just as Morgan finished speaking, her son Jean appeared and informed them that a taxi had arrived to take her home. Their eyes met as Keira walked out the door, and a shaft of pure pleasure coursed through her.

19

Following Morgan downstairs to the basement, Jean was careful to keep his mind well-warded. He had, of course, completely disregarded his mother's demand that he refrains from having fun with her new acolyte. It was delightful, and he wished he hadn't been forced to cover his tracks by wiping the girl's memory of their interlude. But there was a lot more to her than he had expected. He could usually unpick his mother's wards, but there was an area of Keira's mind that seemed to be blocked by something else.

Jean was still mulling this over when he realised that they had arrived at what, to others, would appear to be the end of a corridor lined with rich white marble tiles and lit by a series of muted recessed lights. In the unlikely event that a stranger found their way to this part of the house, there were several doors built into the walls, leading to what appeared to be storage rooms. However, it was highly unlikely that this would ever occur, given the electronic and magical safeguards that had been put in place during the renovation.

He quickly opened his mind and checked that all was as it should be, and, finding that it was, he felt a surge of pride. He had played a significant part in the most recent renovations to what were essentially two Edwardian townhouses, reworked to form one large mansion. Acting as a project and security manager, he orchestrated the build so that the workers were completely unaware of the true dimensions of the changes. Together he and Morgan, who was a master at all things covert, had moved treasures and possessions around the building so as not to cause any unwanted curiosity and subsequent prying into her affairs.

As Morgan took the last few steps before walking into the marbled wall, it suddenly appeared to dissolve into a milky-white, shimmering curtain through which the two disappeared, only to reemerge in a massive hall that stretched before them.

It had been constructed with several types of marble, polished to a high gloss that allowed subtle reflections to emanate around the huge room. When the torches were lit, the walls sparkled as if covered with diamonds.

At the far end of the hall, a huge oak chair stood on an elevated platform flanked by two smaller and less ornately carved siblings. Two portals in a classic gothic arch cut into the wall behind either side of the platform allowed the initiated entrance to several antechambers.

One of the chambers was essentially a small but impressive library, while the other contained urns, jars, cauldrons and a variety of tools reminiscent of a blacksmith's or carpenter's workshop. The place was dimly lit and had a strong, earthy atmosphere created by the fragrances of the aromatic herbs, incense and oils and the musty smell of their ancient receptacles. The combination was mellow rather than pungent and had always reminded Jean of a museum Morgan had taken him to when he was a little boy.

The pleasure for Jean, however, was that this was not a museum but a place where the ancient was still as useful as the day it had been made.

He clearly remembered the day Morgan had introduced him to her inner sanctum. The day that she had deemed Jean old enough to be introduced to the art of magic. Always dramatic, she had raised her arm and swept it in an arc across the room. "From now on, Jean, this will be your most important classroom, your very special classroom. In it, I will teach you true magic."

Jean had been twelve years old at the time and well and truly bored with his regular schooling. In his mind, he had long felt ready to take up the mantle as Morgan's apprentice. He had begged her to release him from the binding spell that prevented him from inadvertently exposing his abilities as a child. Railing against Morgan was, at best, a fool's task, and he had learnt to accept her restrictions and eventually to recognise the danger of being conspicuous. But down here in this room, he had been able to open himself up, releasing the power that sometimes threatened to burst from his skin.

Coming out of his reverie, Jean realised that Morgan had stepped up to the back wall, which was draped by a heavy brocade curtain. A subtle wave of her hand moved it aside to reveal a large mirror hung on the marble wall. As he watched, the mirror's surface grew cloudy and then appeared to transform into what looked like mercury, its surface rippling with subdued waves as if agitated by a slight breeze. Gradually the silvery surface changed to an opaque one, and then, after a little more time, it cleared altogether.

Morgan spoke, using an incantation that would transfer her thoughts to a visual representation, and slowly images began to manifest within the depth of the mirror. A man's face appeared only to be replaced by several others in quick succession. "Take a good look, Jean. I have a job for you. Ancient things are stirring, and I was hoping you could do some mundane investigations for me. That young woman, Keira, is at the centre of it, but I will deal with her."

Jean nodded and moved closer to the mirror so that he could get a good look at the people his mother was so interested in. He had also seen their faces in Keira's mind. Turning back to the mirror, she waved her hand again, this time freezing the face of the blond, well-dressed man in his thirties. "This is Stewart, Keira's bedfellow. We met quite by accident in her apartment." She smiled wryly. "This one is a most interesting man, Jean, and one that will have to be carefully watched."

Morgan paused and studied the captured face in the mirror. "He is a warrior, Jean, in the truest sense of the word. Battle-hardened and intelligent, this man could be a formidable ally as much as a dangerous enemy. It will, I feel, depend very largely on us, which it is going to be."

"Perhaps he would be best dead, Mother," was Jean's laconic response.

Jean, too, had been studying Stewart's face. He felt a twinge of irritation that his mother was so entranced by him, having already been aware of the sexual connection he had with Keira. She had turned around, her look measuring, and replied, "That," her voice edgy, "will be only done if there is absolutely no alternative."

Jean was well aware that Morgan was as capable as he of using whatever means was necessary, but she was not as prepared to go there as he was. He also knew that this disturbed her on several levels, and he used this to keep her just a little unsettled, just a little unsure of how far he would go. She turned back to the mirror, and with another elegant movement of her right hand, another replaced the warrior's face. "This, Jean, is Gavin. You've heard me speak of him from time to time. He is, as I am, one of the twelve."

Jean heard the soft undertone in Morgan's voice and filed that away for further thought. He had, of course, done a lot of personal research on all of the twelve. Well, as much as he could without alerting his mother. Deciding to probe a little, he kept his voice level and neutral as he spoke, "You're fond of this man, Mother?"

"I am, Jean, but it would not stop me from doing what needed to be done." Morgan cocked her head to the side and carefully looked at Jean. "You are not to provoke anything, is that clear? He is, and always will be, mine to deal with.

Jean knew that Morgan meant this in the most earnest way. "You have my word, mother."

Morgan continued speaking as she scrolled through the faces. "Gavin is why I want you to use a modern mundane search process. If we use magic, he will be alerted."

As she was speaking, she was peering closely at a red-headed girl. Jean was startled. He clamped hard down on his thoughts and managed to strengthen his wards, hoping that Morgan's preoccupation with the features of the face in front of her had been enough for her not to notice. She made a satisfied sound as if she had found something and brought up a picture of an apartment building. Jean managed to contain himself, keeping his face impassive as she turned to him.

"Gavin is up to something, and it's tied to an apartment in that building. The owner of the apartment is Rhonwen Tierney, the red-haired girl we just looked at. I want you to find out everything you can about her and her family. She pulled a piece of paper from her pocket and handed it to him, her gaze penetrating and direct. "Here is the address."

Before he could reply, she turned to the mirror and brought up the faces of others who were somehow linked to Keira, as all of these faces had been extracted from her memories. Jean didn't know how to react. For some reason, he hadn't picked up on Keira knowing Rhonwen Tierney. It didn't make sense. He had seen the other faces, they were her work colleagues, but missed this! Keira was associated with the Tierney girl. Could it be a coincidence? His mother's new protege and his first target! Keeping himself contained and remaining the helpful son, he asked, "And these others?"

Without turning, Morgan focused her attention on the faces before her. "I don't know, so I want you to dig around and find out. They all seem to be connected deeply, so we need to know about their families."

Relieved that Morgan had no inkling of the turmoil her little task had caused for him, he listened as she continued with her instructions. "This is Keira's grimoire, Jean, from which she has been working." She found it in the family library, so I am particularly interested in her family."

Morgan waved her hand again, and the image grew larger, making the detail of the book clearer. "Isn't it beautiful? It will make such a great addition to my library, don't you think? I wonder what that leather pocket on the front is for?"

Jean barely heard Morgan's voice which seemed to echo in the distance and, too focused on what to do next, he hardly heard her as she spoke about the grimoire. He needed to get out of there so he could figure out how this was all connected. He quickly pulled out his phone and moved up to stand in front of the mirror. "OK, Mother, I will get on to this straight away. Give me the names as I take a photo of each, and I'll let you know when I have something."

It hadn't taken long for them to compile the list and add the other information Morgan had gleaned from Keira's mind. He knew at least one of those names was on his own list. Brian Poole. His own research had led him to the Poole's, but it had been difficult to locate any information about this particular member of the family. Realising that his mother's interests were now colliding with his was enraging. All these years of careful preparation could be unravelled in seconds if she picked up on what he was planning.

20

Declan was just finishing his third cup of coffee when he saw the door of the building open. Watching Rhonwen walk briskly down the road towards the local shops, he had just started to move when his phone rang. Peering at the small screen, he hesitated, recognising the number, but an inner voice urged him to pick it up rather than let it go to voicemail.

It was his new employer. There had been no contact between them since Marseilles, and Declan instinctively knew that he needed to appear ignorant of Jean Bran's identity. It had taken quite a sophisticated search to find his name. The convoluted way in which the man had been able to conceal himself added another layer of intrigue and danger to this game.

"Hello." He kept his voice neutral, giving nothing away. Declan habitually never used the other person's name and always withheld his own when answering his mobile, a basic model with limited functions that he used only to make and receive calls. The voice on the other phone was equally devoid of emotion and identity. "We have to move quickly. Can you make it happen today?"

"Yes. I'll call you when I'm ready to meet." Declan hung up and, reaching into his pocket, threw a couple of notes on the table and nodded politely to the waiter. The money was enough to cover the coffees he had and a bit of a tip. There was enough there to keep the guy happy but not enough for him to remember Declan should anyone ask about him.

He picked up his trench coat from the chair beside him and slipped into it as he walked out the door. The cold wind and driving rain bit into him. He flicked the collar up and drew the coat around him. It was more for anonymity than cover from the weather, and as he walked the short distance to Rhonwen's apartment block, his heart began to beat a little faster the closer he got.

When he arrived across the road from the building, he stopped and took a deep breath to calm down and relax some accumulated tension in his neck. His hand fiddled nervously with a small toolkit in his pocket. Seeing a break in the traffic, he had just braced himself to step into the flow of cars when he saw a movement at the door of the building. An older woman had energetically flung the door to the building open. She stood in the doorway for a moment, bracing herself against the wind and the rain before stepping into the street. Her impending departure cued him to walk briskly across the road. As he covered the distance to the main entrance, he casually dropped his head as if trying to keep his face out of the chilly wind, all the while keeping his eye on her. She moved quickly away from the door, focused on unfurling her umbrella, and she failed to ensure that the lock clicked behind her, giving Declan just enough time to catch the handle and slip unnoticed into the apartment building.

He smiled, wryly reflecting that the gods must be taking a liking to him to allow him to be that close to being spied on and yet completely avoid detection. He took another deep breath and then casually climbed the stairs to the second floor. Reaching the front door of the apartment, he pulled the little tool kit from his coat pocket. Choosing a small wrench and pick, he quickly looked up and down the corridor before he slipped the tools into the lock. A slight click announced the lock picked, and as he pushed lightly on the door, it swung open.

Without a second of hesitation, Declan stepped into the apartment and shut the door behind him. He looked around. So this is what his boring cousin had done with his inheritance. He shook his head in disgust. About to take a step towards the living room, a large black shape suddenly spat and hissed violently in his direction.

"Shit!" He spun around. "Shut the fuck up!" Declan spat back. He detested cats, and this disgusting beast was making enough fuss to alert the whole neighbourhood. No matter how hard he tried to shoo it out of his way, the cat refused to budge from the door to the living room. Irritated, he tried to shove it away with his foot, but the cat, screaming, spitting and hissing, dropped to the floor, digging its claws into the rug.

In the chaos of noise, Declan lost his temper and landed a kick into the side of the animal. The force of the blow stunned the cat, and it released its grip on the rug. A second later, it crashed against the nearest wall. Declan's attack, however, still failed to silence the animal. In fact, it simply infuriated it to the point where it increased its screaming to such a piercing pitch that Declan realised it was simply a matter of time before someone would hear the noise. For whatever reason, he was unwilling to silence the cat permanently. He decided the best course of action was to ignore it, find what he was looking for and get out of the apartment.

He did not have to look far for what he had come for. Stepping into the living room, the conspicuous mirror with the embedded amulet stared down from its place above the fireplace. He breathed a sigh of relief. He eagerly reached up but found that the amulet was just that bit too far out of reach. He quickly pulled an antique chair closer to the fireplace so that he could climb up and dislodge it from the frame when he heard the apartment door open. Hurriedly, he jumped onto the chair and reached for the jewel, his fist closing around it just as an angry-looking woman poked her head around the door.

"What the hell are you doing?" The woman's voice thundered over the screaming of the cat.

Shocked by the force of the woman's outburst, Declan lost his footing on the chair and, in a desperate attempt to regain his balance, grabbed hold of the frame of the mirror. There was a sudden grinding noise, followed by a final crack reverberating through the room. Declan suddenly found himself and the mirror flying through the air, only to land amidst a chaos of breaking glass and wood.

Stunned by the fall, he lay there for a moment. His hand suddenly felt something warm and wet. He quickly checked to see if he was injured in some way, but what he found was that he had fallen on top of the woman, her limp body now a soft cushion underneath him.

In an instant, Declan leapt to his feet. As his weight lifted off her, she groaned. Declan immediately realised that the woman lying in the debris of wood and glass was seriously injured. He was stunned by this unforeseen turn of events. Standing frozen in the mess, Declan stared at her, mesmerised by the pool of blood slowly spreading around her body. *There could be no witness.* That single thought pierced his mind and spurred him into action. Leaning over her, Declan slipped his hand over her mouth while his other hand slowly closed across her throat, constricting her windpipe.

A creak in the floorboards had him strain to look down into the hallway. Overcome by the urgency to get out of the apartment and his need to dispatch his only witness, Declan quickly increased the pressure on her throat.

Seeing a movement in the corner of his eye, he deftly managed to deflect the incoming blow to his head. It had always stood in Declan's favour that his thin frame belied his strength and agility. This had most adversaries underestimate his ability to defend himself, although he rarely chose to fight and mostly opted for flight as the surest strategy. With the reflexes of an athlete, he jumped to his feet while instantly sizing up his new opponent's physical superiority.

Desperate to escape, Declan realised that the only way out was through the large bay window two storeys above the hectic London street.

With the amulet still firmly grasped in his closed fist, Declan's world suddenly changed permanently. His mind's grasp of the truth shattered like glass, sending shards of reality into every imaginable direction. What was left behind were traces that appeared real but that he sensed were far removed from what he knew as physical existence.

In slow motion, Declan saw the other man reach inside his coat pocket while mouthing something. The sound of a voice should have been clear but it was an unintelligible rumble that rippled through the viscous air that now surrounded Declan. Each successive sound wave rippled towards him like waves on the water, only to break across his eardrums.

Without conscious intent, Declan shifted from logic to faith, his hand clutching the amulet. It felt hot and pulsing, but he had no thought to let it go. As he started to move through the room like a dart speeding through the space around him, Declan watched his opponent struggle to move through the thickened air surrounding him.

In the blink of an eye, Declan launched himself through the window, bursting into the void amidst an expanding cloud of glass shards and wooden splinters. A part of his mind screamed silently in fear, but he was propelled by a greater force that continued to reshape his reality.

ꕥꕥ

The minute the intruder disappeared from Brian's sight, the strange thickness in the air evaporated, and Brian, stunned by what he had seen, instantly regained his well-honed composure and rushed to the broken window. Wrapping the bottom of his coat around his hands to protect them, he brushed the shattered glass aside and then leaned across the window sill to look down the street. He expected to see the body of the intruder lying broken or at least struggling on the pavement below, his escape foiled by his injuries and the growing crowd of onlookers. Instead, he saw a few startled passersby looking up, puzzled by the shower of broken glass and wood bits, trying to see where they had come from.

Stretching to get a better look, Brian scanned the length of the street in both directions. *Nothing!* It was as if the intruder had leapt into the air and had vanished. *That's impossible!* His brain refused to accept what he was seeing; there was no sense to it. As he stood there trying to comprehend what had just happened, he became aware of a tingling heat in his chest beneath the amulet still hanging around his neck, but a pitiful groan forced him to deal with a more urgent matter. The pool of blood beneath the woman on the floor had continued to spread ominously. Ignoring the sticky wetness, he knelt beside her. Retrieving his mobile from his coat pocket, he dialled triple nine.

Trying to reassure the woman, he took her hand, but she was unconscious, her breathing laboured and shallow. Shaking his head in disbelief, he surveyed the mess of broken furniture and glass, a sense of deep foreboding turning his stomach. Another thing to add to the fast-growing list of strange events over the last few days.

21

Locked out of her apartment, which had now been designated a crime scene, Rhonwen had let herself, Brian and Stewart into Lydia's place, where she settled uneasily on the lounge. According to the investigators who were busily photographing everything, dusting for fingerprints and collecting all the physical evidence that they could, it had been made clear to her that it could take several days or even a week before she was able to retake possession of her home.

Brian watched as Rhonwen huddled in the corner of the settee, her legs drawn up tightly to her chest, which was racked with suppressed sobs. Leaning protectively towards her as he sat on a footstool, Brian found himself assailed by images of Lydia's injuries. Particularly persistent was that of a large shard of mirror glass protruding from her abdomen. It was covered in rivulets of red that disappeared into her clothes. Brian sighed. He knew from experience that some images stayed forever. Unfortunately, this was going to be one of them.

He pulled himself together and refocused on Rhonwen. Leaning over, he took her hand and gently squeezed it to attract her attention. "I'm sure that they"ll do all they can for Lydia,

Rhonwen." She looked up at him and smiled weakly. "I know, but her injuries are so awful. And Sooty. Why did they have to hurt him? Do you think Gerry has any news from the vet?"

Brian tried to sound as reassuring as he could when he answered, "Gerry will let us know as soon as he can".

"How long will it take before we can go to the hospital?" She asked, the tears welling in her sad eyes.

"A while yet, I think. We still have to talk with the police."

"I really am grateful to you for Lydia taking care of her till the ambulance came. And Sooty too." She paused for a moment. "I'd hate to think what might have happened had you not come to check on me."

Brian didn't reply. He had not told her that he was convinced that had he not come, Lydia would have been dead and the place completely ransacked. Just then, Stewart emerged from the kitchen carrying a tray. "I thought I would make us some tea." As Stewart started setting up on the coffee table, Rhonwen uncurled herself and sat up with a look of determination crossing her face. "I'll do that. It will help to do something." Nodding in agreement, Stewart went to sit down in one of the other chairs, just as they were interrupted by a knocking on the living room door.

A tall, heavy-set man dressed in a plain black trench coat filled the ample space of the doorway. He cleared his throat noisily as he turned towards Brian. "Ahem, I'm Detective Inspector Riley. If You're ready, Sir, I need to ask you some questions about what you witnessed this afternoon."

Brian nodded and started to rise, assuming that the Detective would want to speak with him alone, but surprisingly, Inspector Riley made himself comfortable on one of the other chairs. Taking out his notebook, he made a fuss of finding his pen before looking at Brian with an expectant expression. "So, in your own words, Mr Poole, could you please tell me what you saw in Ms. Tierney's apartment."

Brian felt a surge of anxiety as he remembered the strange behaviour of the thief. How was he going to describe that without sounding like an idiot? Looking over at Rhonwen, who was close to tears again, he suddenly made a decision to say nothing about the odd time distortion and movie-like slow-motion movements that preceded the thief's disappearance.

"Well, Inspector, I came up to the apartment and saw the door ajar, and I could hear the sound of a struggle, so I pushed the door open and went in. Basically, I saw a man leaning over Lydia with his hands around her neck. Glass and wood were everywhere, and I could see the blood on the floor underneath her. The man looked up, saw me, and suddenly jumped through the window. I mean literally jumped right through the glass! I couldn't believe it. I went over to the window and expected to see him down in the street, but he was nowhere to be found. Then I went back to Lydia and called Emergency Services."

Inspector Riley rubbed his chin and looked closely at Brian. "So you maintain there was another man in Ms. Chamber's apartment and that he leapt through a glass window, fell two stories to the ground, and then disappeared by the time you got to the window."

Suddenly Brian felt a sense of acute apprehension. He hadn't even considered that he would be a suspect, but now the reality of what the inspector was obviously thinking hit him like a ton of bricks. Before he could reply, Rhonwen interjected. "What are you saying, Inspector?

"Well, Ms. Tierney, no one else saw another man anywhere near the window or in the street, so you could say it's a bit of a puzzle as to where he could have gotten to. Don't you think?"

Brian became aware that Stewart was looking at the inspector with a very alert gaze, his eyes narrowed, and his lips thinned and tight. Shifting his weight in the chair, he seemed to grow in size, and in a clipped and carefully modulated voice, he said, "I dare say that some of your answers will be found by the forensic team, Inspector."

Brian hadn't seen Stewart react that way to anything for years. At the same time, he became aware of Rhonwen's eyes flaring with intense rage. "You can't be serious, Inspector. Are you suggesting that Brian isn't telling you the truth?"

"Ms. Tierney, I am merely doing my job." The Inspector turned back to Brian, looking like a predator who had spied his prey. "Could you describe this man that you say you saw, Mr Poole?"

"Of course, I can", replied Brian, who was now starting to feel his own anger rising. "He was of medium height and slim build with blond hair. I would probably be able to recognise him from a mug shot or describe him to a sketch artist."

The Inspector looked around the room at the three of them, and then as if he had gotten the answer he was looking for, he got up and put away his notebook. "Very well, Mr Poole, we will continue this at the Station. I will need you to come back to your apartment, Ms. Tierney, and tell me what exactly is missing. What did this thief want? What did he take?"

Brian was immediately aware of Rhonwen's apprehension at having to return to her apartment. Her eyes seemed to be silently begging for help. Holding out his hand to her Brian nodded. "It's OK. I'll go up with you."

As the other three started to move towards the lounge room door, Stewart started to collect the cups. "I'll sort this out and call Gerry while You're upstairs. He might have some news about Lydia by now."

Brian noticed that this seemed to inspire another of the Inspector's searching looks, and he realised he was having difficulty controlling his anger. It was obvious that the Inspector didn't believe his story. It had been a long time since his word had been questioned, and he didn't like it at all! He was also aware of a warm tingling in his chest directly beneath his amulet. And that was another thing that was unsettling him. He was thinking about that damn thing like it was connected to him, alerting him in some way. *But to what?*

As they entered the apartment, Rhonwen, understandably enough, became intensely emotional, confronted by the bits and pieces of wood that were scattered amongst the glass and debris of the antique mirror. Rhonwen was scanning the room, looking confused and helpless. "I don't know, Inspector. I better check my bedroom, but I don't have anything that valuable."

The Inspector looked at her sharply. "There doesn't seem to be any disturbance to the rest of the flat, Ms. Tierney. In fact, there is no evidence that the thief even entered any of the other rooms. It would seem that the intruder if he was a thief, was after something in this room."

Rhonwen seemed to have missed the Inspector's inference, but Brian didn't, and he could feel his irritation quickly turning into anger. Willing himself into control, he gently squeezed her hand, forcing her to look at him. "Have a good look. I know it just looks like a big mess, but you may figure out if anything is missing.

Rhonwen nodded and started to inspect the bits of wood and glass that she had last seen as a beautiful mirror gracing the wall of her home as if it had always been there. Something nagged at the back of her mind, and as she swept her eyes across the floor, she suddenly realised what it was. "The centrepiece is missing. I can't see it here."

The Inspector, who had been watching this interchange closely, suddenly thrust himself into the conversation. "Describe this centrepiece, Ms. Tierney."

"The top of the mirror had a piece in the middle that looked a little out of place, but I liked it. When I first saw it, I thought it had been an afterthought and added it later. It gave the mirror a slightly whimsical look. It was a large jewel-like piece of polished crystal set like a pendant, but embedded in the frame instead of on a chain."

"What colour was it, Ms. Tierney?"

"It was clear. You know, sort of like a diamond, but not cut into facets, and not as reflective. I had only had it for less than a day." Her voice trailed off as she looked at the Inspector, who was noting everything down in his book.

"Ms. Tierney, are you saying that the only thing that is missing is something you only acquired in the last twenty-four hours?"

"Why, yes Inspector, I bought the mirror yesterday at an Antique shop near Holland Park".

"Well now, that is very interesting. I will need the details of this shop and the invoice. We may well be able to make a little more sense of this after we talk to the shop owner."

Brian could feel the hairs on the back of his neck standing up as he listened to Rhonwen talking to the Inspector. He could barely breathe as he realised that she was describing an amulet. *It couldn't be!* But suddenly, the room was shifting, and the amulet on his chest was burning. He seemed to be watching the Inspector and Rhonwen from some distant place, and everything was somehow stretched. That was the only way he could make any sense of it.

As the Inspector turned towards him and started to speak, everything seemed to snap back to normal. Almost like a giant rubber band had pulled him back to reality.

"Well, Mr Poole, I think that we have finished here for now. I want to you to come down to the station tomorrow morning to try and identify this intruder you saw and give a full statement about the events here this afternoon."

With that, the inspector turned to one of his off siders. "Constable Stapleton, would you get the address of the Antique shop off Ms. Tierney? Oh, and where she will be staying for the next few days? That goes for Mr Poole and Mr Eggleston."

Then without another glance at either of them, he was gone, his bulk filling the hallway as he made his way out of the flat.

22

While Declan had been making his way across the street to Rhonwen's apartment, Gavin was preoccupied with various chores around his workshop. He was working not because it needed to be done but because it helped him to stay grounded. The unease he had been feeling in recent days was back, and it had returned with a sense of urgency and foreboding.

He felt an even stronger trepidation as he swept the wood shavings into a small pile in the middle of the wooden floor. *Something was up, he thought, but what?* He kept sweeping, reflecting quietly on the last few days while the urge to drop in on Rhonwen became stronger and stronger. Suddenly a sharp tingling like electricity raced through his body. The energy was intense enough to rob him of his breath, and he had to steady himself on his broom.

There was no mistaking this unique sensation. Someone had gone through the quickening, that first precious moment when an adept is truly connected to their powers. *And this one was massive, he thought, something big, possibly a shapeshifter or dematerialisation.*

Gavin also knew that whoever it was, happened to be close, very close. *Could it be Rhonwen so soon?*

The tinkling of the bell above the door interrupted him, and he looked up to see Erik weaving his massive frame through the crowded shop towards the workshop, casually wiping his nose with a white handkerchief.

"Damn quickening!" He said, the red stain on the white linen clearly visible.

"Nosebleed?" Gavin asked knowingly.

Erik nodded while quickly slipping out of his trench coat. He stuffed the hanky back into his pocket and then threw the coat onto the workbench. "Well, my friend, what do you make of it all?" Erik's voice boomed while he stepped across the pile of wood shavings to greet Gavin with a generous hug. "Do you think it's Rhonwen? It seemed very close, and she now has the Amulet".

"It was my first thought, but it doesn't make any sense. It was only yesterday when I held her hand, and I couldn't sense any latent power. She would need to be around the Amulet for a considerable time for her talent to emerge.

"So maybe not Rhonwen then", his old friend muttered as he stroked his beard.

"No, but the question is, who has gone through the quickening, and where are they now?" Gavin paused. "You know, Erik, I fear the worst. Think about it. There has been little real magic manifest in the last few centuries, and suddenly, there has been a massive disturbance in just over twenty-four hours. It can only be because elemental forces are being manipulated magically."

Gavin stopped, and running his hand repeatedly through his hair, he looked closely at Erik before continuing.

"And what worries me most is that Morgan is sniffing around like a bloodhound."

"I thought she preferred the shape of a Wolf." Erik grinned.

Gavin frowned. "This is a serious matter, Erik, and you should treat it as such."

"Sorry, Gavin. I couldn't resist." He cleared his throat. "I guess we should pay Ms. Tierney a visit."

"Yes, I think so. If she is the one, then she may have inadvertently opened her senses using the amulet. I am worried. Sophie was convinced that Rhonwen had no idea about her family heritage." He stopped for a moment and ran his hand through his hair again. "If it is Rhonwen Tierney, then she will need all the assistance we can offer her, but she may not want to accept it."

❧ ❧

Morgan had gone out soon after Jean had left, needing to replenish her herbs and obtain a few incidentals. She had been on her way home again when she felt the energy wash through her. It was so intense that she had to pull the Ferrari over to the curb for fear of crashing it into something. When the car had stopped safely, she sighed with relief. She didn't need the complications of having to deal with the local constabulary, who would ask awkward questions.

Although Jean had been very thorough in establishing her identity, one that would stand up to almost any form of scrutiny, she hated this subterfuge she had to engage in. Most importantly, she loathed having to be accountable to anyone.

She had pulled the car in under a tree and decided to sit there quietly and wait till the sensation had passed. Her hands, slightly sweaty and clammy, rested lightly on the leather steering wheel while she slowly regulated her breathing. She tried to reach out with her mind to see if she could discover the source of the quickening, possibly even to get a glimpse of who may have gone through the rite of passage. There was, however, nothing that would even hint at their identity.

Her immediate thought was that Keira must have tried some magical incantation or practice of some kind and experienced her quickening in the absence of a master; that could be a very dangerous and often fatal mistake. But she quickly dismissed the idea. Keira was now aligned with her, and if she had come into her power, Morgan would know without any doubt that it was her.

It was a pity, she thought, as she liked the young woman despite her foolishness in venturing into such dangerous territory as practising magic, on her own, without the relevant guidance and counsel of a high-order witch or warlock. However, in time that could be corrected. *But then, who could it be?* she wondered.

In her mind, the image of Rhonwen slowly took shape. It must be her, Morgan thought; she was the one who had found her way into Gavin's shop of curios. The one that Gavin had tried to hide from her. What was it he had delivered to that apartment? Another witch of true power! Two in one day was unheard of outside of very unusual circumstances.

Morgan was concerned, but she also felt excited by the thought that, here and now, in this century, true magic was once again emerging. But why now? What had set this in motion? It was possible that there were two new witches, both with great power. Starting the car up and moving back into the traffic, Morgan headed home. She needed to do some scrying.

❧ ❧

Jean was busy tracing the identities and origins of the faces that Morgan had showed him earlier in the day when an unease quivered in him, interspersed with a sensation of pure electricity coursing through his body like quicksilver. He had heard Morgan speak of her ability to feel when someone had freed their mind to the power of magic. She had been instantly aware when it had happened to him. She had described how it would send ripples of energy through time and space, allowing all those who shared the gift and knew what to do with it to instantly recognise it as the quickening.

As he sat there quietly, contemplating his own experience of opening his mind to the forces of magic, he wondered who it was that had woken up. *Could it have been Keira? Or someone else, say Brian Poole? He came from the right family, but there was no sign that they had used magic for a very long time.*

For a while now, he had suspected that Declan could, given the right circumstances or opportunity, ascend to being an adept or, at the very least, make use of some of the more rudimentary aspects of magic. After all, the man had come from the right genetic stock, and his uncanny ability to adapt and survive in the most hostile circumstances could only be ascribed to some innate resonance with higher powers.

This could be a problem. If it was Declan and he found out about his potential, he could pose a real threat to Jean's plans. No matter how Jean looked at the man's circumstances, Declan was to have a short life expectancy. For the moment, Jean decided to take the risk and let him live. This was still the best plan for acquiring all of the amulets. He had always known that there was a chance that Declan would figure it out, but without a teacher, his chances of really threatening Jean were limited.

23

When Declan materialised on the pavement a block away from Rhonwen's apartment building, no one could have been more surprised than he. His heart still pounded in his chest, fuelled by the rush of adrenaline from a moment ago. He had leapt impulsively through a window a few storeys up without a single thought of the consequences. He should have been a shattered and bloody corpse on the pavement, but now he was safe, sound, and, most importantly, out of reach of pursuers.

He jumped to his feet from the crouched position he had landed in and hid in a doorway, where he brushed himself down, checking to see if he was injured in any way. Reassured that he was all in one piece, he peered cautiously up and down the lane. To his relief, he found that it was deserted, with the ironic exception of a stray cat strolling nonchalantly around the corner.

A slight burning sensation in his left hand began to irritate him. The heat momentarily intensified, and he quickly unfurled his fingers. Puzzled, he saw that his hand was bathed in a deep orange glow. Despite the discomfort, Declan resisted the urge to let the jewel go, and within a few seconds, the glow and heat had subsided, and it sat benignly in the palm of his hand. Slipping the amulet into his pocket, he leant back against the cold stone of the doorway and took a deep breath. *"Get a hold of yourself!"*

Whatever had just taken place in the apartment defied any rational explanation. Shivering suddenly, he felt exposed and vulnerable. Deciding that the best place right now was the security of his apartment, he peered again from the doorway into the lane and, since it was still deserted, stepped out and quickly made his way home, his mind whirling, searching for an answer.

It wasn't until the lock clicked into place that Declan felt his anxiety subside. Walking across his small the living room to his cluttered desk, he reached for the bottle of whisky and a tumbler almost hidden by the large volume of notepads, pens and books.

Although he wasn't much into alcohol, or any drugs for that matter, he felt that this afternoon's events warranted something to soothe his frayed nerves, and he opened the bottle and poured himself a stiff drink. As the whisky coursed through his system, he sighed deeply and swinging the brown leather desk chair around, he threw himself into its cushioned embrace.

Nursing the glass, he turned to face the window that looked out across the street to another apartment building. The steady hum of traffic from the street below was the only intrusion into the quiet of his apartment. Leaning back, Declan closed his eyes, and the street noise took on a soothing murmur that allowed him to relax.

He took another sip of whiskey but rather than swallowing it immediately, he let the warming liquid settle on his tongue, the smokey flavour a welcome overtone. He held the glass to his cheek and let the coolness of it distract him for a moment.

When Declan felt more settled, he slowly reviewed the afternoon's events. If it hadn't been for that damn cat, then none of this would have happened, he thought angrily. He remembered his surprise when the busybody of a woman had stormed across the room towards him. He had vaguely recognised her, and she, too, appeared to know him. What was her name? Lydia. Yes, that's it, Lydia, something.

Declan couldn't recall her surname but could place her back to the time of the court case. She was a friend of Aunt Sophia's, a meddling sticky beak who stridently took over where his Aunt had left off.

He sat quietly as the picture of her lying in the pool of blood ran through his mind like an old sixteen-millimetre film. *What a mess!* Someone else might have recoiled from the graphic reality, but Declan calmly reviewed his reaction to the woman recognising him. Muttering his name, she had instantly sealed her fate, or at least what should have been her fate. Irritated by his failure to finish her off, he quickly suppressed his rising anger.

Ah, well, shit happens! Declan decided a little more philosophically. He would just have to deal with it. He had no illusions about the fact that he was now in a situation where he was about to appear on numerous wanted lists, here in England and possibly overseas. Whoever that guy in the apartment was, he had gotten a good look at him and would be able to describe him easily. But despite this very real problem, he had a feeling that the police were the least of concerns right now. He knew how to avoid them.

Slipping his hand into his pocket to retrieve the amulet from where it had sat quietly on the walk home, he pulled it out and stared at it. *What was this thing?* Looking at it more closely, he pondered all the questions that had been unanswered since he accepted this job. Jean had explained that the Amulets were actually a set of five jewels. He had assured him that their value was purely in their worth as a matching set of large diamonds and that the glowing picture depicted a myth they had been made to mimic.

But he had seen what he had seen. The thing had glowed. Before he could think any further, he was suddenly aware that the amulet and begun to glow again. Faint at first, but gradually the middle of the stone started to pulse like a heart and it continued to darken until it was red. Shocked, he sat up and put it on the desk, watching it warily. At that very moment, his mobile rang.

"Damn it!" He pulled the phone from his pocket. It was Jean! He was the last person Declan wanted to speak to right now. He placed the phone on the table and let it ring. Thankfully it stopped after a while as the call was diverted to his voicemail. Within seconds the amulet had stopped glowing and now rested innocuously in front of him. He reached across and picked it up, letting it nestle in the palm of his hand. There was a momentary tingle and a faint orange glow, but it too subsided.

Declan knew that the key lay with the amulet or, more precisely, amulets. He also knew that someone out there other than Jean must have the information he needed. As he started to sort out how to access that information, he realised that he had made a decision to keep the amulet. The idea that it was his, that he couldn't part with it seemed to have taken hold of him.

Declan had known from the beginning that Jean was not an ordinary criminal. No, every fibre in his body told him that Jean was far more dangerous than any criminal he had ever dealt with. Jean was a predator. One who would stop at nothing to get what he wanted and to protect himself, and to punish those that crossed him. So the consequences of Declan's decision were pretty dire.

Then again, he had been pretty certain that when he had completed the assignment and found the amulets, handing them over to Jean was assuring his own demise. Once the job was done, why would Jean keep him alive? He had known Jean was going to be a formidable challenge, but he had expected to have longer to work out what to do about it. Now, if he went ahead and kept the Amulet for himself, the problem had become immediate.

As he turned it all over in his mind, there was a part of him questioning his judgment. Why keep this one? He could go ahead with the arrangement and give himself more time. But these thoughts were pushed aside by a powerful urge to not only keep this stone but have it very close to him at all times.

Should he simply drop out of sight or work on a ruse to draw Jean into a trap from which there was no escape? Calculating his chances of success, Declan came to the conclusion that what he needed to do was to drop out of the picture completely, and the best way to do that was to go underground. He was used to doing that, and, more importantly, he was good at it.

As he sat there, he noticed a little tingling sensation that seemed to spread from his hand to his arm and then into his chest. The feeling was not unpleasant, and he continued to stare into the stone while wondering what had happened in the apartment and why. How could he have escaped from what was certain injury, possibly even death?

What had possessed him to jump out of a window two storeys up? Sitting in his chair in the safety of his apartment made that decision seem even more ludicrous than it had a few hours ago. He had to admit, however, that somewhere, deep inside of him, was the knowledge that it had been the right thing to do.

Thinking back to his childhood, Declan remembered the stories his Grandmother told, especially the ones about magic and witchcraft. He had loved the incredible tales and secretly wished them to be true so that one day he, too, could be powerful. It had been Rhonwen's mother, his Aunt Maria, who had always spoiled his dreams. She hated the stories, insisting that they corrupted the innocent and were the devil's work, preying on unsuspecting young minds to seduce them away from the true faith.

His grandmother would never challenge his aunt but would only bow her head and mutter something under her breath. He remembered that on those occasions, the old woman looked sad. Not long after that, there had been some sort of dispute in the family, and Aunt Maria and her own family moved away.

Declan never saw any of them again, and while his grandmother stopped openly talking about magic, he had overheard her and Aunt Sophie whispering about it when they didn't know he was around. His grandmother died only a couple of years later, and he remembered that neither Aunt Maria nor her family had turned up at the funeral. He was, therefore, particularly upset that Aunt Sophie had left her apartment to Rhonwen. It wasn't right after all those years he had spent sucking up to the old bitch.

Looking down at the amulet in his hand, he felt something shift in his thinking, and what he had always just thought of as his family's taste for the unusual and bizarre, suddenly seemed to be a lot more than fairy tales. *What if this was a real magical amulet? What if magic was real?*

24

As Stewart dried up the cups and saucers and carefully placed them on the kitchen bench, he thought about what had happened to Keira. *Where had she gone?* he wondered. After placing the last of the china on the bench, he absentmindedly rubbed his forearms. They had puckered with goosebumps making the hairs stand on end and tingle ominously. It was an early warning system that Stewart had come to rely on.

"How's your spider-sense, Stew?" Brian's voice startled Stewart, and he turned abruptly to face his friend.

The affectionate tease did not by any means imply that Brian thought Stewart's reaction silly; on the contrary. The two men knew that it had saved them from grief on quite a few occasions.

"Well and truly on," said Stewart trying to sound casual.

"You've gotten quite fond of Keira, Haven't' you?" Brian said in a hesitant voice.

Stewart didn't answer immediately. He knew that Brian was right. Over the time they had shared a bed together, Stewart had to admit that she had become more than a casual bed buddy. Amidst the past day's peculiar events, he worried about her, hoping she was out of harm's way. Since the attack on Lydia and the disappearance of the amulet from Rhonwen's mirror, he knew better. She had something that was extremely valuable and obviously coveted by someone very dangerous.

"Have you tried calling her again?" Brian asked.

Stewart shook his head. "No response."

"Well, I've let Gerry know that we're looking for her and he's keeping an eye on her place and has put the word out to the security guys around the pubs and clubs. If she is just out partying, then someone's bound to spot her and let us know."

Brian had just finished speaking when the Pacemakers tune rang out from his pocket. He grinned at Stewart. "Speak of the devil." He nodded. "Yes, what have you got?" Brian nodded, listening carefully. "OK, just text me the address and we'll check it out." He paused again and then said. "No problem. Leave it to me."

Brian tapped on the screen and then slid the phone back into his pocket. "One of Gerry's cabbies saw Keira go to a house in Kensington. He's now got someone keeping an eye on the place, and guess what! The only one that they had seen leave the place in the last few hours was a particularly elegant and beautiful woman who had just returned. Now that's got to be that woman you bumped into at Keira's."

Brian looked over at the phone screen and quickly noted the address. "Right, then we will be able to ID her. That's one more piece for the puzzle."

Stewart looked over at him and quickly glanced at the door to ensure it was shut. "What about the amulets? Two of them are in one small circle of people. That's got to be more than a coincidence."

"You don't know the half of it. Do you know what the thief took from Rhonwen's? A large clear jewel that was a centrepiece in that broken mirror. Stew, she described the amulet."

Stewart's face drained to a sickly white as the implications of what Brian had just told him sunk in. But before they could say anything else, Rhonwen came through the door looking for them. She seemed to have a little more colour in her cheeks as she smiled tentatively at them both.

"I just spoke with the hospital. Lydia has come through the surgery with no problems, and they think she is going to make a complete recovery. I can go and see her in a couple of hours."

"That's great," Brian responded, I'll take you, but first, we need to organise for you to get some of your things. You can't stay here, Rhonwen. Not even here at Lydia's. It's not safe."

Stewart watched Rhonwen's face as she answered. Her reluctance was obvious. "I know. I will have to call my mother."

Before she could say anything else, Brian gently took her hand and offered her a room at his place. Stewart was surprised. The hallowed sanctum of Brian had been a no-go zone for women for a long time now. He wasn't even certain that Victoria, Brian's last girlfriend, had spent much time there. He looked at his old friend and wondered how things had shifted for them both in just a few short hours. And it wasn't just them. The warring emotions crossing Rhonwen's face as she thought about Brian's offer were a testament to that. But in the end, she agreed that this would be better than being several hours away from town at her family's home.

As she left Lydia's to go upstairs and retrieve some clothes and whatever else she would need for a few days, Brian's mobile rang again. It was Gerry telling them that Keira was safely tucked up at her place again. Stewart looked past Brian to the door to check it was securely closed before he declared his intention of going over to check on Keira himself. He saw the concern in Brian's face as he put a hand on his shoulder and advised, "Be careful. We don't know who or what we're dealing with here. I'd hate to see something happen to you."

Stewart grinned. "Easy, my friend. I'm not a geriatric yet! And just because we're in the middle of London doesn't mean I'll let my guard down."

"I know," Brian said, "but we've both been behind a desk for a while now."

Stewart cut him off. "Yes, but neither of us has allowed ourselves to get too soft." He paused and grinned. "I'll be fine. I'll keep you posted every half hour if that makes you feel better." Stewart said reassuringly and headed towards the door. "Catch you later."

"You"d better. By the way, remember that we're dealing with someone who jumps out of the second floor and disappears into thin air." Brian replied.

"Relax, Brian, I know."

ᘐ ᘐ

Brian stood by the kitchen bench and watched his friend slip out of Lydia's apartment. He felt a little foolish treating Stewart with such concern. They had survived numerous combat operations, and neither had ever been seriously injured, unlike many of their companies. Gerry once commented that Brian and Stewart were charmed or had possibly made a pact with the devil. The idea that somehow the two were invincible created a mystique around them and their squad that stuck.

The thief's leap through the window had seriously unsettled him. He couldn't make any sense of the moments before when he had felt like he was moving in slow motion, his limbs heavy and cumbersome. It reminded him of dreams he had as a child, where his efforts to escape from someone or something were futile. An old sense of dread had risen up in him, one he had thought He'd conquered through his training as a soldier and then as a Special Forces operative. His sense of powerlessness had triggered a flashback. A memory he had thought securely locked away, of watching the hooded intruder from the top of the stairs aim a pistol at his mother. He opened his mouth to scream for her to turn, but nothing came out; there was no sound, only a silent terror as an invisible fist seemed to punch into his mother's body, buckling her in two. She appeared suspended in mid-air, frozen for an instant in time. Suddenly sounds of an explosion and screams filled the air, and what a moment ago had been the silent slow motion of the assault had erupted into the chaotic jumble of sounds and movement.

Preoccupied with his thoughts, he didn't hear Rhonwen enter the kitchen.

"Are you OK?"

Startled and still somewhat disorientated, he spun as he grabbed the hand that touched his shoulder and automatically moved to a defensive position.

"Ouch! That hurt, Brian!" She exclaimed, pulling her hand from his and looking at him strangely. He realised that his eyes were moist with tears. Blinking quickly, he gave her a lopsided grin as he apologised. "Sorry Rhonwen, I'm a bit jumpy".

She nodded distractedly, her own face masked by grief. He felt a sudden urge to pull her close to him, to hold and reassure her, not so much for her but for him. He needed to feel her softness and smell her perfume as his material link to reality. He wrapped his arms around her, and she responded, melting into him. He kissed her gently on the forehead. "It will be OK. I'll look after you and make sure that nothing like this happens to you."

"Do you think Lydia will be OK?" she asked, looking up at him. Brian suddenly felt self-conscious and held Rhonwen at arm's length. "I'm not sure. I know she is getting the best care. We just have to wait."

He smiled at her warmly, wanting to reassure her but not to give her false hope. She smiled back and then leaned forward and pecked him on the cheek. "Thank you for being here". Her voice trailed off as a powerful voice boomed through the door.

"Miss Tierney, are you here?" The voice reverberated through the flat like thunder, and in an instant, a blond giant of a man was standing next to Rhonwen. She smiled at him as she disentangled herself from Brian. "Hello, Erik."

The huge Norseman took her hand and lent forward, speaking to her as if they were on their own. "Tell me, what's happened here? Gavin wanted me to drop by to see how the mirror was hanging, but I can see that that is the least of your worries," Erik stopped and looked around. "When I went to your apartment, there were police and people sealing the door. I was worried about you, and they told me to come down to this place."

Slightly annoyed, Brian cleared his throat, and Rhonwen quickly took the cue and said, "I'm sorry, Brian …."

Erik interrupted her and stretched his hand out. "Halo, I am Erik Nordson".

As Brian took the massive hand that wrapped around his own and shook it, he introduced himself, noting that Erik was giving him a measuring look suggestive of a warrior evaluating his opponent. It was Rhonwen's voice that interrupted their unspoken exchange as she explained that Erik worked with the Antiques Dealer, Gavin, who had sold her the mirror the day before.

Her voice faltered, and as Erik turned his puzzled gaze to her, Brian continued for her;

"Rhonwen's apartment was burgled, and the intruder broke the mirror and almost killed her friend Lydia."

Erik shook his head and frowned, turning back to Rhonwen. "How dreadful! Is your friend going to recover?"

"We don't know yet, we'll find out more from the hospital later. The mirror, unfortunately, has been destroyed."

"That is a shame, truly. But may I still take a look? Gavin may be able to repair the piece, Rhonwen."

"No. As you can see, my apartment is part of an investigation, and the pieces are evidence that the police have collected and taken away."

Erik frowned. "I see." He stopped for a second and then asked very carefully, "Is there anything I can do for you?"

It was Brian who answered. "Tell me, Erik, what do you know about the history of the mirror?"

In that instant, Erik's mobile rang, and he put his hand in his pocket to retrieve it. "Sorry."

He turned away from Brian and Rhonwen and stepped into the hallway out of earshot while Rhonwen looked at Brian and whispered. "What are you thinking, Brian?"

Brian shrugged his shoulders. "Nothing really other than Gavin and Erik may have a bit of a history about the mirror that may give us a lead."

"I thought so." Rhonwen looked at her watch, and suddenly there was an urgency in her voice. "Let's get to the hospital, Brian. I really want to know how Lydia is doing, It's getting late and we can catch up with Gavin and Erik tomorrow."

Brian nodded. "You're right. I ... "

He was interrupted as Erik came back into the kitchen. "That was Gavin. He suggested that you come by the shop, and we can fill you in with some of the mirror's history."

Rhonwen smiled warmly. "That's kind of you, but we do need to go to see Lydia. How about we meet at the shop tomorrow."

Brian quickly interjected. "It will have to be late morning because we have to go to the Police Station to give statements."

Although Erik agreed to this arrangement, Brian couldn't help feeling that he was a little put out by the delay. *If I am honest with myself, I'd rather find out about the mirror now than go to the hospital,* Brian thought to himself as he shook hands with Erik and watched him leave the apartment. He noted that he was very light on his feet, and his footsteps were barely discernible for a man of his size.

25

Declan had positioned himself on the corner of Court Street and Whitechapel Road where he could carefully observe the movement of staff and visitors in and out of the Old Royal London. Separating him from the hospital was a river of traffic that steadily flowed along, the air occasionally punctuated by the blaring horns of cars or buses and the random frustrated call for a cab.

Assured that it was safe to approach the hospital undetected, he waited for a small break in the traffic. As he fiddled with the amulet in his pocket, he was conscious of the slight tingling coursing through his fingers and hand. When the traffic slowed for a red light, he dashed across the street and up the old stone stairs. Once out of the drizzling rain, he shook the pearling drops of water from his coat and then made his way into the building, always alert to who was around him.

To his relief, there was no one who appeared to take any notice of him whatsoever, and he casually strolled to the enquiry desk staffed by a friendly-looking young woman who patiently dealt with the various questions thrown at her. "Excuse me," Declan beamed at her, "could you tell me where I could find Ms. Lydia

Chambers? She was admitted here earlier after a very nasty accident."

"Certainly. Let me take a look." She stopped to scan the VDU in front of her while her fingers flew across the keyboard on her desk. "Ah, there." She scribbled a couple of letters and numbers onto a piece of paper and slid it across to Declan.

"Here we go. Just follow the corridor down to the next lift and then up two floors. You can't miss it."

She looked at the screen again and then frowned. "You"ll have to see the Doctor or unit manager first."

Declan smiled again disarmingly. "No problem. Thank you very much for your assistance."

"You're welcome." Her automatic reply faded into the distance as Declan strode purposefully down the corridor, still scanning for anyone he might recognise.

His hand still held the amulet in his pocket, the tingling ebbing and flowing more forcefully up his arm. In the short time since he had taken possession of the piece, he had not just found its touch intriguing, but what was more important, he had come to enjoy the peculiar energy it emitted. Calling the lift, he waited, occasionally looking up and down the busy corridor, and when the metal door opened, he stepped quickly into the empty space and pushed the button. When the door eventually closed, he sighed with relief. *So far, so good,* he thought.

A loud ding announced the arrival of the lift, and the door slid open. Declan was surprised to see the corridor bustling with staff and visitors crowded around the lift. He drew a deep breath, braced himself, and stepped onto the floor, doing his best to blend into the scene. Acutely conscious of not drawing attention to himself, he glanced at the piece of paper the receptionist had given him. Looking around, he quickly oriented himself and walked towards the end of the corridor, where he turned left. He stopped, suddenly riveted to the spot. A uniformed policeman was talking to the Nurse at the desk halfway up the corridor.

Declan wondered if the officer had seen him. *He must have,* he thought. As his mind raced through solutions, Declan suddenly realised that no one was looking at him even though he was standing conspicuously in the centre of the corridor with numerous people flowing around him. His luck was holding. Or was it something else?

At that moment, he chose to do something very risky. He deliberately took a step towards the door of the room he had identified as Lydia's, noting that there was a sink with a water fountain close to it. He figured that if the officer acknowledged him, he could suggest that he was looking for someone and had gotten lost amidst the various corridors and rooms on the floor. The officer, however, continued to talk to the Nurse. Now that he was closer, Declan could see that she was indeed a very pretty young woman and that the officer was completely preoccupied.

Using the sink as a small amount of cover before approaching the door of Lydia's room, he became aware that the tingling in his fingers and hand had spread to the core of his body and become a pulsing beat that seemed to be consuming his whole being. Far from being unpleasant, it provided him with a sensation of power. He felt capable of achieving anything. His fingers clasped the amulet even more tightly, and a comforting familiarity unfolded within the deep recesses of his mind.

On impulse, he closed his eyes, only to see an image of Lydia lying in a bed surrounded by the paraphernalia of modern medicine. Startled by the image, he instantly opened his eyes again and holding his breath, Declan took another step forward. Continuing to keep an eye on the officer, he reached cautiously for the door handle, closed his hand around it and waited. The seconds ticked by, but neither the policeman nor the nurse seemed to notice him. He took the chance to turn the handle of the door.

Declan wasn't sure what happened next but suddenly found himself beside Lydia's bed. He quickly looked back towards the door to check, half expecting the officer to appear in the room suddenly. But the door was closed, and the only sound was that of the respirator and the steady rhythm of the cardiac monitor. He forced himself to take another breath and walked to the other side of the bed from where he could see the door.

Quickly sliding his hand into his pocket, he pulled out a small syringe, popped the protective cover off the needle, and, with the dexterity of a nurse, inserted it into the drip suspended above the unconscious woman. He emptied the contents and then stepped back, casually observing the drip. *This should do the trick,* he thought as he watched the first of the drops of fluid laced with heroin disappear into the tube leading into her arm. *At least she would have a peaceful departure.*

He knew that he had a very small window of opportunity to leave the hospital. Taking one last look at Lydia, he began to walk towards the door quietly. When he got to it, he stopped and pressed his ear to the shiny surface, listening. As he closed his eyes, an image of the corridor popped into his mind with the officer in the same position as he was in when Declan arrived.

A little less surprised than when it had happened earlier, Declan opened his eyes carefully and slid his hand onto the door handle. He took a deep breath and held it. About to apply pressure to it, there was what felt like a blink in space, and in the next instance, he was standing in front of the lift. He quickly looked up, and down the corridor but, as before, no one appeared to notice him.

Pushing the button to summon the lift, Declan waited impatiently, a mix of elation, anxiety and disbelief washing over him. As he stood there, the shrill racket of an alarm rang through the ward, and he watched as numerous staff members raced towards the end of the corridor towards Lydia's.

Automatically Declan's hand closed around the amulet, and in an instant, he stood in the middle of the short lane from which he had observed the hospital. He was almost overwhelmed by the rush of adrenaline and sheer joy. *No wonder Jean wanted the amulets so badly.*

26

The medical resident drew in a deep breath. "I'm sorry, but the news is unfortunately not good."

His vague words seem to drift towards Brian and Rhonwen, the hesitancy in his voice adding to Brian's apprehension since they arrived a few moments ago.

"What? What's happened to Lydia?" Rhonwen's voice broke into a choked sob, and Brian could feel her collapse towards him as the medical resident delivered the devastating news that Lydia had died.

"We're not exactly sure, Ms. Tierney," he paused and sighed heavily. "She had come through surgery safely, and we were expecting her to make a full recovery barring anything unforeseen." He stopped to help Brian settle Rhonwen into one of the many chairs lining the walls of the ward.

Brian reached out a reassuring hand that Rhonwen clutched in desperation. He could see that she was trying to control the burst of sobs erupting from her as she sat down heavily.

"But you must have some idea..." her voice trailed off.

"We'll know more after the autopsy."

Rhonwen sobbed again, unable to collect herself and covered her face in her hands while Brian knelt down beside her. "Rhonwen, listen to me. There's nothing anyone can do now."

Brian was about to say something else, but the large figure of Detective Inspector Riley suddenly loomed over the two of them. Brian looked up, a little surprised to see the detective. "Detective Inspector."

"Mr. Poole, can I have a word with you in private?"

Brian patted Rhonwen's hand. "I'll be back in a minute to take you home." He looked at the young resident and then said reassuringly. "The doctor will stay with you, all right?" Rhonwen nodded and wiped her eyes with the back of her hand.

Brian followed the inspector into one of the empty rooms and watched the large man close the door behind him. He pulled a couple of chairs together and pointed to one of them. "Mr Poole, could you please take me through what happened again when you found Ms. Chambers this morning."

Brian sat down and casually crossed his legs, wondering what the inspector was getting at. He thought he had been quite clear during his first interview with the police. He had told the policeman everything. *Well, not quite*, he thought; *how can you explain the strange magical quality of the experience?*

"I don't think I can add anything further to my account from this morning."

"Mr. Poole," the inspector settled back in the chair, "humour me, please."

As Brian finished repeating what he had told the Inspector earlier, the inspector nodded thoughtfully; the only hint that he was frustrated was a tiny tick in the corner of his left eye. "Yes, yes, you have told me that already." He stopped and scratched his head. "You sure you saw no sign of this intruder below the window after he jumped?

"No," answered Brian. "I really can't explain it to you. I don't think that I took that much time to get to the window, but still, somehow, he had already gotten out of sight."

Riley tilted his head to the side a squinted curiously at Brian. "You're obviously an intelligent man, Mr Poole, and well-credentialed, I must say." He paused and lent forward towards

Brian. "Are you sure you didn't miss something? Perhaps an accomplice, a car leaving the scene?"

Brian sat and scrutinised the man for a moment; his first instincts about Riley had been right; he was certainly no fool. His own experience in interrogation led him to think that the inspector suspected that Brian was leaving something out of his story, which of course, was true. *But what could he say?*

"Well, I didn't see a car pull away, but I guess if he was really crafty, he could have waited for me to pull my head back into the window before leaving."

The inspector nodded slowly and deliberately, observing Brian. "Yes, that's a very plausible theory, Mr Poole, but there appears to be no evidence for an intruder. No one saw anyone, nor did we find any prints anywhere in the apartment."

"So we're talking about someone who is obviously a professional," Brian replied.

Again, Riley nodded. "Yes, most probably." He then lent even closer to Brian. "Don't you think it is a bit strange for a woman of Ms. Chambers's age to confront an intruder in someone else" 's apartment instead of calling the police?"

Brian didn't say anything. He knew that the inspector was prodding him to get a reaction. It was obvious that Riley suspected that there was much more to this situation than was evident. What was abundantly clear to Brian was that Riley was suspicious of him.

"I must say, Inspector, it does seem to be a little foolish. However, I can't really help you much there, as I don't really know Ms. Chambers. She is, was, Ms. Tierney's dear friend."

The inspector suddenly smiled broadly and slapped Brian's thigh with a peculiar familiarity. "Of course, Mr Poole, but I think I'll wait until tomorrow to continue with my questions. I would like to see you both in the morning at the station." He stood up and stretched his back. "A bit stiff when I sit like that. An old war wound, you know." He said. "Thank you for your time, Mr Poole."

Brian got up and replied casually, "Glad to help. Unfortunately, there isn't much more I can add."

The inspector was about to turn and leave the room when Brian said, "By the way, what brought you to the hospital?"

The inspector stopped and faced Brian. "Just following up on things, Mr Poole, doing my job."

27

Keira found the way home torturous and couldn't wait for the enveloping security of her sanctuary. Back in her apartment block, she rushed up the stairs fumbling for her keys to open the front door as fast as possible.

Once she had the key in the lock, it turned abruptly, giving her access to her apartment. She quickly slipped inside and slammed the door behind her, flicking the lock in place and barring anyone from entering. Leaning against the door, she drew a deep breath. This sudden need for security and solitude was new and unfamiliar to her, borne from the oddest sense that she had missed something whilst visiting Morgan. More images, arousing yet at the same time disturbing, tried to crowd forward into her consciousness only to be blocked by the sharper memories of her conversation with Morgan.

Breaking away from the door, she slipped out of her coat and unwound the scarf around her neck, casually dropping them on a chair while heading towards a small sideboard that served as a bar. She quickly turned a shot glass over and, unscrewing a bottle of vodka, poured the clear liquid into the glass, tipped the contents into her mouth and swallowed hard, wanting the alcohol to work its soothing effects as quickly as possible. As the warmth of the first shot spread across the middle of her body, she poured herself another one, but without the same urgency to throw it down.

Carrying the glass, she scooped up her coat and scarf and wandered into the bedroom to put them away, trying to tease the wisps of foggy memories out from behind the clear ones. She looked around the room and was somewhat shocked by the state of it. Putting her drink down, she started to clear up the mess. As she yanked up the sheets, she realised they were torn and smelly. The sense of unease she had felt all day sharpened into fear as she dragged the bedding off the bed.

Deciding that putting her home back in order would help calm her, Keira focused on doing just that for the next hour or so. She had just picked up her Vodka for another sip, as she pottered around her living room when she was startled by a sharp knock on the door. She flinched and froze in her steps. Suddenly she grinned, feeling a little foolish. *Get a grip, girl,* she thought.

There was another knock, a little more urgent than the one before. She felt a stab of irritation as she peered through the spy hole, only to see Stewart waiting on the landing. "Stewart!" She exclaimed, surprised but happy to see the familiar handsome face. She put the glass down and quickly unlocked and opened the door.

"Hi, Keira," Stewart gently kissed her on the cheek as he stepped into the apartment. "I'm glad You're all right. I tried to catch up with you earlier. I must have left a dozen texts on your phone."

Realising that she hadn't even looked at her phone since she had left Morgan's, Keira went over to her bag and retrieved it. Glancing at the messages, she saw that there were indeed quite a few. She also noted that the phone was silent but couldn't remember doing that. Shaking her head, she put the phone down and looked up at Stewart, she was suddenly delighted he was there. A wave of lust almost swamped her as she looked at his handsome face.

Not ready to go there just yet, she offered him a drink and asked him about his day. She wasn't really interested, but she needed to step back from this insane urge to rip his clothes off. Stewart took a gulp of his drink, then started to talk about Rhonwen and Brian.

"Rhonwen had a burglary at her place, and a friend of hers, Lydia, who lives downstairs, seems to have gotten caught up in it. She's very badly hurt in hospital."

Surprised that Stewart would know what was happening in Rhonwen's life, Keira asked, "So how do you know about it all? I didn't know you were that close to Rhonwen."

"Brian called me to let me know. He is helping Rhonwen deal with the police and all of the aftermath. Her place is a complete mess."

Trying to feign polite interest, Keira muttered some polite rejoinder, but her mind was spinning. The news that Brian was with Rhonwen made her furious. Part of the spell had been about winning Brian for herself! The job part worked, so what was Brian doing with Miss Goody Two Shoes?

Looking across at Stewart, she calmed down a little. Why was she so concerned that Brian, whom she had to admit to herself, was more of a political choice than a choice of her heart? Stewart was here now! She liked him, and loved fucking him, so why worry about Brian? Her ambivalence unsettled her, and she loathed the feeling.

Deciding to lighten up a little, she changed the subject. "So, how were you this morning?" She grinned sheepishly at Stewart as she handed him another drink.

He frowned for a second and then smiled back. "A little bruised but otherwise fine. Nothing that a bit of time and a little TLC can't fix."

"We were a little rough, weren't we?" She dropped her eyes for a second and peered at Stewart through her long lashes.

Stewart raised his eyebrows and nodded. "Just a little?" He suddenly looked at her. "You know, You're powerful."

“What, for a girl". She heard herself snap back.

"Keira," there was a decidedly conciliatory tone in his voice, "I'm not saying that You're a weak female at all, but I have never been put in my place like that before by any woman." He paused, then continued, "even a lot of men would not have been able to do what you did."

"Which was to bounce you across the room?"

Stewart grinned. "Yes, that's right. Bounce me across the room."

Keira did not answer immediately. She felt restless, unable to stay still, she found herself wandering over to the bookshelf. Taking a sip of vodka, she probed a little deeper into what Stewart might be thinking.

"Do you think that it's a natural talent that I have?" She stopped to scrutinise Stewart's face. "My strength, I mean."

He grinned. "Oh, that. I thought you meant your sexual prowess." He cleared his throat and injected a more serious note. "Well, it had occurred to me that you are a little, err, a lot stronger than most, despite your very petite frame."

Again she did not respond but looked at the books on the shelf and almost lovingly touched the ribbed, leathery spine of the grimoire.

"Do you believe in magic, Stewart?"

Watching his reaction closely she could see that her question took Stewart by surprise.

"What sort of magic? Like a magic show?" He responded in a sort of lighthearted manner. It irritated her. Such a trite reply. But she felt compelled to continue. "No! Real magic; spells and things.

Stewart sat back in the chair and crossed his legs. She almost laughed. *Such a man. He was threatened and was trying to protect his treasured parts!*

He answered, "Well, I don't know; it's all fantasy, imagination, isn't it? "

Keira knew she could have closed the whole conversation down and turned it into a laugh, but she was torn between her need to tell him about it and her fear of him knowing anything about the spell she had used to get the job. Without making a decision, she slipped the grimoire from between the other books and pulled it close, wrapping her arms about it.

Confused about where she wanted to go with this and why she was talking to Stewart about it, she hesitated and responded quietly. "Is it? Is it really? Are you sure of that?" She was aware that Stewart was very alert; his eyes focused on her in that penetrating way he had as he asked. "Keira, what are you getting at? "

Suddenly very unsure of what to do next, she found herself wandering around the room holding onto the grimoire. Standing in front of a small oval mirror that hung in the hall opposite the door to the living room, staring at her reflection, a part of her was aware that she was caressing the leather cover. The subtle touch of the leather felt reassuring, and she could feel it pressing against her chest and getting warmer. As she held it to her, a slight tingling sensation began seeping into her hand and up her arm.

Her reflection, which had been clear and sharply defined in the glass a minute ago, began to diffuse into a swirling pattern of colours. Mesmerised by the spinning kaleidoscope in the glass, she could feel the tingling become more intense while the heat emanating from the grimoire had now reached a point where she thought she would drop it if it got any hotter.

Keira tried to draw a deep breath but struggled with the effort it required. She moaned softly as she continued to grip the book, her body resonating to the tingling while the heat surrounded her like a shimmering shield. She continued to watch the mirror, transfixed by the colours that seemed to want to draw her into some unknown place. It threatened to pull her into its vortex, but just as she felt that she would lose control, an image began to take shape.

Suddenly the colours merged into organised chaos, revealing a face. Gradually the features became more defined, and Keira gasped. A flaming aura of red and orange framed the stunningly beautiful face. It was at once Keira, and yet it wasn't.

Stewart's grasp on her shoulders broke her paralysed gaze on the image, and she gasped as she felt him pull her away. "Keira!" His voice appeared to echo from afar, yet she could see him right in front of her. Puzzled, she struggled to make sense of the conflicting perceptions that assailed her mind. She could feel him shake her, calling her name again. This time, however, the trance lifted instantly, releasing her mind to perceive the immediate reality around her.

"Stewart?" She puzzled for a moment focussing on his face that was riddled with concern.

"What's happening?" He asked.

"I...I don't know. It's so strange." Her voice trailed off.

"Come and sit down." Stewart gently pulled her aside and guided her towards the settee. She looked down at his hand for a moment and blinked, holding back tears as he guided her away from the strange sense of being split in two. She felt herself responding to his reassurance, and relaxing her grip on the Grimoire, she breathed deeply.

Aware that Stewart was watching her closely, she decided she must now pull herself together. The man sitting next to her was trained to be keenly observant, with a finely tuned intuition, and she shouldn't be at all surprised by his probing. She was, however, not ready to disclose things to him that she felt he might not truly understand. No, those things were between her and Morgan.

She smiled and got up as she walked across to the bookshelf, she said in the most casual tone she could muster. "It's probably all of the excitement about the job and, well, the stress of the lead-up and then the anti-climax of the next day. I'll be fine."

Keira slipped the grimoire carefully back onto the shelf, and when she turned around to face Stewart, she had her best fun girl face on again. Deliberately pitching her voice on a low sexy mode, she winked at him and said.

"So what are we doing tonight?"

Stewart shook his head. It was an almost imperceptible gesture, but Keira registered it nonetheless. He looked up at her and, without any hesitation, followed her lead. "Well, how about a nice bottle of wine, pizza and a quiet night in?"

28

Declan threw himself into the comfortable leather chair by his desk and, with childlike glee, spun it around. He was thrilled by the excitement that he knew could rob him of any reason and logic. The feeling had completely replaced the cynical emptiness that had gnawed at him for most of his life. His head was filled with a multitude of questions and possibilities that left him virtually breathless.

At the same time as the unknown loomed ominously over him, he had found something that was far more valuable than anything he had ever dreamt of. It was something that gave him power beyond his wildest imaginings whilst at the same time, paradoxically, placing him in the greatest peril. Despite the danger and the risk that possessing this amulet could cost him his life, he was determined never to relinquish it to anyone, no matter what.

Declan knew to the very core of his being that this was right, that somehow for whatever reason, this amulet belonged to him, that it was a part of him. He was infused with the certainty that could not be shaken. After all, it belonged to his family. It had obviously been handed down over the generations, so why not to him?

Pulling it from his coat pocket and cradling it in his hands, he carefully examined it. On the surface, it appeared to be a simple piece of antique jewellery. The heavy gold work surrounding the large clear stone was basic, almost primitive. In contrast, the gem was an expertly polished cabochon diamond that sat neatly in the grasp of the metal.

Declan weighed the amulet carefully in his hand. It felt heavier than its size would have at first suggested. A slight tingling in the palm of his hand caught his attention. He had come to suspect that these electric pulses signalled that the amulet had been somehow activated. *But how*, he wondered, *could he control it?*

In a matter of seconds, Declan had decided that he needed to be in a place far away from London, somewhere out of the way, especially from Jean, where he could learn to use and control the amulet, to understand its power as well as its limitations. And he knew where to go. He would head north to Yorkshire, where the family had an old cottage tucked away in a forest. It was a hideaway he had used on several occasions when he had needed to disappear for a while, and he would use it again.

The place had always been a sanctuary for those in the family who wanted time away from the rat race of life. It had been used as a hunting lodge by his own grandfather. Still, over the last few decades, with its lack of civilised amenities and its isolation, it had become less and less attractive to the other members of his family. It had become sorely neglected and almost forgotten, and he was fairly confident that apart from himself, only the family's oldest members even remembered that it was there.

He looked down at the amulet savouring the warmth that radiated from it. Declan grinned and was about to lean back in the chair when his mobile phone rang. Irritated by the intrusion, he looked at the small, scratched screen.

"Jean, you bastard. Can" wait, can you!"

The phone kept ringing while Declan stared at it. It stopped as suddenly as it had begun. He frowned. He knew that if he didn't call Jean back with an update on his progress, it would not take long for Jean to follow up in person. Maybe not Jean himself, but an associate or two! He would have to act quickly. Keenly aware that he was in no position to challenge him at the moment, Declan could make sure that Jean was never going to find him. He would meet Jean again only when he was ready to eliminate him.

Contemplating the upcoming confrontation, Declan instinctively closed his fist tightly around the amulet. In an instant, a burning sensation shot up his arm and his mind was flooded with images of Jean. At first, they were chaotic streams of pictures, but gradually an order appeared as if they were being sorted into a video.

Surprised by the sudden apparent hallucination, Declan gasped and, drawing in a sharp breath, quickly got out of the chair, agitated and alert.

The thought that he was going mad was quickly rejected. Yes, it was all bizarre, but he had managed the unimaginable over the last few hours since he had gained possession of the Amulet. That was a vision of something, but what it was, whether the past, the present or even possibly the future, was the mystery. Frustrated with his lack of understanding of how to use the amulet, Declan slammed his fist into the table.

"Why the fuck didn't this thing come with instructions?" His voice rang through his flat.

His phone rang again, the harsh sound drilling the air. Declan picked it up and silenced it. "Well, then. Bring it on, Jean!"

❧ ❧

As the dial tone persisted with infuriating monotony, Jean paced around the well-appointed living room of his London flat. The tone only stopped when Declan's even more annoying voice replied with his minimalist instruction to "*Leave a message.*"

"Fuck you!" Jean yelled at the phone.

Furious, he threw the mobile against the wall but instantly regretted his impulsive action and reached out, waving his hand. The mobile immediately froze in mid-air. It stayed there, suspended and slowly turning on its own axis as if weightless, while Jean casually walked over to pluck it from its precarious position.

Ah! What to do? Declan was proving to be a problem. He had made a mess not killing that bloody woman, and the disturbance in the fabric of magic yesterday had coincided with Declan's theft of the Amulet. If it was Declan who caused it, then he may well have realised the amulet's potential. It was always a risk that he would touch it and feel some connection, but if he had followed instructions and delivered it immediately, it could have been dealt with easily. A little spell would have cleared his memory, and he would still be useful.

But not now. Jean knew he would have to cut his losses and deal with Declan now. Opening a drawer in his desk, he retrieved a long silver chain from which hung a large crystal. Turning around, he walked across the room to the large table on which an extremely detailed map of London was spread out. With his right arm extended over the map, he dropped the crystal along the length of the chain and left it suspended in the air. Incanting the location spell and focusing it on his target, he allowed the crystal to dangle over the centre of the map, picking up the light from the adjacent window. As the light filtered through the stone, a rose hue gathered at its apex, and he slowly let go of the chain.

Hanging above the table, magically suspended in the air, the crystal slowly drew an ever-decreasing circle over the large map, the rose light seeking its quarry and finally pinpointing Declan's general location. An apartment building. The density of London made it difficult to get a completely accurate reading from this far, but his associate would be able to complete the task from the building's surrounds.

Picking up his phone, he located the number he wanted, and as expected, his call was answered immediately. Jean was aware that his voice had a coldly furious edge as he quickly gave detailed instructions. He also knew that this would signal his man to be sure to carry out his plan to the letter. The question of what level of force was necessary made him hesitate momentarily. He had hoped to use Declan for longer, but the level of risk was too high. "No. I think it's best if you resolve this problem permanently."

Once he had ended the call, Jean found himself feeling intently agitated. He hated having to change tactics midstream. Using Declan Tierney had given him an opportunity to avoid detection and remain at arm's length from this enterprise. Thinking he could double-cross Jean had sealed Declan's fate. Fixing himself a drink, he settled onto the sofa from where he could look out of the window. He waved his hand, and the lights dimmed, allowing him to see the sparkling luminosity of London.

"If you think You're going to get away with this, Declan, think again." He paused and then quietly added. "You, my friend, are a dead man."

꧁ ꧁

Declan felt a sense of extreme urgency as he rummaged through his wardrobe and drawers, throwing clothes and shoes into the medium-sized travel bag sitting in the middle of his bed. His mind was quickly calculating what he would need, as well as what he didn't want found. He had no doubt that Jean would tear the place apart. The cash he held in reserve was hidden in the back of the wardrobe. Opening up the battered-looking box, he scooped it up, and a longish gold chain came with it.

He stopped suddenly, looking at it, an idea taking shape. Retrieving the amulet from his pocket, he threaded the chain through a small loop at the top of the piece and threw the chain over his head. As the stone fell down onto his chest, he could feel the now familiar warm, reassuring tingle as it settled against his skin.

He resumed packing and had just about finished when the Amulet flared a bright red and rapidly heated up against his chest, suddenly becoming searingly hot. Stopped in his tracks, two things happened simultaneously. He intuitively understood that the Amulet was warning him of danger. And at the same time as he heard movement in the next room.

Before he could formulate any coherent thought, he was confronted by the massive figure of a man, and the speed with which he attacked Declan was phenomenal. Within seconds he felt a huge meaty hand close around his throat, and then almost instantaneously, he was slammed against the wall of the bedroom.

"Goin" somewhere, gov?" The man grinned menacingly.

Even if Declan had wanted to answer, it would have been near impossible as the brute strength of his attacker's hand constricted his throat to the point where he could barely breathe. His assailant pushed his face up into Declan's and continued.

"Now, you little, slimy bastard, hand over the Master's property".

On the point of passing out, Declan instinctively closed his eyes. He automatically visualised the Amulet, which seemed to guide his focus to the deep-seated rage that lived in the pit of his being. Drawing on years of resentment and bitterness, he channelled his emotions into a palpable force that suddenly exploded from him, launching the brute across the room and slamming him into the opposite wall.

Declan sensed a sudden change in the air around him as it became a viscous fluid within which everything moved in slow motion. It was as if he was back in Rhonwen's apartment. He watched as the man landed against the wall and slowly slid to the floor where he lay, winded, trying to catch whatever air his body could take.

Suddenly he seemed to regain his strength and his speed, and he jumped back up. The pace of his recovery shocked Declan, who, for a moment at least, had thought He'd overcome the brute. Again he focussed his energy. He felt the connection between his intention and the Amulet as it seemed to synchronise with him and his need to protect himself. Instantly the man began to scream in pain and rage, shaking his head as if something was beating on it. But he still kept coming despite his obvious distress. He threw himself at Declan, who managed to slip out of the way, barely avoiding the grappling arms.

The brute's forward momentum propelled him into the wall, and he collapsed into the corner of the room, writhing and thrashing about, his hands covering his face. He was overcome by whatever Declan and the Amulet had done to repel him, but he wasn't unconscious or quiet. Knowing the noise would bring unwanted attention, Declan grabbed the last few things he needed and followed by a piercing scream from the intruder, he snatched the case from the bed and ran from the room.

As he collected his car keys and some more bundles of cash from a strong box on his desk, he suddenly realised that the thumping and screaming had stopped. Curious, he quickly stepped towards the room and cautiously peered inside what he saw chilled even him. The smell emanating from the room churned his guts as the unmistakable stench of burnt flesh permeated the air. In the corner where he had last seen the intruder now lay his smouldering charred body from which pieces of flesh and bone and bits of clothing protruded.

As Declan scrutinised the room, he noticed that, curiously, none of the surroundings appeared to have been touched by what had incinerated the man's body. As he stared at the pile of remains, he watched them completely disintegrate to dust until only a fine layer of ash remained on the floor.

As he peered at what had been a massive human only a few moments ago, he realised that no one would ever recognise the fine ash for what it was. And if by some chance they did, they wouldn't even find any DNA. Well, this is easy, he thought to himself as he went into the kitchen to find a dustpan and broom. As he swept up the mess, he felt a little sickened and more than a little astonished by the power he had unleashed.

The urgency to get out quickly had lessened, as he knew that Jean would not expect his associate back just yet. So, after emptying the pan into the toilet and flushing his assailant away, he organised his bags and covered his traces as effectively as he could. As he locked the door of the flat and headed out, his mood lifted. It was going to be a long drive north.

29

Brian retrieved Rhonwen from the care of the young doctor and, putting his arm around her, gently led her out of the hospital. He couldn't think of anything to say, and since Rhonwen was completely preoccupied with her thoughts, he felt relieved that he could mull over what had happened as he bundled her into the car and headed home.

Never having been at Brian's home before, she seemed to come out of her mood briefly as she looked around her new surroundings. "I like your place, Brian. Thank you for letting me stay with you."

He could see the tears in the corners of her eyes and moved quickly to put down her bag and settle her onto the lounge. Grateful that she was trying to function at some normal level, he was thinking about what to say when he realised he was hungry. Glancing at his watch, he was astounded to realise it was after 9 pm.

"How about I make us something to eat?"

"I don't know if I could eat anything at the moment but a cup of tea, actually no! Something stronger!" Rhonwen replied, her mouth set with determination. "Have you got some good Whisky?"

Brian nodded, relieved. "Absolutely! Just what we both need. You sit there, and I will sort it," Brian said as he went over to a beautiful glass and chrome cabinet and retrieved a couple of glasses and a bottle of Glenfiddich. "But I think I will also grab something light to eat. I have some cheese and crackers in the kitchen. I will only be a minute."

Obviously not wanting to be alone, Rhonwen got up and followed him into the kitchen to help put a light snack together. Brian started to feel a little less helpless in the face of Rhonwen's grief, but there was still that nagging apprehension in the back of his mind. *How am I going even to begin to tell her about the amulets?*

Deciding that the best thing to do was to wait until after they spoke with the Detective again, and maybe even after they had talked to this Gavin character, Brian pushed it all into the back of his mind and concentrated on helping Rhonwen feel at home and comfortable. They settled themselves in the lounge and sat companionably together, sipping their drinks and looking out at the view through the large picture window. She was exhausted from the emotional nightmare she had been through, and it was taking its toll. He felt that the only thing keeping her together at the moment was the news from Gerry that the vet had let him know that her cat was going to be OK.

After she headed off to bed, Brian poured himself another whisky and as the night deepened and the view of the Thames gave way to the lights of the city, he settled down to puzzle through what had turned out to be another unbelievable day. The last thing he did before going to bed was send a text to Stewart, asking him to be available to meet late the next morning.

Brian would have slept well, at least, as well as an old soldier could under the circumstances, had it not been for the odd noise coming from the guest room during the middle of the night. Brian got up, his amulet glowing softly in the dark and wandered down the corridor, whispers drifting towards him. He stopped to listen at the door. Rhonwen was talking in her sleep—an occasional groan, almost primal, between unintelligible words. Well, let's see how she is in the morning, Brian thought.

He woke to find Rhonwen easily navigating the kitchen, dressed simply in leggings and a white T-shirt. He wondered if she realised that the white cotton was a little sheer, allowing a hint of nipple underneath. He felt a deep stirring of lust as he watched her moving around the room with her hair a loose soft red cloud framing her pale, tired face. A flash of red caught his eye. Glancing at her bare feet he found himself surprised by the perfectly manicured and painted toenails. *Who would have thought it?* There was something about that little incongruity that he found incredibly sexy.

Noticing him in the doorway, Rhonwen blushed and mumbled a greeting as she turned to the sink to fill the jug. Brian used this moment to clamp down on his thoughts and rearrange his clothing to hide any evidence of his imaginings. "Breakfast. Great! Just what I need. How did you sleep?"

Rhonwen, turned towards him with a small smile, her eyes still reflecting her shock and grief from the previous day. "I was very comfortable, and I expect the whisky helped as well." She replied wryly.

Instinctively, Brian knew that the next thing he said would set the tone for the morning. Hoping to avoid opening up Rhonwen's wound around Lydia's death, but needing to acknowledge it, he hesitated briefly before moving over to her, taking her hand and squeezing it. "Are you OK? Is there anything I can do for you at the moment?"

Her eyes glistened with unshed tears as she squeezed his hand back. "Thanks, Brian. I am managing. But if you don't mind, I really can't face the Police again at the moment. Do you think that Inspector Riley needs to see me again today?"

"I don't think so. I think it's just me he wants to see, but I will give them a call and check. OK?" He replied as he went over to the bench and unplugged his phone from the charger. He left Rhonwen in the kitchen and went into the lounge to make the call and check his messages. Returning to the kitchen, he found that she had managed to put together a reasonably decent breakfast for the two of them.

"Good news". Brian said as he came back into the kitchen. "Inspector Riley has been called away, and he only needs me to go down there to try and identify the intruder I saw in your flat. I will be working with one of the other detectives, and because it is all computerised, it shouldn't take too long. It's about eight now, so if I go to the Station about nine, I should be back by ten thirty, eleven."

Relieved, Rhonwen readily agreed to the plan, and they sat down to toast and coffee.

A little later, after calling Gerry to organise a lift, he had a quick shower and headed off to Scotland Yard. Now sitting in the back of the cab on the phone to Stewart, he was trying to get his head around what his old friend was trying to tell him about his evening with Keira. "What do you mean, strange things? Yes, I think that we have a lot to talk about. You need to come over to my place at eleven so we can pool our information, and yes, we do need to tell Rhonwen. Yes, I know, Stewart. It may be necessary to tell Keira as well. Anyway, I will see you at my place."

Looking up through the rear vision mirror, he saw Gerry looking back at him, concern written all over his face.

"What's going on, Gov? That woman in Kensington. The one that Stew's friend, Keira, visited. Well, she has a very interesting ID trail. It's a bit too perfect, if you know what I mean."

Brian nodded. He knew that it was much more complicated than simple theft, but how involved he wanted Gerry to be was another question. "I don't know." He answered honestly. "But it's just getting more confusing and more complex every minute, Gerry, so keep your eyes open and your ears to the ground."

"Will do." Gerry replied as he pulled over to the kerb outside Scotland Yard. "Just give me a call. I'll fetch you when You're ready."

Brian found his way to the right department pretty easily. He was greeted by a Constable who looked like he had barely left high school. Feeling a tad old and tired, he followed him to a specially set up office that housed the equipment that would hopefully produce a likeness of the thief and an identity to go along with it.

They worked at it for about forty-five minutes. In the end, Brian was pretty happy with the result. The face staring out at him from the computer was as close as you could get to the face of the guy, he had seen in Rhonwen's flat. The problem was that he wasn't on the known criminals" national database.

The young Constable excused himself as he needed to discuss this with a senior colleague. Brian nodded politely, and when the door closed behind the officer, he surreptitiously took a photo of the face staring at him from the computer screen. *Maybe his own contacts would have a better chance of identifying him.*

"OK, Mr Poole." The young Constable said as he returned to the office. "You can go now, but Inspector Riley wants you to stay in touch. He will be back later today or tomorrow, so you will need to be available."

"Absolutely," Brian replied as he got up and started towards the door. As he made his way out of the building, he couldn'tt help but reflect that this would probably be the easiest task of the day.

30

Walking through the door of his apartment, Brian immediately sensed that something had changed. He could feel Rhonwen's anger from the front door, and the amulet that had been comfortably nestled in the centre of his chest was noticeably getting warmer by the second. He found Rhonwen pacing the floor. Stewart was sitting at the breakfast bar, wedged against the wall as if trying actually to become part of it. Seeing Brian arrive, a look of intense relief passed over his taut and shocked features.

"What's happened?" Brian asked in a tightly controlled voice. He had found himself instantly on alert, and as he looked at each of them, he realised that Stewart was as puzzled as he was. Rhonwen turned towards him as he spoke, a look of complete fury on her face, her green eyes flashing and her bosom heaving. Brian was suddenly reminded that she had been volatile and moody before Lydia's death, and just as suddenly realised that it had only been in abeyance briefly while she was in shock.

"What's going on, Brian? What aren't you telling me?" Rhonwen almost spat out the words as she retrieved a book from the sideboard and almost flung it at him. It took a few seconds, and then Brian realised that he had forgotten about the book Hayden had lent him. The one with the illustrations of the amulets conveniently bookmarked.

Feeling his own temper start to ignite, Brian resisted the impulse to call Rhonwen on her rudeness. Taking the book and opening it to the appropriate page, he pointed to the picture of the amulets as he calmly sat down at the table. "Does the jewel that the thief stole from your mirror look like this?" He asked in a measured but authoritative voice, hoping that his approach would undermine her emotionality. Unfortunately, it didn't work.

"You know damn well it does. What are you playing at?" She almost snarled back at him.

Stewart, sensibly, had said nothing at this point, but he did unravel himself from his defensive position, a look of alertness evident in the set of his mouth. Brian, recognising the change in Stewart from their days in the army, acknowledged his friend's protective stance with a small hand signal, always keeping his eyes fixed on Rhonwen.

To say that Rhonwen was shocked when Brian pulled the gold chain and amulet from under his shirt would have been an understatement. "Oh my God!" she muttered. She carefully watched the precious jewel shine in the light as it radiated a warm glow and the realisation that it was a match for the one from her mirror sunk into her already traumatised mind.

"Where did you get that from?"

"Well, that is a rather long and strange story."

However, before Brian could go any further, Rhonwen suddenly shouted angrily. "Cut the bullshit, Brian! I want to know what's going on!" As the two men stared at Rhonwen in stunned silence, she paced across the room, every inch of her propelled by fury while her usually generous mouth was set into a thin red line.

"Stop patronising me, Brian; I'm not an idiot!"

"But I'm not .... " Brian started to say, only to be cut short by Rhonwen.

"Really, Brian?" she snorted, "then what is that around your neck?"

Brian was having a very difficult time containing his own anger at this point. Still, somehow he managed to keep his voice even as he set about trying to explain something he didn't actually understand himself. Taking a deep breath, he answered. "This is an amulet that was given to me in the Balkans by a rather strange Gypsy woman many years ago. I have only just found out that it is one of a set of five. The ones illustrated in this book you almost threw at me."

Rhonwen had stopped her agitated pacing and moved a little closer so she could look more closely at the amulet around Brian's neck and the book's open page. Brian could sense her mood shift slightly, so he continued in the same calm voice. "Listen to me, Rhonwen. I know this has been a shocking couple of days. None of us knows what is going on here. Stewart and I have put some pieces of a very large puzzle together over the last twenty-four hours. It appears to involve you, Keira, Stewart, Lydia and myself." Before he could continue, Rhonwen looked at him sharply. "What's Keira got to do with this?" She demanded stridently.

"Rhonwen, think about it. In the last twenty-four hours, there have been several very strange things occur. You saw for yourself that Keira had changed and was nothing like her usual self." He stopped and waited as she processed what he had said, observing her to try and gauge her reaction. She seemed to be turning it over in her mind, and then she looked at him and nodded thoughtfully. She seemed to be a little more receptive, so he continued. "Keira isn't the only one that something odd has happened to. We all have had weird experiences and dreams, and, to be honest with you, Rhonwen, you are not yourself at the moment. These mood swings and your emotionality is not usual for you."

Rhonwen's eyes narrowed for an instant, and Brian quickly moved on. We need your help to work this out. The break-in into your apartment must be an important clue to what is happening. You told me yourself that the only thing stolen was the jewel on top of the mirror. When you drew that picture of the jewel, I recognised that it was one of these Amulets."

Rhonwen broke into the flow of Brian's explanation frowning as she leaned over the open page of the book to look very closely at the illustrations. "So, you are saying that you and I ended up with two of the five amulets."

"It's one of the only things we do know. Our amulets are from a set of five, and they are ancient."

Taking his amulet in his hand, Brian stopped and moved it up into the light where Rhonwen could see it clearly. Then knowing that what he said next was going to rock her completely, he continued. "We also know that a third one is on the front cover of an antique book owned by Keira. Unfortunately, we don't know anything about the other two."

Rhonwen stood there, silently chewing her bottom lip. Then suddenly turning to look quizzically at Stewart, who, until now, had simply sat in silence, she directed her next question to him. "How do you know about Keira's?"

Stewart squirmed a little in his seat, then answered a little defensively. "Let's not get sidetracked. I've been seeing Keira outside work from time to time, which is how I discovered that she has an amulet."

Rhonwen scowled, but before she could say anything, he continued. "I have no idea if she knows what it is as I Haven't'tt spoken to her about it." He paused. "Brian's right, Rhonwen. It's all a little too strange. When I went to Keira's apartment yesterday, she wasn't home, but there was a woman there who claimed she was a friend of Keira's, but the whole thing just felt wrong. She managed to come up with a key that she claimed was a spare, but I know for a fact that Keira has never had a spare key available for her place. I know she was there looking for something, and I interrupted her snooping around. It's all a bit too coincidental that just as she was looking for something at Keira's, there was a thief at your place."

Brian took Rhonwen's hand. "You know, when I burst in on the intruder, the man was about to kill Lydia, but when he saw me, he just leapt through the window and literally disappeared into thin air. It was the oddest thing, and when I looked down into the street, there was no sign of him."

Rhonwen shook her head. She seemed perplexed, even more than before Brian's attempt to explain things. "What are you saying, Brian? I don't understand any of this!"

Rhonwen sat down at the table, tears welling in her eyes, but calmer than she had been earlier. Brian took her hand and squeezed it reassuringly. "We will work this out. I promise. In the meantime, my morning at the Police station did give us another clue."

Brian pulled out his phone and quickly accessed the photo he had taken of the Identikit of the thief. "This is the face of the guy I saw in your apartment, but they don't have him on the database, so we don't know who he is".

When she looked at the photo, he was completely unprepared for Rhonwen's reaction. Rage suffused her face, and she said in a tight, angry voice, "Well, I do. That is my cousin Declan!"
It was Stewart who spoke first. "How could he have known about the mirror? You said you bought it on Friday. Did you tell him about it?"
"Certainly not!" Rhonwen replied hotly. "I hate that little weasel. He is the last person I would talk to. And anyway, I Haven't seen him for years. Not since he tried to have our Aunts" will overturned and take the flat away from me. The last thing I heard about him was that he had moved to Europe."
Brian shook his head. "It just gets stranger, doesn't it? Maybe this Gavin person can give us some information about the mirror at least." Looking across at Rhonwen, who had retreated back into her anger, Brian wondered how he was going to get her to cope with the rest of the afternoon. "Are you OK to come with us to the Antique shop?"
Rhonwen gave him a withering look as she moved away from the table. "Stop treating me like a child. I am perfectly capable of talking to an antique dealer."
It was after midday when they made their way to Gavin's shop. The trip in Gerry's taxi had been difficult, to say the least. Rhonwen had remained distant, her anger a palpable presence. Even Gerry, usually immune to most people's moods, seemed uncomfortable as he drove them through the still-wet streets. The rain was finally easing, and an occasional blue patch was breaking through the gloomy Sunday afternoon.
Brian couldn't believe it had only been two days. It felt like two years since the interviews. He couldn't help reflecting that time was passing in the same peculiar way it did during combat when so much happened in a split second, and your world could change forever.
As they opened the door to the shop, Rhonwen's mood seemed to shift. She became unsure of herself and hesitated before stepping through, her voice betraying her fragility as she called out to alert Gavin to their presence. Realising that she was anxious about this meeting, Brian moved closer to her, taking her elbow. She tensed and almost pulled away but then allowed him to help her thread her way around the antique furniture towards the back of the shop.

Looking through the faintly hazy interior of the large, cramped space, Brian saw a very tall and slender man gliding towards them. When he took Rhonwen's hands in his own, she seemed to relax, and her mood shifted again. Brian felt torn. He found himself feeling jealous and yet relieved. He was confused by what he was experiencing when he was around Rhonwen but now was not the time to deal with that. Glancing at Stewart, who, like him, had been on guard as they approached the shop, he realised that he, too, had relaxed a bit. Then, his attention focused totally on the Antiques Dealer as he spoke to Rhonwen in a beautifully melodious voice.

"Hello, Rhonwen. But for the circumstances, I'd say that it's lovely to see you. Erik has filled me in on what has happened, and I heard about your neighbour Lydia's death on the news. I am so sorry for your loss."

He let go of Rhonwen's hand and turned to the two men to greet them. The elegant, almost feminine hand that shook Brian's belied the power it held. "Gavin Skye. And you would be Brian Poole and Stewart Eggleston."

Brian mused that it was a statement, not a question, as he responded to the greeting. "Call me Brian. I'll get straight to the point. We're hoping you might be able to shed some light on why someone would want to steal the amulet from Rhonwen's mirror." Rhonwen suddenly interjected, her voice firm with anger again. "Not someone. My cousin Declan."

As she said this, Brian saw a flicker of something cross Gavin's well-composed features. It looked like he was just given an answer to something, but the expression was quickly shut down and replaced by a bland look of concern. Turning towards the back of the shop, Gavin smiled at Rhonwen kindly and took her hand. "Come, let's go into my office where we can talk."

Instead of heading towards the far corner, Gavin stepped up to a panel in the wall. Pushing it firmly, it slid to the side, revealing a hidden door. Brian and Stewart looked at each other over Rhonwen's head. Both of them were experiencing the same level of heightened suspicion. There was so much more to this Gavin Skye than they had anticipated.

Brian was sure that Stew's spidie sense was well and truly activated. He followed Rhonwen and Gavin into a beautifully decorated office where the spaciousness of the room belied the small door. As they stood in the room, smells of rich leather and oils flooded their senses, Brian was keenly aware that Rhonwen's mood had shifted again.

"What a lovely, roomy space, Gavin." Rhonwen sighed as she stepped inside.

"It is, isn't it? I like to sit here and ponder the world," Gavin said as he gestured to the huge Chesterfield and several matching chairs. "Please, take a seat and make yourselves comfortable. Would you like some tea or coffee?"

Since they had yet to have had any lunch, they all accepted his offer. Gavin disappeared into another room through a door on the far wall, and Brian could hear the rattling of cups and cutlery. Taking advantage of Gavin's brief absence, Brian gave Stewart an almost imperceptible signal to keep an eye open as he started to scope the room.

He found himself disorientated by the dimensions of the space and what he could remember of the building he had observed as they had arrived. He was still trying to puzzle this out when Gavin returned with a tray laden with the makings of tea and some tempting-looking muffins.

Brian watched him carefully as he organised their afternoon tea. The grace and style in the man's movements reminded him of a predatory cat confident in its own power. When Gavin handed him a plate, he looked straight into Brian's eyes, and Brian had an uncanny sense that Gavin was aware of everything he was thinking at that very moment. But for some reason, he didn't feel threatened or alarmed by this.

Settling them all down into a comfortable circle around the coffee table, and then, looking at each of them in turn, Gavin started pouring the coffee. "Now, I'm sure that you have a lot of questions and, to be clear, I'm not sure that I'll be able to answer all of them, but I will try my best." He said affably.

Brian wasted no time getting to the point. "Gavin, what do you know about the mirror you sold to Rhonwen on Friday? Do you have any paperwork about its provenance?" Rhonwen, who, up to this point, had been quietly sipping her tea, gave Brian a startled look. Then, turning to Gavin, blurted out what had been on Brian's mind since they had first arrived. "Did you know that the centrepiece of the mirror was an old Amulet?"

Brian was stunned. He had failed to recognise that Rhonwen was no longer submersed in her grief. She had asked the question he had been angling towards. Watching Gavin for his reaction, he was perturbed by the lack of any expression on the man's face. Deciding to push him further, he asked Gavin the next most burning question. "Do you know why Rhonwen's cousin would want to steal the Amulet? Why would he be prepared to kill an old lady to get it?"

"That is very regrettable." The frown on Gavin's forehead etched even deeper lines into the translucent skin. Brian carefully watched his reaction and wondered what the peculiar man must be thinking. Gavin rose from his chair and walked across the room past a tall cabinet towards a beautiful antique desk. As he moved, just for an instant, Brian thought he saw a shimmering around his body. He blinked and looked again, but this time saw nothing.

Gavin turned back and looked at him for an instant; the piercing blue eyes locked on Brian's face. Then positioning himself so he could look at all of them at the same time, he continued. "I want you to know that I will help in any way I can, so please, ask me anything you like, and if I can, I will tell you what I know." Brian sat forward on the huge Chesterfield, alerted by Gavin's allusion to there being information that he might keep to himself. "What can you tell us about the mirror, and do you know anything about the Amulet that was its centrepiece."

Brian felt, rather than saw, Rhonwen lean forward as well. Glancing at her quickly, he saw a look of intense concentration on her face. Looking back at Gavin, he noted that the man in front of him was as aware as he was of Rhonwen's volatile emotional state. He smiled gently at her as he spoke. "It might be helpful if you tell me what you already know. It appears that you have some knowledge of the mirror and its decoration."

Before Brian could speak, Rhonwen repeated her question. "Did you know that that jewel is an old Amulet, Gavin?"

Gavin, leaning casually against the desk, his arms crossed across his chest, looked at her kindly, then answered. "Yes. The mirror per se is of little importance. It is the amulet that is of value. According to legend, it is one of five such pieces forged by magic. A magic that empowers its owner with special abilities. The myth states that it was decided that no one person could possess them all, for the temptation to use them for their personal gain would be too strong. So the amulets were entrusted to five families to keep them safe and apart. Hidden, unless they were needed." He stopped and smiled for an instant. "Well, at least so the story goes."

Brian instantly knew that Gavin was being deliberately vague. He had acknowledged that he knew of the story of the Amulets but had told them nothing more than they already knew. "So, knowing that this mirror had one of these legendary Amulets hiding in its decorative frame, you just sold it to Rhonwen." Brian challenged. "Apart from the fact that it would be a valuable archaeological find, what if someone did believe in the old stories? Someone like Declan Tierney? Brian asked.

"Then they would probably want to get their hands on all five as that would make them, at least in their mind, immensely powerful." Gavin's mouth formed a tight grim line. "Perhaps by any means necessary."

He heard Rhonwen's sharp inhale as she took in what Gavin had just admitted. "But it's all just a myth. A fantasy, surely, she argued.

"Does the name Scáthach mean anything to you?" Interjected Stewart from the other side of the room.

A startled look passed over Gavin's face so quickly that Brian would have missed it if he hadn't been watching so closely. But although he had been quick to conceal his chagrin at the sound of the name, his body language said something very interesting. Gavin's whole body had tensed into a very familiar state. Glancing at Stewart, Brian knew that he had seen it too. Gavin reacted to that name like a warrior reacting to a grave threat.

His voice even, with no hint of his disquiet, Gavin casually asked them. "How much do any of you know of Celtic mythology?" It was Rhonwen who replied, her voice hinting that her mood had shifted again to controlled anger. "Celtic history is a hobby of just about everyone in my family except for my parents. Aunt Sophie and my grandmother were very knowledgeable, but I didn't spend much time with them after moving away. The amulets are Celtic, aren't they?"

"And so is this Scáthach, I assume," Stewart interjected, feeling compelled to follow the trail but acutely aware that in doing so, he was going to expose Keira's strange behaviour to the others. "Why do you ask, Stewart? Where did you hear this name?" Gavin asked quietly.

Reluctantly, Stewart filled them in on some of the experiences he had in Keira's flat the night before. Not all of them, of course. A very censured version, but still, he could see that Gavin understood more than he had actually explicitly reported. The looks on both Brian's and Rhonwen's faces were enough for him to feel that he had violated Keira's privacy. He felt extremely uncomfortable. However, he also felt compelled by a powerful need to tell Gavin what he had seen.

Brian watched Gavin closely, looking for some hint of what he was thinking, as Stewart told them about what could only be called a bizarre and unbelievable phenomenon. He felt like he was in some episode of the Twilight Zone, and he could feel Rhonwen's discomfort radiating from her as she sat next to him on the lounge.

Gavin proved to be a cool customer. Using a voice that reminded Brian of a school teacher, he explained. "Well, legend has it that Scáthach was a Celtic warrior queen who lived on the Isle of Skye. She eventually rose to divinity in order to lead the dead on the Journey of the Soul".

"This warrior queen became immortal?" Asked Stewart.

"So the legend goes." Replied Gavin.

"And the five amulets. Where do they fit in? After all, if this is only legend, how come they actually exist?" Brian pressed, acutely aware of the one nestled amongst the hair on his chest.

Gavin shifted his weight in the chair. "What I'm about to tell you is partly myth and part fact. It is entirely up to you which you choose to believe. As I said before, five families were chosen to take possession of the amulets and, more importantly, guard them. Each family came from a special bloodline. Scáthach was ultimately banished to the otherworld through the power of the five amulets, wielded by a member of each of those five families. It is also said that the Amulets possess the power to release her from her otherworldly prison."

Gavin paused and looked at Rhonwen. "Rhonwen, your family was the original owner of the amulet on the mirror. That is why I sold you the mirror. It is, in fact, your inheritance, but you needed to choose to own it."

He paused for a moment so she could digest this and then continued. "The families were sworn to keep them hidden from those that would use them for their own immoral purposes and, if need be, to defend them against misuse. However, with the passage of time, fewer members of the families took on the responsibility of their guardianship, and eventually, much of the knowledge surrounding the amulets was completely lost. Soon the amulets themselves had disappeared." He stopped, and when he continued, it was more for himself. "They have now begun to reappear, one by one, but for what reason, for what purpose?"

Gavin stopped, aware of their curiosity and no longer able to completely hide his concern. "It appears that the three of you and Keira have been drawn into a scheme to recover the amulets by someone who appears to believe in the old legends." Looking intently at Brian, he continued, "And you, Brian, are from one of the other of the five families".

For some strange reason, Brian knew that Gavin was telling the truth. He could feel the warmth of the Amulet against his skin and the slight pulsing that underscored the sensation that the Amulet was alive. Slowly, he eased the gem out through his shirt front and exposed it to the others. Gavin walked over to stand in front of him and then said in a hushed but somehow powerful voice. "You need to know that with its possession comes a great responsibility, Brian." The sombre words echoed in Brian's head as he stared at Gavin. "The question is, will you accept that responsibility?"

31

Reclining in his favourite chair, the new moon shining through his lounge room window, Brian crossed his arms behind his head. Taking advantage of Rhonwen being too exhausted to do anything but go straight to bed, he looked out over the city, enjoying just being alone for a while. Finally having relaxed, he allowed himself to carefully sift through the day's events trying to make some sense of it all, ordering what he knew into categories, looking for patterns and connections.

Gavin Skye was an enigma, and Brian found that he had quite ambivalent feelings about the man, but he had been able to give them some useful information. Thinking back on the afternoon, Brian recognised that they had also given Gavin some answers, but to what exactly, he wasn't sure. Gavin had been particularly interested in the story of the Gypsy woman and had asked for detailed information about the village.

His other main interest had been Keira, which was understandable given what Stewart had disclosed about the bizarre stuff he had witnessed. Brian wanted to believe that Keira was either unstable or had been playing around with some drug, but it didn't fit. Just like his experience in Rhonwen's flat didn't fit. It defied normal reality, yet he hadn't sensed any disbelief from Gavin as he described the encounter. In fact, none of what they said seemed to shock the man.

Brain admitted to having nightmares, but not the content. He couldn't go there, not in front of Rhonwen, but it had prompted her to tell them about something of her own experience. She was also holding back; it had been obvious to them all. She had become distressed again and refused to go into too much detail. He was glad Gavin hadn't pushed her. The man had shown a lot of kindness and sensitivity to Rhonwen, and Brian felt pretty confident it had nothing to do with being attracted to her.

Looking at his mental lists, he realised that the question of how Gavin came to be in possession of the mirror remained to a large part, unanswered. Gavin had been evasive when he had spoken about it being part of a deceased estate. Whose estate? Why hadn't any of them asked more detailed questions about that? It left him with the very uncomfortable feeling that somehow, he had been out manoeuvred. It suddenly occurred to him that Gavin had not explained how he knew about his and Rhonwen's families. Five amulets, five families, and he and Rhonwen coincidently both working at the same firm. And what about Keira? If she had an Amulet, where did she get hers? And all of these allusions to the supernatural!

Now, assessing all of the bits of information he had gathered, Brian found himself rather desperately trying to avoid the conclusion, unbelievable as it was, that the common element in all of this was Magic! He just couldn't accept it. The whole idea of magic was outside his tolerance for the strange and unexplainable. But just how did Declan jump out of the window and disappear?

Restless and a bit agitated, Brian got out of the chair, pacing around the room, trying to force the facts to align with a different explanation. But he couldn't escape the most glaring fact that the Amulets were somehow the key. He quietly went into his study to his desk. Lifting the gold chain with the amulet over his head and placing it carefully onto the desktop, he retrieved a large magnifying glass from one of the drawers. He methodically began to study the stone and its settings.

After a few minutes, he sat back, frustrated. It looked the same as the last time he had examined it. Just like an ordinary antique, with no sign of anything special, but he had seen it glow and felt its heat. As he sat there staring at it, he felt a wave of tiredness wash over him. A little puzzled by his sudden fatigue, given it wasn't that late, he picked up the Amulet to put it back around his neck. Immediately, he felt the now familiar tingle of energy tracing itself through his fingers and up his arms. As the Amulet came to rest on his chest, he felt a surge of power through every muscle in his body.

Drawing a sharp breath, he stood up as a flicker of light caught his eye, and he noticed his reflection in the window pane. His shadowy silhouette was surrounded by a halo of light that shimmered in a multitude of colours not unlike what he had observed around Gavin earlier that day. It wasn't just the immediate boost of energy; his sense of smell also seemed more acute. Standing still and taking stock, he realised he was able to hear the steady rhythm of Rhonwen's breathing even though she was two rooms away.

He was considering the notion that the Amulet amplified the wearer's senses when he heard footsteps on the hall's marble floor outside his apartment. The moment he was aware of them, he was confronted with the image of Inspector Riley walking towards his apartment. Before he could even begin to understand what he was seeing, the doorbell chime sounded, and in the next instant, he was at the door. It all happened so quickly that Brian barely had time to get his bearings as he automatically reached for the door handle.

"That was quick!" Riley looked puzzled, obviously surprised at the speed with which Brian had answered the door. "May I come in?"

Brian was more than a little perplexed himself. Still trying to work out what had just happened to him, he realised the officer standing in front of him was watching him closely. Quickly putting all those thoughts aside, as he knew he couldn't afford to be distracted, he motioned for Riley to enter. "Of course. Let me take your coat."

"Much obliged, Mr Poole. I would like to speak with Miss Tierney. Is she here?"

Brian steered the Inspector towards his study, hoping not to disturb Rhonwen, who remained unpredictable and fragile. He wanted to avoid any chance of her exposing any of their recent findings inadvertently. He lied, explaining that she was asleep and saying she had taken a sleeping pill. He was half expecting the Inspector to insist, but he accepted Brian's excuse and followed him into the study.

Closing the door quietly, Brian offered him a chair and a drink. "No, thank you. Just had a coffee earlier. Anything else, well, I am on duty." Brian nodded. "I understand. Is there any news?" Riley nodded, and as he sat down and crossed his legs, he asked, "What do you know about a man called Declan Tierney?"

Years in military intelligence meant that Brian's face revealed little, but knowing that the Inspector was watching him closely, it was all the more important that he gave nothing away. "Declan? Not a lot, really. I think he is a cousin of Ms. Tierney."

"Yes, that's right. A bit of a shady character, that one." He paused and squinted at Brian. "Ever meet him?"

Brian sat down in his desk chair and reclined casually. "Can" say I have, actually. Rhonwen mentioned him briefly. He apparently gave her a frightful time over an inheritance." Again, the Inspector nodded. "That he did, Mr Poole, that he did."

The man uncrossed his legs and lent forward. "That was some years ago. Did you know that he completely disappeared immediately after the court case? Curious thing to do, wouldn't you say, Mr Poole?"

Brian almost smiled at the Inspector's manner but carefully maintained his casual attitude. The fact that he was asking questions about Declan meant that they must have somehow identified him from the likeness Brian had given them earlier in the day.

Changing tack, the Inspector looked around the study admiringly. "This is a very nice place, Mr Poole. Do you normally live here by yourself?"

"Yes, I do, as a matter of fact. Why do you ask?"

"Bear with me, Mr Poole, but as you can appreciate, my line of work makes me a very inquisitive sort of a bloke. I am just trying to clarify the exact nature of your relationship with Ms. Tierney".

Brian smiled, thinking to himself that the Inspector wasn't the only one who needed to know the answer to that question. "She has been a work colleague for the last few years. Given the circumstances, I felt she would be more comfortable here as my guest. Her family live out of town."

The inspector nodded knowingly and then frowned. "You suspect that she is in some sort of danger?"

Brian shrugged his shoulders. "In my line of work, it pays to anticipate the worst."

"Yes, I suppose it would." The Inspector said.

He then sat up, squaring his shoulders in the process. "I should tell you that we have been able to identify Miss Chamber's assailant from your description. The picture that our artist drew was a match for Declan Tierney. I will need to speak with Ms. Tierney and any other family members who may know of his current whereabouts. Also, I am sad to inform you that Ms. Chambers did not die of her injuries. Instead of manslaughter, I am now investigating a homicide."

"A homicide?" Brian asked. "Do you mean that Lydia ..."

Riley nodded. "The pathology report came back late this afternoon. Ms. Chamber died of respiratory arrest brought on by a narcotic analgesic, most likely heroin."

"She died of an overdose?"

"Yes, that's right, an overdose." Riley stopped for a moment, a little theatrically, Brian thought, and then continued. "The drug was delivered through the cannula in her arm. This would suggest that she knew her attacker, and he was making sure she didn't identify him. This adds weight to the other evidence that Declan Tierney broke into the apartment."

Brian was very aware of the scrutiny he was under as he digested this news. He allowed himself to look shocked, hoping that he didn't overdo it.

"I had hoped to speak with Miss Tierney about this tonight." The Inspector said hopefully.

"She is asleep, Inspector. Could we do this tomorrow? She is devastated by all of this, and finding out that her cousin broke into her home and killed her friend is going to be very traumatic."

Looking at his watch, the Inspector seemed undecided, and for a minute, Brian thought he would insist on seeing Rhonwen immediately.

"All right, Mr Poole. Bring her down to the station in the morning."

With that, the Inspector hauled himself out of the chair he had been sitting in, and Brian ushered him to the door. Just as the Inspector walked out into the hall, he turned and looked at Brian, his brow furrowed, he asked.

"How long have you known Ms. Tierney, Mr Poole?"

It was at that moment that Brian realised that the Inspector's suspicions now included Rhonwen as well as himself.

"As I said earlier, we have worked together for a number of years now, Inspector. I have complete faith in her integrity. After all, the firm we work for ensures that all of its employees are thoroughly screened."

The Inspector nodded and, putting on his hat, walked towards the elevator. "I'll see you both tomorrow morning, Mr Poole."

32

The empty bottle of wine on the bedside table took the full brunt of Keira's arm. Had it not been for the thick carpet that covered the bedroom floor, it would have smashed as it hit the ground, shattering into a multitude of shards. As it was, neither Keira nor Stewart could be distracted from their passionate lovemaking. Here and now, in the semi-dark bedroom, what had once been simply sex had somehow transformed into a tender and consuming interlude that swept the two lovers along an ardent river of passion, undulating in its primitive landscape.

What Stewart was unaware of was that there was a raging conflict that had begun to tear at Keira's mind. With each erotic moment, with each kiss, and each caress, that conflict grew, and she struggled more and more to suppress the urgency to overpower Stewart, to tear him from the bed and throw him to the floor in a triumphant struggle for supremacy.

It wasn't Keira who wanted to vanquish her lover. Keira's struggle was with Scáthach, who once more wanted to burst into her consciousness, take over her mind, and take possession of her body. As the mental struggle intensified, the physical signs began to manifest. Slowly at first, then with growing intensity, her muscles shuddered and contracted like earthquakes, erupting in a final spasm and snapping Keira's head back.

Shocked, Stewart tore himself from Keira, whose arms had clamped around him like the coils of a serpent. She fell back onto the bed; her breathing laboured while her face was a strange, contorted mask where the whites of her eyes were eerily visible in the semi-dark of the room.

At first, Stewart thought that she was experiencing an unusually intense orgasm. Still, in seconds he realised that what he was witnessing was more akin to a seizure than anything like a sexual climax. He leapt out of bed and threw the light switch on the small bedside lamp.

"Keira!" he shook her forcefully and then rolled her onto her side, "Come on, girl, snap out of it."

Keira groaned as another spasm shook her. As it ebbed away, she visibly relaxed, her body stretching out along the length of the bed while the pained and aggravated look on her face dissolved. Stewart sat back on the bed and drew her into his lap, resting her head on his thighs while gently stroking her sweaty forehead and brushing back the wet hair. "Keira, can you hear me?"

"Hmmm." It was a languid reply, and a wisp of a smile spread across her mouth. "Stewart?" her faint voice drifted up towards him. "Yes, it's me, sweetie. Are you OK?" Keira frowned as if the question was too much for her overloaded mind to deal with. "Ah, I'm not sure. A bit sore, I guess."

She reached up and lightly touched Stewart's face. "What about you? I didn't hurt you again, did I?"

Relieved that Keira was able to respond to him, Stewart shook his head. "No, I'm OK. But what about you? Can you tell me what just happened?"

The question seemed to trigger something in Keira. Sitting up, she wrapped her arms about her drawn-up knees and shook her head. "I'm not sure," she hesitated and looked intently at Stewart. "If I tell you something, you must promise not to think that I'm mad." He smiled, trying to cheer her up. "No more than usual."

This time her smile was stronger than before. "OK, OK." She hesitated, then looked straight into his eyes. "I know this will sound really out there, but I've sort of been dabbling in magic." She stopped and searched Stewart's face for any reaction but could find nothing to make her think that he was anything but curious. "You know, witchcraft."

When Stewart didn't say anything, she continued. "I found this book at the Manor, and it was full of spells and things." She pulled her legs closer to her body as if she was holding herself together, then continued. "Ever since then, some really weird shit has been happening to me."

Stewart reached out and touched her arm, encouraging her to go on. "Like what?"

"Like what happened just now, where I felt like someone or something was trying to take over my mind," Keira paused and rubbed her arm, "and I guess my body."

" Have you spoken to anyone else about it?"

Keira smiled sarcastically. "And tell them what? That I turn into this sex-crazed fury that throws my boyfriend around the room like a rag doll, and I feel possessed." She sneered. "That"ll get me a pass straight into Maudsley, won't it?"

Stewart sat back. She was right; who would not think that she was having a mental breakdown? He had to admit that he had wondered about her himself before speaking with Gavin earlier in the day.

Keira glanced at Stewart again. She felt his warmth as he sat beside her, trying to be a reassuring presence for her. She was about to tell him about Morgan and her visit there, but somehow she decided that that was not necessarily a good idea. In that moment, it dawned on her that she was getting much too fond of Stewart. She knew she could trust him, but something stopped her.

33

Brian sat back in his chair and stared at the computer screen. After the Inspector left, He'd decided it was time to do what he was good at, gathering intelligence. In as short space of time, he had compiled a small dossier on Gavin, Erik, and a woman by the name of Morgan Wood, who held the title to the property in Kensington.

The dossier was small because he couldn't find very much on any of them. It appeared that Gavin Skye had bought the shop some thirty years ago but had only recently taken over the actual running of the day-to-day business. Up till six months ago, he had been resident at his home on the Isle of Skye. A house that had belonged to his family for as long as records had been kept, and strangely, all of the owners had been named Gavin. He appeared to have no living relatives.

His financial records were interesting. It seemed a complex family trust was the main source of his money, and the shop had been purchased with cash from this fund. His day-to-day banking was unremarkable. The shop did well, and he had the usual spread of bank accounts, but the records all looked too tidy. He had neither a driver's licence nor any sign of owning a passport, and even more curious was the lack of health and educational records.

Erik Nordson was another enigma. He also lacked the usual historical markers, the electronic trail accompanying the modern person. A citizen of Norway, he had moved to the UK and settled in Cornwall at some point that was not recorded anywhere apart from the date of the purchase of a property. He seemed to possess independent wealth, and although there were records of consulting fees adding to his funds, they all originated from jobs he did for Gavin. There was no record of him having worked for anyone else. He also had no living relatives.

As for the woman, Morgan Woods, just as Gerry had remarked earlier in the day, the records were just too perfect in the way that smacked of invention. They reminded him of the histories used by intelligence agencies to provide backgrounds for their operatives. She at least had a stepson but no known blood relatives.

Continuing to trawl through various security databases and records, he focused his search on the movement of antiques. Trying to find a timeline for Gavin's business, he was looking for records of purchases when he stumbled on a peculiar picture held by Sotheby's. It depicted the illustrator Manuel Orazi in 1895. The man was a native of Rome and had moved to Paris in 1892, where he quickly gained a reputation as a highly talented Art Nouveau illustrator and poster designer.

The picture caught Brian's attention not because he had any interest in Orazi but because there, standing beside the illustrator, was a character that looked uncannily like Gavin. Brian sat back, scratching his head. *It couldn't be*, he thought. He lent forward again, looking more closely at the old photograph. There was no denying that the person in the picture bore a striking resemblance to the antique dealer.

Brian concluded that the man must be a direct relation to Gavin because the alternative was more than Brian could even begin to accept. On further reading, he learnt that Orazi had a peculiar fascination with magic and sorcery and showed a talent in combining the esoteric with the aesthetic. Whether Brian liked it or not, magic appeared to be a persistent theme that emerged whenever he delved into the events of the last few days.

As he sat there by his desk, contemplating the photo on the screen, he could feel the amulet warming the skin on his chest, and slowly, ever so slowly, it began to pulse. It was only a matter of seconds before he realised that it was in sync with his heartbeat. His first instinct was to deny the connection, but as the rhythm of the Amulet's pulsing continued to match his own, even as it increased in response to his increasing agitation, he found it harder to deny.

Brian couldn't sit still any longer. Getting up, he started to pace, remonstrating with himself to stop being illogical. *It's the twenty-first century! There are always logical explanations for everything.* But his mind kept returning to the picture of Orazi, and he couldn't shake the idea that it was Gavin. The more he tried to deny it, the stronger the idea got. As he stared out at the night sky, the rhythm of the Amulet's pulse changed; its beat became more rapid, and it started to heat up. As he looked at his reflection, he could see the tinge of orange through his T-shirt that told him it had started to glow.

In the same instant that he became aware of the Amulet's glow, the air in the room began to whirl madly, tearing at the papers across his desk, scattering them across the floor like pieces of large confetti. The increased air pressure now began to push against his eardrums, reminding Brian of a rapid descent into the depths of the ocean. At the same time, the slight humming that had initially filled the room had now pitched into a sort of low musical tone that reverberated through his body like a base note from a guitar.

He was in the middle of wondering if the noise had woken Rhonwen when a flicker of blue caught his attention, and the space between him and the door seemed to fill with a swirling pulsing blue light. It shaped itself into an oval, with the light moving outwards until there appeared to be a dark sort of emptiness in the middle. Suddenly Brian recognised a shape moving towards him. Shocked, he stepped back. As the skin on his arms puckered and the hairs on the back of his neck stood to attention, he watched a tall, lean figure emerge from the whirling vortex by the door.

With utter disbelief Brian watched Gavin step towards him and casually wave his hand. The air instantly stilled, and the silence that came with it seemed to Brian almost more disturbing than the deeply primitive sound that had filled the room just a moment earlier. He instinctively dropped his weight into his knees, taking up a combative posture preparing for whatever was to come.

"Relax, Brian. There is no need for that." Gavin's voice was calm, deep and soothing to Brian's frazzled nerves; he felt himself relax his muscles slightly, but he was not prepared to stand down completely. His mind was racing, desperate to find some acceptable explanation for what he had just witnessed.

"What the ..." Brian didn't finish the question as Gavin interrupted him.

"You wanted an explanation, and you shall have it.

"How ... how did you do this?" he stuttered. His mind was in total disarray and he felt stupid asking what seemed to be obvious, but he was still looking for another explanation.

Gavin looked at Brian and drew a breath. "It is what you have been trying to dismiss, Brian. It's magic."

The last couple of words hung in the air between the two men. Brian kept shaking his head as if to reorganise Gavin's comments into something that would be more logical, but failing to do that, he simply repeated them. "It's magic?"

"Yes, Brian, magic. I am what you would call a magician, a warlock." He held his hand out, and a small ball of fire appeared, hovering just above the palm of his hand. The fireball began to spin, slowly at first, then faster and faster when it suddenly exploded into a shower of stars. Startled, Brian instinctively backed away from the fiery spray crashing into the corner of his desk.

"Shit!" he exclaimed, trying to catch the falling lamp with one hand while rubbing his corked thigh with the other. Having managed to secure the light, Brian quickly placed it back onto the desk. Looking back at his visitor, he asked the first question that came to mind. "What are you doing here?"

"As I said, Brian, I am here to tell you what's going on. To help you understand that everything has changed. At least you already have many of the skills you will need because we need to get a move on. This is urgent. Someone is trying to acquire the Amulets, and that must not happen under any circumstance."

"Skills! For what?" Brian managed to get out.

"You, my friend, are about to embark on what is most likely going to be the most important mission of your life."

"What mission?" Brian exclaimed. He knew he sounded stupid, but he was struggling to form a logical thought.

Gavin walked across the room to one of the easy chairs and sat down. He looked at Brian, frowning.

"Take your time. Breathe and relax."

While Gavin was talking, Brian had automatically moved over to his favourite chair and, without any obvious intention on his part, had sat down. However, he had none of the calm, relaxed poise of the magician. Instead, he was perched on the edge of the chair like a bird of prey, ready to take flight at a second's notice.

Having settled further into his chair, Gavin started talking again, his voice resonant and even.

"It has been a long time since magic has had a place in this world. In fact, much of it has almost died out. But some of the bloodlines still exist, unbroken and able to be reawakened to the ancient power. Brian, have you ever wondered why you have come through so many dangerous experiences unscathed? And why people gravitate to you in a certain way?" Gavin stopped for an instant, and when Brian didn't answer, he continued. "How would you explain what has happened over the last few days if there is no magic? Recently, you have had dreams that are different from any you have had before. More real, more intense, deeper than normal dreams."

Brian looked at him sharply. He nodded his head, not really prepared to acknowledge the truth of it but unable to deny it. Gavin continued. "Your job is to assess threats and solve puzzles, military and security puzzles that impact the safety of this nation. What is your assessment of what is happening now?"

Brian didn't answer immediately. He had no idea what he even believed any more. Finally, taking hold of the still pulsing Amulet, he asked. "So the legend. The myth about the Amulets is real?"

Gavin looked at Brian with the sort of expression a schoolmaster usually reserves for a gifted student who is not performing to expectations. "As I have already explained, you have inherited a special legacy. The Tierney family, your family and three other families are keepers of bloodlines that reach back to the beginning of mankind, families that have kept a vigil against forces that would destroy humanity and all it has achieved. Now, for some reason that we have yet to discover, you are being called to your family's obligations. But we will face this threat together, and for that, my friend, I will have to prepare you."

As Gavin stroked the amulet, his mind seemed to open up to memories he hadn't thought of for years. His mother's death, times when he had been clearly in danger, perilously close to death but had somehow escaped. He saw parts of dreams that he now felt had a possibly deeper meaning than he had given them before Gavin's revelation. Brian was distracted from his memories by Gavin slowly brushing his long hair back with both hands. There was something about the gesture that he found intriguing. It had a certain ritualistic feel to it, and somehow it brought him back to the reality of the moment. He was sitting in his study with a Magician!

Looking at Gavin, his mind was in turmoil; he had so many questions but didn't know where to start. He wasn't sure why he trusted the man across from him, but somehow he knew he must. As if he had read his mind, Gavin spoke. "It's all right, Brian. I know this is hard, but sooner or later, you will know that your trust in me is warranted. We all have our obligations in this, and I am responsible for guiding you. Will you trust me with your Amulet now?"

Gavin's voice was reassuring, and Brian found himself pulling the chain over his head. He was surprised at how reluctant he felt about handing it over to someone else, but he held the Amulet out to the magician. It lay in the palm of his hand, a glowing orange pulse illuminating his extended fingers and some of his forearm.

Gavin did not reach out as Brian had expected. Instead, with its chain dangling between his fingers, the amulet suddenly levitated from Brian's hand and floated away to hover in mid-air between the two men. The familiar orange glow had now been replaced by a piercing icy blue light that gave the room an eerie cave-like feel.

Gavin smiled while he watched Brian's fascinated expression. "Now, Brian. This amulet is the conduit to the magic that will be yours if you choose to embrace all that comes with it. The rights, as well as the responsibilities, shall be yours as they rightfully should have been."

Gavin's voice lost its reassuring tone to be replaced by a deep, resonant timbre that reverberated in the room like a Gregorian chant. "You, Bryn, are one of the chosen. Will you now stand and take your place amongst the few who have served so well?"

In the instant that Brian heard his name in the ancient tongue, a portal opened in his mind, releasing a flood of visions. Like a wave rolling inexorably towards him from the beginning of time, sweeping him up in a maelstrom of sights, smells and sounds that assailed his senses, threatening to overpower his mind.

He struggled against this tidal rush and strained to come back to the reality that was now. He forced himself to focus and managed to conjure up an image of the amulet in his mind. He reached out to it, calling it to him. A shrillness suddenly exploded in his head, so painful that he instantly withdrew his mind from the image.

"What the fuck!" Brian exclaimed. He shook his head in the vain hope of clearing his ears of the painful sound, only to find that the noise was in his head.

"Stop and take a deep breath, Brian." Gavin's soothing voice whispered to him.

Brian wasn't sure if he heard Gavin or, like the shrill screeching noise, it originated clearly in his head. Confused, he looked at Gavin. "And then what?" was Brian's impatient reply.

"Try it and see."

Once more, he closed his eyes and, focusing on the image of the amulet, Brian brought that image back into the centre of his mind. He resolutely refused to let anything distract him from taking the Amulet back into his possession. Instantly the screeching sound assailed his mind again, but unlike before, he gathered all of his strength of will and clung to the image of the Amulet. The screeching suddenly stopped. Opening his eyes, Brian saw the Amulet slowly drifting towards him and holding out his hand; it slipped gently into his grasp. It felt right. Although his rational side was still trying to tell him that he was delusional, he knew he had taken a step beyond his previous experience or expectations. "It's all so unreal!" He muttered, almost to himself.

"You don't believe your own eyes, Brian?" Gavin mused.

Brian smiled ruefully. His intellect still fought against acceptance, but deep down in the very core of his being, he found a sense of intense joy. It bubbled up through his consciousness, undeniable, powerful. He felt complete. "What is it that has just happened?" He asked the man sitting across from him. "I feel changed in some fundamental way."

Gavin made a delicate sign with his right hand. It reminded Brian of a religious benediction, but he felt a wave of power emanate from that gesture that he had never felt before. "That is called a quickening. You have completed the ritual that links you with your own inheritance. That links you with your Amulet and your potential as a wielder of magic."

Brian started. Over the last few days, he had carefully constructed a set of explanations and rationalisations that he could no longer believe. But despite everything he had seen and heard, he hadn't grasped that as an Amulet's owner, he would be able to use magic. Of course, you had to actually believe in magic, and up until this very moment, he had steadfastly refused to do so.

"Why don't you try it again?" Gavin suggested.

"What?" Brian asked, unsure of what Gavin was referring to.

Gavin smiled with a mischievous twinkle in his eyes. "Magic."

It was like Gavin knew what he had been thinking. Did he? Brian wondered as he turned his Amulet over in his hand, looking at it with totally new eyes.

"Go on, I'm serious. Try it." Gavin urged Brian.

"Try what?" Brian said. He had no idea what to do, and he was acutely aware that for the first time in many, many years, he was a novice at a skill he wanted to master. He looked at Gavin. He knew nothing about this man. How did he know he could trust him?

He could see that Gavin was watching him speculatively. The man abruptly moved and, within a split second, was towering over Brian, his body seemingly to have expanded, and a black shadow appeared to envelop both of them. Instantly the amulet glowed, and an electric pulse surged into Brian's hand and up his arm. Brian intuitively reacted. A barrier suddenly appeared between himself and the other man. Brian became conscious of a shimmering shield between them. Almost as quickly as it happened, it was over. Gavin was back on the lounge, a quizzical smile playing across his mouth. "And that, my friend, is magic."

Before either of them could say anything else, they heard a choked sound at the doorway, and they both turned to find Rhonwen looking at them. Her face twisted with rage, and she hissed. "What the hell is going on?"

Rhonwen, her whole body shaking with fury, glared at Brian, and then she turned her attention to Gavin. Brian rose from his chair, but as he took a step towards her, she turned back to him. "You bastard! You fucking bastard!" She choked on another sob. "You've known this all along and yet kept me in the fucking dark!"

Brian wanted to go to her, to reassure her that it wasn't so, but she turned and darted down the hall towards the front door. Before he could blink, Gavin was at the door waiting for her, and she almost collided with him. Before she could do anything else, he reached out and gently touched her on the shoulder. Instantly calmed, her face serene, she allowed him to guide her back. Brian, having got about halfway down the hall by this time, indicated the spare bedroom, and Gavin gently led her back to the room, where he sat her down on the edge of the bed. "I was afraid of this," he said quietly, possibly more to himself, Brian suspected, than to him.

Brian, disoriented by Gavin's sudden relocation into the hallway, struggled to order his thoughts. "Is she OK?" he asked somewhat tentatively.

Gavin looked across at him. "She will be." He stopped and then asked, "What about you?"

"I ... I don't know, really." He looked at Gavin, trying to fathom if the man really was a friend. "You know, it's just all bit sudden. I mean this whole thing about magic!"

"It's never easy to find something like this out, Brian. But I need you to get a grip because we don't have much time." Laying Rhonwen back onto the bed, Gavin gently covered her with the quilt. She complied like a small child, and Brian noticed that she even had that beatific smile on her face that little girls could have when there was nothing to be afraid of. He shuddered. The look on her face was completely out of place, and it sent a chill down his spine.

Gavin sat down on the edge of the bed for a moment, watching Rhonwen's face and the rhythm of her breathing. It was as if he was looking for something. He suddenly nodded and then got up. "Come, let's go back to your study."

The two men walked back to Brian's study, and when they were inside, the door swung quietly closed behind them. When the lock clicked shut, Brian jumped. "Please, Gavin! Give me at least some warning when You're doing whatever it is you do. It's a bit unnerving, you know."

Gavin smiled and cocked his head, his long hair flowing down the side of his face, obscuring it slightly. "Get used to it, Brian. After all, it is your legacy."

Settling himself backing the chair he had occupied earlier, Gavin gestured for Brian also to relax and asked:

"Brian, tell me. Who are the people you trust most?"

34

Morgan was instantly awake. She lay there while the energy pulsed through her. *Another one! But not the same. This one is stronger, directed.* As soon as she had regulated her breathing, she jumped out of bed. This quickening had the feel of being guided, and there was only one person who could be responsible. *Was it Keira? Had Gavin found her?*

Moving quickly, she teleported herself to the basement skrying mirror. She had set up a spell to enable her to keep tabs on Keira. Waving her hand across the surface to enact the spell, she was relieved but puzzled by the image of a sleeping Keira. *If not her, who?* She tried skrying for Gavin, not expecting to locate him, as he undoubtedly would have warded himself. *Nothing!*

Becoming aware that she was still a little queasy from the power of the magic that had propelled her out of bed, she took some deep breaths and calmed her racing thoughts. Something big was happening. It had been so long since this much magic had been evident anywhere in London, and now, within months of Gavin returning to the vicinity, there had been two Quickenings. Shivering from the cold, she padded across the floor in her bare feet towards the door. The flavour of this magic was teasing her with its familiarity. She recognised it as being ancient, but she couldn't quite pin it down, and she was still musing about its origins as she headed back upstairs. Suddenly it clicked into place in her mind. Both these magicians belonged to the five families. *The amulets!* Realising that finding out who Keira really was had become urgent, Morgan was on her way to the library when she heard Jean coming through the front door. Instantly warding her thoughts, she put a welcoming smile on her lips and turned to greet him as he came through the hall door.

ᘛ ᘛ

Jean had gone to Declan's when his associate had failed to return. It hadn't taken him long to scry the faint telltale signs that someone had died in that flat. It just hadn't been Declan. He was staring at the spot on the floor where one of his most experienced and valuable employees had been disintegrated when he had been hit by the surge of magic that announced the emergence of another new magician. Although there had been something different about how this quickening felt, he recognised the association with the amulets. The implications rocked him. It had been close. In London, somewhere nearby.

Frustration was starting to tear away at his self-control. He had been banking on having his and the Tierney Amulet to help him find and recover the others. He was furious with himself for underestimating Declan. Not only had he run off with the amulet, but ignorant and untutored, he had somehow managed to link with the magic. How could they have got it so wrong? He had been sure it was the Tierney girl who had the talent.

One thing had gone well today, at least. Not everything had gone awry. Despite Morgan's secretiveness, he had managed to circumvent her wards around her new Acolyte. Morgan had been very keen to protect her, but his own little spell had worked a treat, and he had been able to get in without leaving any evidence behind. He had gleaned enough from Keira's mind to know that she was very talented and that she had been mucking around with some pretty obscure magic. Strangely ignorant and raw, she seemed to be self-taught. Whoever she was, she was undoubtedly the sexiest baby witch he had ever tasted.

Thinking about this afternoon was distracting. He needed to focus. Morgan had been talking about the Grimoire. He had seen an image of what looked like a very old one in Keira's mind. Nowadays, there are so many fakes around it is rare to find something real, but maybe this one was a true magical text. Everything was leading towards the Amulets. He had been so busy chasing around after Declan that he hadn't focused on the girl. *What if she was from one of the families and had an amulet? What was Morgan really up to?*

As he drove back to Kensington, Jean started formulating a plan to give him access to Keira. He was certain that Morgan had no idea that he had found out about his own family's history. He was going to exploit her arrogant belief that she had succeeded in hiding it from him. He would continue to play the dutiful son and run around doing her little jobs while he bided his time. His mood had brightened considerably as he parked the car outside the mansion, and, checking that the wards around his mind were firmly in place, he headed into the house through the front door.

☙ ☙

Declan had been dozing fitfully on the hard, narrow bed in the only bedroom that was habitable in the old cottage, when he woke suddenly and completely. He felt as if He'd split in two; a part of him was watching himself from somewhere else. His nerve endings tingled. Yes, that was the word, tingle. That word described precisely what he was feeling. It was an electric feeling. It seemed to go on and on, and yet, he intuitively knew that it was, in fact, only a few minutes.

Suddenly back in his body, he sat up. He swung his legs over the edge of the bed. *What the fuck was that?* The Amulet, still hanging around his neck, was hot and pulsing and had a golden glow. Getting out of bed, he moved restlessly around the room, trying to calm himself down. As his breathing settled, his mind cleared, and the Amulet settled back to its normal warm, reassuring presence.

He really needed to find out more about this new power. As the thought coalesced, it took the shape of a question, and he felt the Amulet warm up again, but this time it was a bluish colour. Without any conscious intent, he let his eyes drift around the room and noticed a loose board in the timber cladding of the wall next to the fireplace. He knew he needed to look behind it the moment he saw it. Prying the piece of wood looser and ripping the board away, he peered into a cavity in the wall.

Lying on a hidden shelf was an old metal box. Slipping his hand into the hiding place, his eager fingers closing around the box, he pulled it out and, sitting back on his haunches, placed it on the floor. It was big and heavy and covered in many years' worth of dirt and cobwebs. He peered at it suspiciously, his natural caution at war with an overwhelming desire to open it immediately. The serendipitous way in which he had found this thing, just as he thought about needing information, excited him. He felt confident that he had been directed to it by his Amulet. But what exactly had he found?

Thinking carefully about all that he had learned, he realised that the Amulet had always warned him of danger. Since it was not doing so now, he decided, he was probably safe to open it. Lifting it up, he went to the kitchen and, using an old rag, wiped off the encrusted dirt. Standing as far back as he could and still open the lid, he carefully undid the catch. Nothing happened, so emboldened, he lifted the lid and peered inside, finding that the box contained a bulky object wrapped in some old oiled leather and bound by leather cords knotted in intricate patterns.

As he picked up the package, the Amulet's blue light became more intense. Instinctively knowing that this was not a warning, he undid the bindings and unwrapped what turned out to be a book. Focusing on the book in front of him, his Amulet having gone back to a golden glow with a faint pulse, a feeling of anticipation filled him with excitement. As he opened the front cover, he felt his whole being throb in tune with the amulet. For the first time in his life, Declan felt somewhere deep within himself, completely whole.

35

The acrid smoke filled his nose and stung his eyes as he smashed his way through the burning hall. He barely registered the screams of pain and fear coming from the villagers as they scattered before him. He had spied his prize and his whole being centred on her. Surges of lust drove him forward through the falling timbers, and with his vision blurred by the red haze of blood, the men who died on the end of his sword were of no consequence to him. Finally reaching her, he grabbed a long yellow braid and yanked hard, pulling her towards him. Seeing a gap in the side wall where the burning timbers had collapsed, he dragged her out to the compound. Looking around, he spied a break in the surrounding palisade. The girl screamed and twisted as she tried to evade his grasp, but somehow her struggle only inflamed his desire. With barely any effort, he dragged her out of the hall and over to the edge of the forest.

Erik had been wakened earlier by the surge of magic that heralded a quickening. Knowing that Gavin had planned to go to Brian and offer him his guidance, he had not been surprised. But this! Propelled back into the past, the violence of his mortal life shocked and disturbed him. He needed to speak with

Gavin. Quickly pulling some clothes on, he teleported to the park across the street from Gavin's shop and, seeing the light on upstairs, made his way around the side of the building.

Knocking loudly as he walked through the door to Gavin's lounge, he found him in a robe, damp and flushed. He felt so agitated that he didn't even greet his old friend before he almost shouted. "What the fuck! And I mean fuck! Was that Scáthach? Because it really felt like it could be, and I really had a hard time not dragging some poor woman off the streets?"

"OK! I know it was strong, Erik, but you are going to have just to manage it!" Gavin responded, his voice slightly cracking at the effort to sound calm. Erik, realising he had been overbearing and aggressive, took a deep breath. "I know," he said ruefully, "but it caught me by surprise. I was my old Viking self for a couple of minutes. Is it her?"

"You are right. It was Scáthach. She's close, really close. It's this girl, Keira, that we need to worry about. She is the portal; every time she has sex; she gets closer to the moment when she will be lost and Scáthach will be back. I messed up, Erik. I should have told Stewart to stay away from her."

Gavin stopped, the worry about what this meant etched on his face. "I don't know if we can win this time!"

Erik looked at him, wanting to reassure him, but he was too worried himself. Gavin seemed to sense his mood because he came over, put his large hand on Erik's shoulder, and smiled reassuringly before saying.

"Come, we can forget sleeping for tonight as it is almost dawn. I'll brew us some coffee, and we can plan what to do next."

As they made their way to Gavin's kitchen, he continued. "The good news is that Brian has accepted his Amulet and its obligations". "Yes," Erik replied. "It was his quickening that woke me initially".

Just as they entered the kitchen, Gavin's mobile went off. Erik watched him tense up as he saw the identity of his caller. "Shit! This is all I need. Bloody Connell!"

Erik couldn't help himself. He flashed a wicked grin at Gavin and headed for the kitchen. "I'll make the coffee then." Digging around in Gavin's fridge, he found some food to add to the promised coffee and took it back out to the living room, where Gavin was still talking to Connell. Erik liked Connell. He was the patriarch of the Banach family and the current guardian of their Amulet. They were a large, close-knit group whose ties to the old ways remained strong. And they were the only family amongst the five to have kept to their obligations continuously throughout the centuries.

Connell and his wife lived on the northwest coast of Yorkshire, and he often spent time with them. Having stayed connected to their powers meant that they were long-lived people, and so he had been able to forge reasonably long-term relationships with them. The sadness of losing friends to their mortal lifespans never did get any easier, Erik thought sadly.

Putting these thoughts to the side, he looked up as Gavin ended his call. "Well, it was to be expected that Connell would make contact after all of the upheavals of the last few days." Gavin mused as he joined Erik at the table. He just nodded and waited, knowing that Gavin's relationship with the Banachs was strained at best. He thought both sides had a responsibility for the problems, but this was not the time to stir up old history, so he refrained from comment. Gavin poured himself some coffee, having obviously settled something in his own mind. "Well, I am sure you will be pleased to hear that Connell and his boy Rouan will be here later today."

Erik was pleased. He had a bad feeling about what was going on, and having some support from Connell, who was a very talented magician in his own right, was more than welcome. But Gavin's next comment almost had him choke on his coffee. "I think they might be the best people to take over the care of Rhonwen."

Erik's bewilderment obviously showed on his face as Gavin quickly continued. "I Haven't had a chance to tell you, but Rhonwen is falling apart. If there had been enough time before its theft, I have no doubt she would have bonded to the Tierney Amulet. She was starting to open up to it, so the loss has been traumatic." He paused as if trying to find the right words before continuing. "I have come to realise that she is a very conflicted young woman, and this whole experience may push her over the edge."

Gavin filled Erik in on everything that had happened at Brian's during the evening while they ate their early breakfast. It left Erik feeling very sad for Rhonwen. He had liked her, and now she had not only lost her inheritance and a friend, but she was also emotionally fragile as well. Gavin was right about the Banachs. They would be a good influence on her.

36

Brian was struggling to keep it together as he and Rhonwen waited for the Inspector to see them. He was completely exhausted after another night where he had hardly slept, having been too restless to sleep after Gavin had left in the early hours. A part of him was excited and invigorated by what Gavin had called his quickening, but his rational part was in shock. He had paced around the apartment for a time, regularly checking in on Rhonwen.

But that wasn't the worst of it. If he had been asleep, at least he would have been dreaming, but he had been wide awake. He was hard-pressed to think of any time in the past when he had experienced such a powerful sense of lust and rage. It had hit him out of the blue, his Amulet suddenly flaring red and pulsing madly on his chest; he had known that something dangerous was happening. Hearing Rhonwen thrashing around in the bed, he was pretty certain that she had been affected too.

He had just settled down again when Stewart had called and filled him in on his night. The connection was obvious, but he had no idea what it meant. Having to play cat and mouse with the Inspector this morning was going to be exceedingly difficult. He would much rather be at Gavin's with Stewart. Startled out of his revere by one of the Officers coming to collect them, they followed him to a small, crowded space and settled onto hard, uncomfortable chairs.

The Inspector focused his attention on Rhonwen, almost ignoring him, which was to some degree a relief as it enabled him to observe the Inspector in action. He had begun his questioning predictably enough, but now he was looking intently at Rhonwen, who was obviously very emotional and anxious. His gaze was calculating, and Brian recognised the interrogation technique he was using. *He couldn't seriously believe Rhonwen had anything to do with Lydia's death.*

Immediately alert, he focused on the Inspector challenging Rhonwen's official statement.

"Are you absolutely sure, Ms. Tierney, that you have had no contact with your cousin in the last three years?"

"Why on earth would I, Inspector?! He tried to steal my inheritance."

Rhonwen sounded genuinely perplexed by the Inspector's questions, and Brian was acutely aware that she was becoming increasingly angry. A knock on the door interrupted them, and the Inspector excused himself and left the room. Brian couldn't help but wonder if this was another strategy. Leave them alone and see what they do, or maybe hear what they said. If he hadn't been so tired, he would have realised that the room was probably monitored despite the age of the place. Sure enough, a small unobtrusive camera hung in the corner near the ceiling.

Rhonwen's anger and distress was palpable. Brian, well aware of what she may have experienced, having experienced it himself, was loath to try and comfort her. Just getting themselves organised to get to this appointment this morning had taken every scrap of energy either of them had. Whatever their relationship had been before, it had been shattered beyond repair. *I just have to get her through this interview, and then Gavin will take over and look after her.* Brian used this as a mantra to calm himself. He hadn't told Rhonwen that he was taking her to Gavin after this meeting. That was, of course, if Inspector Riley let either of them go. He was well aware that the Inspector suspected them both of being somehow involved in Lydia's death.

Just as he finished that train of thought, the Inspector returned, accompanied by an elegant, blond woman in her early 60s. He was immediately aware of Rhonwen's reaction. She seemed to shrink into herself.

"Well, Rhonwen, I can see you are still the simpering moron you were the last time I saw you."

Turning to the Inspector, she captured him with her imperious gaze. "And don't you think you are going to blame my son for this silly business, Inspector?" She almost spat the words out at him as she sat down in the other chair next to where Brian was sitting.

"I don't think murder is silly business, Madam." The Inspector replied in a chilly voice.

Turning to Brian, he introduced the woman as Elizabeth Tierney. Then, looking back at Rhonwen, the Inspector regarded her with somewhat kinder eyes than previously. "Well, Ms. Tierney, your Aunt here confirms your claim that you have no communication with your cousin or anyone on that side of your family".

Brian had the distinct impression that the Inspector had not completed the sentence that was actually in his mind. That Rhonwen's avoidance of this side of her family was completely understandable! He certainly was in no doubt that the woman who had joined them was a total bitch. Still standing near the open office door, Inspector Riley continued. "I have asked my Sergeant to get you two some tea or coffee, if you prefer, while I speak with Mrs Tierney. If you could wait outside. I still have some questions that need to be answered."

Sitting in the noisy outer office, with phones going off and people coming and going all around them, Rhonwen continued to hold herself aloof from him. There was no point in trying to converse with her because every time he tried, she cut him off and turned her head away.

Brian was not that unhappy about her silence. He wanted to focus on his own thoughts. *What could the Inspector wish to ask them about now?* He was so busy sifting through the information he thought the Inspector might know that he was startled by the sudden shift in the atmosphere as Elizabeth Tierney stormed past them and out of the office. Looking up as she swept by, he saw her throw a deeply malevolent glare in Rhonwen's direction, but she said nothing to either of them. The Inspector had followed her out and now stood before them. "If you will come back inside now, please."

Settling themselves back into his office, they watched the Inspector shuffle some papers and fiddle with his computer. He was obviously trying to frame his questions in his mind before speaking, and Brian could feel Rhonwen tensing up as the seconds expanded into minutes. Finally, the Inspector looked up and directly at Rhonwen. "What do you know about Lydia Chambers, Ms. Tierney?"

This was completely unexpected. Brian was still processing his surprise when he heard Rhonwen's bewildered reply. "What do you mean, Inspector?

"Well, Ms. Tierney, what do you know about her family and where she comes from? Surely as friends, you spoke about these things. It's pretty normal to do so, wouldn't you say?"

"I, I don't know," Rhonwen replied in a small puzzled voice. She hesitated, and it was obvious that she was thinking deeply. "When I think about it now, we always seemed to talk about me and my family. You know, she was so supportive and kind to me." Distressed and tearful, Rhonwen looked up at the Inspector. "I can't believe I know so little about her. How could I be such a terrible friend?" And with that, Rhonwen burst into sobs of anguish.

The Inspector passed over a box of tissues, and Brian tried to comfort her by putting his arm around her. For a brief moment, she let herself lean against him, then pulled herself away and, gulping air into her lungs, she worked at calming herself down. Brian noted that the Inspector was watching her like a hawk. There was more to this than he had immediately assumed. "Haven't' you been able to contact her family Inspector?" Brian asked.

"Well now, that is the problem, Mr Poole. Not only do we have no family, we have no Lydia Chambers! She doesn't seem to exist. At least not in any records we have been able to find." The title deeds to the apartment are apparently a forgery, and the previous owner, a Michael Jones, also doesn't seem to have any records. None of the other neighbours seems to have been around long enough to remember him, as those apartments have all changed hands in the last ten years."

Rhonwen just stared at the Inspector. She had become completely still and quiet as he had spoken, barely breathing as she listened to him. "What are you saying Inspector?" She almost whispered in a tight voice.

"I am saying, Ms. Tierney, that your close friend Lydia Chambers was not who she appeared to be. I have no idea what she was up to, but her false identity leads me to suspect that her murder is linked with something a lot bigger than the theft of a jewel."

Half an hour later they had been allowed to leave. Inspector Riley had decided that they were obviously not going to be able to provide him with any further information. Although Brian was relieved that the Inspector seemed to have decided that he wasn't a suspect, the mystery of who Lydia was had him feeling very uncomfortable. He felt like his brain was opening up like the file on a computer, as a series of questions kept popping up. Shit! This was huge! He knew instinctively that the Inspector was wrong. This was all about the jewel. It was all about the Amulet. His own was gently pulsing against his chest, and had been since the moment the Inspector had told them Lydia was a fake.

Gerry had been waiting for them on the opposite side of the road and, grabbing Rhonwen's elbow, Brian started to cross the street. He felt a tug as Rhonwen pulled out of his grasp. "I'm not going anywhere with you, Brian". She snarled. "I can look after myself and I certainly don't need you".

And with that she bolted down the street and around the corner of the building. By the time Brian got to the corner, she was across the road and running into the park. He found himself dashing through the traffic, trying to follow her, calling her name. As he ran through the gate and wove his way through the lunchtime joggers, almost tripping over a stroller, he watched her disappear amongst the trees. Peering into the dark amongst the branches, he swore under his breath. "Fuck you." Sorely tempted to just let her go, but knowing he couldn't, he headed across the lawn.

37

Rhonwen felt a rush of panic as she wove through the trees, trying to hide her direction from Brian. Her rage was driving her, and it felt uncomfortable and wrong. She had never been an angry person, and yet this was all that she thought about now. In fact, since the nightmares had started, she had either been terrified or furious.

She just had to get away and think. She couldn't trust any of them. Brian and Gavin seemed to believe she was an idiot, but she had been aware that they were trying to control her. When Gavin used magic on her, she had known for sure that he was not to be relied on. They were in this, whatever this was, together. Magic! She couldn't believe it.

Breathless, she slowed her pace and, looking around for a hiding spot where she could rest, she saw a dark-shaded area under a large tree with overhanging branches. Cautiously moving towards it, she cursed her lack of fitness, the stitch in her side and her breathlessness making her feel like she would collapse at any moment. Sitting down amongst the large protruding roots, Rhonwen pulled up her legs and, wrapping her arms around herself, tried to shrink back out of sight.

Slowly as her breath settled she felt the rage relax its grip on her mind. Tears came unbidden and she just let them fall, too exhausted, saddened and confused even to wipe them away. Wishing that she could disappear for a while, she looked out across the park. It occurred to her that it was really quite empty of people, despite it being a warm day, and she suddenly remembered that it was Monday. The rage was instantly back, a throbbing heat washing across her body, every muscle rigid, she could feel her nails digging into the flesh of her arms. It was Monday! She should have been at work getting herself ready for her new job, but it wasn't her job because that bitch Keira had stolen it from her. More than that, somehow Rhonwen just knew that everything that had happened was Keira's fault. She didn't know how. She couldn't even begin to work out how Lydia's death, the whole crazy business of magic, or Declan fitted into it. But she just knew that it was all connected to Keira. A sense of intense hatred filled her as she thought about how everything she had worked for had been destroyed.

The images from the nightmares haunted her. Last night's had been truly awful, and she had no idea how she should interpret the role that Brian, or at least a Brian look alike, had played in that terrible moment when she died. The tears welled up again and a wave of sadness and despair rolled over her.

The soft crunch of feet on the ground startled her. She was not alone. Assuming that it was Brian, Rhonwen did not bother moving. She felt completely helpless, but she wasn't going to be bullied into going with him so she spoke without even looking up. "I am not going with you, Brian. You can just bugger off."

"Well now, what a sad little thing you are, sitting all by yourself under this tree."

The sound of a strange woman's voice startled Rhonwen into looking around the edge of the root she had been hiding behind. Standing only a couple of feet away from her was a youngish woman in jeans and runners. Her warm coat was buttoned up and her hands were hidden in its pockets. She had a rather beautiful face, but somehow it wasn't attractive. In fact, Rhonwen felt wary the moment she looked into the woman's eyes. There was something very sinister about the way she lifted her head and looked around. Rhonwen felt the hairs on the back of her neck stand up as the women looked back at her and a slow predatory smile crossed her mouth.

Rhonwen felt rage surge through her, as her heightened senses recognised that was she in danger. Energised by fear she jumped up to her feet, and looking across the park saw Brian heading towards her. As she turned, ready to run she looked back at the woman. It was immediately apparent that she had also seen Brian, as she was now backing away from Rhonwen. "Fuck off, bitch! I am not some sad little thing," was all Rhonwen could think to say as she jumped over the roots and headed out onto the lawn.

In the few minutes it took her to get into the middle of the open space, she realised, that at this very moment, she had no choice but to stick with Brian. She literally had no where else to go except her mother's, and she"d be dammed if she asked her for help. Calming her breathing, she slowed to a walk. Deciding not to tell Brian anything, she waited for him to reach her, noting the look of fury on his face. Sadness warring with anger she couldn't believe what was happening. *Was it really only a couple of days ago that she thought she loved this man?*

His expression changed as he realised she was waiting for him and the anger was replaced by a bland distant look that hid what he was really thinking. Deciding to take some control back Rhonwen spoke first. "I just needed to get away, to run. It has been just too much and I don't know what to think of any of it." *There was no way she was going to apologise. He would have to just accept that and do with it what he wanted.*

Brian didn't attempt to touch her. He just stood there and watched her before replying. "OK, I guess its understandable, but I am not the bad guy here. We have to work together and try to figure this out." Not trusting herself to speak, she just nodded her head in ascent. He continued. "Gerry is waiting for us at the North gate. I think we should get back to Gavin's and try to put some of these pieces together. I've called the office. They"re not expecting us to come in for the rest of the week."

She nodded again, and let him lead her across the park towards the gate, surreptitiously looking around for any sign of the woman who had been lurking under the tree. She wouldn't have been surprised to find out she was working for Gavin, or maybe even Brian himself. He had plenty of connections that she didn't know about. In fact she realised she didn't know him at all. Just like she hadn't really known Lydia.

38

Stewart had hardly slept at all. He had been so worried about what Keira had told him, and how it fitted into what he had learned from Gavin, that he had spent the rest of the night guarding her as she slept. He had been to the bathroom and was in the hallway when He'd felt a strange tingling, and the hairs on his arms had stood up. A wave of energy buffeted him and the front door to the apartment swung open, slamming him against the wall. Stunned, he had stood there, as the very women who had been snooping around the place on Saturday strode down the hall.

She had barely glanced at him, she strode into Keira's bedroom and slammed the door shut in his face. He had tried to open the door but it was locked. More than locked, it was impenetrable. Something made it resist every effort he used to get in. Then, just as suddenly, the door had opened and Keira, now dressed, was bundled out into the hall and being propelled towards the front door.

Seeing him, Keira had smiled weakly and told him it was alright. She had been a bit cagey about what she said, but she had alluded to their discussion about her using magic. That had made the other woman look at him with a penetrating gaze that bore a hole through his head. He'd felt like his brain was being reamed and it hurt! Suddenly it had stopped, and the women smiled and nodded as if she had found something. Taking Keira by the arm, she had started towards the door again and at the same time, looking over her shoulder, she had told him to tell Gavin that she would deal with this. Obviously expecting that Stewart knew what this was. It was only as the door closed behind them that Stewart had realised she had the Grimoire tucked under her other arm.

Only minutes before she had stormed into the place, he had been examining the Amulet by the light of a lamp on Keira's desk. Rushing into the living room he had not been able to believe his luck. It was still where he had left it under a cushion on the lounge. He was still looking at it wondering what to do when his phone rang.

It was Brian on the line, but before Stewart could say anything, Brian had launched into a stream of almost indecipherable words.

"Hold on, Brian!" Stewart snapped. He quickly dragged his mind back into order and, breathing deeply, slowed his heart rate. It helped to contain the anger that was threatening to sweep over him. "Before you go any further, I have to tell you what just happened here—that woman, the one that I ran into here the other day. Well, Keira knows her. Her name's Morgan. Apparently, she knows Gavin too and has just taken Keira off to God knows where. She told me to tell Gavin."

"What do you mean? I should have stopped her! You have no bloody idea what she was like! And anyway, Keira wanted to go with her. She thinks this Morgan can help her with the mess she made playing with magic."

After briefly filling each other in on their night's experiences, they decided that they needed to speak with Gavin. Because Brian still had to deal with Rhonwen and the Police, Stewart called Gavin and, after speaking with him, felt a great deal better. He had promised to go to Morgan's and check on Keira.

Stewart's sense of being out over a precipice, about to fall, had faded now that he had been given some jobs to do. The big, blond Viking, Erik, was going to pick him up, and they were to take Keira's amulet back to Gavin's for safekeeping. Then, while Brian and Rhonwen kept their appointment with Inspector Riley, the two of them went to the office to use the company resources. Stewart found it somewhat reassuring that modern intelligence gathering was still useful. All this magical stuff was making him very anxious.

ꕥ ꕥ

Gavin was furious with himself for having let Morgan get to Keira first. Keeping his feelings tightly under control, he had not reacted too negatively to the news, and thankfully, Erik was taking his lead in this. Stewart was worried enough as it was. He had impressed Gavin with his measured intelligence. His carefully constructed persona of the lightweight man about town didn't fool Gavin for a second. He had been pleased that Stewart had dispensed with it the moment they met.

Holding Keira's Amulet, wondering how Morgan had missed it he asked Stewart, who explained that when he had removed it from the pocket at the front of the Grimoire, he had refastened the flap, just in case Keira had woken up while he was examining it.

"Keira had hidden the book from me amongst some other stuff in her bedroom, so it was out of sight. The Amulet looked like it was part of the actual cover, almost completely embedded into the leather. I think it had been glued in because I needed to tug it pretty hard to remove it. And the flap itself was fastened in such a way as to make it look like decoration. I don't know if she had any idea it was separate from the book, and I think she hid the Grimoire out of embarrassment, you know, about messing around with spells."

"Just as well. I know Morgan. If she had any idea that Keira was in possession of an amulet, she would have taken it."

Stewart looked at him with a penetrating gaze as if he was trying to weigh up the truth of what he had been told. "So who is she then? This Morgan Woods. You must know that we did a search on her the first time she had Keira in her clutches. What we found was a very good fake identity. Somewhat like the one I found when I searched for you."

Erik let out a hoot of laughter from the other side of the room. "He doesn't hold back, does he?"

Gavin decided that it was time to give Stewart a little more information. He was sure that Brian had shared most, if not all, of what he knew, but Stewart's own background and his own family's inheritance had not been disclosed to Brian.

"What do you know about your family's history, Stewart?" Gavin asked in a quiet voice.

Stewart looked puzzled by the question. "How is my family involved with this Morgan Woods?

"The answer to who she is lies in the history of the Amulets, and your family is as involved as the five families charged with safeguarding those Amulets."

Stewart, who had been standing up until this moment, abruptly sat down on one of the chairs, a look of disbelief on his face. "You're not telling me I have magic too, are you?"

"Well, not like Brian, no, but just as Brian is the inheritor of his family's magic in this generation, you are also the inheritor of your family's sacred task—the protection of the Amulets. You see, Stewart, you are Brian's protector. Your family has been associated with Brian's throughout the millennia, since the time when the Amulets were forged."

The look on Stewart's face told Gavin that this was going to take time. Looking over at Erik, who had been quietly watching the exchange, he smiled. "Erik, I think you could be a little useful here. Would you show Stewart the research you did last night, please?" Turning back to Stewart, Gavin continued in a kind voice. "Stewart, I sensed who you were, but Erik has confirmed it with modern research methods. He has the information on his computer, and it might be easier for you to come to grips with the details if you look at it. This would free me up to go and check up on Keira."

Stewart immediately sat forward, ready to jump up from the chair. "No! I'll go with you to this Morgan's place. Keira's frightened and she doesn't know you. I want to be sure she is safe. I can find out about my family later."

Gavin was determined to keep Stewart away from Morgan for now. She had only scratched the surface of his mind, or she would already know about the amulet. "Keira will be safer if Morgan doesn't know who she is for now. I am sorry, Stewart, but one thing you must accept is that Morgan is very powerful, and she will get information out of your mind if she has access to you for any length of time."

Aware that Stewart was conflicted, Gavin briefly entertained the idea of a gentle spell but dismissed it immediately. No, Stewart had to accept his role without any coercion. It was vital if they were to prevent Scáthach from re-entering the world of man. He stilled his own anxiety, letting the man in front of him weigh up what he had just heard in his own time. Stewart finally looked over at Erik and, with a wry smile, said. "Well, I guess that will give you a chance to tell me how you fit into all of this as well, won'tt it?"

Gavin narrowed his eyes, looking keenly at this young man. He was beginning to like him very much. "Fair enough!"

As Erik and Stewart settled themselves into the study, Gavin prepared to leave. Normally he would have driven, but it was still peak hour, and the traffic would be a nightmare. He wanted to be back at the shop when Brian and Rhonwen arrived after their interview with the Inspector so that he couldn't waste time. On the other hand, using magic to move around the world ate up your energy, and needing time to replenish left you vulnerable. *Oh well, it's only a few miles.*

The park across the road from Morgan's provided an easy point of access. Small and heavily planted with bushy trees, it was rarely used on weekdays, as it offered no space for the modern obsession with exercise. The likelihood of anyone actually noticing him was minimal. Crossing the quiet street, he made his way to the front door and rang the bell. Gavin hadn't decided just how he was going to broach the subject of Keira with Morgan. As the door opened, he felt a rush of energy fill him. His automatic response to threat switched itself on as he looked into the face of the boy Morgan had adopted almost thirty years ago.

No. No longer a boy. Gavin could sense the magic in the man standing in front of him. There was the answer to why Morgan had done something so out of character and offered this child a home. But not the complete solution. Putting on a pleasant, friendly smile, Gavin simply announced himself and asked to see Morgan. He saw a flicker of something in the young man's eyes before it was quickly shut down, and he was politely welcomed into the hall and directed to an elegantly furnished reception room.

While Gavin waited for Morgan to arrive, he looked out the French doors to the garden. He really didn't know how he wanted to approach her. She was difficult and dangerous and had used her power in a self-serving and reckless manner many times. Having had so little to do with her over the last few centuries, Gavin was not sure that she remained loyal to her responsibilities as an Immortal.

Sensing her arrival, he turned from the window to find her standing in the doorway. The small smile, lifting the corners of her beautiful mouth, didn't distract him from the calculating look that she wasn't bothering to conceal. "Well, Gavin. It's been a long time since you made an effort to call on me at home. Could it be that I am right?"

Watching her as closely as he would have watched a snake, Gavin decided to get straight to the heart of the matter. "I won't pretend that I am not seeking an alliance in this, Morgan. We both know that over the last few days, there has been a fundamental shift in the boundaries between the dimensions."

Morgan didn't respond immediately as he had expected. He saw her tense and felt her wards strengthen a second before he felt the presence of the man who now emerged into his line of sight. *Ah! So not a happy family.* Turning towards the young man, Morgan nodded her acceptance of his presence and ushered him into the room. "Gavin, you haven't met my son, Jean. Jean, this is Gavin Skye, an old friend of mine."

The two men moved towards each other, holding their hands to shake for the whole world like they were two ordinary men meeting in normal circumstances. Gavin had no idea how much Jean knew about Morgan or himself, but he found it interesting that Morgan obviously did not trust him.

"Jean, could you ask Emily to make us some tea and then join us in the study?"

As Jean left the room, Morgan led the way through another set of doors into her study and gestured with a perfectly manicured hand towards a lounge. "Take a seat, Gavin. And tell me all about your little group of new friends."

Gavin smiled. "Been doing your homework, have you, Morgan?"

"Well, no, actually, Jean has been very helpful with this as I am busy with more important tasks," she replied as she sat in a lovely Rosewood chair near the window.

Gavin smiled at the artful manner in which she arranged her stunning long legs so that he could glimpse the seductive lines of her thighs. Before he could broach the subject of Keira, Jean arrived, followed closely by a pretty young woman dressed in an old-fashioned maid's uniform and carrying a tea tray. There were the usual few minutes of ordering the tray onto the table, and then she left, quietly shutting the door behind her—the impression of a well-controlled and ordered home having been played out for his benefit.

As Jean passed the tea around, Morgan looked directly into Gavin's eyes, and he felt a small, directed thought to enter his mind, slipping past his wards. He was as astounded by the skill and elegance of her probe as much as by the content of her thought. *Don't mention Scáthach!*

Realising that there would be no open discussion while Jean was with them, Gavin launched into an easygoing conversation that two old friends catching up would be expected to have. Once they had bored Jean out of the room, they were able to speak more openly. Gavin left Morgan reassured that her agenda was to protect Keira. She felt confident that Scáthach was still locked behind the boundary but, like Gavin, was aware that it had thinned significantly over the last twenty-four hours.

They had both agreed that Keira was better off not knowing the full extent of the danger she was currently facing. He had met Keira briefly, letting her know he was Stewart's friend. A simple probe showed him that she was still in control of her mind and was happy to stay with Morgan for now. But it wouldn't be long before Morgan knew who Keira really was and came looking for that Amulet.

39

The constant vigilance needed to maintain his wards against the two Immortals had proved to be quite tiring, so Jean had driven to his office. Despite many years of practice with Morgan, Jean had found it difficult to defend his thoughts from Gavin. He still didn't know if either of them were aware of his interest in the Amulets, but he felt confident that Morgan still knew nothing of his having found his own Amulet. At least with Keira staying at the house, she was now more accessible.

He had found it prudent not only to separate his personal business from the work he did for Morgan but also to manage his affairs on premises she knew nothing about. Situated on the ground floor of a modest building in the CBD, his rooms were at the back and had the advantage of a door leading onto a short alley. As no windows overlooked that part of the alley, his associates could come and go without being noticed.

He had set up a meeting with a couple of his people so that he could get some feedback about the tasks he had set them. *Declan, Declan!* Jean was still pissed off that he had underestimated that little thug. Not only had he gotten away with the amulet, but he had killed George. George had been a very useful employee, a minor talent with magic, but a devoted acolyte.

Jean had been intermittently skrying for Declan for the last twenty-four hours, but there was still no sign of him. That meant he was warded, and that meant that he was either being protected by someone or had somehow figured out how to use the amulet to protect himself. The only way Jean was going to be able to find him was to use his own amulet. Since he couldn't risk Morgan knowing he had it, Jean kept his family's amulet at the office. Checking his watch, he realised that he didn't have enough time to look for Declan before Emma was due to arrive, so he settled himself at his desk and started constructing a mental list of things to do.

He was still deep in thought about his next move when he heard the office door open. Looking through into the outer office, he saw that it was Emma. Giving her an approving nod, he greeted her. “Good. Right on time."

She smiled with pleasure, her face betraying her desire to please him. "Oh, I was worried I'd be late with the traffic." She gushed at him as she came through the door, shrugging a large backpack off her shoulders. "I didn't have any trouble at the apartment. The police hadn't been there, so I found everything you wanted exactly where you said it would be."

Bending over, she rummaged through the pack and pulled out a parcel of documents, a smartphone and a rather beautiful old wooden box. Having put them on Jean's desk, she hesitated, letting her hands linger on the box. He knew she could feel the power in it. He would have to be careful. He needed her to remain completely in his thrall for now, but there was no way she could have the box.

Moving around the desk so he was standing close to her, he took her face in his hands and smiled, looking deeply into her eyes. Had Emma not been enthralled, she would have seen the brittleness in the smile and the hardness in his eyes. Jean used a subtle spell to amplify her desire for him and, therefore, forget about the box. She was quite a pretty girl. Her pale skin, a palette whereon colour stood out, her face framed by an auburn pageboy sitting neatly on top of her shoulders. Jean was drawn to her hourglass figure, where the curves of her breasts complemented the subtle lines of her hips. He had enjoyed seducing her and her total surrender and devotion to him. There was nothing she would not do for him. All he needed to do was to command, and it would be done.

Feeling her breath increase and the hardness of her nipples pressing against his chest, he realised he was disappointed it wasn't Keira. The instant he thought of her, an urgent desire coursed through him. Happy to take what was at hand, he let Emma feel his lust, rubbing his cock against her mound. Feeling her melting into him, he hungrily kissed her lips, then taking a breath, he gently pushed her away.

"Later, my sweet." He turned her towards the door, using his body to hide the box, and gently pushed her towards it. "Your place at five. OK?"

She smiled back at him over her shoulder as she walked towards the outer door and replied somewhat breathlessly. "Lovely."

As soon as she was gone, Jean turned back to the desk and took the box over to the window so he could look at it in the light. *Yes. It was what he had expected. The old witch had been holding out on him.* Lifting the lid, he was surprised by the interior. He had expected it to be bigger than the exterior had suggested, but there was a significant difference. This was not only a very special magical artefact. It was filled with objects that were brimming with power. It seemed that Declan had done him a favour. That's one loose end tied up.

Taking the box, he went over to a shabby-looking cupboard tucked behind the office door and, passing his hand over the handles, muttered a spell. As the doors opened, he heard the quiet tinkle of a bell that announced the working of significant magic. This cupboard was one of his greatest finds and was completely secure against magic and brute force. Placing the box on one of the shelves, he retrieved his amulet and returned to his desk.

This time his scrying was enhanced by the power of his amulet. After a considerable amount of effort, he managed to get a sense of Declan in the north of England. Disappointed that his quarry remained hidden, he at least knew he hadn't left the country. Deep in thought, he replaced his amulet in the cupboard and, glancing at his watch, realised that another of his associates was due any minute.

Quickly clearing his desk, he was just about to check his messages when his phone rang. Looking at the caller ID, he saw it was Cecily. She had been sent to watch Rhonwen Tierney. Listening to Cecily's report, he was puzzled by the Tierney girl's behaviour. She seemed to be somewhat impulsive and chaotic. There could be some advantage in that for Jean. He wasn't sure yet how he could use her, but she was Declan's cousin and might know something useful, even if she didn't know it.

As he gave Cecily her instructions, he heard Max at the door, and glancing up he nodded to let him know to come in. Max had been at the State Archives, searching for the family backgrounds of Keira and the two men Morgan had asked him to check on. He already knew they all worked together, including the Tierney girl. Their current occupations and educational backgrounds were easy to access through an internet search, but Morgan's interest in Keira had made him want to look deeper. So he had sent Max to do some digging.

Max was one of Jean's most trusted acolytes. He was more than simply muscle, unlike George. Max had a moderate amount of power and had been a keen and dedicated student of Jean's for over a decade. More importantly, he had no personal ambition. Jean used him for more sensitive tasks, so he knew more of Jean's actual plans than anyone else. And luckily, he was totally unconnected to any living relatives. Should anything happen to him, no one would miss him.

"You wouldn't believe it, boss!" He said, grinning from ear to ear as he flung himself down in the chair near the desk. "That Keira Blair is one of *the* Blairs. Rich, old money rich. And connected. But the best bit is that they changed their name a few centuries ago. She is the direct descendent of Lucas Ninian."

Jean was stunned. He couldn't believe it. She had been right there in his grasp, literally. He had felt something there in her mind, but the ward had been too strong, and he had been too preoccupied with her wonderful body. Pulling himself back to the present, he became aware that Max hadn't finished. "And you know that Poole guy? Well, he is from one of the other families, and they are based in Wales. The Pooles used to be the Cuinn!"

"And Stewart Eggleston?" Jean asked quietly, excitement spreading through him with a burning intensity. "Who is he?"

"Well, now, that is quite interesting, too. You see, the Eggleston's are a very old family from the north, up near Whitehaven, where the Banachs are located. And, as you know, the Banachs have been there, literally, for thousands of years. The Eggleston's appear to have moved to Wales at around the same time as the Poole's did in the seventeenth century."

Slowly, pearls of laughter bubbled up in Jean. *Timing! It was bloody brilliant. After all these years, here they were, all together, and right where he could get to them.* Max, knowing his master well, grinned with pleasure. He had done well to bring back such welcome news. He would be well rewarded. "So, boss, what next?"

Jean, leaning back in his chair, narrowed his eyes. It was a look Max knew only too well. An idea, a plan, had taken shape. "You know what, Max, I think you have earned a night off, but tomorrow, I want you to go up to Yorkshire and see if you can find any sign of Declan Tierney. I'll email you the addresses of all the family properties I already know about, but look for something less obvious. He's hiding out somewhere."

After Max left, Jean remained at his desk, contemplating the synchronicity of recent events. It was all coming together. He was going to win! Yes, it was going to be his. It was going to come together, and he would be the most powerful immortal on the planet! Just thinking about it made him randy. As he felt his jeans tightening, he glanced at the clock, and realising it was after four, he grinned. Emma! Perfect!

Walking into Emma's small apartment thirty minutes later, Jean felt the rush he always felt when he was in total control. Emma came out of the kitchen with a welcoming smile, her eyes filled with devotion as she looked up at him. "Can I get you a drink, something to eat, or perhaps something else?" Her voice trailed off.

Jean smiled. He slapped her on the bottom. "Let's start with the drink, and then we can go to something else."

He walked into Emma's sparsely decorated but tasteful living room and threw himself into the recliner. A minute later, Emma arrived with a tumbler.

"How was the rest of your afternoon?

"Max did well." Jean took a sip, put the glass down, and reached for Emma's hands. He looked into her eyes. "Come, let's do something else." As if on cue, Emma turned, walked across to a cabinet set against the wall, and reached for the remote control. Music began to fill the room with slow and seductive sounds, and Emma turned around and started to undo the fastenings of her shirt. Jean relaxed back into the chair, watching Emma's body move in time with the beat of the music, her eyes closed as she seemed to disappear into herself. As her hands began tracing her body's curves, sliding up and cupping her breasts, she danced towards him.

40

Inspector Riley had decided to take a close look at Lydia Chambers's apartment. It hadn't seemed like an urgent task yesterday, but now he was looking for answers to who this woman really was. How did the mystery of her identity fit in with her murder and the theft? He was still mulling over all of the information he already had when they arrived at the apartment building—his morning mapped out. He would supervise the apartment search, then go and see the antique dealer who sold the Tierney girl the mirror.

It was cool this morning, the patchy rain washing across the city in sporadic showers. Uncomfortable in his trench coat, tired and grumpy from lack of sleep, he had barely spoken to the constable driving the car. He stared out at the building as they parked. His mood started to lift. This, after all, was why he was a detective. He did love solving a puzzle.

Standing in the middle of the lounge room, he orientated himself. This apartment was on the other side of the building from the Tierney place, mirroring it exactly in proportion and layout. Furnished attractively, it spoke of a woman with good taste and a reasonable income—all the hallmarks of the middle class. Wandering over to the bookshelves, he took note of the titles of what were predominately paperbacks. What he was looking for would not be on display.

Something odd about the photographs lined the mantle above the fireplace. He couldn't quite put his finger on it. He had a system of categorising information as he came across it. A little mental trick his father had taught him. The photos got filed under suspicion, and he turned towards the desk near the window.

The constable came in through the door just as he was opening the top drawer. He had sent him to retrieve any mail left in the letterbox down in the hall, and he had a couple of letters in his hand. "There was nothing in the post box, but these were just delivered. One is the power bill, and the other is a Credit card offer. He said as he placed them on the coffee table. The inspector checked the top of the desk. *No recently opened mail. Another entry in the suspicious section.*

Returning to his search of the desk, he found nothing of interest. All of the drawers were organised and tidy. There was no sign of any identifying documents, and all of the bills and invoices were in the name of Lydia Chambers. Turning back towards the centre of the room, he noticed that the Constable was waiting for instructions. He liked this young man. He was smart and quiet, which meant he didn't chatter all the time like some. The Inspector liked that in an off-sider.

"Come with me, Stapleton. We will have a look around the bedroom. Look for her personal papers. Birth certificates, passports, that sort of thing."

The moment the Inspector walked into the bedroom, he felt it. There was something incongruent about this room and the lounge room. The fabrics in the bedding were a more exotic, less bland middle class than those in the furnishings in the rest of the flat. Behind the door, out of sight of anyone looking into the room from the hall, stood a dressing table, its top covered by the bits and pieces that women everywhere kept in their bedrooms. On one side, a large photo dominated the space. It was a group shot of what looked like a large family. There were about ten people of various ages, including children, and they all carried a similar likeness to the woman who had called herself Lydia Chalmers.

He felt it like a palpable click. The photos in the living room were, for the most part, fake, apart from the one of Lydia with another woman her own age who, he was pretty sure, was the Aunt who had left the unit to Rhonwen Tierney. He would bet money on it. A little smile chased its way across his mouth. He knew there was more to find.

He turned towards the other side of the room just as Stapleton opened the wardrobe doors. There was a large empty shelf staring at him. The rest of the space was filled with clothes, arranged in the same way that most people set their stuff, but right in front of him, exactly where a woman of Lydia Chalmers's size would put something she accessed regularly, the cupboard was bare.

Watching the constable start to reach towards the empty shelf, he almost shouted. "Don't touch anything, Stapleton".

The younger man almost literally jumped back away from the wardrobe. "Sir?"

Striding across the room, the Inspector patted him on the shoulder gently. "Sorry, Constable, but I think this is very important. Something is missing."

Looking closely at the shelf, he could see a pattern of dust that had surrounded what looked to have been a large rectangular shape. The dust was scrapped away on the outer edge as if whatever had been there had been pulled across the shelf to remove it. He was still looking at the dust when a tiny sliver of wood caught his eye.

"Constable! An evidence bag, if you please."

He pulled out his gloves and quickly and efficiently picked up the little piece of wood, turning it over so that he could look at it more closely. "Well now, I think whatever was here was removed rather hastily. I also think that it was removed in the last twenty-four hours. Look here, Stapleton, there hasn't been time for more dust to accumulate on the edge of the shelf."

The Constable held out an open plastic evidence bag for the Inspector as he followed the Inspector's gaze towards the shelf. "Do you mean that someone has been here since the lady died, Sir?"

"I am not sure yet, Stapleton, but it's a possibility. Now let's see if we can find anything else."

With that said, the Inspector carefully placed the wooden sliver into the evidence bag and sealed it. He was about to turn away when he spotted several shoe boxes tucked behind a hamper at the other end of the wardrobe. Moving the hamper, he reached down to retrieve them and, in doing so, disturbed a rolled-up piece of soft cardboard. Taking his finds across to the bed, he carefully unrolled the paper. It was a family tree. One that went back through more than a dozen generations. Hand drawn and highly detailed. It outlined the history of the Tierney family.

Noise in the hallway alerted the Inspector and Stapleton to the arrival of the Forensic team. Turning towards the younger man, the Inspector nodded towards the door into the hall. "Off you go then. Tell them to dust for prints out there first while I look at this stuff." The Constable had just started towards the door when the Inspector spoke again. "Keep an eye on them. I want this done properly."

Well now. Let's have a look. He lifted the lid on one of the shoe boxes and found it full of papers and photos. Putting the images to one side, he started sifting through the documents, many of which were to do with the purchase of the flat over fifteen years earlier. They were all in the name of Chambers, including a copy of a birth certificate. He was impressed. She had everything she needed to support her false identity, and no one would have ever guessed if she hadn't been murdered.

Picking up the photos, he quickly realised that the subjects were the same people as in the large family portrait on the dressing table. Taking careful note of the hairstyles and clothes, the Inspector came to the conclusion that none of them were recent. He carefully put all the photos on the bed and, using the family shot as a reference, he started to pick individuals out, matching the single photographs to the people in the group.

There were three people who were not part of the family group. He moved them to one side and then looked more closely at the backgrounds of all the photos. A large stone house figured in about a third of the family photos. It looked old but well cared for. There might be a way to find it if it was a listed house.

Gathering up all the documents and photos into a neat pile, he put them back into the shoebox and turned his attention to the second box. This box was also full of photographs, but they were all of the same person and spanned a lifetime from birth to about thirty years. Inspector Riley knew surveillance when he saw it. Whoever this person was, he had been watched almost continuously all of his life. In fact, it looked like there were very few gaps in the record.

Frustrated, the Inspector put the photos back in their box and turned towards the bedside tables. He didn't really expect to find anything, so he was stunned by what he saw when he opened the drawer. Staring up at him was the face of Declan Tierney. It was a recent photo taken from a distance. Picking it up and heading over to the window, he looked at it more closely. It occurred to him that Declan wasn't looking into the camera. The Inspector shook his head, and a wry grin spread over his face.

Going back to the bedside table, he checked that there was nothing else of importance to be found there, placed the photo in his pocket and headed back out to the lounge room.

He spied Stapleton down on his knees, gently prizing something out of the carpet at the side of the settee.

"What have you got there?" He asked, allowing himself to feel a little more optimistic now that he had something to go on.

"A few strands of hair, Sir. They have a reddish tone so I thought they might belong to that Tierney girl, but you never know." He replied as he rose, carefully depositing his find into an evidence bag.

"Good. Have you got anything else?" The Inspector asked as he peered over the shoulder of one of the Forensic Team who was gathering up some ash and partially burnt paper from the fireplace.

"Not really, Sir." Stapleton responded in a disappointed voice.

Looking at his watch, he realised it was after twelve, and he still had to go to the Antique Shop. Quickly calculating the time it would take to get there, he decided they should get going. Noticing that Murray, the Forensic team leader, was in the kitchen, he headed over to him and quickly sorted out what he wanted to be done. As he returned to the lounge, he signalled to Stapleton to join him, and they made their way out of the apartment, a faint grumbling in his stomach reminding him that he hadn't eaten for a while.

"Come on, Stapleton, we'll get some lunch on the way."

41

Gavin found Erik and Stewart deep in conversation over coffee and sandwiches, their companionable and relaxed demeanour reassuring after the last few days. These two, so alike, and born to their destinies as warrior companions, had bonded easily, and he greeted them warmly. "How did you two go?"

Stewart looked up at him and grinned. "I have to say, Gavin, it has been really amazing finding out all that stuff about my family. Up until now, I only knew what my grandfather had told me, and he only knew about the last few generations. My head is still reeling from it all. I never really bothered to look into it before." He paused thoughtfully. "But then again, I didn't have any reason to, did I?"

"I like this modern world of technology, this modern magic," Erik added. "Although I am constantly amazed at what information is retained and what gets lost. We were able to piece together a lot from the official records and your archives. But what about you? I see you have emerged from the wicked witches" den alive and intact."

Instantly, Stewart sat up. "Keira! Christ! I almost forgot. How is she?"

"She is safe for now, Stewart. I saw her, and she told me to let you know that she wants to stay with Morgan for now. I can assure you she was not being compelled or held against her will. Keira wants to be there. She believes that Morgan can teach her how to manage magic, which of course, is true. I spoke with her, and I doubt she will let Morgan dominate or control her. She appears to have a very sharp mind and is sensibly very cautious and watchful. For now, at least, neither of them knows about the Amulet, but it won't take long for Morgan to figure out who Keira really is."

He was about to continue when he felt Brian and Rhonwen arrive. Erik jumped up, his senses as acute as Gavin's, and headed for the shop, saying, "I'll let them in." Seeing the startled look on Stewart's face, he was reminded that this was all still very new to him. Gavin thought ruefully that he could almost relate to what he was feeling. He was still trying to adjust to the way in which everything had changed overnight himself.

He had started gathering his thoughts when they came through the door; the tension between Rhonwen and Brian preceded the two of them like a wall, its heat burning a path before them. She was enraged and scared. Brian was shut down. His anger was tightly contained. There had been a shift in his attachment to Rhonwen in the last few hours. Gavin sensed that he was disappointed in her lack of resilience. As he gently probed Rhonwen's mind, he realised that her coherence was fraying around the edges and that she was in a worse state now than she had been the previous night. He looked at Erik as he followed them in and sent him a request.

Putting on a welcoming smile for Rhonwen's benefit, Gavin greeted them and then, having offered coffee, went to the kitchen to organise it while Erik, using his most charming smile, took Rhonwen under his wing. He shepherded her over to the lounge near the window, muttering a gentle spell to soothe her mind. Once she had settled and was happy to sit looking out the window at the garden, Erik turned to join the other men, both of whom were watching him intently. "What did you do to her?" Brian whispered.

Having returned from the kitchen, Gavin smiled reassuringly and deliberately banged the china a bit so Rhonwen wouldn't overhear them. He had always found Erik's interpretation interesting. His experience of magic before he and Gavin met still lingered in how he approached the craft. The Viking would never disappear completely, no matter how many centuries passed. The influence of the Wends had been strong in Erik's youth, and there was still a raw, visceral quality to his spell-casting. It seemed to make sense to Brian, who, like Stewart, had warmed to Erik quickly.

Pouring the coffee and settling down with one of the leftover sandwiches, Gavin let himself relax for the first time since the previous night. He knew it wouldn't last long, but he had hoped for more than five minutes. Suddenly alert to two men crossing the street, purposefully heading towards the door of the shop, Gavin heaved a sigh and started to get up. Erik, similarly aware of their approach, glanced over at him quizzically.

"It's OK, Erik. I expected the police to come calling. They will want to know if I am connected to Declan. After all, it was less than twenty-four hours after I sold the mirror to Rhonwen that he broke in and stole it. In fact, I hope to get some information out of them."

Brian jumped up and, looking quickly over towards Rhonwen, moved closer to Gavin. "I Haven't had a chance to tell you yet. Lydia has turned out to be a fake. She was using false ID, and the cops don't have a clue who she really was." He paused. "Well, at least they didn't when I spoke with them earlier this morning."

Gavin sensed that this new information was really important, but before they could talk more, he heard the shop door alarm go off. "OK! I will go and talk to the Police. You all stay back here, and when I am finished, we can try and put all the pieces we have together and see what we are dealing with."

Putting on his most urbane twenty-first-century face, Gavin headed out to the front of the shop. "Hello, gentlemen; how can I help you this morning?"

Pulling out his Badge, Inspector Riley introduced himself and the Constable. He seemed affable and pleasant, but Gavin was instantly aware of the quick and incisive intelligence behind the Inspector's grey eyes. He was also aware that the Inspector was not going to disclose anything he knew willingly.

"Well, now, Mr Skye." His eyes narrowed ever so slightly. "An item that you sold to a Miss Rhonwen Tierney on Friday was stolen from her home on Saturday. I am curious about how that may have come about. Miss Tierney states that she didn't tell anyone about her purchase, yet it seems to have been the object the thief was after."

Gavin let himself visibly pale and appeared to be blindsided by the news as he replied. "This is shocking, Inspector. Are you talking about that robbery that was on the news yesterday, where that poor woman was attacked? Don't tell me it was Miss Tierney?"

Without answering Gavin's question, the Inspector reached into his coat pocket and pulled out a photograph. "Do you know this man, Mr Skye?"

Looking at the photo very carefully, Gavin considered the face that stared out at him for a full minute before looking back up at the Inspector. "I don't think so. Certainly, he isn't someone I actually know, but there is something about him that I can't quite put my finger on."

"What do you mean by that, Mr Skye?" The Inspector asked, staring straight into Gavin's eyes.

"I don't know. There is just something about his face that tugs at my memory even though I don't have any recollection of ever meeting this man. Of course, I dealt with many people over the course of my business, so that I could have seen him somewhere. He may just have one of those faces."

"Mmm," was all the Inspector said as he put the photo back into his pocket. He studiously looked around the clutter of the shop. "So, tell me, where did you get the mirror? I presume you have all the proper documentation, given that it is a valuable antique."

"Oh, of course, Inspector. I am very careful to know the provenance of all of the more important pieces I sell. If you want to come to the counter, I'll get it for you."

Having expected this inquiry, Gavin had put together a false set of documents the previous evening. Officially, the mirror had been part of a large number of antiques found in the attic of a deceased estate with no connection to the Tierney family. Since there was a large mirror in the collection, it was easy to alter the description on the invoice. The seller, a distant relative of the deceased, had not bothered to examine the items closely and had quickly returned to his home in Canada once he had put the house up for sale. Retrieving the paperwork from the filing cabinet, Gavin handed it over to the Inspector.

"You didn't tell me if Miss Tierney is all right, Inspector. The news broadcast said that it was a serious injury."

The Inspector gave Gavin a long flat look before he replied. "We are not releasing any information about the details of the crime at this time, Mr Skye. If you don't mind, I'll take this paperwork with me. We may have some more questions for you at a later stage."

With that, the Inspector called to his Constable, who had been looking around the shop in a rather haphazard fashion. As the pair moved towards the door, Gavin noted that the Constable had a quiet word in the Inspector's ear. The Inspector retraced his steps back to the counter. "Now, Mr Skye, my Constable has quite rightly pointed out that you don't seem to have any security camera equipment. I'm surprised, given the price of many of the items you sell. Seems a bit odd. Surely your insurance company would have insisted on it?"

Gavin smiled winningly at the pair as he replied. "Well, as you would be aware, Inspector, there are CTV cameras watching this street, and one of them has a direct line of sight of my door. I have a camera at the back loading dock that is out of sight and, therefore difficult for any would-be thief to tamper with. There are alarms linked to motion sensors inside the shop, and the Insurance Company has its own Security people who monitor those alarms. It's quite secure, I can assure you."

The Inspector nodded. "Well, then, that's all for now. I'll be in touch should I need anything else."

Gavin watched them closely as they left the shop and headed for their car. Casting a subtle spell, he listened in on their conversation as they walked down the street. The Inspector seemed keen to look at the film from the CTV camera across the street.

Gavin chuckled to himself. The Inspector was going to be very disappointed to learn that it broke down early Saturday morning. However, it would be returned to service quickly, so Brian and Stewart would have to use the back door. Or better yet, they should probably move over to Erik's. Connell could meet them there just as easily as here. Gavin quickly sent a message to the Banach patriarch, who, he could sense, was just getting to the edge of London along the M6. Closing the shop up and setting the alarms, he headed back to the others.

42

Morgan quietly closed the door of the guest bedroom, leaving Keira in a natural sleep. She was exhausted from Scáthach's assault on her mind and body, so Morgan had woven a net of protective magic around her. *That should keep the Warrior Goddess at bay, at least for now.* She thought as she headed downstairs. As long as Keira didn't have any sexual experiences, she was reasonably safe.

The problem was, of course, that Scáthach's influence on Keira's own desire was profound. The girl was suffused with lust. She had managed to keep Jean away from her this morning, but the question was how long she could keep that up with Keira in the house. Morgan was well aware that Jean was a sexual predator. She had watched him develop his magic and seen the way he incorporated sexual dominance into the very fabric of his spells.

All of this is connected. Jean is up to something, and somehow, it's stirred up Scáthach. That thought disturbed Morgan more than she wanted to acknowledge. It went to the core of her relationship with Jean and the way she had raised him. She felt a sense of unease that she had created a monster. Quickly dismissing that conclusion, she reminded herself that he was already a product of his mother's lifestyle long before she adopted him.

Thankfully he had left the house soon after Gavin had arrived. He was getting very powerful, but he still couldn't ward against two Immortals at the same time. At least, not for long. Letting her thoughts drift, she allowed the natural sorting and cataloguing of information to take its own direction. She could feel the threads of information starting to weave into a pattern. Two men and two women, all of whom were connected in this time and world, but also in the past. Keira had to be the key, but Keira herself didn't know anything. That Grimoire was important. Keira's family had kept a Grimoire over many generations without knowing its value or using it to practice magic.

Where did Keira get her considerable talent from? Morgan had accessed all of Keira's memories of her family and found nothing of use. Pulling a vial from her pocket, she held it up to the light—Keira's blood. Morgan could feel tendrils of excitement playing across her skin, and a deep sense of joy bubbled up as she started collecting the ingredients of the spell she was about to cast. She loved magic with a visceral and lustful drive, and this sort of magic, old magic, was a rare pleasure in this modern world.

As she let herself into her inner sanctum, she started the ritual cleansing of the space. She needed to free the environment of all traces of anyone but herself before she started the spell she needed to cast. Stripping off her clothes, she placed them at the arch and moved further into the room, loosening her hair. Cleansing her hands in the basin by the wall, she gathered what she needed and set to work at the fire pit she had brought with her through the centuries. She kept the ancient stone bowl in every home she had ever lived in. In it, she had made history, and now she had a feeling she was going to be doing so again.

Focusing all her energies on the task at hand, she kindled a fire using the wood she sourced from the remnants of the old Caledonian forest above the Allt Ruadh and poured in some pure distilled water using her favourite small caldron. Returning to the basin, she washed her hands and face and completed the cleansing ritual before turning to the small wooden table next to the fire to prepare the ingredients. Picking up the herbs, she gently shredded them and placed them into the cauldron as she spoke the incantation that would start the spell.

As they settled into the now hot water, the release of odours from the herbs triggered a responding warmth that flowed through her body. The increasing heat of the water was mirrored by the rising heat of her abdomen and groin as she continued to add the various ingredients. When the water came to the very edge of boiling, she spoke the final invocation, quivering with pleasure at the rush of magic coursing through her.

Maintaining her concentration through the waves of her own climax, she used an ancient silver ladle from the hook above her work table to fill a ceramic bowl with the solution from the cauldron. It would have to cool to body temperature before she mixed it with the blood to ensure the result. As this would only take a couple of minutes, Morgan used this time to retrieve an old leather-bound journal from it's hiding place. Over the millennia, she had collected the blood of all of the important magical families and recorded their properties. She was confident that she would find Keira's amongst them.

Returning to her work table, she felt the ceramic bowl with the magical solution in it, and deciding that it was at the right temperature, she opened the vial of Keira's blood and very gently added it as she cast the spell of revelation. Watching as the two mixed and settled into a unique pattern, Morgan was startled by what she saw. She didn't need her journal. She recognised the signature of the Ninian bloodline. *No wonder Scáthach picked Keira!*

Morgan knew immediately what this meant. She had known that four of the families had ceased to practice magic over the last few centuries. Jean's family had all but disappeared. Decimated by the deaths of the men in the previous two wars and ruined financially during the Depression. She had found no trace of their Amulet. And now here was another one of the five, but no Amulet. She needed to look at the Grimoire again. There may be some clue as to the Amulet's whereabouts.

Turning it all over in her mind, Morgan wondered if Jean had somehow gotten past her safeguards. She had hidden all knowledge of his family's inheritance from him, taking great pains to eliminate all reference to the Amulets from her library. Watching him closely over the last few years, she was no longer confident that this had been enough. Scáthach trying to break back into this world after so many centuries, had to be linked to the Amulets. Gavin's sudden move back to London and his re-connection to the Tierney's was too big a coincidence.

Gathering up her clothes, she quickly dressed and cleared away the evidence of her spell casting. Secreting her journal back in its usual hiding place, she headed back up upstairs to the Library where she had left Keira's Grimoire. It didn't take more than a minute for her to realise that the pocket at the front of the book was big enough and had the right-sized indentation in the cover to hold an Amulet. Did Keira have it somewhere? Given her inexperience, it would make sense for her to have been able to access so much power with her spell. But on the other hand, she had found no hint of it in Keira's memories.

Glancing at the time, she made a decision. Emily was gone for the day, so she headed for the kitchen to make some tea. As she organised afternoon tea and a light snack, she continued to sift through the information she already had. Who, besides Keira, had had access to the Grimoire? The image of a handsome young man hovering in the hallway of Keira's apartment immediately came to mind. *Aha! The warrior! One of Gavin's new friends!*

Anger flared, hot and sharp, at the thought that Gavin may well have Keira's Amulet. Taking a breath, she calmed herself and, picking up the tray, went upstairs to wake Keira. Knocking softly on the door, simultaneously releasing the spell that had kept Keira undisturbed, she went in and put the tray on a small occasional table. Opening the curtains to let in the late afternoon sun, she looked over at the sleeping girl. *It is time to tell Keira who she is!*

43

Rhonwen felt warm and comfortable looking out at the small garden tucked down the side of the building that housed Gavin's Antique Shop. She was surprised to see that it even attracted birdlife, and she contentedly watched the comings and goings of a family of wrens, only distantly aware of the others in the room.

She wasn't sure what triggered her mind to tune in to the conversation between the three men, but she found herself becoming more aware of what they were talking about. At first, she felt a sense of irritation. Her anger at Brian sat like a great big lump of lead in the pit of her stomach. She didn't want to be aware of him or anyone. She just wanted to be left alone in peace.

Ah! That was it. They had mentioned Keira! That bitch! Wanting to hear what they were saying about her, Rhonwen focused her attention behind her, careful not to alert the men to her interest. They were talking about magic and their families. Rhonwen was appalled to realise that Keira was a significant part of all of this. That she came from a family that owned an Amulet. She felt her rage starting to gnaw at her just thinking about it. Yet underneath it all, she was suddenly very afraid.

Recognising that she had been mentally and emotionally unravelling, she didn't understand how she could have become so irrational over the last few days. She had worked hard to remain sensible and practical, locked into life's pragmatic, solid and reliable areas. It had been a very long time since she had allowed her emotions to control her. But so much had happened that didn't make sense to her! It just didn't fit into her ideas about reality.

The very idea of magic had been so terrifying to her. First, she had refused to allow herself to accept what she had seen with her own eyes. Hearing Brian and Stewart talking about it, she sensed that, unlike her, they could both now accept its existence. They didn't seem to shy away from what they had all seen over the last twenty-four hours. Chiding herself for being a coward, she made up her mind to take back control.

Remembering some of the breathing exercises her yoga teacher had taught her, she quietly concentrated on calming herself, and, using a little trick she had learnt dealing with her mother, she locked her anger up in a corner of her mind. Breathing deeply, she felt the tension in her shoulders and arms start to ease. Looking down into her lap, she realised she had been grasping hold of her scarf and twisting it into knots, so she consciously unclenched her fists.

Feeling more like herself, she let herself settle back into the comfort of the lounge and re-focus her attention on the three men at the other end of the room. Erik's voice, louder than the others, captured her attention. He was talking about Stewart's family. Listening to him explain that Brian's and Stewart's families had been connected for millennia, Rhonwen suddenly understood that she could no longer hide from the fact that she, and her family, were somehow involved in all of this. After all, it was her cousin who had broken into her flat, attacked her neighbour, and stolen this Amulet that was apparently so important.

She rarely allowed herself to think about her childhood. It had been too painful and frightening. Her mother had been cold and angry, and her father weak and ineffectual. Their lives had been dominated by her mother's church, and Rhonwen had always felt that she was somehow bad but had not been able to understand why. When she was really young, she thought that it was her fault that they hardly ever saw the rest of the family. She had long ago come to the conclusion that this wasn't true. After all, Aunt Sophie had left her the flat. She wouldn't have done that if she hated her.

Thinking back, Rhonwen tried to remember why she had thought she was to blame for the split in her family. As she tried to grasp hold of a long-forgotten time in her life, she felt the cold blade of fear. Just for a moment, she was almost paralysed. The fear of delving too closely into the past was so great that the only defence she had, was to feel the heat of her anger. Clamping down on her emotions with the full force of her will, she made herself face her memories.

An image of her mother, a snarl of rage and loathing on her face, screaming at two older women. "*This family has been involved with evil for far too long, and I'll be dammed if I am going to let you embroil my daughter in it.*" Followed by another image of her Grandmother and her Aunt Sophie, staring at her mother in shock. She clearly saw her Grandmother's face.

Rhonwen felt a wave of grief. Unlike her mother, her Grandmother had been kind and loving. Another image came into Rhonwen's mind. This time, it was a memory of another confrontation between her mother and Aunt Sophie, talking about her, Rhonwen. And again, there had been accusations of the family being evil. Fragments of other conversations, hushed and secretive, drifted back into Rhonwen's consciousness. She felt like her childhood had been filled with conversations that always ended abruptly when the adults realised that she was listening.

Turning it over in her mind, she realised that this had all started when her Uncle, her mother's only brother, had died. She clearly remembered, amongst all the other sad regrets about his death, that her Grandmother had focused most especially on the fact that he was childless.

Rhonwen had always been aware of her mother's obsession with evil. She prayed daily for her God to keep her safe from it and had always implied that Rhonwen was somehow tainted with it. Her parents claimed that they had moved away from the family because of her father's work. Their excuse for not visiting had been that they were too busy. As she grew up, Rhonwen realised this wasn't true. But she had never challenged her parents, mostly because she was afraid of her mother's cruel tongue.

Now, thinking about the story of the Amulets and their protectors, she started to put some of these memories into a different context. It made sense that her mother would reject anyone that had anything to do with magic. It would be at total odds with her own beliefs. Magic would be evil in her mother's eyes. Rhonwen had turned away from her mother's beliefs by the time she was a teenager and based her life on the principle that there was no such thing as the supernatural. Just as her mother had embraced her religion, Rhonwen had embraced reason and science.

And now she was being asked to revise all of that and accept that magic existed. Remembering the previous night at Brian's, she was again confronted by the image of a floating Amulet and of Brian controlling it with his mind. This was quickly followed by an image of Gavin, and then nothing until she woke up this morning. He had done something to her! *Who the hell is he?*

Hearing laughter from the other end of the room, Rhonwen turned around and looked at the three men as they spoke to each other, their growing friendship so apparent to any onlooker. She felt a niggle of resentment. *It's so easy for them!* They had all been keeping secrets from her. The rage that was still sitting deep inside of her seemed to grow a little hotter with this thought.

Seeing Gavin return, Rhonwen carefully hid her thoughts behind a pleasant smile. He immediately came to her side and asked her how she was faring. He seemed kind, but she wasn't sure she liked Gavin anymore. She felt like he was treating her like a child. Looking directly into Gavin's eyes, Rhonwen spoke in the calmest voice she could manage.

"I think it's about time you all told me what is really happening here."

Looking at her closely, Gavin nodded, almost as if to himself, and replied.

"You are right. It is time we sat down, talked about it, and pooled our information. You not only have a right to know, you need to know. However, I think it would be prudent if we moved over to Erik's place for now. The Inspector intends to set a watch on the shop to ensure Declan isn't my associate. He has no other leads, so he wants to make sure that the shop is the dead end it appears to be."

Realising that this would delay returning to Brian's, Rhonwen was happy to go along with the plan. Typically, her willingness to go along with the men's plans was a great relief to them. Brian visibly relaxed and, taking her hand, apologised to her for being a "*little harsh*" earlier. Defending himself with the excuse that he had been worried about her.

Having all agreed, it was surprising how efficiently they orchestrated the move to Erik's home in Shepherd's Bush. Brian's mate, Gerry, was called to come and pick them up in his Taxi. Since Gavin needed the police to think he was still in the shop and that the shop was open for business, he would travel separately. She couldn't figure out how he was planning on doing this but decided not to ask too many questions.

In just over an hour, they were walking through Erik's front door. Rhonwen felt immediately at home. The place had that Scandinavian, Ikea sort of feel about it. All light-coloured woods and bright fabrics. It was surprisingly large for a London flat, taking up a floor of an old converted townhouse.

Allowing Erik to fuss over her and giving Stewart and Brian warm, friendly looks, all three men ceased their surreptitious monitoring of her emotional state and their deliberate censoring of their conversation. It was Stewart's excitement and awe at the news that his ancestors had "messed around with magic" that lightened the mood the most. He had always thought of them as stuffy and conservative, claiming that the Manor House, where the last eight generations had lived, was filled with the trappings of farmers rather than magicians.

They had hardly enough time to settle into the lounge before another couple of people arrived. More men, she thought ruefully. This time it was a father and son. It was obvious that Erik knew them well, and the three of them greeted each other with a lot of noisy pleasure. As the introductions were made, she noted that the younger man, Rouan, became a little distant, especially with Brian.

Although she felt an immediate liking for Connell, his massive warm hands enveloping hers with obvious pleasure, Rhonwen was a little puzzled by their arrival. After letting go of her hands, Connell turned towards Erik and, with a slight edge to his voice, asked where Gavin was.

Before Erik could answer him, the man himself arrived, walking in through the kitchen door. Rhonwen, who was quite close to the door, heard a faint sound of a bell ringing and saw a brightening of the light in the kitchen at the same time as he appeared. Feeling a little startled by the ordinariness of this apparent working of magic, she was reassured to see that both Brian and Stewart had reacted similarly to her. Stewart's jaw literally dropped, much to the amusement of the others in the room.

"I don't know if I will get used to that." He muttered to Rhonwen as he made himself comfortable on the chair next to her. Overhearing his comment, Erik gave a hoot of laughter, and looking at his watch, he looked around the room and offered them all a drink. "After all, this is a momentous occasion. We have representatives of three of the families in the same room for the first time in centuries."

"And no weapons visible!" Replied Rouan with a grin.

It was Connell who spoke next. Turning to Gavin, an eyebrow raised quizzically, "Is it as urgent as it feels?"

"I am afraid so." Replied Gavin as he accepted a drink from Erik. "But I think we may have a chance to stop it".

Stop what, thought Rhonwen. She really wished they would just get on with explaining it all to her. Almost as if he had read her mind, Gavin turned to Rhonwen, and smiling warmly, he directed his words to her. "You have been the most injured by the events of the last few days. Your inheritance has been stolen, your friend killed. But it will be humanity that will suffer if the evil currently knocking at the door is allowed to enter."

"Then it is Scáthach!" Connell said in a quiet voice loaded with concern. Turning to him, Gavin nodded. "Yes, she is trying to get back into the world, and she has found a vessel." Gavin sat down on one of the dining room chairs that Erik had put around the room, and gesturing to the others to all sit; he started telling them what he now knew about the events of the last few days.

Rhonwen was stunned. She wasn't surprised that Keira was a conduit for evil. She had always known that the girl was a slut. The fact that she so obviously wanted Brian, but was willing to screw around with Stewart, said it all, as far as she was concerned. The reaction of the Banach men to the news that Keira was currently in the safekeeping of the woman Morgan was interesting. Connell had become almost explosive;

"You have always given that woman far too much leeway, Gavin! She can't be trusted," and, pointing an accusing finger at

Gavin, exclaimed, "and you know it! Beltane is only a week from now, remember!"

Rhonwen felt Stewart start to fidget. Turning to him, she saw the worry on his face and realised that he cared for Keira more than she had thought. Having sat there quietly next to her, he now blurted out. "Are you sure she is safe, Gavin? I have only left her there because you said she would be."

Gavin turned to him. "She is all right for now, Stewart. But remember, this is Keira's choice. We can't control her. Morgan is aware of the danger. As long as Keira isn't sexually active, Scáthach can't use her. She is not my biggest concern at the moment." It was then that Gavin informed them that Morgan's adopted son was none other than the heir to the fifth family's Amulet.

Rhonwen had been a little chuffed with the way Connell berated Gavin about this. "Are you mad? You left this girl, Keira, in the same house as a Bran? What is Morgan up to, adopting this boy? She must have a plan, and if I know anything about that woman, it won't be in our best interests, I can tell you."

Connell started pacing around the room in an agitated state, pointing his finger at Gavin and accusing him of stupidity. Rhonwen was enjoying it. She relished Gavin being put in his place. However, the icy air that suddenly filled the room stopped her gloating. Puzzled, she looked at Brian and Stewart. The two men had become very still and alert. Connell, too, had stopped in his tracks, wariness written all over his face. It was Rouan's face that said it all. Fear. That's what Rhonwen realised it was; unadulterated fear.

Rhonwen glanced back at Gavin. What she saw made no rational sense, but she felt something, something that electrified every fibre of her being. So strong it left her immobilised. Gavin, or at least his persona, filled the room. Colossal and very dangerous, his steely eyes fixed on Connell. His implacable voice boomed within her body. In reality, however, it was very quiet, and the words were simple; "That is enough! You forget who you are speaking to!"

The effect was instant. Dropping onto one knee, Connell meekly bowed his head. "I am sorry, Gavin," a heartbeat later, he plucked up courage and looked up, "But Morgan is a problem."

The air in the room changed. Gavin returned to his usual self. He calmly acknowledged Connell's retreat, then said, "Yes, Morgan is an unpredictable and uncontrollable force, but she has always been on our side against Scáthach. You know this from the archives. I know it from experience. I don't know what her plans are when it comes to her son, but I do know that she is deliberately keeping him in the dark about this."

Rhonwen, still trying to process what she had just witnessed, was brought back to the present when Gavin mentioned Declan. "We all felt the quickening. The problem is that not only is he a criminal and a murderer, he has no one to teach him how to handle the Amulet." Gavin sighed. "He is a major threat, and we have no idea where he is. He has obviously found somewhere shielded, somewhere to hole up in because I can't scry him out."

Keeping her voice as calm as possible, Rhonwen asked the question at the forefront of her mind while she listened to Gavin and Connell. "Was it an accident that I found the mirror in your shop, Gavin?"

Turning towards her, Gavin shook his head; "No, you were led to it by your familial connection to the Amulet. Your Aunt Sophie was well aware that leaving you her flat was likely to create a furore in the family. She gave me the mirror to protect, in the hope that you would find your way to me and your inheritance.

"But why me?" Rhonwen asked, trying to ignore the slightly shrill sound of her voice.

Gavin gave her a penetrating look as he replied, "You are in the direct line of power through your mother. Her rejection of the family's heritage was a bitter blow to your grandmother. It might seem strange to you, but there was a certain amount of prestige in your family for being the protector of the Amulet. Your grandmother was particularly upset that this honour might end up in the hands of her cousin's side of the family. It was a matter of pride for her that the Amulet had come down to Sophie from their father and his father before him."

Rhonwen was still confused. "I still don't understand why she didn't just leave me the mirror with the flat. How did she think I was going meet you?"

"I was going to approach you as an old friend of the family. That's why I moved back to London and re-opened the shop. You see, when your mother abandoned the family and separated you from her, Sophie made it her business to get to know you from a distance.

She had sensed you had magical talent. But knowing you were being brought up with a different set of beliefs, she also forged links with Elizabeth and her family in case you embraced your mother's prejudices. Declan also has the talent, and so he was her backup".

Gavin paused for a moment, looking at her, his eyes keenly watching her reactions to what he was saying before he continued.

"Of course, it didn't take her long to realise that Elizabeth was an extremely unpleasant woman and that Declan was following in her footsteps. Sophie was convinced that they had no idea that the family was in possession of such an important artefact, and she made sure they didn't find out. She planned to approach you when you were an adult, hoping to have time to build a relationship with you, but she became ill before she could do this."

Thinking about what Gavin had just told her, Rhonwen felt a tightness in her chest. She was still appalled at the idea of magic. It frightened her, and Gavin frightened her because he used magic. And now Brian wasn't the same man she had known because he had this talent. Looking around the room, she realised that some of the others must also use magic. "Did Aunt Sophie practice magic?" She asked in a small voice.

It was Connell who replied. "She didn't. In fact, no one in your family has practised magic for several generations. A lot of knowledge was lost over the years. One of Sophie's great regrets was that she could never locate the family's Grimoire. She searched all through the family's papers for some hint of where it might be hidden, but it is still missing."

"The big mystery is Declan." Stewart interjected. As he continued, Rhonwen recognised that he was echoing her own thoughts. "How did he know that Rhonwen had the Amulet when she had only just bought the mirror the day before?"

Rouan, having sat quietly in the background up until now, responded to his question in a voice filled with venom. "It could be connected in some way to Morgan. We know she can't be trusted, and if that stepson of hers is a Bran, this could all be part of some scheme of hers."

Gavin and Connell looked at each other, Gavin shaking his head slowly as if he didn't believe it, but Connell obviously thought there was something in his son's idea. It was Erik who startled them all, leaping up from his chair in an agitated state. Turning towards

Gavin, he said. "It makes sense, Gavin. She was in the shop within minutes of Rhonwen having bought the mirror. I know you don't want to believe it, but how else can you explain how Declan knew where the mirror was? In fact, how else would he have known anything about the Amulet and its value to him?"

Brian added in a thoughtful voice. "He used magic to get away. I saw him jump out the window and disappear. And we still have to find out who Lydia really was."

Rhonwen looked over to him and saw he was looking at her with compassion as he continued. "What was her agenda, and who is she connected to? Obviously not Declan because he killed her. I bet he is the one who finished her off at the hospital. No one saw anything, and yet she is somehow given a fatal overdose of heroin. Maybe this is where Stewart and I could help. We're pretty good at tracing people, and finding out who Lydia was and what she was up to might give us some leads."

Feeling a sense of deep sadness, Rhonwen tried to stop herself from crying. Stewart must have been aware of her feelings because as they sat there listening to the others discussing what to do next, she felt him lean closer to her, and taking her hand, he squeezed it reassuringly. Unsure of what hurt the most, Lydia's duplicity, or her death, Rhonwen just felt like curling up and sobbing.

44

Stepping out of the elevator, Brian walked straight into Michael, who was hurrying down the hall. It was pretty apparent from the look on the man's face that he was not expecting to see Brian in the office. "Oh, hello! I thought you were working from home today. How's Rhonwen? Poor girl, after that interview disaster on Friday, to have her home burgled and a friend killed!"

Brian smiled warmly at the harried man in front of him. "She is coping pretty well, really. Friends are looking after her for the next week or so. Her place is a crime scene, so it will be a few more days before she can go home."

Looking at his watch, Michael shook his head. "I've got to go to the weekly HR meeting, but if you could let us know where we can send her some flowers, I would like to let her know we care."

"Absolutely!" Brian replied. And with that, they parted, each heading off to opposite ends of the hall. Brian had barely unlocked his office door when Stewart appeared beside him. He looked perturbed. "You wouldn't believe it! Gabrielle at the front desk told me that Keira's in her office."

Stewart was right. Brian had not been expecting that. This was going to get complicated. They had no idea what Keira knew and what she thought she knew, and, of course, she was still Keira. He could feel his Amulet warming up just at the thought of it. It was Stewart who voiced his first thought. "Do you think she knows that she should have an Amulet? Gavin said that Morgan would figure it out pretty quickly. She might have told her it was in the front of the Grimoire."

Stewart's obvious discomfort at the thought of having to face an angry Keira did nothing to ease his tension, and Brian was quite sure they could expect a visit from her sooner rather than later. Pushing open the office door, he gestured to Stewart to precede him into the room. "Come on, let's get on with it before the storm arrives. We can both work here, so we are a united force when she strikes." Stewart relaxed a little and, nodding his head towards the laptop he was carrying, muttered his thanks.

Turning on his computer, Brian took a quick look at his emails and efficiently sorted out what needed to be addressed immediately and what could wait. He had already spoken with Stewart about their main tasks of the day. One was to try and track Declan over the last few years. Not just to get an idea of what he had been up to but to see if they could find any connection to Morgan. The other was to find out who Lydia really was.

They had been at it for about two hours, using some of their contacts within Interpol and several European intelligence agencies. They had managed to build a reasonable picture of Declan's career as a con man and petty criminal in the South of France when a sharp rap on the office door interrupted the peace. They both jumped up like two schoolboys having been caught out. Brian almost burst out laughing at the look on Stewart's face. Chuckling, he went over to unlock the door, having secured it earlier so they wouldn't be surprised by Keira just walking in.

He had barely undone the lock when the door was pushed inwards. Keira swept into the room, no longer the goth. She was dressed like she had been for the interviews on the previous Friday. This, and her aura of confidence, threw him. He had known how to deal with the old Keira. This Keira was different, and an image from his erotic dream about her intruded into the front of his mind as she brushed past him. He could sense a slight blurring to the edges of her physical form, and suddenly everything Gavin had told him about Scáthach returned to him. He could feel his Amulet heat up and was glad it was now safely tucked into a little black pouch. He had no desire to try and explain to the rather ferocious woman standing in front of him why his chest was glowing.

"Well, here you are." Keira said in a sarcastic, edgy voice. "Hiding behind locked doors. Afraid of someone? Surely not!" Turning into the room, she saw Stewart. There was a sudden shift in her demeanour, and she seemed to hesitate. When she spoke, her voice carried a slightly puzzled tone. "I'm supposed to stay away from you, Stewart!" Then, her expression changed, and she flashed him a brilliant smile. Coquettishly tossing her head, she headed straight over to him. When she was in striking distance, she trailed a scarlet fingernail like a scalpel down the line of his jaw.

"But I do what I want!"

It was as if an electrical charge arced between the two of them. In the connection that had them both transfixed Keira seemed to expand. It was Stewart who managed to pull back from her caress. He nimbly twisted around, slipping across to the window, leaving Keira shocked and shaken. Stewart stayed where he was, watching her closely as she seemed to deflate back to her usual self, the blurring a little fainter than when she first arrived. Her confidence was gone. Keira just stood where she was. She looked confused and more than a little scared.

Feeling compassion for her, Brian spoke gently, "It's all right, Keira, come and sit over here. I know a lot of strange stuff is going on, so it's probably a good idea if we talk about it." When he saw her suspicious look, he quickly continued. "We do know a bit about what's happened, so we might be able to help".

Surprised by the startled look Keira gave Stewart, Brian immediately regretted his words. He watched her face contort with rage. She turned her back on him and vented her fury on Stewart in a blistering attack, castigating him for his presumption that she would ever need his help. Viciously articulate, her words assaulted Stewart. She tore away at his sophisticated veneer. As she continued to spray him with scorn, her physical appearance changed again, and her vocabulary became cruder. The outline of her body blurred, giving her presence a dark and menacing aura. Brian could feel the hairs on the back of his neck bristle while the heat of his Amulet felt like it was going to burn a hole in his chest.

Stewart, who at first hadn't reacted to this onslaught, tried to interject. Speaking gently and softly, he tried to reassure her. Then suddenly, Keira deflated, quite literally, back to her normal-looking self. A war of emotions washed across her lovely features. She looked at Brian and then again at Stewart. Finally, in a sad small voice, she quietly accused Stewart of betrayal. "You had no right to talk about us. It was private. I trusted you!"

Just for a moment, she seemed vulnerable. Stewart reached out to her, but the remorse in his expression acted like a spark to gunpowder. Pulling herself up to her full height, she slapped his hand away. This time, her nails left a trail of blood. She spun on her heel, heading for the office door. Before she opened it, she turned back to them. Nostril's flared, her mouth a thin line of disdain. She hissed, "I had no idea that you were a thief, Stewart. You are to return what you stole, and then we are done!"

As the door slammed behind her, Brian looked across to Stewart. He was surprised to see grief in his friend's eyes. It had been a long, long time since a woman had gotten to him. Brian was puzzled that Keira, of all women, had been the one to do it. He knew there was nothing he could say, so he decided to give Stewart some space to get his head around what had just happened. When their eyes met, Brian acknowledged Stewart's need for silence with a brief nod and went back to his desk.

Scanning the screen of his computer, he realised there had been a response to his last query about Declan. He had sent a photo of him to a contact who had extensive knowledge of the cartels and syndicates that operated out of Marseille. Opening the email and quickly reading its contents, he swore softly under his breath. Rhonwen's cousin might seem to be a petty con man on the surface, but he had, in fact, been a very successful player for the last few years.

Amongst the attached photos of Declan meeting various criminals was one that showed Declan leaving a luxurious mansion. What caught Brian's attention was the face of a man watching Declan from one of the French windows. Manipulating the size of the picture, the face of Jean Bran became clearly visible. "Got you!"

Sensing Stewart moving around the desk to his side, he realised he had spoken aloud. "Look at this, Stew! Proof that Declan has met with Jean Bran, Morgan's stepson."

"Is there a time reference for the photo?" Stewart asked as he scanned the image in front of him. "Yes. It was taken only a few weeks ago, in March." Brian replied, looking at the information that came with the photo. Sizing up Stewart, he recognised the familiar set of his jaw and the flat look in his eyes. Stewart was ready to get back to work, his feelings neatly filed away somewhere.

"Well, this suggests that either Morgan is playing Gavin or Jean is running this show. What was it Gavin said? Morgan was very careful to alert him not to mention Scáthach in front of Jean. Now that could be a ploy to give her credibility with Gavin. We don't know."

Stewart, rubbing his chin as he did when his intuition was fully switched on, looked closely at the image of Jean. "I think that if we track Jean, we may well find Declan. Even if Morgan is in on it, it looks like Jean will most likely lead us to him."

Brian, acknowledging Stewart's assessment with a nod, scrolled down through the other photos so Stewart could get a feel for the company that Declan had been seen to keep. "This guy hangs around with some real sleaze bags, which is why Mario was interested enough to follow him to this meeting. I'll email him and see if he has any other images or info about Jean."

Stretching his back as he moved over to his computer, Stewart offered to call Gerry to do a bit of surveillance. Brian was about to agree when an image of Gerry sprawled out in an alley suddenly came into his mind. His Amulet was pulsing rapidly against his chest, and he was experiencing a strong sense of dread. Shocked by the intrusion of what had to be magic, he slowed his breathing and focused inwardly to try and capture its essence, the way Gavin had taught him.

It wasn't that different from any other threat situation. He went into a hyper-alert state, but instead of looking outward for the danger, he was trying to capture an inner comprehension of a threat yet to present itself. The image of Gerry, dead and discarded remained, but a firm and unshakable knowledge now accompanied that. Jean was far too dangerous for Gerry to deal with.

The sharp intake of Stewart's breath brought him back, and seeing the look on his friend's face, he realised that what had felt like a completely inner experience to him must have had some marker that Stewart could read.

"That was magic, wasn't it? That thing you just did, closing down. Your eyes changed, and you went very still." Stewart said in an awed voice.

Brian was about to reply when there was a knock on the door. Quickly shifting his computer around so the screen wasn't visible, he invited the visitor in. As he sauntered into the office, a huge grin seemed to precede the blond Viking. "Hello, boys. Found anything useful?"

Smiling back at their new friend, Brian greeted him with some relief. "Your timing is perfect". Barely waiting for Erik to settle into a vacant chair, Brian launched into a description of what he had just experienced. Seeking reassurance that what he had seen was somehow real, Brian told Erik about the way the vision, or whatever it was, had been triggered.

"This friend of yours, Gerry, you are close?" Erik inquired.

"Absolutely! All three of us spent years together. Training, fighting, and depending on each other. Soldiers. That's the strange part. Before that vision, I wouldn't have doubted Gerry's ability to look after himself in any situation."

Before he could go on, Stewart interjected. "Gerry has saved both of our skins more times than I can count, just the same way as we have saved his."

Erik looked at both of them thoughtfully. "I know you trust your friend, but trust your instinct more. Everything is different when magic is involved. Take your vision at face value. Leave your friend out of this. Remember, Jean has been trained as a magician by one of the best. Morgan is far beyond your ken at this stage. You boys are only just starting to get some small idea of what's at stake here."

Brian, thinking about how Declan had vanished out of Rhonwen's apartment, wondered aloud if Jean, in turn, had trained Declan. "Stewart's right. I think Jean is the key. Whether Morgan is in on it or not, the connection is between Jean and Declan, so we need to find out more about them. If we can't use Gerry to shadow Jean, we must find another way to track him."

Erik gave him a broad smile. "That's a job I can put my hand up for. I am more than a match for this guy. I'll let Gavin know about what you have found. I have been thinking about this and decided that Morgan's involvement in this doesn't make sense. She was instrumental in banishing Scáthach. They hated each other."

Brian looked at this new friend of theirs with more than a bit of awe. He still felt like he was in some sort of fantasy novel and that none of this was real. Reaching up to touch the Amulet nestled against his chest, he looked at Stewart. Was it really only a few days ago that they were living in a rational world where they thought they knew what they could expect from most situations they encountered? The look on Stewart's face mirrored what he was feeling.

Erik, obviously aware that they were struggling, smiled reassuringly. Rising, he unfurled the long limbs he had somehow found space for in the rather inadequate lounge. "How about I keep an eye on our friend, Jean, and you guys can continue to look for Declan."

Stewart suddenly shook his head. Speaking with a certain amount of hesitancy in his voice, he turned to look directly at Erik. "We have another problem. Keira knows about the Amulet, and she has demanded it back."

Brian, picking up on Stewart's unease, started to explain what had happened earlier, but Stewart interrupted. This time with a little more resolve, he put it to Erik that it was Keira" Amulet and that he didn't think it was morally right to keep it from her. Brian watched Erik closely, wondering how he was going to react. It seemed to him that there were some real risks in giving Keira the Amulet. But Stewart was right.

With a wry, lopsided smile, Erik gently replied. "Your sentiments are commendable. However, there is a much more compelling reason to give it back to her. If we don't, Morgan will come and get it, and all hell will break loose."

Brian was startled by his answer. As Erik continued to explain, he felt a growing sense of unease. Apparently, Gavin had been expecting either Keira or Morgan herself to make this demand. He had decided the risk was greater if they tried to keep it. Even with this new information about Jean, Erik was sure that Gavin would want them to give it back. "When did she say she wanted it by?" Erik asked Stewart, who somehow managed to look relieved and spooked at the same time. "End of Business today". Stewart replied.

Erik seemed to do some quick calculating, and then with a reassuring grin, he gently slapped Stewart on the back. "I'll have it here by mid-afternoon. It won't take me long to speak with Gavin and retrieve it from my place."

Bidding them both farewell, he quickly left the office, the door closing behind him, seemingly on its own. Brian looked across at Stewart and shook his head in bewilderment. "I feel like a little boy trying to work out what the adults are up to!"

Stewart looked at him momentarily and then burst into semi-hysterical laughter. "You and me both! Everything I ever believed has been turned on its head. I have a feeling in my gut that it hasn't been there since our first mission in Kosovo. We are way out of our league!"

Taking a deep breath, Brian forced himself to release the tension in his shoulders by shrugging to loosen them up. Watching his friend, he recognised that they had both been pushed close to their limits by the events of the last few days. Like Stewart, he was only just starting to acknowledge that they were no longer in control. They were the grunts, not the leaders. He wasn't used to it, and he didn't like it.

They needed to get some space. To have some time out to assimilate the new paradigm they had found themselves in. Making a decision, he spoke. "Well, we need a break, and I, for one, am hungry. Let's go and get some lunch while we wait for replies to our inquiries. When we get back, we can search for Lydia. We've survived madness and mayhem before. Let's work on doing so again."

45

Keira felt like she was about to explode. Holding her head high and maintaining a neutral expression on her face, she walked purposefully back to her office. She managed to get through the door and close it against prying eyes just in time. She collapsed in her chair, heaving great gulps of air, her stomach lurching as if she was about to throw up.

Morgan had been right! This may not have been a good idea. But after Morgan had told her the truth about her heritage, she felt so empowered! The spell she had cast had worked because she, Keira, was special. Not just some wanna-be witch, but a real one. She had been so sure about coming to work today. She had planned to confront Stewart herself about the Amulet. It had just not occurred to her that he would tell Brian about her using magic. She had trusted him!

Nausea washed over her again, and she gripped the edge of her desk, wondering how she was going to make it through the day. Thinking about what happened in Brian's office made her very uneasy. She hadn't been entirely in control. She just didn't understand what was happening to her, and she didn't like that feeling. Her whole body felt odd.

After a few minutes, her stomach more settled, she decided to call Morgan. The woman had warned her to expect some physical adjustment to having used powerful magic for the first time. But that had been four days ago, and Keira had felt fine this morning. Taking a deep breath, she clamped down on her anxiety and made up her mind to take control back. She was determined to make it through the day. There was no way she would let Stewart or Brian see her as weak.

Knowing that Morgan had been irritated that she hadn't taken her advice and stayed at the house in Kensington, Keira was hesitant to ask her for help. She wasn't convinced that Morgan's agenda was entirely in her best interests. She instinctively knew that Morgan hadn't given her the whole truth. There was a lot more going on than the fallout of one little spell. Keira was not prepared to put herself completely at Morgan's mercy but, on the other hand she needed some help.

She was still tossing it all up in her mind when another wave of nausea hit her. Making a decision, she grabbed at the phone and made the call. Morgan answered immediately. Once Keira had told her what was happening and how ill she was feeling, Morgan suggested she return to Kensington. When Keira demurred, Morgan, to her credit, let it go and didn't try to force the issue. She did, however, demand a fairly detailed description of what Keira was experiencing before offering advice.

Deciding to remain cautious, Keira held back a lot of the stranger stuff. Anyway, how could she even begin to describe it? The rush of lust mixed with anger and the odd sense of herself slipping out of herself! She had no idea what it meant, but she wasn't ready to tell anyone about that just yet. She certainly didn't feel that it was something she wanted to disclose to a woman who was a total stranger.

Morgan proved to have some good ideas about how Keira could restore her equilibrium. As she focused on her core self, repeating the simple spell that Morgan had given her, she felt a sense of calm return and her anxiety fade. Feeling more confident, she then followed the second of Morgan's suggestions, which was to do what were, in essence, basic relaxation exercises.

Thirty minutes later, feeling like herself again, she grabbed her handbag and left the office as discretely as she could. She needed to avoid Stewart and Brian at all costs. She had felt perfectly OK until she had gone to Brian's office. It irked her that she was not as in control as she had expected. Surely her heritage meant she had the upper hand!

Making it downstairs without running into anyone, Keira headed for the local Vegetarian Cafe. She wouldn't normally go anywhere near all that Mung bean and Tofu nonsense, but she knew they would have the tea Morgan had recommended. She needed to think. Morgan was much more than some Coven leaders. Her knowledge of Keira's family had been creepy. And the Grimoire and Amulet! Keira was still reeling from being told they had been in her family for centuries. She still couldn't believe that her boring, staid old family were the descendent's of real witches with absolute power.

Tucking herself into the corner of a booth where she could watch the street and the door of the cafe, she picked up the menu and looked for a tea based on Camomile. Surprisingly, she found some of the offerings appealing and realised she was hungry. Ordering her lunch, she sat back and started to review what Morgan had told her about her family. Ninian! No wonder they changed it. It really was an awful name, straight out of some old-world fairy tale. Or worse! A fantasy novel!

Staring out the window, Keira let her mind drift as she watched the lunchtime crowds rushing along the street. It was all well and good to have the upper hand by using a bit of magic, but there was a lot to this that she needed to learn. Thinking about the spell she had cast, vivid images of those strange sexual experiences intruded. How much had Stewart told Brian? How could he? Biting her lip, Keira suppressed the emotions that threatened to swamp her. She was more than angry with Stewart. She was infuriated that this was going to undermine all of her plans for Brian.

Her chain of thought was interrupted by the waitress bringing her lunch, and as she settled back into her solitary contemplation, she found her thoughts moved on to a different tack. Did it really matter any more what Brian thought of her? Maybe the original plan needed modifying anyway. Now that she knew she had other more intriguing opportunities, a management role in a security firm might not be her next step. This thought started to take shape, and as she sipped her tea, Keira allowed her mind to roam around these new possibilities.

46

Jean found Morgan in her study. Sensing that she was warded to the same level as the previous day, he realised that it hadn't been just Gavin she was suspicious of during that meeting. Filing that insight away to think about later, he smiled warmly, making sure it reached his eyes and bent down to hug her as he greeted her. Putting the folder he was carrying on the desk, he moved around to stand next to her.

"You will be pleased to know that my research has been quite successful. The people you wanted to know about are all involved in some way with Gavin."

"What all of them? That's interesting." She replied in a neutral voice. Nothing about her reaction betrayed her thoughts, but Jean hadn't spent the last three decades living with this woman without learning how to read her. She was guarded and watchful. He wondered briefly if she had already known this before continuing.

Jean had spent the morning figuring out how he would protect his interests and keep Morgan from figuring out that he was after the amulets. Looking through all of the information Max had given him, he realised that with a bit of misdirection, he could destroy the fragile alliance that was forming between the two immortals. If he could fan Morgan's rage against Gavin, he would have a better chance of slipping under her radar.

Bending down, he flipped open the folder. Pointing to the photos of Brian Poole and Stewart Eggleston, he continued, "These two are not easy to find. They work for one of the biggest security organisations in the country, so I knew they would be protective of personal information. I didn't expect to find them on Facebook, but there is practically no public record of either of them apart from their birth and educational records. They are the same age, come from affluent families and went to Eton and Cambridge together."

Morgan looked up at him sharply. "So, what *did* you find?" Jean grinned down at her. He had the upper hand, and she knew it. She had managed not to react to their names, but there was no way she hadn't recognised them. He continued, "For a start, the only way to trace these guys is by hacking into government records. When someone leaves such a light footprint in today's world, it's deliberate. I eventually found them in a secure defence personnel database. They were Special Forces. That's why the secrecy. But the interesting thing is that they both still have active IDs."

Morgan interjected. "So You're saying they still work for the government".

"That's right. The firm they work for is not what it seems." Jean replied.

Morgan sat back in her chair, her face revealing nothing, but an increase in her heart rate alerted Jean to her interest. Her expression remained neutral as she responded. "Well, Keira told me she worked with this Stewart. He was the one at her apartment when I invited her to visit me here. They have a relationship that is probably more important than she realises. "What did you find out about Keira?"

Carefully keeping his own wards as tight as possible, Jean turned the documents over to reveal the information he had gathered about Keira and her family. He had carefully culled any hint of the family's change of name several centuries earlier. "As you can see, there is more to her as she is a modern girl who uses social media. However, I was impressed by her caution. She doesn't expose herself."

Jean observed Morgan as she looked through the information. He knew that Morgan would have already accessed all of this and more in her time with the girl, but he didn't know how much Keira knew about her ancestry. Turning over the papers, Morgan came across the photo of Rhonwen and cocked her head. Her eyebrows arched as she looked at him. Jean smiled in acknowledgment of her interest as he continued with his report.

"You were right, this is Rhonwen Tierney, and she works at the same company as Poole's Executive Assistant".

Seeing a slight flaring of Morgan's nostrils, Jean knew she had started to put it together as he continued to outline what he had decided to tell her.

"She doesn't seem as engaged in social media as Keira, so there isn't much about her apart from the usual records of her birth and schooling. She went to the University of London and didn't seem to be connected to either of the men or Keira prior to them working together."

Jean bent down and rummaged through the folder as he continued, pulling out a photo of Declan. "The most interesting fact about her is that she is related to this other guy. He is another face you asked me to follow up on."

Morgan picked up the photo and looked closely at Declan's sharp features. She asked, "What's his name?" Jean replied. "He is her cousin, Declan Tierney, and I found him easily on the Police database because he is wanted for murder."

That made Morgan sit up. "So, how is he connected to Gavin? I knew that Gavin knew Stewart because he came here specifically, on Stewart's behalf, to check that Keira was happy to stay here with me. But he said they were acquaintances and that Stewart had no idea Keira was playing around with real magic."

Keeping a tight rein on his satisfaction at how well this briefing was going, Jean looked into Morgan's eyes as he spoke, "I don't know if he knows Gavin, but I know that the other three are connected to Gavin because they have all been at his place for a fair chunk of the last few days."

He saw a flicker of anger, quickly hidden and felt her tense up as he continued, "This Declan character is some sort of petty criminal, and the Police are interested in his connection to Gavin because he stole something that Gavin sold Rhonwen. That was on Saturday. He broke into Rhonwen's flat and killed a friend during the robbery."

"What did Declan steal from Rhonwen?"

"Some antique. I am not sure what because the Police have kept it under wraps, but it was small, and I think it might have been jewellery."

He couldn't help but respect how well-controlled Morgan really was, given the bombshell or was it bombshells he had just delivered into her lap? In the research he had done when he first found out about the amulets, it had been evident that she had been associated with all of the families in the past.

As she looked through the file, her mouth a little tight and her jaw just that bit too clenched, he made himself comfortable in one of the chairs across from her desk. It was time to direct her thinking away from him. "So what do you think Gavin is up to?"

He paused before continuing. "Do you think that this girl your looking after is genuine?"

47

Having left the boys huddled over their computers, Erik headed back to his place to bring Gavin up to speed. The moment he stepped through the door, he could feel the tension. Gavin and the Banach men had obviously been at each other again. The problem was that he needed to understand where they were all coming from. Morgan was dangerous and deceptive. She had proven herself untrustworthy time and time again. But despite it all, she wasn't evil, just incredibly self-centred. Morgan was definitely all about Morgan! *And always has been and always will be.*

"Hello!" He called as he made his way down the hall. As he went through the door into the lounge, he put a big grin on his face. "You know the rules, boys! No unsheathed weapons, mundane or magical, in my house. OK?"

He saw Gavin visibly relax as he gave him a lopsided smile. "Glad You're back."

"As am I," Rouan retorted as he put a coffee pot and some mugs on the table. "Perhaps you can talk some sense into Gavin about trusting Morgan".

Glancing around, Erik realised that Connell and Rhonwen weren't in the room. Before he could ask after them, Gavin, having noted his look, informed him that the Inspector had called Rhonwen. "Since she is still unable to go home, he offered her the opportunity to get some more of her things. He is hunting, of course. Trying to see if he can get any more information from her. Connell is with her, not just to keep the Inspector at bay, but to protect her."

"Why? What's happened?" Erik said in a puzzled voice.

Rouan and Gavin exchanged a worried look, and Gavin pulling a chair out from the table, invited him to sit, replying. "A lot!"

As Rouan organised the coffee, Gavin filled him in on the story Rhonwen had told him earlier. Erik listened closely as Gavin told him what Rhonwen had said about the woman in the park.

"So, after she and Brian left the Inspector yesterday, they fought, and she ran off into the park on her own, right?"

Gavin nodded and continued. "She was completely out of Brian's sight and hiding from him under one of those old trees where the foliage almost hits the ground. She was approached by a woman who was extremely menacing. She really frightened Rhonwen badly."

"What makes you think this was something other than the usual random violence that happens all the time?" Erik asked, feeling alert in response to Gavin and Rouan's obvious concern.

"Nothing we can put a finger on, but all three of us had the same instinctive reaction, and we are all positive it wasn't random." Gavin replied.

Thinking about it, Erik had to concede that there was a lot about this whole situation that didn't make sense. Yet! "There are a lot of seemingly unconnected pieces to this puzzle, Gavin." Erik finally announced. "I have just come back from Brian's office. The boys have found a connection between Declan and Jean Bran."

Before he could continue, Rouan interjected, turning to Gavin with a smug look on his face. "See! We were right about Morgan."

Erik, seeing the look on Gavin's face, was quick to explain further. "Well, we have no proof that she is connected to Declan or that she knows anything about what Jean is up to. But we are pretty sure that Jean could lead us to Declan."

Erik went on to tell them everything that the boys had uncovered about Declan and his activities in Europe. When he told them about

Brian's premonition about his friend Gerry, Gavin agreed it was best if Gerry was left out of any surveillance. Pouring himself another coffee, Erik went on to tell the others about Keira's demand to have her Amulet returned to her.

"Well, we knew that was coming," responded Rouan.

Looking across at Gavin, Erik waited to see his reaction. He was still undecided and was interested in Gavin's opinion. Knowing Gavin as well as he did, he was not surprised to see warring emotions and indecision in his expression.

"I have been thinking about this all morning." Gavin replied slowly. "I believe that it is in all our interests for Keira to have possession of her Amulet. She needs to be told about its protective power." Seeing the look on Rouan's face, he held up his hand to forestall his comment and continued. "From what you have told me of her conversation with Brian and Stewart, it doesn't look like Morgan told her the whole truth of her inheritance. Or of the danger she is in."

"Are you sure?" Erik asked, looking over towards Rouan.

He had spent many years observing Rouan as he grew up and trusted his intuitive and intelligent grasp of things. What he saw now was a very thoughtful look that suggested that, like Gavin, he could see a benefit in this plan. Turning back towards Gavin, he saw that he was also keenly watching Rouan for his reaction.

"You think you can use this to give Keira more power in her relationship with Morgan, aren'tyou?" Mused Rouan, a slow smile crossing his mouth.

Gavin seemed to relax a little with this response. "Yes. Even if Morgan isn't part of whatever Jean and Declan are up to, I think it will work better for us if Keira is not fully aligned with her. This could inject a sliver of distrust if we handle it properly."

They spent half an hour tossing around ideas, finally coming up with a plan they could all agree on. Erik was preparing to head back to Brian's office when Connell and Rhonwen returned. He was pleased to see that Rhonwen had relaxed a little. It was obvious she liked Connell and had responded to his fatherly approach. She had agreed to go up to Whitehaven with the Banachs for the next few days, and he was relieved about that. She was fragile and emotional at the moment, and he had always found the Banach household full of warmth and security. It had always been a bit of a Haven't of his own. Every generation had been the same. It was their gift and their strength. They had used their magic to bind themselves to the good, and that was why they had weathered the centuries intact and strong. The other families had all fallen into division and greed. Their magic lost through complacency, inattention or rivalry. It would help Rhonwen to appreciate her heritage and to see magic as a positive manifestation within the world.

He was just about to leave when Gavin pulled him aside. Looking deeply into his eyes, he spoke quietly, "I might have been wrong about Morgan, Erik. I hope not, but if I am, this task of watching Jean is very dangerous. I have no doubt you can handle Jean, but if Morgan is involved, we will need help. I am going to try and find Finn. He has been off in Eastern Europe on some errand he wouldn't talk about, but he is accessible. I might have to actually go to him in person, but I will try to avoid being out of town for long. If for no other reason than Inspector Riley will be watching for me to slip up. He still thinks I'm his best suspect."

Thinking about what Gavin had said, Erik found the idea of another Immortal helping out reassuring. He had no personal experience of dealing with Scáthach, but he had no doubt that she was as formidable as he had heard. There was a real risk that if Morgan was involved, this was already too big for the two of them to deal with.

"It's OK. I'll be careful not to let either of them know I'm watching. I'll call you if I find anything important before you get back." He replied with a smile. Clasping each other's arms, they said their goodbyes, and he headed out the door.

48

Stewart observed Keira turn her Amulet over in her hands. He could sense the connection as if the stone had a life of its own. She looked up at him, eyes filled with wonder. "I can feel it!" She frowned. "How did you know about it?"

"I was looking at the book, and as I ran my hands over the engraving on the front, I heard the little click of the lock". He answered truthfully.

"But why didn't you tell me about it?" Keira demanded as she held the Amulet up to the light of the window.

"Because it's not the first one I have seen, and I didn't know what to do." Stewart said quietly. He sat back, waiting for a reaction.

Startled, Keira looked at Stewart, a suspicious look in her eyes. "What do you mean it's not the only one?"

At that moment, as if on cue, Brian and Erik came through the door. Keira's expression froze. Stewart got the distinct impression that she was about to start shouting. He was relieved when she didn't. Following her gaze, he saw that she was staring at Erik, who was smiling at her as if she was the only person on the planet. Stewart felt a tug of sheer rage. It occurred to him that he was jealous. The sadness he felt at the conflict between Keira and himself was only just below the surface and a threat to his emotional equilibrium. Taking a deep breath, he pushed it all backdown and focused on what was going to be a very difficult conversation.

Walking across the room, Erik held out his hand to Keira to introduce himself. She automatically reached out to shake his hand. The touch visibly relaxed her. She appeared oblivious to Brian, who followed Erik into the room. He closed the door behind them. Continuing to speak to her as he held her tiny hand in what, for all intent and purpose, was an embrace, Erik explained that he was there as a friend. "This beautiful object you are holding is your inheritance. It is an Amulet of Power and rightfully belongs to you, but it is an enormous responsibility. Will you let me tell you about it?"

Stewart looked over at Brian and saw his feeling of awe reflected in his friend's expression. Erik was smooth. Stewart doubted if any woman could resist him. Certainly not Keira. Not at this moment in time. She allowed him to take her over to the lounge under the window, where he sat her down, asking if she was comfortable. He then turned and waved both Stewart and Brian over to some chairs that had been placed strategically across from the lounge.

Keira looked puzzled by this and a little waspishly asked, "What has this got to do with them?" This was when Erik, holding her gaze, calmly explained that her Amulet was one of five. As he went on to explain that there were five families of ancient linage who owned them, Brian retrieved his from the little pouch under his shirt. "Stewart recognised your Amulet because he had seen Brian's."

Looking over at Brian, Keira immediately saw his Amulet nestled in the centre of his now exposed chest. "I don't understand." She whispered. "That's why I am here." Erik responded kindly.

It was an hour later. They were all a little rung out from the intensity of the experience. Keira had needed a lot of careful managing through the revelations about Scáthach and the possibility that she was trying to use her to get back into the world. Stewart felt that he had been stripped bare and exposed. He did not doubt that Keira felt the same. Only for her, there was the added dimension of a real threat to her safety.

Erik had taken a lot of time to explain how she could use the Amulet to protect herself. He gave her a gold chain he had brought with him, so he helped her thread the Amulet onto it and put it around her neck.

"Keep this on at all times. It will warm if you are under threat. The hotter it gets, indicates how much danger you are in."

Looking up from her new necklace, Keira asked the question they were all hoping she would ask. "How much does Morgan know about the Amulets? She knows who my family are and that they had changed their name."

Erik had been careful to avoid any mention of Morgan's immortality but had affirmed that she was a very knowledgeable and skilled practitioner of magic. He was now able to honestly tell her that since she knew what family Keira came from, she would also know about all the other families who possessed an Amulet.

Stewart was just starting to allow himself to relax when he saw a calculating look flash on Keira's face. Turning away from Erik, she looked straight at Brian. "What about the other three families? Who are they?"

That question was still hanging between them, dangerous and menacing when they were all startled by the sound of knocking at the door. Stewart, whose office they were sitting in, jumped out of his chair and went over to the door. They had asked not to be disturbed, so he was surprised by the intrusion. Opening the door, he saw Sylvia, Michael's PA, outside in the hall, looking flustered and distracted. "I am sorry, Mr Eggleston, but the Detective insisted that I announce him."

In that instant, Stewart became aware that Inspector Riley was standing off to the side.

Quickly evaluating the chances of being able to re-direct the Inspector to Brian's office as unlikely, Stewart greeted him in a loud enough voice to alert the others. He hoped that by taking his time to thank Sylvia for her help, Brian and Keira would have enough time to secrete their amulets under their clothes.

As he ushered Inspector Riley into the office, he felt a slight chill and heard a very faint tinkle of a bell. Looking around, he realised that Erik and Keira were no longer sitting on the lounge. Keira, a slightly startled look on her face, was being ushered towards the door by Brian while Erik, looking totally different, followed them.

"Thank you, Ms. Blair. Mr North, if you don't mind waiting in my office, we will continue this meeting in a short while."

Feeling greatly relieved, Stewart offered the Inspector the recently vacated chair and sat on the lounge.

Having closed the door behind the others, Brian took the lead and greeted him politely. "What brings you here today, Inspector? Have you found Declan Tierney yet?"

"No." There was a tone of frustration in his voice. "I am here because I have just had a very interesting chat with a Professor Hayden Cooper. He tells me that you two have met." Then, turning towards Stewart, he continued. "In fact, he met both of you here at this office on Saturday morning. Is that correct?"

Brian answered. "Yes, that is correct. May I ask what Professor Cooper said about that meeting?"

The Inspector made a show of unbuttoning his coat and taking out his notepad. "Well, as you know, identifying the object of a theft is pretty standard, so one of my Constables put the drawing of the "jewel" that Ms. Tierney described into a database of known antique jewellery. He found an entry that matched the description with Dr Cooper's contact details attached."

His eyes narrowing, the Inspector stared closely at Brian. "Your meeting with Dr Cooper, happily for you and Mr Eggleston here, provides you both with an alibi for the actual theft at Ms. Tierney's apartment. However, there are serious questions about what it was that was stolen, and you know more about that than you have led me to believe."

Before Brian could respond, the Inspector, shifting around so that he could undo his coat, retrieved a sheaf of documents from his pocket and continued.

"When exactly were you planning on telling me that you possess one of these, ah, Amulets that Dr Cooper is so excited about? He seems to think that the jewel stolen from Ms. Tierney's mirror is either one of these amulets or a copy. Surely you recognised the similarity from the description Ms. Tierney gave me of the missing piece?"

Stewart felt himself sinking further into the lounge, a fervent hope that the Inspector would forget he was there filling his mind.

49

Having been initially startled by the sudden shift in Erik's appearance and being unceremoniously expelled from Stewart's office, Keira quickly regained her equilibrium. As soon as Erik closed the door, he reverted to his appearance and Keira, hearing the faint chime again, immediately picked up on the relationship. "That sound. Like a bell or something. Does that always happen when you do magic?"

She noticed Erik looking at her thoughtfully. After a few moments, having obviously decided, he gestured towards the lounge. "Come, let's sit and talk while we wait for the others." Keira followed him, and as they settled into the comfortable old leather, Erik folded himself into the corner to look at Keira and continued.

"When the magic comes from within, formed by your will and focused through you, it makes a sound. But only those with talent can hear it."

"What do you mean?" Keira asked in a puzzled voice. "I worked a spell from the book and didn't hear a bell".

Erik smiled as he replied. "Well, you used a spell that was not personal to you. It was a generic spell that had been compiled by other witches, somewhat like a recipe. These are very useful, and all talented magic users can use them to affect the world around them, but they don't have the same level of power as unique intrinsic magic."

Keira turned this idea over in her mind. She liked the idea of having her own personal power. Instinctively reaching for the Amulet nestled between her breasts under her shirt, she felt the same strange connection she had felt earlier. It was like the stone was part of her, and as she held it, she felt her mind sharpening, her perceptions becoming more acute. Looking across at Erik, she became aware of his gaze and immediately recognised that he was immensely more powerful than she had ever imagined.

"Morgan doesn't need spells, does she?" She asked quietly, watching him closely for his reaction, trying to figure out the underlying tensions between these people she had just met. Erik answered in the same gentle and unemotional manner that he had used consistently over the last hour or so. "No, she doesn't. Morgan is very adept and very dangerous. It would be best if you were very careful around her. She always has her agenda, which is always about what she wants."

"But my amulet will protect me. You said that it would tell me when I am in danger."

"That's right". Erik replied. "But you have no knowledge or experience. You are vulnerable at this time. Magic isn't a game. It's not to be used frivolously."

Erik continued speaking about the different types of magic in the world and the training she would need to safely navigate this new domain. Keira listened politely, but this guy, cute though he was, didn't seem to be interested in telling her anything she wanted to know. Stroking her Amulet, she felt her mind opening up, and intuitively she knew that this magic was nothing like she had expected. Morgan might be dangerous, but she was interesting. And she wasn't the only one with an agenda. Keira was becoming convinced that Erik was working some magic on her. She felt too calm. She didn't trust Stewart or Brian, but for some reason, she was sitting here, just waiting for them.

Keira focused on keeping her anger under control. She still had a whole heap of questions, and she would not let emotion distract her. She decided to take advantage of being alone with Erik and put on her most charming smile.

"We were interrupted before you could tell me about the other three families. Do you know them? Are they aware of their heritage?"

As Erik started to answer her, she realised that the pitch of his voice was very low. There was a sort of lulling quality to it that she could feel reverberating through her chest. *So it's how he uses his voice. That's a neat trick. I want to be able to do that.*

As Erik spoke about how nearly all the old knowledge had been lost over the centuries, Keira became increasingly frustrated. *Another bloody history lesson!* Why didn't he want to tell her who the other families were? Something was teasing at the edges of her mind—a vague memory of something Morgan had said intruded and started to take shape.

"Stewart!" She almost hissed his name. All her calmness having suddenly evaporated, she felt a whole lot of different sensations at once, but mostly rage. "What has Stewart got to do with all of this? He doesn't have an Amulet, does he? But he is involved. I know it."

Before Erik could respond, the door opened to let Brian and Stewart into the office. They had obviously heard her. Both looked guilty somehow. Then, it struck her. What were they doing talking to the Police? That must be about that drama over the weekend with Rhonwen. She looked at Erik and realised he had disguised himself to hide from that Inspector.

She had picked up on the fact that some jewellery had been stolen from Rhonwen's place. Which was surprising, given Rhonwen's complete lack of style. That she would own anything anyone else wanted didn't make sense. But now? *No! She couldn't stand it. Not her!* Her rage felt like a visceral living entity. She almost spat out her next words. "I think it's time you told me about this robbery and what Rhonwen has to do with all of this?" And looking directly at Stewart, she added. "And how exactly are you involved, because you are not some innocent bystander?"

Keira watched a strange look pass between Brian and Erik. Then Brian turned towards her and looked intently into her eyes as he replied. "Rhonwen's family are also one of the five families. It was her family's Amulet that was stolen on Saturday."

Keira took a big breath, sucking the air in and holding it, to give herself time to calm down. She marvelled at how well she was keeping it together. In reality, what she really wanted to do was to hit someone. Deliberately modulating her voice, she asked as calmly as she could, "Did Rhonwen know about her Amulet?"

Brian hesitated. She knew he was choosing his words very carefully. "No. Rhonwen's family, like yours and mine, didn't pass on their family history, so she didn't know that she had possession of an Amulet."

Keira felt a surge of hope as she asked. "So she doesn't have any magic or power?"

Brian gave her a stern look, obviously having picked up on the main thrust of her interest. But it was Erik who answered her question in a gently chiding voice. "Rhonwen is a victim in this, Keira. She had no idea of her inheritance, and before she could be introduced to her family history, her Amulet was stolen."

Keira didn't need to be told Rhonwen was a victim. That girl was a born victim, and Keira was sick of everyone wanting her to care. Looking straight at Brian, rather than responding to Erik, she felt herself willing him to tell her everything that was going on. "I don't get it. You're telling me that you, Rhonwen and I are all descendants of three of the five families, and we happen to be all working here together."

Before he could answer, she forged on, her voice becoming more demanding and shriller. Turning towards Stewart, who up to that moment had remained utterly still and quiet, she continued. "And what about you? How do you fit into all of this, Stewart?"

50

"Well, that went well." Stewart said wryly as he poured himself a Whisky and offered the decanter to the other two men. Erik gave himself a generous nip and gulped it straight down before responding.

"I underestimated that girl. She slipped out of my control the moment the Inspector interrupted us. Although I must say, it was probably pretty shaky already."

Brian ran his hand through his hair and, taking his own rather full glass with him, wandered over to the window to stare out at the city. His head hurt. Keira's rage had been palpable. In fact, it had been loud! He needed to think. Nothing had gone to plan. Keira was now in possession of most of the information they had, and knowing her, it wouldn't be long before she figured out what they hadn't told her.

"I am particularly concerned by her interest in the thief." He muttered; his back still turned from the others. "At least she doesn't know it was Declan or his connection with Rhonwen."

He felt, more than he saw, Stewart moving across the room to stand beside him. "Yes. Frankly, I was a bit stunned at how easily she ignored the fact that he actually killed someone to get to the Amulet," responded Stewart.

Still holding the Decanter, he poured himself another shot and offered to top up Brian's. "No, thanks, Stew. I think I need to eat something before I have any more to drink." Turning back to look at Erik, he asked, "So! What's our next step?"

"Well, I have to keep an eye on Morgan and Jean, so I had better get going". Replied Erik. "You should let Gavin and the Banachs know about our spectacular failure to align Keira with us. We probably need to watch her too. She has plans. I could see them forming in that sly brain of hers. With that said Erik placed his empty glass on Brian's desk and, collecting his coat, left the boys to their thoughts.

Almost a lifetime spent together, in some of the most challenging circumstances possible, meant that Brian and Stewart were comfortable with long silences between them. Both cradled their glasses and focused on their thoughts. Brian was acutely aware of Stewart's conflicted feelings about Keira, and he found them echoed in his confusion about Rhonwen. She had disappointed him with her lack of emotional strength, yet he felt he was being far too harsh in his judgement.

Eventually, having thought about it from every angle, he decided to pack it away for now and get on with the practical realities of their situation. The Inspector remained suspicious but seemed to have accepted their story for now. It was plausible, since neither of them had seen the stolen jewel, and Rhonwen had not seen Brian's Amulet, they would not have put it together immediately.

Brian, maintaining his persona as a completely rational Security Executive, had suggested that the diamond's value as a stone had attracted Declan. Using what he had hoped were his best persuasive powers, he had downplayed the archeological significance and the attached mythology as a factor. Now, reflecting on the conversation, he wondered if he had been kidding himself. Turning to Stewart, he interrupted his friend's thoughts. "What do you think the Inspector's next move will be?"

Stewart looked up from contemplating the whisky in the bottom of his glass, his expression thoughtful. He hesitated for a minute before answering. "Probably what we would do. He will watch us, and Rhonwen, hoping we will do the work for him. There is no way he wouldn't realise that we will investigate this ourselves. He will have already done his homework on the company and know that we have better resources than he does."

"I agree. We are going to have to give him the opportunity to tag along but somehow keep him in the dark about the real story." Replied Brian.

"Well then, he can tag along while we have dinner," said Stewart with a laugh. I Haven't eaten since breakfast. We had better call Gavin first and organise how to meet without the Inspector's watchers seeing us."

51

Keira couldn't believe the fuss Michael was making about her wanting some time off. For heaven's sake, it was only a week! You"d think the world would end if she weren't at her desk. He hadn't blinked an eye when that bitch Rhonwen didn't come in this week. Well, tough! She had the leave owing, and she was going to take it. And now he was in Brian's office whinging to the boys. If only he knew what those two have been up to!

Letting herself out the security door and heading to the lift, Keira took a very deep breath. She had bigger fish to fry than this little fucking company. If Michael had any idea of what she was capable of, he would have kept his mouth shut. After the last few days, Keira was feeling very good about herself. Morgan had introduced her to a world she hadn't known existed. Keira wasn't stupid, she knew Morgan had her own agenda, but on the other hand, Keira knew she needed to come up to speed with this magic stuff quickly.

Taking the lift down to the ground floor, she made her way out to the street. She had organised a car through the co-op she belonged to and wanted to pick it up and do a few errands while she was at lunch. Hailing a taxi, she gave the driver the address and then focused on checking her emails. She couldn't believe her luck. Her parents had gone to the south of France for a couple of weeks, and her brother was still in New Zealand so that she would have the family house to herself.

Over the last few days, using Morgan's experience and training, she had been learning to use a new form of memory retrieval. She had been careful to censor what she told Morgan. There was no way she would let that woman have any power over her. Then, last night while she was practising on her own at home, she had had a particularly useful breakthrough. She had remembered the secret door in the library of her family's home.

Dismissing the sense of unease that suddenly intruded into her consciousness, she had pushed through the barrier in her mind. The nausea and dizziness resolved as the memory cleared. She had been a child of maybe four or five when she had seen her Aunt Judith emerge from the wall next to the fireplace. Looking at the images now as an adult, she could see that Judith had been excited, her face flushed. When she had seen Keira watching, she had looked back over her shoulder and shaken her head, then touched the carving beside the mantle piece. The opening in the wall had slid quietly closed.

After that, Keira could only remember Judith coming across the room and smiling down at her. Until Morgan had taught her to seek out her past experiences, Keira hadn't conceived of the possibility that there were spells that could either cover up or altogether remove memories. And now, she had not only found out that her memories had been tampered with, but she had also found out that at least one member of her family was still practising magic when she was a child.

The present intruded as the taxi pulled up to the curb outside the garage. Glancing at the time as she closed her mail, Keira realised she wouldn't return to the office much before two. She was irritated at having to comply with other people's timetables. But as she stowed her bag in the car and settled in behind the wheel, she felt the anger melt away. She didn't need to put up with this for much longer.

Driving out of the garage, she thought about all of the possibilities that were now open to her. Keira could feel a visceral excitement filling her with a real rush. It was as good as sex. *Oh well, maybe not that good, but almost!* She just loved magic. She knew it was the power that it gave her or rather the way it filled her, that she loved. Keira felt a little tug of common sense, reminding her that anything that felt this good was bound to be addictive, but she easily pushed it back out of her mind.

52

Brian had been chasing up some of the clues to his family history given to him by his father, while Stewart followed up some of his own leads. He was frustrated by the ordinariness of what he had found and glad of the interruption as Stewart entered the office. An affluent and well-connected family, the Pooles had contributed their sons to the defence forces of England for centuries. Through well-planned marriages, their daughters had aligned them with most of the other old families in Wales, where Brian's parents still lived.

"Found anything useful?" Stewart inquired as he settled himself into a chair near the window.

"Not really. But Dad said there are boxes of papers in the attic in the townhouse in Aberystwyth. I think I will have to head down there tomorrow. I thought the army's records would give me a lead on when the Amulet went to Europe. I was sure I would find that one of my forbearers had died while stationed in the Balkans, but it doesn't look like it. At least not for the last three hundred years. What about you?"

Stewart grinned, a mischievous twinkle lighting up his blue eyes. "Actually, I have just had a fascinating conversation with my great aunt Mary. She said that when you and I met at school, her mother, my great-grandmother, made a comment that she had never forgotten. In fact, she remembered the words exactly. Apparently, Grandma said, “We're in for trouble. The Pooles and the Egglestons always come together when the darkness comes”."

Brian felt a cold shiver up his spine. "You know, I also looked for your family in the army's records. They appear pretty regularly in the same regiments and theatres of war as the Pooles. Not every generation, but a fair number of them. We need to widen the search beyond the obvious. Which reminds me, Hayden called earlier. He hasn't had much luck, either. Although the original sources mention the story of the Amulets, there is very little detail."

Stewart wriggled into the chair as he replied:

"Yes, when I spoke with him on Wednesday, he said he was looking for the names of the other families but couldn't find any reference to their identities".

"Just as well, really", mused Brian. "The problem is that he is a bit like a dog with a bone. His interest really spiked when the Inspector told him there was a second Amulet."

Brian had planned to ask Stewart about Keira, but their conversation was interrupted by a knock on the door. It was Michael, his mouth set and his eyes hard. "Did either of you talk to Keira today?" He said in a tight, infuriated voice.

Brian knew Michael had been swamped with extra work with Rhonwen on unexpected leave. It had left a considerable gap in the team. Although he and Stewart had worked hard to keep their projects on track, it had been Michael who had to answer to the clients. Brian looked over to Stewart, who suddenly looked wary. He shifted in his chair uneasily as he answered in the negative. He hadn't seen Keira all day, and over the last few days, he had been very aware of her in the office. Her demeanour had been brittle and distant as she had gone about her work, and she had only spoken to him when she absolutely had to.

It turned out that Stewart had seen her arrive earlier in the morning but had not spoken with her. Michael then told them that she had just informed him that she needed to take leave because of some family emergency. When he had tried to negotiate with her, citing the pressure of deadlines already agreed to, she had refused to be flexible and had threatened to resign.

"You know what!" Michael said. "I am tempted to let her, but finding replacements is very time-consuming, and as you know, we can't just use temps".

He suddenly slumped down into the other chair next to Stewart. He looked tired. Brian felt sorry for him. With their sensitive work, it wasn't easy to have two staff members off. Brian knew he needed to devise a solution that didn't involve either Stewart or himself working over the weekend. Gavin was back, and they had a lot to do. Thinking quickly, he came up with an idea.

"What about Jennifer? She is smart and ambitious. Rhonwen has been training her up over the last few months. I'm sure she would love the opportunity to prove herself."

Michael's face lightened considerably as he thought about it. Looking at his watch, he jumped up from the chair and headed for the door. "Thanks, Brian. I should be able to catch her before she goes to lunch. She can hand over her portfolio to Felicity this afternoon, and I will orientate her to Keira's project on Monday." He grinned at them as he opened the door. "This will unsettle the status quo. It could be a good thing.

Stewart looked at Brian. "Keira won't like him giving Jennifer her project. I really don't want to be around for the slaughter. I have some work to do at the Ministry, so I think I'll head over there now." He said with a rueful smile.

Brian, who wouldn't have minded being able to disappear himself, just grinned at him. "It's OK. I'll meet you at my place. Erik and Gavin will get there later on, and I'll get Gerry to stop off at the Indian place for some food when he drives me home."

53

Rhonwen was staring out the window, watching the ocean teasing the rocks. Gentle little waves just touched the edge of the land before quickly retreating into the bay. She had been at the Banachs for the last few days and had found it peaceful and inviting. She felt like she was starting to regain some of her sense of the Rhonwen she was before all of this happened. Connell and Rouan's family were warm and welcoming. Their attention and care had enveloped her, and yet, at the same time, she had been given space and time for herself. Sitting here, she was tempted to let the rest sort all of this out. Part of her still didn't want to know about magic. It somehow felt out of place in the twenty-first century. But she was not prepared to be excluded from what was rightfully hers.

The mere thought of Keira and Brian in possession of these powerful artefacts, while hers was in the hands of the cousin, gnawed at her. She knew she had become obsessed but hated being excluded and powerless. All because that weasel Declan had stolen her birthright. Taking one last look at the little cove below the house, she got up and made her way down the hall to the room she had been given. Everyone was out, so this was her chance to slip away for a while. She would walk into the village and call a cab from there. Grabbing her coat and bag, her iPad already tucked into the side pocket, she quietly let herself out of the house. Neve,

Connell's wife, was down at the far end of the property in the greenhouse, so it would be a while before she knew Rhonwen was gone.

She had a pretty good idea of where she needed to go. Knott's Wood was a fair distance, so she had booked a hire car from a firm in Whitehaven. If she was right, Declan was hiding out at the old hunting lodge. No one had been there for decades, but it had remained in the family, almost forgotten, and she was positive Declan knew about it. She also knew he was dangerous, but she refused to allow herself to hesitate. Her common sense told her this was stupid, that she was mad even to consider it, but it was her Amulet, and she would get it back.

It was lunchtime by the time she arrived at the edge of the lake. Parking the car, she started preparing for her plan's next stage. She quickly changed into walking boots and transferred all of her stuff from her handbag to a day pack. The parcel on the back seat was next. Unwrapping the packaging, she exposed the wicked-looking hunting knife she had bought from the sports shop. She looked at it, turning it over in her hand, her heart pounding with fear but also with rage. Deliberately squashing her feelings, she took a deep breath to calm herself and stowed it in her pack.

Once she locked the car, she hefted the pack onto her back. She started off towards the cabin, following the path around the lake. She had estimated that she had two hours of walking ahead of her and that it would be early afternoon when she arrived. As she hiked through the woods, enjoying the lovely warm spring day, she found herself thinking about Declan. Her plan was to watch the cabin to see if he was there, and if he was, she could tell Connell. Then he and the others could sort Declan out and get her Amulet back. But something felt wrong. Shaking her head, she tried to grasp hold of an idea that seemed to be sliding around her mind but not taking shape. As her confidence in her plan wavered, she was overwhelmed by a sudden rush of fear. She could have just told Connell and Rouan about this place. *What was she doing here on her own?* Stopping dead in her tracks, she felt like she had just woken up from some sort of dream. And then the headache hit her like a sledgehammer. Dropping to her knees, dizzy and nauseated, the last thing she saw was the vague outline of someone emerging from the brush next to her.

ꟷꟷ

As he walked across the lawn towards the house, Rouan felt a little spark of excitement. He had been aware that his desire had been ignited from the first time he had seen Rhonwen, and he had enjoyed the last few days. Knowing it was a bad idea didn't change the fact that he was looking forward to spending some time with her.

He had decided to try and distract her by taking her down to the cove. It was a special place, a place of power, and its magic was one of healing. An excellent place to go if you are troubled. Stamping his feet on the mat to shake off the loose mud, he opened the back door. The moment he entered the house; he felt its emptiness. Having spoken to his mother down at the greenhouse, he knew that Rhonwen was supposed to be there. His mother had left her in the kitchen eating breakfast. Rouan's sense of alarm started to grow as he quickly checked the house and found that not only was Rhonwen gone, she had been gone for well over an hour. There was no sign of anyone else having been in the house. All the wards were still in place.

Why would she go out? His father had been very clear after yesterday, when she had gone for a stroll around the village, that she needed to be accompanied by one of the family to ensure her safety. He didn't believe she had just forgotten and gone off on some silly errand. But on the other hand, there was no sign that the house wards had been tampered with. Something was seriously amiss, and the only thing he could do was follow her trail.

She had obviously gone out the front door, and as he moved along the path, he could sense her easily. Quickly connecting his mind to his mother's, he told her that Rhonwen was missing and then started off towards the village, following the faint traces of her aura. As he walked along the road, Rouan turned over in his mind what he now knew about Jean Bran, and adding that to the incident in the park in London, his fear that she was in trouble coalesced into certainty.

Rouan had spent the last few days researching the Bran family. Using his own family's archives, kept safely in his grandmother's house, he had come to suspect that the woman Lydia was a Bran. This meant that Rhonwen had been watched for years. But why? Was it simply to get their hands on the Tierney

Amulet? If it was, they failed. Declan got it first. But how did he know about it? He must have been watching as well, or were they aligned?

Coming into the village, he followed the traces of Rhonwen's passing around the corner of the pub, where they abruptly stopped at the bus stop. Rouan had lived here all his life. He knew the bus timetable by heart. He did not doubt that she had caught the bus to Whitehaven. Just as he turned to head back, his father pulled up next to him, looking deeply concerned. Rouan quickly walked around and got into the passenger side of the car. He had barely closed the door when Connell took off down the street.

"Your mother told me about Rhonwen, and I have just been talking to Gavin. Finn remembered that the Tierney's had a place over near Ambleside. Gavin thinks Declan might be hiding there, but it's warded, so we can't be sure. He will be back from the Continent later tonight, but that will be too late if that's where Rhonwen's heading".

"Surely she's not that stupid"! Rouan replied. But even as he said it, he knew that was where she had gone, and she was in trouble. The sense of foreboding that had been building since he had discovered her missing was clearly mirrored in his father's features as he manoeuvred the car through the small village and onto the link road.

54

Max lent down and rolled the girl over to see her face. He was surprised she had broken through the spell. It was unexpected but not a big problem. She had already led them far enough. Cecile had informed him about the cabin she had spotted half a kilometre further along the track, and she was now moving into position. Lifting the Tierney girl easily, he moved quickly back into the brush and stashed her out of sight. He incanted a binding spell to make sure she didn't wake up before he came back and then started to make his way along the edge of the track, keeping to the trees so as not to be seen.

He found a little glade that ran around to the right and, following it, moved slowly forward. Just ahead, through the trees, he caught a glimpse of a small building, and a sense of triumph coursed through him. He did not doubt that Declan was there. He felt Cecile long before she reached him. She had been circling the cabin and come back up behind him.

"Someone is definitely there". She whispered close to his ear. "The window upstairs is open, and there's a car parked at the edge of the clearing, tucked into the brush, well hidden from the lane along the front".

Max nodded. He dug into the pocket of his jeans, and retrieving his mobile, he quickly texted Jean with the location. Then he and Cecile settled down to watch and wait.

Having decided to see if the Tierney girl would lead him to Declan, Jean had been surprised that initially, he had found it hard to scry for her. Luckily he had been looking for her at the right time. While she was in London, she had obviously been warded, probably by Gavin. But once she left London to travel north, he could locate her. When she had ended up in Whitehaven and then promptly disappeared from view, he had realised she had been handed over to the care of the Banach family. Organising to meet up with Max Jean had been in Whitehaven for a couple of days.

Rhonwen's little wander around the village yesterday had given him the chance he had been waiting for. She had been surprisingly well defended, and her memories well warded, but her rage had given him his in. A few well-placed suggestions, and he had a fair idea of Declan's location, and now he had Rhonwen as well. He had sensed the talent in her the moment he had slid into her mind. Subverting her into an alignment with him would start to even up the balance a bit.

Now as he joined the other two in a well-concealed hollow at the back of the cabin, he saw that ancient spells cleverly secured it. Sending out his senses, he felt the strength of the wards. He might not be able to scry into the cabin, but he could use his Amulet to confirm that another Amulet was nearby. Taking hold of the stone that now hung securely around his neck, he focused his mind and felt an instantaneous linking of the two stones. Smiling with delight, he sat back. This would be easy.

Jean felt, rather than saw, a movement behind the window at the back of the cabin. He was warded and concealed by spells, but Declan had proved to be unexpectedly effective at spoiling his plans before. This was why he had the other two with him. Jean felt confident he could subdue Declan with a spell as long as he didn't have time to realise what was happening. It was tempting just to kill the little shit, but he was curious about how he had become so adept with magic so quickly.

With Cecile ready to approach the front door and Max at the back of the house, Jean stayed out of sight and watched as she hobbled up to the cabin. He saw a shadow at the window, so he knew that

Declan was aware of her before she knocked on the door, but he was taking his time answering. Jean was getting very irritated. It had become evident that Declan had decided to stay hidden and wouldn't answer the door. Deciding that he would just have to use brute force, he slipped back and around to the back of the cabin. He was instantly aware of two things as he emerged from the brush. First, Max was in a crumpled heap on the ground; secondly, the cabin's back door was wide open. He couldn't believe it. How was this happening? The car was still under the overhanging trees, but he knew Declan was gone. He couldn't sense him, and his Amulet had lost connection. An uncomfortable feeling of apprehension was nagging at the edges of his mind. Declan had somehow moved from novice to adept without any training in a very short space of time. This was not good.

Cecile came out of the cabin through the back door with a bewildered look on her face. Seeing Max on the ground, she stopped in her tracks. "What the fuck!"

"Wake up Max. Maybe he can tell us," Jean said, frustrated at his failure to capture Declan. Having to wait while Max recovered just increased his fury.

Several hours later, just as they were turning out of the laneway to the cabin, they almost hit a police car. Cecile managed to avoid the collision, and they got past the other vehicle before the occupants managed to get a good look at them. Still enraged by his failure to kill Declan and retrieve the Tierney amulet, Jean almost erupted right then and there, but he held himself in check. Speaking very quietly through gritted teeth, he addressed Cecile, who was driving. "We will have to get rid of this van quickly."

She glanced at him as she negotiated the country roads back towards Whitehaven and nodded. "No problem."

Sitting morosely in the back next to Declan's unconscious cousin, Max spoke for the first time since they had left the cabin. "Do you think those coppers are after Declan or on some other business?"

"There's not much else down that road except that cabin, but on the other hand, there is no record of it belonging to the Tierneys, or we would have found it without the girl," Jean replied in a thoughtful voice.

"What about the girl? Do you think they might be looking for her?" asked Cecile.

"I doubt it". He answered. "I made sure she believed it was necessary to act on her own".

As they drove, he weighed up his next move. He would have to wait for another time to get to Declan. He would have doubled his power if he could get hold of even one more Amulet. So how could he find another one? Where was Keira's Amulet? She hadn't known anything about it last weekend, but a lot had happened since then. Morgan knew he was out of town, so she might relax her guard enough for Max and Cecile to get to Keira. They could stash her at the office where it was well warded and keep her unconscious till he got back.

By the time they got to Kendal, where he had left his car, Cecile and Max knew what he wanted of them and just how important it was that they got it right. The transfer of a still unconscious Rhonwen to his back seat, safely disguised by a spell to look like a pile of blankets, went smoothly, and he sent the others on their way.

Jean immediately headed off to his farm. He had let the other two think he would take Rhonwen somewhere remote, empty her mind of useful information, and dispose of her. They would return to London and grab the Blair girl, who foolishly had decided not to stay with his mother. No one knew about the farm but him. He had bought the place on the edge of the Yorkshire Dales several years ago under an alias, then carefully established himself in the local community, weaving an identity that evoked no interest amongst the locals. As far as they were concerned, he was a hobby farmer who only used his farm for holidays. There were subtle spells warding the place that deflected interest in anyone who came near the boundaries.

Arriving at the farm late, Jean deposited his unconscious guest onto one of the spare beds and settled in for the night. Wandering into the room where he had left her over an hour before, a glass of excellent old brandy in his hand, he looked down at her. He would need to wake her so she could be re-settled into a regular sleep. And since he wanted her to be helpful, he would need to keep her hydrated and fed. Watching her, he noted that she was actually quite beautiful. The curve of her breasts outlined by the way the fabric of her teeshirt was pulled tautly around her body was alluring. Her jeans emphasised the length of her legs, and her skin was unblemished and naked of makeup. Lust warmed his groin as he peeled off her clothes with his eyes and smiled. He was looking forward to a slow magical seduction.

Lydia had given him quite a lot of information about her that he could use. Her lack of experience with men would be his biggest advantage in weaving the spell he had in mind. But the fact that she was so angry and ambivalent would be just as valuable. He had already gleaned enough to know that Brian Poole and his protector would be formidable enemies. He would need to weave this spell with great care and leave no memories behind for her or anyone else to access.

55

Declan had remained where he was for quite some time after the Van had left. He was still clutching his Amulet, his other hand protecting an old leather satchel against his body. The spell had worked. He was hyper-alert, his whole body tingling with arousal. *Fuck! This is better than sex! Or at least it's equal.*

Sitting back against the tree he had been sheltering behind, he let his mind roam over the experience, looking at the way the spell had shaped and reshaped reality. He grinned, and almost laughed out loud as a new thought made its way to his consciousness. *Yes! It's a bloody star trek moment! A cloaking spell!* It had indeed been effective. He had walked straight past the dyke that had come in through the front, and she hadn't sensed him at all. And Jean! That bastard hadn't a clue he was watching him the whole fucking time.

He could feel himself getting aroused again just thinking about it, when his amulet suddenly flared up, hot and insistent. Almost simultaneously he heard the sound of a car pulling up at the front of the cabin. Quickly muttering the spell and visualising himself as blending with the forrest, he peered through the brush. His hearing enhanced by the spell, he listened to the crunch of boots as they stomped around the side of the small building.

Having expected it to be Jean returning to try and trap him, he was surprised to see a cute-looking policewoman. She was looking around the clearing and peering into the door of the cabin. Then he heard another set of footsteps, this time in the cabin, and an older policeman emerged from the back door, shaking his head. He could hear everything they said despite being a good fifty metres away.

It quickly became obvious that they weren't looking for him specifically, but for whoever was using the cabin. Locals had reported that they had seen lights in the abandoned building and had reported it to the local police. He felt a sense of intense anger at the nosy busybodies who had to interfere, but almost immediately it was redirected to his cousin. Jean had found him, thanks to that bitch, Rhonwen. Even if the police hadn't turned up he would have had to leave the shelter of the cabin because of her. The voices of the police interrupted his thoughts.

"I don't know, Sir, there's no sign of anyone around, but the cabin's wide open, and there's a car parked here and another one down at the parking area. I can't put my finger on it, but it just feels wrong, if you know what I mean."

Listening in to the police speculating with each other and over the radio to their colleagues, Declan was reassured that he was right. They didn't know he had been here. Having had the car's owner identified from the licence plate as no one of interest to the police seemed to reassure them, and they eventually decided that whoever was using the cabin might possibly return at dark, probably from a walk. Closing the doors and tucking a card with the local station details on it into the crack, they headed off.

Sitting back, he started thinking about his next move. It was still safe to use his car, which was registered in a fictitious name, but not for too long. The other car must be the one Rhonwen used, and now she was in Jean's clutches, she might end up being reported as missing. That will lead them right back here. Well, he would be long gone by the time the coppers realised that there was no Mark Dunne. It was irritating, though. That alias had stood him in good stead for a long time now.

Caressing the satchel, he experienced a feeling of profound relief mixed with a strange sense of desire as his hands felt the outlines of the books it held. The sensuousness of the experience continued to surprise him. He had spent the last few days studying the hidden cache he had found at the cabin. The notebooks were a mix of journals and instructions written by his ancestors over a period of several centuries. The most recent had been written by his great-grandmother and had been an instruction manual for using the spells in a book she called The Grimoire.

Pouring through her notes, he realised that she had known her knowledge might be lost over the next generation or two. She had been the one who had hidden the collection of the family's artefacts in the cabin. His predecessors had been very helpful. Their notes had given him a lot of stuff to think about as well as information. Knowing more about his Amulet had enabled him to start practising with it, and a kernel of an idea about his next step had been taking shape when Jean and his henchmen had descended on him.

Once he had realised that Jean was from one of the other families that owned Amulets, he quickly understood the danger he was in. No one outside the family could have any idea about the cabin, but this magic stuff was very potent. Look at what he had managed without knowing anything. If Jean had one of these Amulets and knew what to do with it, he, Declan, was in trouble.

He had been greatly relieved to find out from his great-grandmother's notes that the cabin was protected from magical searches. Warded from magic by magic. Well, he had managed to fool Jean with his own magic, and there was no reason he couldn't get on with his plans. His stuff was hidden in the cabin, so that was the first priority. Thinking about the various possibilities, he stood up, only to almost collapse, his legs like jelly. Only then did he realise he had been continually using magic to hide himself for several hours.

Remembering a warning he had read in one of the notebooks about the energy used doing magic, Declan sat back down. Opening up the satchel, he dug out his own notebook and looked up the spell he had sourced from the Grimoire that would undo the casting. As he became visible again, he could feel his energy starting to return and was startled to find himself absolutely ravenous. And not just for food. He was still seriously aroused, and his need was urgent.

Checking the Police card, he saw that they had come from Ambleside, so he decided to head to Kendal in the opposite direction. The town was big enough for him to access everything he needed without being noticed. Not that he would look anything like Declan Tierney, anyway.

56

Connell's sudden arrival in the middle of Brian's lounge room startled them all. They had been sharing the information that each had gathered over the last few days. Gavin had been feeling a little more optimistic after talking to his oldest friend, Finn. Another immortal Finn had spent the last hundred years or so living in what was now the country of Austria. Always a voice of reason and calm, he loved to keep records. His archives, a treasury of information that few knew even existed, could be considered one of the world's greatest wonders.

Seeing Stewart standing in the doorway with his mouth hanging open, Gavin couldn't help but laugh. These boys were so new to what their heritage called them to, yet here they were stepping up. Magic had been a fairy story for them both only a week ago, and now they were witnessing translocation spells. Brian turned to him reproachfully. "You can't tell me you don't find that just a little disconcerting".

Before Gavin could reply, he became aware of the Connell's expression, and his humour quickly faded.

"What's happened?" He asked, instantly aware that something was seriously wrong.

"Rhonwen! She's missing. She left the house alone without a word, and when we tracked her, it became pretty obvious that she knew about the cabin in Knott's Wood. When we got there, the stink of magic was everywhere, but no sign of Rhonwen, apart from the hire car in the car park at the park gate."

Looking closely at Connell, Gavin could see the guilt and anger warring within the man in front of him. His angry retort to Connell at not having protected Rhonwen better, bitten back, he calmed his frustration. Squashing his anger, he took a breath before responding. Glancing at the boys, he saw them still struggling to process the news, so taking the opportunity their silence offered, he quickly stepped over to Connell and put his hand on his shoulder.

"You weren't to know she had any knowledge about that cabin, Connell. She played her own hand in this. You know as well as I do that destiny will find a way to lead people where she wants them to go."

Connell, nodding in agreement and taking a deep breath, looked into Gavin's eyes. They had not always been the best of friends, but they both knew that no matter how strong their own powers were, there were other forces at work that they had no control over. "Yes. You're right, I know, but she has no idea what she is up against."

Gavin turned back to find both Brian and Stewart watching them closely. Their worry was etched clearly on their faces. Turning back to Connell, he led him over to the lounge and gestured to the other two men to join them. "Tell us more about what you found at the cabin."

Sitting heavily in the chair, Connell composed himself before he answered. It was obvious to Gavin that he was careful in his choice of words knowing that Brian and Stewart both knew and cared for Rhonwen. "It was obvious someone has been living there these last few days", Connell replied. "But they have covered their tracks well. There is evidence of a car having been parked there in the same spot, and it looks like it was driven away only in the last few hours. There are signs of two other cars. One was parked out of sight of the cabin, the other at the front door. Both arrived and left around late afternoon. There are signs of a scuffle at the back of the cabin".

Brian piped in. "Are you sure Rhonwen isn't in the woods making her way back to the hire car or lost or hurt?"

Connell looked at him, shaking his head sadly. "I am sorry, son, but we did a full sweep of the surrounds, on foot and using my Amulet. There was no sign of her or Declan. Since he has an Amulet, he would have to be warded for me not to find him using my Amulet. You know that they pick up on each other, don't you? If you know how to use them." With a look of puzzlement on his face, he turned back to Gavin. "I thought this Declan character was untrained, but he obviously has some knowledge. He's vanished."

It was a little after eight, and they had been tossing around ideas about how to track Rhonwen when they heard Erik arriving. Gavin turned towards the door and was immediately struck by the look of bewilderment on Erik's face. At first, he thought it was that Erik had spied Connell, but he quickly realised that something else was the cause of his old ally's unease. Before he could say anything, Erik threw himself into his favourite chair and looked around the room moodily. Speaking quietly, he informed them that he had lost Jean.

Failing at his task, which was obviously weighing heavily on him, he explained that he had no idea how Jean had outwitted him. He had realised by late morning that Jean wasn't at the Kensington house, so when Morgan left, he decided to see if he could break into the house and check it out.

"It's very well guarded. There is no way you can get in there. I have spent the whole day waiting for that little dick to return, and there has been no sign of him. I did manage to set an alert spell that will go off when he does come back, but I have a bad feeling that he isn't planning to come home anytime soon."

Connell responded first, with a look of sympathy on his face as he informed his old friend that he had lost Rhonwen. Gavin sat there listening to the others discussing the day's disasters, a feeling of inevitability taking hold of him. Turning all of the information over and over, he kept looking for the links. It seemed pretty coincidental that Declan, Rhonwen and Jean were all missing at the same time. And the timing itself with Beltane only days away.

The question of who was working with whom was still unresolved. He thought of Keira, and at that moment, he felt a sense of prescience, and the hairs on the back of his neck stood up. Turning to Brian, he interrupted the conversation. "What is Keira doing? Do you have any idea of her plans?"

Brian looked stunned for a minute, and then, suddenly alert, he answered that she had demanded to take a week off. It had something to do with family stuff. She hasn't spoken to either of us since we gave her back her Amulet."

Gavin turned to Connell. "Can you locate Keira for me? She won't have warded herself, so you should be able to use the link between the Amulets." Connell quickly retrieved his amulet from the pouch around his neck, a look of relief on his face. Being helpful was medicinal for Connell. Turning to Brian, he asked him to bring his Amulet over, explaining that using two of them together increased the power of the spell. Always an excellent teacher, Connell quickly instructed Brian on what he needed to do, and together they worked the spell.

They didn't take long to find her, obviously in transit and heading north. "Well, that's the right direction if she is heading home. Her family are in Carlisle". Stewart commented. "Maybe Jean has gone with her for some reason. She's been spending a lot of time with Morgan". He continued.

"It's possible". Gavin replied. It does make sense for Morgan to want to keep an eye on her. But I got the feeling that Morgan didn't trust Jean, and Scáthach was just waiting for an opportunity. Remember, she nearly got through the last time Keira had sex and Jean's a predator. If he seduces Keira, we could be in real trouble."

They were all still digesting this when Connell's phone rang. It didn't take long for them to pick up on the fact that it was Rouan filling his father in on what he had found. Or rather what he hadn't found. It was now after nine in the evening, and there was no sign of Rhonwen. They had to assume that she was in trouble, and the most logical conclusion was that her disappearance had something to do with Declan.

As Connell ended the call, Brian started speaking.

"When she doesn't return the hire car, the local police are going to come looking for her. They will flag it in their system, and that will get picked up by Inspector Riley's team. He knows she is supposed to be at your place, Connell, so he will send them there first."

"That's right." Interjected Stewart. "Your place will be the first place they will look, and if you have no idea where she is, it will look dodgy that you Haven't' reported her missing".

"Absolutely!" Continued Brian. "But we have a bit of time. We don't know how long she hired the car for, but even if it were only for the day, the company wouldn't alert the police until the morning."

Gavin realised that if they couldn't track Rhonwen magically, then letting the police do the job might be the next best option. As worried as he was about Rhonwen, the fact that Declan hadn't just killed her outright was significant. He had a much more urgent feeling about Scáthach. Especially if Keira was with Jean. Listening to the others tossing ideas around, he came to a decision. Interrupting the discussion, he outlined his plan. Connell was to go home and, in the morning, call the local police to report Rhonwen missing. Erik was to follow Keira to Carlisle. They needed to know if Jean really had gone with her. As for himself, well, it was time to find out what was going on and if Morgan was part of it. "What about us?" Brian asked.

"Your original plan was to go to Wales and check into your respective family archives this weekend. I think that this is still important. I have this nagging feeling that we are missing some clue to why Scáthach has chosen now to try and come back. We really do need to know how your family's Amulet ended in the hands of a Gypsy family in Eastern Europe".

As everyone organised themselves to leave, he pulled Connell aside. "We need to speak about next week. I assume you have celebrations planned." He said quietly so the others wouldn't overhear him. Connell nodded his head and replied in an equally quiet tone. "Yes, Neve has already thought of that. She realised immediately that having Beltane festivities might be a problem."

Gavin was relieved. "So, are you going to cancel?" He asked. "No, we have just alerted everyone that it will be a magic-free gathering. There has been a bit of grumbling, but we can't take the risk. Not with Scáthach knocking at the dimensional door, so to speak."

57

The Inspector put the phone down just as Stapleton arrived with some coffee. Taking the cup offered, he walked over to the board he had been using to map the case and stared at it thoughtfully. Despite being in the office on a Saturday, he had been feeling quite positive earlier in the day. The house in the photo he had found in Lydia Chamber's flat had been identified. Checking the catalogue of listed houses had paid off. He was now reasonably sure she had been a member of the family that had owned the house for several centuries until the 1970s. The Brans. They seem to have made some disastrous financial investments and lost everything, including the house down in Dorset. He had planned to go down there himself, but now it looked like he would have to change his plans. Turning to Stapleton, he quickly filled him in.

"I've just had a call from the local Police in Whitehaven. That family Rhonwen Tierney was staying with has just alerted the local station that she's missing. Apparently went out yesterday morning and hasn't returned. They have triangulated her phone, and it looks like the location is Knott's Wood, a few hours east of the coast. I am waiting for an update from the locals".

Riley mused the fact that it was so easy with today's technology to find people, yet so many still managed to vanish. *Hopefully, not this young lady.* Deliberately taking his time, he sifted through his mental list, making a decision about what to prioritise. Looking across at the constable, he asked him to start a search for any other members of the Bran family in the local area directories. With a nod of his head, the Constable sat down at his computer and got to work.

Thankful that he didn't have to work with one of the more talkative members of the squad, Riley sat staring at the board in front of him. He had a few irons in the fire, so to speak, but he decided to check in with the Constable watching Poole and Eggleston. He was absolutely sure they knew more than they had let on and that there was a lot more to all of this than was currently apparent. After being reassured that they were still well within the sights of their tails, he sat down reluctantly to wade through the paperwork he had been sent from the Registry Office. The somewhat convoluted inheritance trail of the Bran family was giving him a headache. It looked like there had been some schism in the family after the Second World War. There was a name change lodged for one of the daughters in the early seventies, at about the same time as there had been a challenge to the will by a cousin of some sort. There was a notation in the paperwork directing him to court documents.

It couldn't have been more than five minutes later that Stapleton made a rather disturbing noise that sounded somewhat like a war cry. "Sir, I have found something. There is a Jean Bran living here in London in Kensington. I've just pulled up his driving licence. He is a dead ringer for that fellow in the surveillance photos we found in Lydia Chambers's flat."

Sending a silent thanks to whatever powers run the universe, Riley shoved the file he had been scrutinising away from him and, with a grin on his face, said.

"Great! Let's go and see what he has to say."

Grabbing his coat and making a beeline for the door, he felt a great sense of relief to be able actually to do something. He hated being stuck in the office. He was already at the lift when Stapleton hurriedly joined him, pulling his own coat on.

They were halfway to the Kensington address when he got the call from the officers watching Brian Poole. He had picked up Eggleston from his apartment a few minutes ago. He authorised the officers to follow them wherever they went. Then deciding to check in on the officer watching the Antique Shop, he dialled the precinct and asked to be put through. After a brief wait, he was speaking with Constable Grey. He vaguely recalled her, a pretty blond who was more intelligent than she looked. She reported that the shop had opened at the usual time of trading by the proprietor and that nothing of note had occurred so far.

He instinctively knew that this Antiques Dealer was somehow involved. The strange thing was that he also had this sense of certainty that they were somehow on the same side. This case was very odd—so many questions. So many people were, on the surface, respectable, law-abiding citizens, yet not innocent. Breathing deeply, he deliberately released the tension from his shoulders and looked out the car window at the drizzly London landscape. He had a sense that, somehow this case was going to change something fundamental in him, and he wasn't sure if he was excited or alarmed by that thought.

Arriving at a very swish address in Kensington, he was immediately aware that he knew this place or at least had heard of the address before. It was Stapleton who, swearing under his breath as he turned off the engine, triggered his memory. "Sir, I just realised this is the address of the place where that Blair girl has been spending her evenings". Michael Riley felt the machinery of his mind start to whir as little pieces of the puzzle moved into place. Everything was connected. He had put a watch on the Blair girl because of how Brian Poole attempted to divert his attention away from her. That she was connected to this Bran fellow was unexpected. "Right!" he said as he readied himself to get out of the car. "First, we find out why this Jean Bran is so interesting and how that is connected to Rhonwen Tierney. That's the connection. Lydia Chambers, or whoever she was.

"Now, tell me, does Jean Bran own this house?"

"No, Sir, the owner is his adopted mother, Morgan Woods. I did a search on her but there are no flags. She isn't known in our system."

"OK, let's meet this Jean Bran".

With that, they both headed across the road.

Waiting in the elegant entrance hall they had been ushered into, Michael Riley mulled over what he knew and, more importantly, what he didn't. The address, the decor and the servant who answered the door all pointed to serious money. The sound of a door opening interrupted his thoughts, and he turned around to find a lovely-looking woman moving across the hall to greet him.

"Good morning, Inspector. I am Morgan Woods. I am afraid my son is not currently at home. May I be of some help?" Taking her offered hand, he introduced himself and Stapleton, then watching closely for her reaction, he said. "We would have liked to speak with Mr Bran about some rather disturbing information that we have come across during a murder investigation".

He saw a flicker of something in her eyes. He wasn't really sure what, but he was instantly alert. It had been there and gone so fast that he could have been mistaken, but he didn't think so. This was no ordinary woman. She allowed herself to look shocked and concerned as she replied. "What sort of information, Inspector? How could Jean be involved?" Indicating a door to the right of them, she continued. "Let's go into my study so you can tell me all about it."

He was on his way through the door when he realised that he hadn't actually made a decision to speak further with this woman about the case. He felt puzzled, and then, as he relaxed into the chair she had offered him, he felt his focus shift back to the woman in front of him.

Crossing the street to reach the car, the Inspector glanced at his watch and realised it was now after two in the afternoon. The sound of the remote lock clicking as the Constable reached the car brought him to an abrupt halt. He felt a little disorientated. Looking back towards the house they had just left, he had the distinct feeling that he had not led the conversation he had just been a part of.

As he settled into the car, he glanced over at Stapleton and noted a rather bemused look on his face. Pulling his notebook out of his pocket and flipping through the pages, he found that, for some reason, he had written no notes about the interview with Ms. Woods. Trying to focus on the content of the discussion, he realised that he knew no more now than he had before. He didn't know what had just happened, and he didn't know why he didn't know. Michael Riley suddenly felt very angry and very puzzled.

"Stapleton!" He barked gruffly. "Did you take notes during that interview?" The constable looked at him in confusion and pulled his own notebook out of his pocket, rifling through it to the most recent entry. There in front of him was a one-page notation about the interview. "I don't understand, Sir. You always take your own notes." Then, his face red with embarrassment, the Constable passed his notebook over. After a quick perusal of the content, the Inspector looked at Stapleton thoughtfully. "You do well to feel embarrassed, lad if that's the quality of your work. Let's get back to the Station."

As they drove back through the traffic, Riley thumbed his way through the Constable's notebook and found it very interesting indeed. Stapleton was typically very pedantic and inclusive in his note-taking and could be accused of putting in too much extraneous information. But the notes of the interview they had both just been part of were skimpy to say the least. "You know what, Stapleton. When we get back, we are both going to go through these notes of yours and try to make sense of them."

He looked out the window as they drove through the traffic, letting his mind roam through what he knew without trying to order it in any way. It was a mental trick that sometimes worked, allowing him to remember small items of information that didn't fit with the overall pattern. He was missing something. He knew it.

His phone interrupted his musings. As he listened to the report, he tried to make sense of how the information he had just been given made any sense in light of what he already knew. Ending the call, he sat there staring at the windscreen. It was Stapleton's voice that brought him back to himself. "Tell me, Stapleton. He said as he turned to look at his offsider's profile. "Would you have thought that Rhonwen Tierney was working with her cousin Declan?"

He watched Stapleton's face crumple into a frown as he thought about his answer. "No Sir, I wouldn't have. It doesn't make any sense. She didn't need to steal the Jewel. She already owned it."

"Exactly. So why do you think she went off to some isolated, abandoned cabin in the woods, where some unknown person has been staying for the last few days?"

🙞 🙞

Morgan was sitting in her study thinking about what she had learned from Inspector Riley when her maid knocked on the door and informed her that Gavin was waiting to see her. Despite her initial plan to align with Gavin, Morgan now felt a strong sense of ambivalence. It wasn't just that she preferred her independence, she was unsure if she could persuade Gavin to follow her lead. However, Jean had forced her hand. Telling the maid to show him in, she gracefully arose from her chair and put on her most charming smile.

The moment he walked through the door, she knew it was going to be a difficult conversation. Gavin was wearing a charming smile, but he was fully warded, and there was a stiffness to the way he held his shoulders that spoke volumes. Taking the lead, she deliberately swung her hips in a subtle but suggestive manner as she glided over to him, and, taking his hand, kissed him lightly on the cheek. Drawing him into the room and exerting just the right amount of welcome to put him at ease, Morgan offered him a drink.

"No. Thank you, Morgan. Not just now. I need to speak with you about Jean, and it's very important that we do so with candour." Gavin said in a firm voice.

Morgan was not surprised after having spoken with the Inspector earlier. However, she was a little startled by the way Gavin had launched into the subject immediately. Over the many centuries that they had known each other, they had become used to a certain approach to conversing. They had rarely been straightforward with each other so quickly in a conversation, always preferring to assess each other, to get the upper hand by trying to get past each other's wards.

Looking straight into Gavin's eyes, Morgan realised that this was not the time to play games. Her own suspicions had been sharpened with the information Inspector Riley had unwittingly given her earlier in the day. She had already come to the conclusion that she would have to intervene. Now it was just a matter of how to do so.

"Take a seat, Gavin, and tell me what you know."

Gavin looked at her for a minute and then, obviously making a decision, started speaking.

"We need to collaborate, Morgan. I think that Jean has been instrumental in opening up a door that should have remained locked. I think the threat of Scáthach is directly linked to him and that he is dangerous."

Morgan waited, sitting still and not showing her consternation. She knew this and had been worried about Jean's arrogance and narrow vision. He had always been completely self-absorbed, and her failure to align him totally to her had been a significant irritant over the years. Now to hear this, coming out of Gavin's mouth, a direct statement of her failure to control a junior warlock. And from Gavin, who had warned her years ago of the intrinsic instability of the Brans.

Gavin shifted in his chair, then continued. "There is no way that it is a coincidence that Jean's last remaining relative was living in the same building as Rhonwen Tierney. That is who that Lydia Chambers woman was, you know. Margarita Bran! I just discovered it this morning. The police are all over this, and everything is at risk."

When she didn't respond, he continued, his blue eyes icy and penetrating. "I have been thinking about the way the Amulets, forgotten and hidden for the most part for so long, are now suddenly exposed, and some in the hands of amateurs. I know you have been teaching Keira. I need to know. Are you and Jean working together? Are you or Jean teaching Declan Tierney?"

This was not what she had expected. Having gleaned a lot of information from Inspector Riley earlier, she had already surmised that somehow Jean was involved with the Tierney boy, but teach him? No, that was not Jean's style. Taking a deep breath, she answered. "I certainly have had nothing to do with that little criminal. I know, Jean. He covets magic and power. He is not a sharer. I do not think that he would teach Declan. Use him, yes, but not teach him. The risk would be too great that Declan could be more powerful than him."

She could tell that Gavin accepted this and that it fits somehow with his own thinking. It was time. She knew that this situation would need them both, despite their differences, and maybe some of the others, to contain it. "You are right. We need to collaborate. There is a distinct risk that this is far more complex than a greedy psychopathic warlock like Jean trying to grab power."

Gavin flinched at her honesty. "Oh, yes, I am well aware of what he is". She continued. "I have tried to direct him, but I got to him too late. He had been managing on his own for too many years for me to have any real influence over his character. You know that. You told me so yourself twenty-five years ago. Not that you needed to. I knew what I was taking on, but having him out there in the world unsupervised, even without his Amulet, was not a risk I was willing to take."

She could tell Gavin knew there was more to that story, but it was basically irrelevant now. Jean had become the problem they had feared anyway. The last few days had demonstrated that very clearly. Ordering her thoughts so that the disparate bits of information she had gleaned from various sources over the last week made sense, she started to fill Gavin in on what she had discovered.

58

Parking the car at the side of the house, Keira retrieved her bag off the passenger seat, the weight of the Grimoire still stashed in its depths, almost breaking her arm. Tired from the drive and eager for a bath, she locked the car and headed around the back. It had been a long drive, and it was almost dawn. She normally wouldn't have done it in one stretch, but she had been too excited to stop over anywhere for the night.

Making her way through the house to her own room, she briefly thought about getting something to eat, but exhaustion was starting to set in. Changing her mind about the bath, she stripped off her clothes and quickly showered before collapsing into bed. Thanking her mother silently for always keeping everything ready for her, she snuggled under the quilt and was asleep immediately.

It was hunger that woke her. She looked dreamily towards the window and realised from the position of the sun that it must be late in the afternoon. Wriggling her legs to stretch, she felt the sheets slide seductively around her naked body. Food wasn't the only thing she was hungry for. The lust was intense, and she knew that if there had been anyone even remotely attractive anywhere near her, she would have trouble restraining herself.

Morgan had warned her not to give in to it. She had been adamant that any sexual encounter could be a disaster. Just the memory of the way Scáthach had tried to get into her when she and Stewart had fucked the last time helped squash her desire. One thing about Morgan, she had been useful. Apart from all the information she had given her about her family and magic, she had given her a little potion and showed her a spell she could use to deal with this incredible randiness.

Getting out of bed, she opened her wardrobe and grabbed her old dressing gown off the peg. Then finding her toiletries bag, she rummaged through it for the potion. It tasted terrible, but she only needed a small sip. She had the recipe but needed to figure out where to get the ingredients. Looking closely at the bottle, she noted that she probably had enough to last four or five days so as she dragged a brush through her hair she started to formulate a plan for the evening.

The potion worked quickly, so by the time she walked into the kitchen, she felt relaxed and focused. There was nothing fresh in the fridge since her parents had not expected her to be at home while they were away. However, her mother was a particularly organised woman, and there would be long-life milk in the cupboard and leftovers in the freezer. Gathering what she wanted, she started to make herself some dinner. She could go into town tomorrow and get some fresh food, but this would do for now.

About an hour later, dressed in a warm jumper and leggings, fed and with a glass of her father's whiskey in one hand, Keira was in the library, staring at the section of wall where she had seen her aunt emerge when she was little. She was savouring it. The grimoire lay open on the coffee table in front of her, a spell for *Opening what is Hidden* on the page, and her amulet warm and reassuring in her other hand. Taking a sip from the fine crystal tumbler, she put it down carefully beside her. It was time!

Reading the spell out loud while she held her amulet, she directed her energy towards the wall next to the fireplace. She heard an audible click, and then a section of panelling swung inward leaving a dark empty space. She could feel an incredible rush of air, and as she slowly walked towards the opening she could see cobwebs stirring around the edges. Keira peered intently into the darkness but she couldn't see, or sense anything. She picked up the torch she had ready, took a deep breath and, clutching her Amulet firmly in her left hand, stepped through.

Shinning the torch around the space, she realised she was in a corridor that led back for a few feet and then turned to the right. She tried to picture in her mind the dimensions and how this worked within the wall space as she crept towards the bend, then stopped, and using the torch illuminated the area. After about two feet the floor of the passage turned into stairs that descended quite steeply into the dark. Carefully moving down the stairs she felt the temperature drop and realised she was heading underground.

As she came to the bottom of the stairs, she turned and shone the light back up them. It looked like she was about fifteen feet down. Calculating the direction, she thought she must be somewhere behind the wall of the cellar where her father kept his wine. She had just taken another couple of steps along the passage when her Amulet suddenly flared with a bright blue shaft of light. She heard another click and immediately a warm glow filtered down the passage from a door that was opening about ten feet ahead of her.

Excitement filled her. Her heart was racing and she felt a giggle bubbling out of her. Her Amulet was the key. It felt so right. It was all going to be hers. She had the Amulet and the Grimoire, and now she had found the secret place her aunt had tried to hide from her. She had thought about how her aunt had tampered with her memory while she was driving up from London. Aunt Judith had been killed in a car accident when Keira was ten years old. Was she really the only one in the family to have known about the magic? Judith had been her father's sister. He had another brother and sister, and they both lived locally. Yet no one had noticed that the Grimoire had been missing from the library for the last six months!

Shaking her head, she put it all into the back of her mind. She would worry about that later. Pushing the door open, she walked through into a large room with a sandstone floor and walls lined with shelves. There was a large wooden table in the middle, covered with dust, and in the far corner, a pedestal with a large metal basin resting on top of it.

She couldn't see the source of the light that illuminated the room. Looking up, she saw a ceiling light that looked like it was at least a hundred years old, and sure enough, on the wall next to the door was an old black light switch, but it was turned off. Deciding that it must be magical, she continued to look around the room.

Turning she was confronted by a large ornate mirror on the wall next to the door. At first she couldn't figure out what was odd about it, and the suddenly she saw what was so strange. Everything else in the room was covered in years of dust, but the mirror was perfectly clean. There wasn't a speck of dirt or dust on it or, for that matter around it. It was obviously very old and yet there was no sign of the usual deterioration you would see in old mirrors. It looked newer than the one in her room.

Moving closer she glanced down at the floor and stopped in her tracks. In the dust there were clear footprints leading away from the mirror towards the shelves, and then another set leading back again. *There's no dust in them.* Fear vied with curiosity. She followed the footprints over to the shelves and using the torch, looked around, careful not to disturb anything. On the shelf just above her eye level there was a noticeable gap in the neatly stacked but dusty books and scrolls. Something was missing. More to the point, someone had taken something from this room, and they had done it very recently.

59

Having arrived soon after Kiera, Erik had searched the house and surrounding area for any sign of Jean while she slept. There was nothing, either physical or magical, to suggest that he had ever been anywhere near the Blair house. Now, hidden by a simple spell, he watched her through the window of the library as she discovered the passageway behind the wall. Once she had entered the hidden door, he slipped quietly through the front door.

He was heading into the library, when he felt a prickle up his back that always signified the use of magic. Stilling himself he sent out feelers and was surprised to find that there was someone else using magic near by. Checking the direction, he knew it wasn't Keira. He had already felt the particular signature of her Amulet being used. No, this wasn't Keira, it was too far away and outside of the house.

Moving quickly he entered the door in the wall and closing it behind him, navigated his way down to the spell room. Having left it undisturbed earlier, he now took his time to ensure there were no twraps. But just like the rest of the house, there were only remnant wisps of magic, that told him that no one had practiced the art in this house for many years.

Keira was looking at something behind the door when he came to a holt at the threshold of the room. He watched her lovely deep grey eyes widen with shock as she saw him. Putting his finger to his mouth to alert her to be silent, he took a step into the room sweeping it with a neutralising spell in case there was a magical alarm. Sure enough, there was. But that wasn't what stopped him in his tracks. The foot prints in the dust that did not belong to Keira were a glaring anomaly amongst the general neglect of the place. Pointing to them, he spoke very quietly, staying where he was so she wouldn't react abruptly. "This isn't your only problem. There is someone using magical stealth to approach the house. Could it be any of your family?"

He had to hand it to her. She recovered quickly. She replied in a similarly hushed tone. "I don't know if any one else knows about the magic, but both my Uncle and Aunt live in the area". Quickly making a decision, he smiled cheekily at her. "Well lets not be the ones to let them in on the secret. How about we go upstairs and pretend we are just here for the weekend and see who has come to visit".

She hesitated and looked at him suspiciously. Her voice still hushed but with a strident edge, she demanded. "Why are you here?"

Erik decided to be completely honest with her. " To keep you safe from Morgan's stepson, Jean. He is a pretty nasty character and he is up to something to do with the Amulets. He is also a very skilled warlock".

Seeing that she was still unsure, Erik reached out and took her hand—the one holding her Amulet. "If I was a danger to you, your amulet would have reacted. It would have warned you I was around. We need to get moving. Whoever it is, they are almost at the back door."

Erik didn't kid himself that she trusted him, but she allowed him to manoeuvre her out of the room and up the stairs to the library. The door had only just slid flush with the wall when he heard footsteps in the hall. Erik quickly moved them to the centre of the room and pushed Keira behind him. His own senses on high alert, he could feel his power building but strangely, Keira's amulet remained quiescent, giving no sign of alarm.

A short man in his sixties sauntered into the room, a quizzical look on his face. "It OK, son." He said in a soft voice, filed with irony. "I am not here to hurt the lassie. You can power down now".

Erik, sensing the truth in the man's words, relaxed and as he did so, he felt Kiera move sideways so she could see her guest. Spying her, he beamed a brilliant smile filled with honest warmth and said. "Aye, this would be little Keira all grown up. And a very lovely lady to boot. You have the look of my Judith, but darker."

"Your Judith! Who are you? And why did you just walk into my house without the courtesy of knocking on the door?" Keira replied haughtily.

Erik could see the real Keira starting to emerge now that she was no longer threatened. Quickly intervening before she got too nasty, he turned to her and using his favourite calming spell, he attempted to ease the situation. It seemed to work initially, she relaxed and softened, but before he could consolidate the process, she was shaking her head and looking him in a calculating manner that he found somewhat disconcerting.

"Stop doing that! Its not going to work anymore. I don't want you, or anyone else for that matter, to ensorcel me".

He heard a sudden guffaw from the entrance to the room, where their visitor had remained throughout the exchange. "She's a Blair, then. There've all got tempers on them".

Erik saw Kiera turn towards the old guy and he could feel her wrath, but just before she could retort, he felt a little push and saw her stop. "Don't turn on me, lassie. I cut my teeth dealing with your Aunt. Now why don't we sit down like civilised people and I'll tell ye why I'm here. A wee dram of that whiskey would be a nice welcoming gesture, given that its turned quite cold this evening". He moved a little further into the room obviously conscious that Keira would need time, and then in a voice suddenly tinged with sadness he introduced himself. "My name is John McWilliams and I was Judith Blair's closest friend."

Erik had a sense of familiarity with the name but he couldn't place it and looking at Kiera, he could still sense a level of irritability beneath her curiosity. Taking the lead he introduced himself. "Well, Mr Mc Williams, I am Erik Nordson, and I am very interested in why you are here. How about I pour us all that drink while you begin?"

Erik moved over to the drinks cabinet while the other two settled into their chairs and listened as John started to tell his story. "Judith and I went to school together. We were always friends. We started going out together as teenagers and we started living together in our early twenties. We didn't marry for all sorts of reasons, including your grandfather's disapproval of me".

Erik handed him a drink and he paused to take a sip. Erik could see that his grief was still deep, even now after twenty-odd years. John looked straight at Keira and continued in a gentle voice. "Judith had no idea that she came from a magical family. Your family had stopped using magic over a century ago, and no one had been born with the talent for two generations. Or that was what we all thought. You see my family is also magical, and we had been associated with your family since they moved to the area. Anyway it was time for my training to start, and initially my mother took on that task. Your aunt used to help me practice and that is when my mother recognised she had the talent".

John paused for a minute, a smile playing around his mouth as he remembered. " My mother realised Judith needed a more skilled practitioner, so she contacted one of the elders, and he took on our training. Over the years, it became obvious that Judith was much more powerful than anyone had anticipated, so this set our teacher to wondering who she was. He questioned her about her family, and did some research. That is when we found out that the family had changed its name".

John paused to take another sip of his drink. Then putting it down on the table next to him, he leaned forward in the chair and looked very intently at Keira. "He became obsessed with Judith's family. He told her that her family was one of five very important and powerful families, and that they must have hidden their tools and heirlooms somewhere. He encouraged her to search through the house, but warned her not to tell anyone. He started to create division between us, and if we hadn't been so close he would have succeeded".

Keira had been listening intently up to this point. Interrupting him she asked in a tight voice. "What did he want?" John, looking at her intently and nodding towards her hand still tightly curled around her Amulet, replied in a quiet, angry voice. "He wanted her inheritance. He wanted to steal her Amulet".

Erik was startled by the boldness of it. "Who is he?" He demanded. This was all starting to feel very worrying, and he would need to speak with Gavin quickly. "His name is Marcus Neville". John answered, his voice filled with hatred.

Erik knew that name. A cold sense of dread filled him as he asked: "Is he still in the area?"

"Long gone". The other man replied. "He worked hard to get to Judith. Because of his insistence that there must be remnants of the families magic in this house, she did find the secret room, and the Grimoire. The problem was that she daren' take the book away from the house. It wasn't safe at our place, too easy to access and no hidden spaces, so we warded this house". Turning to Erik John continued. "Thats how I knew you were here. Anyone with magic talent who isn't a Blair, trips the alarm. I have been monitoring it ever since he killed Judith".

Kiera was obviously startled by this disclosure. "What do you mean, he killed Aunt Judith? She died in a car accident."

John shook his head sadly. "No, my dear. It just looked like a car accident. She knew she was at risk. Thats why she hid the Grimoire amongst the old books in the Library. She had guessed that you had talent, and she wanted you to be able to find it".

Erik interjected. "But surely that was dangerous. Anyone could have found it".

John smiled. "Judith was very powerful. She spelled it so that only Keira would even see it".

Watching Keira, Erik saw that this made sense to her. She looked up at John and said. "That's why none of my family ever realised that it was missing from the shelf. I couldn't work out how they wouldn't have noticed".

Erik sat across from John as he and Keira talked about Judith and her magic. He told her about Judith's tenuous relationship with the family, and how difficult it had been for her to access the hidden room. They had belonged to a local coven which John now led, and the members had kept an eye on the house and any sign of Neville, but no one had seen him since the night he killed Judith.

Listening to John speak, and mulling it all over Erik decided to mention the footprints. Turning to John he asked. "Have you been in this house in the last few weeks? Specifically, have you been in the spell room?" John's response told Erik what he needed to know. It hadn't been him. He quickly filled him in on the footprints they had found leading from the mirror and the empty space on the shelf, where something had been taken.

John was obviously stunned by this news. He took it all in then shaking his head he replied grimly. "This is worse than you think. Its not my spell that's been circumvented, its Judith's. She used the Amulet to set the wards on the Spell Room".

Seeing Kiera startled by this revelation, Erik immediately tried to reassure her but she was brittle and volatile. The fact that her Amulet might not protect her completely had unsettled her badly, and he could feel her mood changing. John seemed to understand this as well. Without needing to be told, he seemed to know that she needed reassurance. He also seemed to know how to go about dealing with her. Erik watched in wonder as he navigated around the currents and eddies of her emotional reactiveness.

Erik was pretty sure, that it hadn't been Jean who had accessed the spell room, but it had to be someone very powerful. The real question was whether it had anything to do with the current threat from Scáthach. That this incursion was very recent was too coincidental. Turning to John, who was explaining to Kiera how all the wards on the house worked, he asked. "Would you know what is missing from the documents downstairs?"

John shook his head in the negative as he answered. "Remember, Judith didn't live here. It was Kiera's father's house and he knew nothing of what was going on. She didn't have access via the mirror because we hadn't sourced another portal yet, so she had to go in through that door." John pointed to the wall next to the fireplace.

"I remember seeing her coming out of there once". Kiera said quietly. I was pretty angry a few days ago when I remembered, and realised she had tampered with my memory". Looking at John, she gave him a small smile. "I guess I understand now".

John nodded. "I only saw the room a couple of times myself. Your father didn't like me, so I didn't get invited to the house, and your parents rarely went away in those days".

Looking at the clock, Erik realised that it was getting late. He didn't feel comfortable with Kiera staying at the house alone, but had no idea how to persuade her to leave. Fortunately, John was obviously of the same mind on this. He announced that he could do with a bit of supper and invited them both to his home to stay. He reminded Kiera that it had once been her Aunts home, and that it was likely to be safer than staying in this house.

Erik could sense that she was inclined to refuse at first, but somehow John persuaded her. He certainly knew how to respond to her, and then there had been that mention of food. That was enough for him. He was suddenly starving and realised he hadn't eaten all day. As soon as Kiera left the room to go and retrieve her things from upstairs, John looked at him with a penetrating glare and then as if he had made up his mind about something, he spoke in a quiet voice, obviously not wanting Kiera to overhear him. “You're not her boyfriend and you’re not her teacher. And you are far more than a body guard. Something big is going on, isn't it?"

Erik stared at John for a moment and then just nodded. John sighed. "It's OK, you don't have to tell me. I'll look after Kiera for Judith's sake".

60

Leaving Morgan's, Gavin was undecided about his next move. They still had no idea who had summoned Scáthach or why. Having gone over all the information they had, both he and Morgan had come to the same conclusion. This was a deliberate attempt on someone's part to bring her back into the world. Morgan was certain it wasn't Jean and had to agree with her. All the evidence pointed to him wanting to collect all the Amulets, but for another purpose entirely.

There were so many unanswered questions about all of this. Making a decision, he made his way to Erik's and used his portal to slip into his private quarters at the shop. It was closing time so he would need to make an appearance as the police were still monitoring his movements, and his little spell to keep customers from venturing in needed to be refreshed.

After that, his first priority was to check in on Erik and Kiera. They could be in danger if Jean decided to try to steal her Amulet next. Morgan had been very clear that he used mundane means, as readily as magical ones, to achieve his ends. Erik would not be expecting Jean to arrive with a gang of henchmen carrying guns.

As he put the CLOSED sign in the window of the shop and made a show of shutting the door, he sent a little probe out to the policewoman sitting in the unmarked car down the street. Her boredom was palpable. Smiling to himself, he subtly reinforced her thought that this was a waste of time and a little push encouraging her to argue against continuing with it when she next saw the Inspector.

He was back at Erik's within a few minutes and, quickly scrying his location, was surprised to find him in the local village and not at the Blair house. A quick check told him that Kiera was with him. He could sense magical wards around them. They were the product of old and solid magic, and he recognised their signature. Funny, though, that family had never been that strong before. Sensing nothing dangerous, he sent a message to Erik and waited.

He could feel the worry in his old friend's response. Erik wanted to speak with him urgently. They were safe, but he did not want to leave Kiera. It was obvious to Gavin that Erik needed to meet face-to-face with him, as he also sent through an image of a garden with an ancient oak at its boundary. Using this as an anchor, Gavin translocated using Erik's portal as a gateway, arriving just as Erik emerged from a cottage about twenty metres away.

Looking around him, Gavin did a quick survey and found no threats. Making his way up the slight slope to meet Erik, he was aware of his friend's relief. Looking past him, he saw an older man waiting quietly in the doorway. As he approached the porch, he recognised the awe in the waiting man's eyes. He smiled reassuringly and stopped. Erik, aware that the protocols should be maintained, announced Gavin by his formal titles. Gavin of Skye, Second of the Twelve, Protector of the Craft, this is John Mc Williams, our host.

Executing a graceful bow, John welcomed him into the cottage, stepping aside so Gavin could enter. He quickly ushered Erik in behind him and firmly closed the door. Gavin was instantly aware of Kiera. She was watching him from across the room, a wariness and also a little hostility evident in her eyes. Pulling a little packet out of his pocket, he held it up as he covered the few steps that got him to where she was seated. Bending down, he offered it to her and said. "Morgan sent you some more of the herbs you need to make the potion she gave you". Turning towards John, he continued. "I expect, however, that John would have them all here in his garden".

He saw John start. "Morgan!" He muttered quietly. "It is big then, isn't it? I'll just go and check on dinner." And with that, he hurried out to the kitchen. Keira stared back at him and took the proffered packet. "So, you two are working together now, are you?" She almost sneered.

Gavin decided not to react. She was out of her depth, and she knew it. Kiera was a product of the modern world, and her lack of respect was not going to change overnight. Getting up, he turned to Erik. "So, no sign of Jean?" He asked as they settled down on a lounge near the fireplace. "No, but another name from the past has come up. Marcus Neville."

Feeling like the nasty bits of news were never going to stop, Gavin dreaded what he was going to hear. "How is he involved?" The answer was unexpected and very worrying. Neville had been a very talented warlock, but his greed for power had finally outstripped his own innate capacity, and he had turned away from the guidance of the council. Gavin knew that he had been involved in some way in the death of Connell's daughter, Riona, but now listening to Erik retell what he had learned about the death of Judith Blair, gave him a whole new perspective on Riona's death.

He was acutely aware of Kiera listening to their discussion and John, not far away in the kitchen, organising their supper. This was not the time or place to fill Erik in on what he had learned from Morgan. Thinking about what he had discovered over the last twenty-four hours, he was reassured that his assessment that Jean was not involved in trying to bring Scáthach back was right. Jean would realise that Keira was his best bet, and he hadn't made any move towards her so far. And time was ticking away, it would be Beltane in just a few days and that would be the perfect time to cast the spell.

He was pulled out of his reverie by John bustling into the room with a large dish of fried rice. A little flustered, he placed it on the table and looking at Gavin, said somewhat ruefully. "I am a single man and I wasn't expecting guests, so we are going to have to make do". Sniffing the delicious aromas wafting towards him from the dish, Gavin felt a rush of genuine liking for this gentle man.

"If this is making do, then I might visit you again," interjected Erik, who looked a bit like a ravenous wolf slavering over the food. John disappeared back into the kitchen to return a few minutes later with some plates and cutlery. Setting the table quickly and efficiently, he looked across to Kiera and invited her to join them. Gavin noted that he seemed to know how to handle her, and that she responded well to him. She smiled for the first time since he had arrived, and gracefully unfolding herself from the chair she had been sitting in, came over to the table.

Sitting around John's table in his comfortable cottage, he focused on being a good guest. John deserved to be treated with respect and courtesy, and since he couldn't talk freely anyway, he decided to find out more about the local coven and the level of knowledge about magic still held by them. He was surprised to find that it was a thriving community. John had led them for the last ten years, and his own skill was significant. Indeed the wards that protected this cottage were of a high quality.

Having come to accept the absence of magic in the modern world, Gavin found himself a little ambivalent about what he was learning. John, unaware of his eminent guest's conflicted ideas about the usefulness of magic in a world of technology, proudly spoke of the magic school he ran out of his bookshop. He was in touch with similar covens all through the lowlands, and the north of England, and he held a great deal of knowledge in trust. As he sat there listening to this good man, Gavin chastised himself for his lack of attention to what was really going on. He was supposed to be the protector of the craft, and he had selfishly allowed himself to drift away from his responsibility.

He saw Erik watching him closely. His old friend had been quite vocal over the years about what he saw as Gavin's gradual retreat from the magical world. He hadn't always been gentle about it either. Acknowledging his mistakes was not easy. Especially now, when he couldn't help but accept that his failure to properly monitor the five families had left them open to attack. He had known that the Bran family had almost died out, but he hadn't known that the Poole Amulet had been missing for more than a century. He had just accepted that the family were no longer interested in practicing magic, and left them alone.

Pondering this thought, he suddenly had a clear picture of Adrian Poole sitting in the drawing room of the London townhouse, in slightly dishevelled clothing with blood shot eyes. His discourteous manner had been insulting. He had informed Gavin that he had put the families Amulet away for safe keeping. He had no talent of his own, and neither did his son, so they would wait and see if any of the grandchildren showed signs of talent. He had promised to let Gavin know if this should eventuate.

He felt a stab of guilt as he acknowledged that he had not challenged Adrian. He had been preoccupied with his own life, and fed up with the centuries of responsibility. Relieved that he didn't have to put time aside to train and mentor another initiate, he had happily accepted Adrian's assurances . It had been the same with the Blair's. He had so readily accepted their rejection of their inheritance. The fact that these families, so strong in magic for so many centuries, no longer had talented progeny, just reinforced his own belief that magic was fading from the earth.

Kiera's voice brought him out of himself. He had indulged in too much self absorption and now was not the time to whip himself with guilt. He needed to look at all of this in the context of what was happening now. He needed to be honest and accept the help of those who had been braver and truer. He focused on the conversation around him. Kiera was questioning Erik about his history and role. She had a strident quality to her voice that he found irritating, even though he knew that it hid her insecurity. Again it was John who deftly intervened and turned the conversation back to the present, and the vital issue of desert.

While John and Erik cleared the table, Gavin focused his attention on Kiera. She certainly had a strong resemblance to several of her ancestors. Despite the modern, somewhat harsh and edgy persona, there were depths to this young woman. Gavin realised he would have to find a way to relate to her if he was going to get her to trust him, but for the life of him, he couldn't work out how. Morgan had given him a brief outline of the knowledge and basic skills, she had introduced to Kiera over the last few days. She had been impressed by her aptitude and intelligence.

Kiera had obviously also decided that she needed to approach him differently. Using her considerable beauty as her tool, she smiled at him in a seductive and alluring manner and asked him questions about himself and Erik. He knew from Morgan that Kiera was unaware that they were immortal. Morgan had not felt it was safe to give her too much information. Watching her now he thought that Morgan had been right. There was a cunning and calculating aspect to this woman.

Having heard Erik introduce him, Kiera was very aware of John's deference to him, and to a lesser degree to Erik.. He needed to provide her with answers that made sense. She already understood that there were levels of skill, as well as inherited responsibilities, among those that practiced magic. Building on this, he explained to her, that in the past, as a member of one of the five families, she would have known and been taught by a member of the council. That it is the responsibility of the council to monitor the practice of magic, ensuring that it remained within the defined areas that had been determined millennia ago.

He was aware that John and Erik, having returned from the kitchen with tea and cake, were listening closely to what he said, and how much he said. He assumed that Erik had already cautioned John about giving Kiera too much information. Quickly glancing at his host, he saw that he was wearing a neutral expression that gave nothing away, so he continued. And explained that if her family had continued to practice magic he would have overseen her training as current bearer of the Amulet, since this was his role on the council.

Unlike previous junior members of the community, Kiera didn't simply accept his pronouncements. She wanted to try and prise information out of him. He was starting to feel his ire build, when John distracted her with an offer of a cup of tea. It was obvious that her initial reaction to being diverted from her target was irritation, but somehow John was able to diffuse and deflect her emotional reactiveness, and she accepted, not only the tea, but the closure of any further questioning.

As they all focused on tea and cake, and Erik and John entertained Kiera, Gavin started formulating his next step. Having had some of his questions answered by Morgan and now this new information from John, he had realised that this scheme to return the warrior goddess had been a long time in the making. He wasn't going to solve it tonight. What he did need to do was ensure Kiera's safety. Scáthach had already partially infiltrated this realm through

Kiera. Libido killing herbs were all well and good, but that didn't stop someone using force rather than seduction.

He also needed to find out what happened to Rhonwen. Did Declan have her? That didn't make much sense. He did not need her, and taking her with him would have been risky. No. If he had gotten his hands on her he wouldn't have hesitated to kill her. The mystery was that no one had been able to scry her. This meant she was somewhere warded. If not Declan, who? Almost before the question was fully formed in his mind, he thought of Jean Bran, and a nasty taste in his mouth developed as the workings of his intuition told him the truth about it.

61

Sitting at his desk, staring through the window, Brian felt completely alien and out of step with the routines of the office. Was it only just over a week since his whole understanding of the world had so fundamentally shifted? He had finally processed some of what had happened as he and Stewart had driven to Wales and back. He still couldn't believe it, and yet apparently it was real.

The Amulet dangling off it's leather cord against his chest, was a constant reminder that he wasn't dreaming. Or would that be a nightmare?! He felt the constant warmth of this thing. This connection to something he didn't really want to believe in, and yet, there was also something reassuring about it at the same time. He felt safer with it. The real puzzle was that he hadn't felt unsafe before, so what had changed?

He had spent a lot of time thinking about it since Saturday. Rummaging around in the stuff he had found in the attic of his father's townhouse, he was stunned at what was there. When he had asked his father about the family, he had vaguely directed him to the boxes and mentioned that there was more in a trunk that his great-aunts had stored in the attic. On closer questioning, it became apparent that his father had never been interested in the family's history. "That stuff is just what the women collected", was his dismissive answer.

He had happily gone off to play golf and left Brian to himself. The first shock had been that it was obvious that someone had already been there before him. The layer of dust suggested that it had been many years ago. Papers had been rifled through and then hastily crumpled and squashed back into the boxes with no semblance of order. Nevertheless, it had been an emotional experience, especially finding his mother's papers. But nothing about any of it offered a clue to the family's magical inheritance.

The trunk his father had spoken about wasn't in the attic. He had found that stashed at the back of the garage behind a collection of discarded furniture. It had been an entirely different matter. As soon as he had cleared away all of the rubbish, his Amulet started to warm up and make a strange humming noise. He had been inspecting the old and intricate lock when there had been a sudden sound of a bell, and it had just clicked open. He immediately understood that the Amulet was the key.

He had sat there for maybe half an hour, just looking at the designs on the surface of the wooden trunk. It felt foolish now, but he had been afraid to open it. Somehow, despite everything that had happened, he knew that it was all going to be too real once he looked inside. As he had waited for himself to be ready to face it, he had come to understand that he was afraid. That all of this digging up of the past had propelled him back into his grief over his mother's death. He had no wish to experience that loss again.

It had been finding the family Grimoire that had really brought it all home to him. It had been wrapped up in a sheepskin, with a beautifully worked leather cord of several different colours tying it into a neat bundle. There were lots of other objects that he had no understanding of, although he recognised some of them from one of the books Haden Cooper had given him.

Then, of course, there was the diary. The last entry was in the spidery hand of the elderly, but there were several different peoples handwriting evident. It had been kept by several members of his family, but the most recent set of entries had been made during the latter part of the eighteenth century. Using a family tree that he had found in the attic, he had worked out that the diarist was his thrice great-grandfather, Adrian.

There was a considerable gap in the record. Adrian had made entries all through the eighteen-eighties and nineties and then abruptly stopped. He wrote of family matters, the births of his children and his business's success, but the last entry was totally different. He had been well into his seventies, and the date of the entry was only weeks before his death. Brian was still appalled by what he had read. Even now, when he had had time to digest it, the idea that one of his family had been so disreputable was unsettling.

Still immersed in his thoughts, he was suddenly aware of a knocking on his door. Looking up, he saw Felicity hovering at the doorway. She had a hesitant smile on her face and a bundle of papers in her arms. Pulling himself back out of his reverie, he brought his mind back to the present and, with that, acknowledged her, inviting her in for the Monday debrief. He would need to put it all on the back burner until tonight. The others weren't far behind Felicity, and they had a lot of work to get through.

It was around six when he made his way to the lift. He could see Stewart waiting for him. It had been a hectic day, but the decision to give Jennifer a shot at Kiera's project had proven to be a winner. Michael was happy, and there was a sense of order back in the department. He felt a level of reluctance to end his working day. It was reassuringly familiar and left him with no ambiguities. Gerry was downstairs waiting to take them to Erik's, where they were set to meet with Gavin and pool their information. He was very curious but also very apprehensive.

Once they were safely tucked up in the back of Gerry's taxi, Stewart informed him that he had spoken with Erik and Kiera wouldn't be joining them. Stewart's relief was palpable. His own family research informed him of several interesting facts. Still, one that he hadn't been too keen on was that the Eggleston men apparently had a bit of a fatal attraction to the Ninian women. There were several of them in his family tree.

Brian felt himself relax a bit. "It will be much easier to talk about all of this without her there, all hostile and bitchy". He commented. He and Stewart had already exchanged their news on the drive back to town last night. They both felt as bemused as each other. Stewart had confessed to being extremely ambivalent about the fact that, although he was somehow involved, he wasn't a key player. It sort of tied in with an ongoing theme he saw in his life, of being what he had called the support act.

Brian wanted to be supportive, but his own resources were wearing thin at the moment. He was worried and tired. And tired of being worried. A big part of him just wanted his life back. And there was still the Inspector to contend with. Not long before he had left the office, he had had a call from him, seeking to interview him again tomorrow. He had said it was to clarify some of Rhonwen's details, as they had been unable to locate her since she was reported missing on Saturday. But Brian had a sixth sense that the Inspector knew something. He just had no clue what he could know.

It was Gavin who opened the door to Erik's. He seemed to sense that they were both a bit overwrought. Brian felt a gentle touch on his mind, filled with kindness and understanding. Surprisingly, instead of feeling irritated by the presumption, he felt relieved. He had been dreading this. He was already struggling with information overload. As Gavin ushered them into the lounge, Erik emerged from the kitchen with a platter piled high with antipasto and bread, and Connell offered them a glass of wine.

The ordinariness of it seemed to dispel the rest of his anxiety, and as he took a sip of what turned out to be an exceedingly good red, he sat down on the lounge and relaxed for the first time in days. The general consensus was that they should settle in and eat and let the sharing of information wait until they were replenished. He looked across at Stewart, his friend of so many years. They had been through so much together. This was not going to defeat them. Almost as if he could read his mind, Stewart turned towards him and lifted his glass.

It was only ten o"clock, but it seemed like they had been talking for hours. Connell had been particularly impressed by the workmanship of the coloured leather cord wrapped around the Poole Grimoire. Brian had not known that there were spells woven into the pattern of knots and that no one but the bearer of the Amulet could have untied it. Stewart's dagger, found in a secret stash of old weaponry at his family home, had elicited an equal amount of praise. Gavin had even become a little sentimental remembering the last time he had seen it in action.

It hadn't been anywhere near as complex as he had thought it would be to explain how his Amulet had ended up in Europe. That his great-grandfather had gambled it away in the South of France was humiliating. His justification, written just before he died, was that the crash of the Bank of England had wiped out the family fortune, and he had been trying to salvage what he could.

The others were suitably incensed on his family's behalf, but it was Gavin's reaction that surprised him. Telling them about his conversation with Adrian over a century ago, he expressed regret that he had allowed himself to accept Adrian's lies, confessing that he had been lax in his responsibilities.

The news that Morgan had found Jean's signature in some of the magic used around the cabin in Knott's Wood had been profoundly worrying. It seemed pretty conclusive to all of them that Jean had Rhonwen. Connell was furious, feeling the guilt of having lost her very deeply. No one had any idea where he may have taken her. Morgan had supplied Gavin with as much as she knew, working together to pool their considerable power. They had located his flat. Although Gavin had checked it out while Morgan was up at Knott's Wood, he had found no clues as to where Jean may have taken Rhonwen. What evidence he did find was to do with Jean's connection to Declan.

Then while they were still trying to come to terms with the fact that Rhonwen was in the hands of a very dangerous warlock, Gavin told them about Marcus Neville. Poor Connell was so enraged by the very name he had been almost speechless. Gavin's explanation of what had occurred twenty-odd years ago, leading to the death of Connell's daughter, had set Brian's alarms off. Adding that to the story of Judith's death at the hands of the same man, Brian could see a pattern emerging. The frightening thing about that pattern was that his own mother's murder had occurred at around the same time.

Stewart, obviously thinking along the same lines, looked at him, almost asking for permission, at the same time as he spoke. As he asked him when exactly his mother had been murdered, Brian became aware that the room was suddenly silent. As he answered, he could see them all doing the same calculations. All three deaths had been in the same six-month period.

It was Erik who broke the silence. Looking at Gavin, he quietly asked: "When did Jean's mother die from that overdose? Gavin looked up, startled. Answering thoughtfully, he replied that it was probably about thirty years ago, maybe a year or two less, as Jean had been around seven years old at the time."

"So not the same time frame then". Erik mused.

Brian felt that there had to be something else. It was teasing around the edges of his mind, but he knew that pushing wouldn't help. He needed to let what he had learnt tonight settle into his mind and look at it again with fresh eyes. Sighing deeply, he stretched out his legs, and looking around the room at the other men, he saw the same tiredness in their faces.

His attention was grabbed again by Connell talking about Beltane. He knew little about the old pagan festival, but as he listened, he became aware that Gavin and Connell took it very seriously. Directing his question to Gavin, he asked what they were talking about.

"Beltane is an ancient festival. It is held at the beginning of May and is based on the movement of the stars and the change of seasons. Its celebrations are focused on the fertility of the herds and the coming of summer. It is also a time when the Otherworld is closest to this world. When the boundaries can be crossed more easily."

It was Stewart who spoke first. "Isn't Beltane when you were allowed to have sex with whoever you wanted?" Connell laughed for the first time that night. Erik's eyes twinkled, and he grinned as he answered. "Not quite. There were some groups that allowed the young to spend the night together as couples, but it wasn't some free-for-all."

"Pity." Stewart's reply had them all burst out laughing.

But it was Gavin's more serious response that interested Brian. He told them that the risk of Beltane was that the veil was thinned, and with Scáthach already focused on passing from the Otherworld to this one, she might be able to do so if she had the right level of magic being used on this side and a vessel. "You see, that is why it is so important that Keira be kept safe and that she has no sexual contact during this time. Scáthach has already infiltrated this realm. She just hasn't been able to stay. She could take over Keira's body with the right spell, and then she would be back."

"So this Scáthach was banished centuries ago, right"? Stewart said. When Gavin nodded in agreement, Stewart continued. "Has she ever tried to get back before?"

"She can't initiate a return from where she is now". Gavin replied. "She has to be called back."

Stewart looked puzzled. "So, You're saying that Keira inadvertently called her back using a spell."

"It looks that way," Gavin replied thoughtfully.

"Isn't it a bit strange that no one else has accidentally called her back before?" Stewart continued.

"I mean, after all, Keira can't be the first inexperienced person to use that spell".

"More to the point, I think, is who would want to use Keira's mistake to bring Scáthach back?" Erik said quietly.

"And is it connected to Marcus Neville and whatever he is up to?" Connell added, his voice hardened by rage.

62

Inspector Riley was feeling particularly frustrated this morning. There was no sign of Rhonwen Tierney, no evidence of her being in that cabin up north, apart from the hire car being parked near its location, nothing. He hadn't really thought she was in league with her cousin, but in this case, anything was possible.

He had decided to try a new tack. Hayden Cooper and Brian Poole were due soon. He had spoken to the Archeologist at some length the previous day, and a plan had been formulating in his mind ever since. He was pretty confident that Poole knew more than he had disclosed about these Amulets, and his little trip down to the family home over the weekend had to be connected. In fact, everything seemed to be connected; it was just that he didn't know how!

He was still planning his approach when they were both announced. Hauling himself out of his chair, he went out to the waiting area and arrived just in time to see the two men greet each other. Both surprised, but neither showed any sign of being flustered or anxious. Using a very matter-of-fact sort of tone, he said, "Good, You're both here. Will you come with me, please?." And he ushered them into the interview room.

Watching them as they found their seats, he quickly ordered his thoughts, and then before they could get too comfortable, he started. "Now, Mr Poole, this Amulet that you claim was given to you by a Gypsy Woman in Kosovo. You do realise that it is an archeological artefact and, as such, belongs to the nation." He was gratified to see a startled look on Poole's face as the man digested what he was saying.

Looking at the other man, he continued. "Mr Cooper, you informed me yesterday that five of these Amulets are part of a set integral to Britain's ancient historical record." Having given the archeologist his opening, he sat back and watched. "Absolutely, Inspector. And there are legal requirements that must be taken into consideration when a piece of our national history is discovered."

He saw a flicker of irritation in Poole's eyes. It had been quickly extinguished, and his expression was bland and neutral, but he was not happy about where Cooper seemed to want to take this. He hoped that this might be the way to crack Poole. When Cooper had told him yesterday about his findings, and his interest in obtaining at least one of the Amulets for research, it had occurred to him that he had an opportunity.

Poole did not answer immediately, so he decided to stir it up a bit. "So Mr Poole, this Amulet currently in your possession is of historical significance. Mr Cooper here feels it should be handed over to his University for study. What are your thoughts on this?" He was prepared to listen to all sorts of arguments, prevarications, whatever Poole came up with in the hope that he would learn more about what was really going on.

Poole looked directly at the Archeologist. Obviously choosing his words carefully, he replied. "It is my understanding that those legal requirements do not relate to objects that are owned and inherited within families." Cooper started to look a little flustered. He had probably thought that, being in the middle of a police station, Poole would just agree to give it to him.

"Well, yes, obviously private property is excluded from the law, although most families are happy to loan them to us to study." This was where Riley decided to interpose with his own question. "Are you suggesting, Mr Poole, that this object belongs to your family?" He was surprised to see Poole's mouth curve into a smile as he replied. "That is exactly what I am saying, Inspector."

"But you told both Mr Cooper and myself that it had been given to you by a Gypsy."

"That is true. It was returned to me by a Gypsy. However, it had originally belonged to my family."

Riley could see Cooper's shocked expression, his face slack and his mouth dropping open. He looked a bit like a fish. He might have been amused if he hadn't been somewhat surprised by this response.

"How do you come to that belief, Mr Poole?" The archeologist almost stuttered.

Poole turned to look directly at him instead of Cooper as he replied. "As you know, Inspector, I spent the weekend down at my family home. I did so because of what I had been told by that Gypsy woman when she gave me the Amulet. She implied that it belonged to me and that she was returning it. So I went looking for any evidence that this was the case, and I found out that she was right. It belonged to my family for many generations before being lost in Europe."

Before he could respond to this announcement, Cooper jumped up and almost knocked over his chair. "Are you claiming that you own this as part of your family's inheritance?" As Poole acknowledged this with a simple yes, Cooper started pacing around the small space, an excited sort of agitation evident in his expression as he continued. "So what about the other one? The Amulet that was stolen? Was it a family heirloom of Ms. Tierney"? Looking at the other man, he seemed to be weighing something up. "Well, of course, you will need to have proof, but more importantly, tracing its movements through time would give us so much more information. Does Ms. Tierney know anything about the other one?"

Riley found himself captured by the Archeologist's gaze as the man started talking about the National Interest with a look of intensity that was a little unnerving. A slight flare of light at the centre of Poole's chest caught his eye, and looking up, he saw wariness in the man's expression as they listened to Cooper talk about moral responsibility to the state and not hoarding artefacts in private collections. With a closed and implacable expression on his face, Poole cut in to inform the Archeologist that he did not believe there was any urgency for him to make a decision and that he would consider the matter.

This was not going anywhere near where he had originally surmised it might. The disappointment on Cooper's face mirrored his own. He had hoped that he would get something to help him find the pattern to all of the threads in this case, but Poole's assertion that his Amulet was actually a family heirloom, well, that was unexpected. Realising that he would have to ask Poole to provide the evidence to appease Cooper, he spent the next ten minutes negotiating between the men about how this would be managed and then let Cooper leave.

"OK, Mr Poole." He said as the door closed behind Cooper. "I am well aware that not only you but your colleagues, Stewart Eggleston and Keira Blair, all visited your family homes over the weekend. In fact, Ms. Blair has not returned to London as yet. Ms. Tierney, another colleague, is missing. Don't you think it is time that you let me in on what exactly is going on?"

"Inspector, I can't talk for Ms. Blair. She has taken leave, and we did not discuss where she spent her time off. However, as you can imagine, Ms. Tierney's disappearance has been very unsettling. I felt the need to see my family and follow up about the ownership of the Amulet, and as Mr Eggleston's family are close by, he hitched a ride so he could spend some time with them."

Riley could see that he wasn't going to get anywhere from this angle, so he tried another. "Mr Poole, are you aware that Lydia Chambers appears to have been monitoring both Ms. Tierney and another person by the name of Jean Bran?"

He had expected more of a reaction about this information, but all he saw was a flicker of interest in the other man's eyes as he replied. "No, Inspector. How is this Jean Bran involved?"

"I don't know Mr Poole. However, I do know that Ms. Blair has been spending a lot of time at his home over the last week before she left town. He also seems to have left town. I was wondering if you knew anything about a possible relationship between the two of them?"

Again, the poker face. Poole had not been forthcoming with any information, claiming ignorance. Since there was no further reason to keep him at the station, he let him go, reminding him to provide proof of his ownership of the Amulet. Sitting at his desk, staring moodily at his case board, he went over it all in his mind again. He hadn't really expected much. He had done his research. Brian Poole was seen as one of the best intelligence operatives in the business. He had connections and clout. From his own dealings with him, Riley had concluded that he could, in fact, be invaluable in this investigation if only he would share information. The very fact that he seemed to be holding back meant that there was something going on apart from a basic robbery and murder.

Riley couldn't help wondering if it was all part of some business with Poole's firm. Which, of course, meant that it was government business. However, if he had somehow become embroiled with some MI5 business, he would have expected a discrete communique telling him to butt out. And, of course, all of this crap about magical Amulets that Hayden Cooper had told him was just plain silly. He had actually wondered if the man was a little touched.

He was just thinking about getting some lunch when Stapleton came bursting into his office. He opened his mouth to rebuke him when he saw the excitement in his face. "What is it? What have you found?" He demanded of his offsider.

Stapleton almost threw the papers he was holding onto the desk in front of him. "Look at this, Sir!" Riley looked down at what appeared to be some court documents and, as he read through the headings, realised that this was the information alluded to about the Bran inheritance. And right in front of him, highlighted was the name Margarite Bran. Stapleton, obviously impatient to impart his news, pointed to another section of the documents. "See, she changed her name to Lydia Chambers over twenty-five years ago. It was in the old system, so it took more time to access it, but it's there. Lydia was Margarite and is some sort of third cousin to Jean Bran."

Riley read through the documents. So Margarite had tried to challenge a will that had left her out of the line of inheritance. She had already changed her name at that time but had to use her birth name to support her claim. She had lost. They already knew that. But it still didn't explain why she was stalking Jean Bran. He didn't get anything in the will. In fact, he would have been a tiny child at the time.

He knew Stapleton was waiting for his response but didn't know where it fitted in. Looking up at his board, there was no apparent solution emerging from this new piece of the puzzle. "Well, we might just have to wait until we can talk to Jean Bran himself to see how this fits in." He said as he added the documents to the growing file on his desk. Glancing up at Stapleton, he could see his disappointment. "Come on, lad, let's go and get some lunch, and we can talk it through."

63

Gavin had decided to check in on Keira before heading to bed. He had left her in the care of John McWilliams, where he felt she would be safe. As long as she stayed within his warded property, no one would be able to scry her. She had been a little reluctant at first, but when John explained that he could teach her more about her talent while she stayed with him, she agreed.

Morgan had not been overly happy with the plan, wanting to control the emergence of Keira's talent herself. However, she could see that, for now, at least, her home was not a safe place for Keira.

Passing his hand across the mirror in front of him, he sent a request through to John. It was only a couple of minutes before he saw the older man outlined in front of him, smiling and relaxed. Gavin was still a little perplexed about how easily John managed Keira and her mercurial moods. They spoke for a few minutes, and reassured that they were both safe, Gavin closed the portal and headed to bed.

The following day having finally managed to get some sleep, he opened up the shop, making his presence obvious to the ever-present police surveillance, wondering how long this was going to continue. It was more than a little irritating since the police were going to start to wonder how he ever made any money, as the spell he had cast around the shop meant that he never had any customers.

Setting the alarms so he would know if anyone came near the premises, he returned to the mirror and opened a portal to Erik's. Hopefully, Rouan would have some news about Rhonwen's location. It was a long shot but worth trying. Morgan had helped Rouan acquaint himself with the signature of Jean's magic, separating it from Declan's, and Rouan had spent the last couple of days trying to find some trace of it around the area. Even if they just got an idea of the direction he went in, it would help.

He arrived just after the Banachs, and it is evident that Connell was tired. It was not just the stress of the last week and all of the use of significant magic that was wearing him down. Being so harshly reminded of his grief and rage over the death of his daughter showed in the deepening of the lines around his mouth, his eyes more deeply set in his face, and a slump in his shoulders.

Rouan also looked flat and frustrated. He reported that he had found a faint trace of something about twenty miles from the cabin heading north, but it had been localised to that spot only. "This guy Jean knows how to cover his tracks." He said despondently.

"What about Declan?" Connell asked. "Do you think he is with Jean and Rhonwen? That they are still working together?"

"I don't know yet. Stewart would let us know the moment he comes up with anything that could give us a clue, but if he isn't with Jean, then Stewart thinks he will head back to Europe and go to ground.

Erik looked at his watch. "Well, Brian is with the Inspector right now, so maybe he will have more information when he returns. The boys have to look like they are just following their normal routine for now, so I will go to the cafe near the office where they have lunch and catch up with them. Neither of them wants to use their phones at the moment. Seems a bit paranoid to me, but anyway. What about you? What is your next step, Gavin?"

"Well, with Beltane only another twenty-four hours away, I have to try and get to as many of the covens as I can to request they keep all festivities mundane this year. Fortunately, most of them do so anyway because of the influx of neopagans at all of their gatherings. Morgan has already reached out to all of her contacts. The less use of magic at the moment, the better."

"Have you informed the council?" Connell asked in a quiet voice. Gavin looked around the room, knowing what they were all thinking. If Scáthach made it back into this world, the opportunity for her to create mayhem was immense. "Yes. And I have asked for a meeting of the full council. But as you know, that is not easy to organise and will take some time."

They all sat quietly with their own thoughts, drinking their coffee. He was loath to mention the name, but they had to address the burning issue. What was Marcus Neville's part in all of this? Twenty years ago, there were three deaths. All suspicious. Judith and Riona were both owners of Amulets. Rouan had become the heir only after his sister's death. Brian's mother had been an only child. Did Neville assume she was talented and that she had an Amulet in her possession?

He was still turning it over in his mind when Connell spoke. "It's time we focused on Neville. He disappeared after Riona's death, but that doesn't mean he isn't still involved in some way."

Gavin nodded in agreement. "Yes. This is a long plan in the making, and I do not think we know anything like the full extent of it. Jean would have been too young to initiate it. He must be either working with someone else, for someone else or being used by someone else. Morgan told me that she had thought his Amulet lost and that she had deliberately withheld the knowledge of the Amulets from him.

"Do you believe her?" Rouan asked.

Gavin understood the Banachs antipathy towards Morgan. She was a ruthless manipulator and had always followed her own agenda, irrespective of who got hurt along the way. But having had an opportunity to talk openly with her over the last few days, he did believe her.

"Yes, Rouan. In this I do, because she has nothing to gain and quite a lot to lose if Scáthach returns to this world."

"So, we need to find Marcus Neville," Connell said in a firm voice. "I, for one, would very much like to get my hands on that man." He continued with a look of determination in the set of his jaw. Having all agreed, they started to look at how they would do that. "We need something of his. An item he touched would be a help, but some part of him would be better." Erik offered as a first thought. The look on Connell's face said what he was thinking long before he spoke the words. "I only wish I had some bit of him, preferably his head on a stick! But he was very careful not to leave a trace of himself."

"That's right. I remember Mum telling me you only knew it was him because Riona managed to send you a message before she died." Rouan added.

Father and son, who had been sitting together on the lounge, clasped each other's hands, sharing their anger and grief. Gavin watched them. Nothing broke this family's bonds. The other four families had splintered apart from rivalry and greed for power. But the resilience of the Banachs over the many centuries had kept them true to their responsibilities and each other.

It was Erik's voice that brought him back to the moment.

"What about John McWilliams? Neville was part of that coven before he disappeared. They might still have something that was his or that he used".

"That's as good a place to start as any". Connell replied.

Thinking over their options, it came to Gavin that this was where modern technology might be of help. "You know, I think that we can ask Brian and Stewart to help with this as well. Erik, you could go and see John and, with any luck, find something we can use for a magical trace, and I will ask Brian to use his considerable skills at modern hunting to see what he can find."

Rouan suddenly sat up, a bright look in his eyes. I hadn't thought about it before, but they might be able to find out if Jean has any property that we don't know about yet. I mean, he must have Rhonwen somewhere, right? From what you have told me, they are possibly the only people who might be able to follow his trail through various government records."

"That's right!" Erik exclaimed excitedly. "It's been so long since we have dealt with anything like this, we've been a bit slow to recognise the possibilities".

"Rouan, that is a great idea." Connell agreed.

"And I could ask them about it when I see them at lunch." Erik offered.

"You better ask them to find out all they can about Margarite Bran while they"re at it." Gavin said. "Living there at the apartment house all those years, first watching Sophie and then Rhonwen. What was her game?"

"Jean's only remaining blood relative," Rouan noted.

"Yes, and it all started twenty-odd years ago. So, whose plan is it?" Erik responded.

"And who else is involved? That is what we need to find out. Why try to bring Scáthach back?" It was Rouan who voiced the nagging worry they all had. "Even if we get through Beltane with no mishaps, that's not going to be the end of it."

"For the life of me, I don't understand why?" Connell said in a puzzled voice.

"Maybe so we are forced to gather the five Amulets together in one place to work the ritual to return her. They have been kept apart for centuries, and now three of the five are already linked again." Rouan answered.

"But they can't possibly think they are strong enough to get past all of us, surely". Erik exclaimed.

Looking at the other men, Gavin couldn't help but ask the same question. Even without help from the council, between Morgan, Erik and himself, not to mention the considerable power of those that wielded the Amulets, they were a formidable force. He was missing something. Deciding not to alarm the others before he had any more information, he kept his thoughts to himself.

64

They had been at it all afternoon, ever since they spoke with Erik over lunch. Brian had been relieved he could do something useful with the tools he understood. He knew that Stewart felt the same. Both of them had been pragmatic and accepted that the world as they knew it had changed. That it now included magic. But Stewart did not have a new quiver for his bow; his weapons remained the same. While Brian's own "talent," as Gavin called it, was more a hindrance than a help.

He and Stewart had talked about it a lot over the weekend. Having a talent didn't mean much if you didn't know how to use it. Brian felt so totally out of his depth, despite the help that both Gavin and Erik had tried to give him. He was a soldier. He knew full well that a dangerous weapon in the hands of the untrained was even more dangerous and likely to get you killed. Although it was handy to have your personal warning system, he thought, as he touched the Amulet nestled under his shirt and currently lying quietly on his chest.

Stewart's little yelp from the other side of the desk brought his attention back to their task. "Have you found something, Stew?" he asked, hoping the answer would be yes. It was well after nine at night, and he was starving. *Selfish.* His inner voice scolded. *Rhonwen was in grave danger, and You're worried about food.*

"I have been given permission to ask permission to search through a security site that follows up on the purchase of large properties," Stewart said excitedly. "It's one of those sites that they set up after 9/11, so I have had to go through a lot of channels".

"How long will it take?" Brian asked, a sinking feeling in his stomach that they would be here all night.

"It's not that easy, my friend. "As I said, I can ask. That means waiting until tomorrow morning."

Brian thought it through. They had already exhausted the easily accessible sites for real estate transactions. Cross-referencing, using Jean's name, had come up with zilch. He had obviously used a different name, but knowing the addresses of Jean's flat and now his office had helped because they could trace the money used to purchase both places. That led them to watch for any other purchases that could be linked with that money trail—the sheer amount of information they had to search through meant that it would take time. Brian had set up the search parameters and an automatic signal for if a match was found, but there was nothing more he could do with that particular inquiry at the moment.

Jean could have taken Rhonwen anywhere in the country. Not knowing where to start was the most frustrating part of the search. But it was Stewart who voiced what he was thinking. "I don't know how the guys down on level five can stand this". He said a little forlornly. Brian almost laughed at the look on his face. "I know!" He replied wryly. "I wish we could have handed it over to them, but it's not company business, so we're stuck with it."

"And that bloody Marcus Neville character! He has covered his tracks so well there is hardly any reference to him even having been alive." Stewart continued.

"Yes, according to Erik, he hasn't been seen by anyone who knows him for over twenty years. He could be dead for all we know."

"Well, that would be one less evil dude to deal with." Stewart replied with a grin.

They had done all they could for now, and they might as well go home. As they made their way to the lift, he sifted through the information they had and tried to make some sense of it all. "You know, Stewart, that information the Inspector gave me about

Margarite stalking Jean, as well as Rhonwen, doesn't seem to fit anywhere. Erik had no idea what it could mean either. Do you think she was playing her own game in this?"

"Could be. But then again, maybe she was playing with and against Jean. You know. She was really keen to get her hands on the family's inheritance." Stewart said as they headed into the lift.

"Yes, You're right. Who did get that stuff? It must have been some other branch of the family. I think I will check into that tomorrow." Brian mused as they headed down to the foyer. "We could ask Morgan. She might know." He continued.

"How about we get Gavin to ask Morgan." Stewart responded. "You Haven't' met her. She is really scary."

Brian was a little startled by this. "Oh, come on, Stew. I know she bested you at Keira's, but...." Before he could finish, Stewart had stopped walking and pulled his arm to turn him so they faced each other. "Brian, that woman is not just formidable. She is as powerful as Gavin, and she is like a shark. Don't think that because you can do a little bit of magic, you will ever be in her league."

Brian stood still, looking closely at his oldest friend. Stewart was deadly serious, and he knew better than to discount Stewart's threat assessments. They had kept him alive more times than he could remember. "OK, Stew. We will ask Gavin to talk to Morgan." He replied quietly, watching relief wash over his friend's features. A quiet beep interrupted them, and he turned to see Gerry waiting. "Let's eat and go home."

None of them were aware of the eyes that watched them from a dark doorway across the street. As Gerry's cab pulled away from the kerb, quickly followed by the police car set to watch them, a tall, slim woman emerged from the shadows.

An hour later, as he entered the foyer of his apartment building, Brian's Amulet flared red through his shirt, its heat pulsing against his chest. At the same time, he became aware of four shadows detaching themselves from the walls in the darkened area. Instead of solidifying into recognisable thugs as the light hit them, they remained insubstantial and ghostlike. The stink of decay surrounding them made his stomach heave as he crouched low in a defensive stance, watching them as they surrounded him.

He found it challenging to keep a fix on the position of each of the four as they hovered, menacing but not coming close enough for him to strike at. He wondered if his hand would just go straight through them if he did manage a hit. As they circled him, he tried to plan a strategy. He noted that they had the semblance of faces and what appeared to be remnants of clothing, and filing away the details for later, he chose his first adversary. Before he could make a move, the lights of the foyer suddenly flared, and a low growl accompanied the blur of Stewart, crouched low as he forced his way past the creatures.

As Stewart knocked one of the spectres flying, Brian became aware that there was someone else standing to his left in the corner, near the stairs. The sense of threat was so overwhelming that he reached for his Amulet and grasped hold of it without a thought. Some part of him, the old Brian, watched detached as his other hand swept the room, a blue light streaming from his fingertips. He heard his voice crying out to Stewart to duck, and he felt like he was filling up with light and power.

The sound was earsplitting as the ghouls vanished, replaced by tendrils of smoke. Brian became immediately aware of several things at once. The snarling face of a woman as she disappeared, the look of amazement on Stewart's face, his family's dagger in his hand, and Gerry and a Policeman standing at the door of his apartment building, watching them both with disbelief.

65

Rhonwen woke up with a start. She was freezing, and there was something hard pushing against her back. Opening her eyes, she blinked a few times to clear her vision. As she tried to move, the lump at her back dug in even further, causing a sharp pain that she instinctively rolled away from. This landed her almost on her face, and that's when she realised she was on the ground.

She tried to focus and immediately felt a shaft of pain through the centre of her head, behind her eyes. Even though she knew it was dark, she felt like her eyes were hurting from too much light, so she automatically closed them, and the pain receded. Feeling herself drift back into unconsciousness, she shook her head to wake herself up, which caused excruciating pain. Then everything was black.

The next time she woke up, it was the feeling of being lifted by strong but gentle hands around her shoulders. She could hear voices that seemed a great distance away, but somehow she knew they were close. Forcing her eyes open, the light blinded her for a moment, but she didn't feel the pain this time. As her vision cleared, she found herself looking at the interior of a car; no, not a car, she realised. An Ambulance. Just as she recognised where she was, a woman's face smiled down at her, and a warm hand brushed the hair away from her face.

"Well, hello, young lady. The woman said. "Can you tell me who you are? What is your name?"

She had to think about it for a minute, and then she knew. "Rhonwen, Rhonwen Tierney." She replied in a voice that sounded very rough to her ears. She suddenly felt very dry and thirsty. "Can I have some water, please?"

She was given a few sips of water, and then as she relaxed back against the trolley, she was aware of the woman lifting her arm. "I am just going to take your blood pressure and check you over." The voice said, but Rhonwen was already drifting back to the comfort of sleep. She woke with a start to the clatter of metal somewhere close and opened her eyes. This time she found herself looking at the face of Rouan Banach. She saw relief written in his expression as he leaned over to take her hand. "Are you OK?" He asked in a quiet voice.

She thought about it for a minute. Doing an inventory of her body, she found that she was a little sore but otherwise felt normal. Her head didn't hurt, thank goodness, because that had been unbelievably painful.

"Where am I?" She asked, puzzled.

"Whitehaven Hospital," Rouan answered. "You were found on the side of the road just out of town early this morning." He continued.

Before she could ask any more questions, she became aware that they weren't alone. A Policewoman was moving across the room towards them. Rhonwen was confused. She didn't understand what she was doing on the side of the road. As she tried to think about it, she felt a twinge of pain behind her eyes, but she pushed through and remembered waking up on the ground in the dark.

The Policewoman looked at her closely and asked in a brusque sort of voice. "Ms. Tierney, I have been sent to protect you while you recover. It would be best if we leave the questions for now until Inspector Riley arrives from London."

Rhonwen was puzzled about why she needed police protection but was happy not to have to talk to them right now. Turning back to Rouan, she saw his lips thin and his eyes flash with irritation at the interruption, but he said nothing. "It's all right. I will stay with you for as long as you want." He said gently.

Over the course of the next few hours, the Nursing staff monitored her blood pressure and temperature and shone torches into her eyes. They felt her neck and asked if she felt any stiffness or if she was nauseated. Finally, a Doctor arrived and, looking at her and her results, proclaimed she wasn't exhibiting any signs of a head injury and could sit up and have something to eat.

Rhonwen suddenly realised she was ravenous. As the nurses helped her sit up and organised the pillows, a sound at the door caught her attention. It was Rouan's father, Connell. His caring smile warmed her heart when he saw her sitting up with a tray of food in front of her. It was genuine and honest. But his gaze was also questioning, and she was terrified that she had no answers.

She and Rouan had managed to exchange a few words without attracting the Police woman's attention, so she knew that she had been missing for the better part of four days. She had no explanation of where she had been, and looking at these two men who had been so kind, she felt guilty that she had caused them such worry.

She could feel the tears fill her eyes as she looked at Connell. "I am so sorry. I know it was stupid, but..." Her tears spilled over, and she started sobbing. Rouan grabbed her hand, his eyes full of sympathy, and Connell, having reached the bedside, put a reassuring arm around her shoulders as he comforted her. "At least You're safe now, lass."

Before they could speak further, the Policewoman was back, censure in her face. "Please, Ms. Tierney, Inspector Riley has asked for you not to talk to anyone about your experience before he gets here."

“And just how long will that be?" Rouan demanded.

The Policewoman looked irritated at having to explain herself, but she took a breath and said calmly. "The Inspector will be here in the morning. The doctors want Ms. Tierney to stay here overnight to be observed and suggested she not be questioned before the morning."

Rhonwen saw Connell frown, but he didn't argue. Instead, he moved around to the side of the bed and pulled a chair up next to his son's. "Well, I am sure you won't mind if we stay with her to keep her company for a while."

Rhonwen expected the woman to object, but instead, she nodded at Connell and returned to the chair beside the door where she had been sitting.

"Good," Connell muttered. Then taking a big, folded handkerchief out of his pocket, he gently wiped Rhonwen's tears from her face. It was such a fatherly gesture, and it brought a little smile to her lips. "It's OK, lass. It's probably best if you get more rest before we try and figure it all out. The doctor's right."

It was Rouan who reminded her that she had some food waiting on the tray in front of her, and he helped her navigate the packaged cutlery. She managed to eat most of the rather bland curry, and drink some juice, listening to the men chat about ordinary things to do with their lives. Rhonwen felt an enormous sense of relief that Connell and Rouan would be staying with her, and as she relaxed back into the pillows, a wave of exhaustion claimed her and she drifted back to sleep.

She couldn't believe how noisy hospitals were. All night the comings and goings of staff, the lights, and the noise of equipment had kept her half awake. Feeling like she had just drifted off, a harassed-looking nurse had woken her to take her blood pressure. But apart from not feeling rested, she actually felt OK as the morning dawned. Returning to her room from the bathroom, she was startled to find her mother waiting for her and the Banach men, nowhere to be seen. What was even more shocking was that she felt happy to see her mother.

It had been a long time since Rhonwen had felt loved by her mother, and seeing the look of genuine love on her mother's face as she came back into the room was as unexpected as it was beautiful.

"Oh, my darling!" Her mother exclaimed. "I have been so frantic since the police told me you were missing."

And with that, Rhonwen found herself enfolded in her mother's arms, feeling like she wanted to be nowhere else.

Before they could even begin to talk, there was an abrupt knock on the door of the room, and Inspector Riley strode in, another policewoman on his heels.

"Well, Ms. Tierney, the doctors tell me you are recovered enough to be questioned, and I have a few questions for you."

She felt her mother stiffen and found herself moved around so that she was half hidden behind her mother's body. "And exactly who are you?" She heard her mother demand. "My daughter has been through a trauma of some sort, and I will not have her harassed." She continued.

Rhonwen watched as the Inspector raised his eyebrows and looked appraisingly at her mother. "Mrs Tierney, I am sure you understand that, given the circumstances, it is imperative that we find out where your daughter has been for the last four days. I am Inspector Riley, and I am investigating the theft and murder that occurred in your daughter's apartment last week."

Rhonwen smiled to herself; he had no idea who he was dealing with. And sure enough, her mother quickly and firmly negotiated the terms she would accept, which was that she would stay with her daughter throughout the questioning. And so she found herself settled into a chair, her mother next to her, the Inspector across from her, and the policewoman taking notes.

"Now, Ms. Tierney, would you please tell me why you didn't inform me that you knew where your cousin Declan was hiding?"

She saw her mother's head jerk up at the mention of Declan. But before her mother could say anything, she answered. "I didn't know. I remembered about the cabin and thought that he might be hiding there."

"Oh, come now, Ms. Tierney, do you expect me to believe that you came up to the vicinity of that cabin, staying only a couple of hours drive away, without knowing that your cousin was hiding there?"

And the interview went on like that for over an hour. The Inspector basically accused her of being in league with Declan. Even her mother's dismissal of the idea as ridiculous didn't seem to have any real effect on his thinking. She couldn't convince him she had no memory of the last four days. He kept stating that the doctors had determined that she did not have a head injury.

She had become increasingly frustrated and enraged. How could she explain anything when she didn't know anything? Her integrity was impugned, and her rationality was questioned. The Inspector had finally left, making it clear that he was not convinced of her innocence and that she was to remain accessible for any further questions he might have. But, she thought to herself, what about my questions? Why have I no memory of the last few days? Even more scary was that she had no idea of what had happened to her during that time.

66

He was still feeling shattered. It was like he had been emptied out and left a shell, a husk with no substance. A movement at the door caught his attention, and he saw Stewart watching him from the hallway, worry written all over his face.

"I'm all right, Stew. Gavin said that I would recover by tonight".

Stewart came into the lounge and sat gingerly on the chair across from where Brian was ensconced. He had bruised his hip when instead of bowling over the creature he had aimed at, he had gone straight through it and hit the floor. "I feel like an old man". His friend said ruefully as he positioned himself more comfortably.

Before he could respond, Erik came bustling into the room with a tray of drinks. "OK, you two, I have some healing tea here, and I don't care that it tastes like dead socks; you have to drink it. We have to get you back into action, and Connell swears by it."

Erik had been looking after them and basically guarding them, at his place, since the attack the previous night. Brian was still trying to piece it all together. Somehow he had dredged up a tremendous amount of power and projected it at their assailants. Gavin had told him later that the sound of so much magic being used had alerted every magic user in the greater metropolitan area. He had teleported in almost immediately, quickly followed by Morgan. They had handled his curious neighbours very efficiently and dealt with Gerry and the constable. Both men now have no memory of what they saw.

His thoughts were interrupted by Erik passing a glass of greenish-looking stuff over to him. Realising that he was unfocused and vague, he took a deep breath and made himself drink the concoction. He needed to get back to normal. Rhonwen had been found, and he was no use to her, or anyone else, the way he was feeling.

"Have you heard any more from Connell about Rhonwen"? He asked, looking over at Erik.

The frown on his new friend's face was not reassuring.

"Rouan sent Gavin a message to tell him that Rhonwen's memory has been tampered with. It was a very sophisticated spell that can't be undone, which we think confirms that she had been with Jean. Declan is proving to be extremely adept at magic, but this type of spell could only be cast by a highly trained practitioner".

"So she doesn't remember anything that happened to her?" Stewart interjected from the other side of the room.

"No. But Rouan said that although she is very frightened and confused, she is not injured and won't have any residual problems with her memory."

Brian's initial reaction was one of relief, but as he turned it over in his mind, he realised that this would leave Rhonwen in a difficult position with the police. Inspector Riley had been very clear that he considered her actions suspicious. He was irritated that he wasn't able to get up to Whitehaven to be with her, not that she necessarily would want him there. He stared moodily out the window, vaguely aware that Stewart was working on his laptop but finding it difficult to focus his own mind on anything.

It was the sound of Stewart's voice calling his name that brought him back out of his reverie.

"I've found something. Brian, wake up over there. There's a farm up in Yorkshire, purchased five years ago through a holding company that is owned by none other than Jean Bran."

Brian became instantly alert, and as he did so, he realised he had been asleep. Glancing at his watch, he was stunned to find that he had been off in some sort of dreamworld for the last two hours. Getting up to go over to the desk where Stewart was working, he felt the strength returning to his limbs and his mind starting to clear.

"That potion of Connell's seems to have worked." He muttered as he breathed deeply, the muscles that had been so useless only a few hours ago now feeling strong and powerful again. Focusing his attention on the map that Stewart had googled, he noted that it wouldn't have taken that long to travel from the farm across to Whitehaven, where Rhonwen was found. They were still discussing the implications when Gavin arrived. As he turned to tell him the news, he was immediately aware that something was wrong.

"What's happened?" Erik demanded before Brian could formulate the same question.

"It's Keira. Morgan went up to John Mc Williams to provide some extra support for tonight and found him unconscious, and Keira was gone." Gavin informed them in a tight, angry voice.

"Does Morgan know what happened?" Brian asked, a feeling of foreboding starting to take hold as he thought about the implications.

"John was attacked. His wards were dismantled by someone with a lot of power. Morgan said that there was no sign of Jean's magic anywhere in the area. She is tending to John, but he is badly injured, and we will have to wait for him to come around to find out if he saw his attacker."

"Meanwhile, someone has Keira.". Stewart said in a quiet, tight voice. His worry was obvious to them all.

How could so much shit happen in less than two weeks? Brian thought, taking a deep breath to settle the initial anger that coursed through him. Today was Beltane. Two weeks ago, he wouldn't have even known about it, and it would have held no meaning for him. Now, he and a group of people he had only just met were circling the wagons, so to speak, using magic to protect the world from some warrior goddess. First, they lost Rhonwen, who thankfully was safe, but now they had lost Keira!

"We have been played, Haven't' we?" Brian asked in a quiet voice as he looked at the other men. Before any of them could answer him, the room was suddenly filled with blue light, and a voice called out from somewhere within a vortex that appeared at the door. "Erik, it's Finn here. May I enter your home?"

This was accompanied by a low-pitched sound that seemed to carry within it several different musical notes. Brian saw that both Erik and Gavin were startled but not alarmed. Erik waved his hand in a peculiar way, and the vortex dissipated, leaving a tall, finely-made man standing before them. His beautiful pale face, surrounded by a mane of blue-black hair was arresting, to say the least. Dressed elegantly, the grey and black hues of his clothes emphasising his slender form, this was a man you would never miss in a crowd.

Erik moved quickly to greet him. Their friendship was obvious from their embrace. Letting go of the Norseman, he turned to Gavin, his expression swiftly changing. With a look of distress in his eyes, he announced that he had made a terrible discovery. "It is worse than we could ever have imagined!

"What have you found?" Gavin asked, trepidation making his slight Irish brogue more pronounced.

"One of the twelve is involved in this plot. I don't know who." He held his hand up to forestall Gavin's immediate reaction before continuing. "All the evidence points to a council member, but they have covered their tracks so completely that I can't identify them."

Both Gavin and Erik looked as stricken by this news as Finn had in delivering it. Erik glanced at Gavin and then, addressing Finn and choosing his words carefully, asked: "Could it be Morgan?"

Finn didn't answer straight away. He looked thoughtful and then shook his head in the negative. "No, I don't think so. Morgan was one of the most outspoken against Scáthach. After all, she had been personally injured by Scáthach's warmongering and rampaging across the south of Scotland. Her own people were decimated".

Brian suddenly realised that he knew nothing of the history of what had precipitated the banishment of the Warrior Goddess in the first place, and as he thought about it, an image formed of the procession with the red-haired girl. As more memories flooded his mind, he was almost wretched as nausea overwhelmed him. He felt Erik's arm around his shoulders, and from a distance, he could hear Stewart demanding to know what was happening. Gradually the nausea faded, and his head cleared. As he looked up into Gavin's eyes, he saw that he knew what had just happened. "It's OK, Stew, he muttered; it was a flashback, just not my own.

The other men watched him, alert and focused. As his head cleared, he asked the question that had been at the edge of his consciousness all week.

"Rhonwen, or at least her ancestor, was killed by Scáthach, wasn't she?"

"Yes." Gavin said quietly. "There is a reason why the Tierney's were picked to be one of the families that were given an Amulet, apart from the strength of their inborn talent. Like all of the five families at that time, they had proved themselves morally incorruptible, but they had also lost one of their children to Scáthach".

Brian had somehow refused to look at the implications of the nightmare, being so appalled by the immediacy of his physical response to the dream. If he was honest with himself, he found the idea that he was witnessing a real event, something that had happened to his ancestor, not only disturbing but frightening on a level that had never affected him before now.

67

Standing in front of the mirror, looking at the dark circles and the lines of tension around her eyes, Rhonwen felt disconnected from herself. She didn't recognise the angry, fragile being she seemed to have become over the last couple of weeks, and as she pulled a brush through her hair, she yanked hard in helpless frustration. A knock on the door startled her, and she glanced through the mirror to see her mother poke her head around the widening crack as the door opened.

"Are you ready? They have processed all the paperwork, and you can come home."

Go home! Whose home? Rhonwen suddenly realised that she had agreed to go to her mother's. Looking back at her mother, she felt somehow powerless to make any other decision. She wanted to go to her own home, but she knew she couldn't; it wasn't safe. Maybe she could go back to Connell's or a hotel! Actually, anywhere else but her mother's, where she would be interrogated endlessly about everything that had happened.

As her mother retreated and the door swung closed, Rhonwen felt a sense of pressure building up inside her head. It wasn't really a headache; it was different, it was like something was pushing against her brain. Recognising that she had felt this before, earlier in the day, her immediate response was to pull back, but this time, something stopped her. Instead of retreating, she took a deep breath and pushed back with every fibre of her being against the pressure. She felt something pop, and her world changed.

A rush of power surged through her brain, sweeping away the webs that had tied up her thinking. It was like something had opened up a door in her mind, and she was able to see everything clearly for the first time. She saw the face of the man who had held her captive, and at the same time as she recognised who he was, she regained a complete memory of the last four days.

At first, she was horrified by the way she had been so misused by Jean Bran. Then rage threatened to take over her reason, swamping her with emotion so intense she had to grip the edge of the sink to remain standing. Looking at herself in the mirror, she was suddenly assailed by an image from the nightmare she had been having for the last week. Only this time, it was utterly and vividly real, and this time she understood its meaning.

All the pieces of information that she had been told or overheard started to form into a coherent stream of knowledge, and she instantly knew she needed to speak with Gavin. Her mistrust of him, and her anger with Brian were forgotten in this moment of recognition of her own responsibility to step forward and help deal with the threat Jean and whomever he was working for posed to them all.

Thinking of Brian, she saw his face clearly, and without realising what she was doing, her mind sought his. She was shocked to find him answering, his own surprise obvious. It lasted only a few seconds, but it was enough for her to acknowledge at last that not only was magic real but that she had talent that worked without an Amulet. Instead of the fear and dread that the idea of magic had caused her only a few days ago, she felt a sense of wholeness that invigorated her.

As she started to collect her things and put them in a bag, she became aware of a commotion outside the bathroom. Her mother's raised voice, filled with irritation, reminded her that she needed to address some practical problems right now. Emerging into the ward, she found her mother toe-to-toe with Connell, who was trying to tell her that he was a friend of Rhonwen's.

"It's all right, Mother, Rhonwen said. This is Connell Banach, and he is a friend, and I do want to speak with him."

As her mother stepped back and changed her confrontational stance, Rhonwen proceeded to introduce her to Connell and then very gently asked her mother if they could have a few minutes alone. Her reluctance was obvious, but she relented, and the moment the ward door closed behind her, Connell spoke, his voice hushed, his eyes filled with approval. "You've found your power, Haven't' you? I could feel the transformation from outside in the hall."

“Yes," Rhonwen answered simply, basking in this new sense of confidence in herself.

His hug and kind words of friendship warmed her heart. As he let her go and held her at arm's length, obviously wanting to say something, his phone went off. He quickly retrieved it from his top pocket and answered the call.

"It's Brian for you." He said as he handed her the phone.

Rhonwen took the phone from him, then glancing at the door to make sure it was still securely closed, she started speaking. Brian's relief that she was safe and ready to leave the hospital was obvious, but it was his excitement at her having made contact with him with her mind that she found the most reassuring. That he did not mind such an intrusion from her, especially after how complicated their relationship had been in the last week, was a relief. She quickly explained that she had her memories back and confirmed that it was Jean who had abducted her, adding that she needed to speak with Gavin.

"He is here with me now; I'll give him the phone". Brian responded.

As Gavin greeted her, Rhonwen moved further away from the door, and lowered her voice. "Gavin, I overheard a couple of things when Jean thought I was under his spells. Jean and Declan were working together, but Declan has broken off all contact and disappeared after he apparently killed one of Jean's friends. I heard him talking about it with someone called Max."

As Rhonwen told Gavin what she had heard Jean say about Keira, she was surprised to find herself feeling sorry for the woman. "No, I don't think he realised I wasn't completely under his control all the time." She answered Gavin's query.

She knew Gavin was being careful not to alarm her, but his reaction to the news that Jean had been able to access Keira through some sort of spell was obviously important. The look on Connell's face as he listened in confirmed it. Passing the phone back to Connell, she listened carefully to his side of the conversation and started to realise that there was a lot that she didn't know. For a start, what was so important about Beltane?

A loud rapping on the door interrupted them, and then her mother abruptly stormed into the room, impatience and irritation on her face. Before she could hear anything, Connell ended the call and, putting on a charming smile, turned and greeted her as if everything was completely normal. Rhonwen, who had automatically reacted like she always did to her mother's moods by retreating into passivity, watched in amazement as her mother suddenly stopped dead still, the door swinging closed behind her.

Marie Tierney had a beatific sort of smile on her face, but her eyes were glazed, and Rhonwen instantly recognised that she was under a spell. Connell came over to her side, and they moved as far from her mother as they could; then before he could say anything, she blurted out the first thing that came to her mind. "Could you teach me that?"

Rhonwen felt a twinge of guilt about her response to her mother being magically silenced, but the idea that she could learn to do it for herself was very seductive.

"It won't last long." Connell said, obviously trying to keep a straight face. "We need to sort out what you want to do. I know you have agreed to go to your mother's but we will need to all put our heads together to work out what it was that Jean wanted from you. You are welcome at my home any time lass."

Rhonwen had been thinking about how to get out of going to her mother's, but just in the last few minutes, she had changed her mind. An image of the family home where her mother now lived had become increasingly vivid. It was a room in the old part of the house up on the second floor. She had found it when she was a child, and now she very clearly remembered her Aunt Sophie deliberately diverting her attention from it. In fact, right up to this very moment she had never thought about it again.

"You know what Connell? Much as I appreciate your invitation, I think it might be important for me to go home. I Haven't been there for nearly a year. My father has been sick, and, well"; She hesitated glancing at her still quiescent mother. "She has been trying, and she would be really hurt if I didn't go with her. It's not too far from you and we can get together in a couple of days."

Connell took her hand and smiled gently at her. "You're a good lass." She squeezed his hand back and smiled gratefully. "But I would still like you to teach me how to stop her in full flight."

Connell laughed as he let her hand go and then turning to her mother, he made a small gesture and whispered something. Her mother regained her momentum, a warm smile on her face as she asked Rhonwen if she was ready to go.

68

Opening his eyes, Declan's first impression was that he was lying in a rather gloomy stone room. Trying to get a feel for the strange place he had found himself in, he turned his head to look around, while at the same time trying to take an inventory of his body. He was surprised to find that he didn't hurt anywhere so he decided to sit up, but to his horror, Declan realised that his head was the only thing he could move, and just as this registered so did the fact that his Amulet was gone. He lowered his chin to his chest desperate to be wrong, but he knew it was gone because he felt naked, almost hollow, and then a wave of pain and loss so huge and intense swept over him and he was overwhelmed; fear gripping his guts.

Declan's breathing quickened uncontrollably and he was on the verge of blacking out, when he heard a groan. Following the sound with his head he turned and found himself looking at the profile of a beautiful, dark haired girl. She was lying next to him on the other side of what he now realised, was a very large bed. Watching her breathe, it dawned on him that she was unconscious. Somehow the fact that he wasn't alone, helped him re-focus. Declan's natural instinct for survival kicked in, and he pulled himself back from the edge of hysteria.

His breathing slowly settled down as he turned his head in each direction trying to get an idea of the size of the room and it's features. But all he could see were shadows. They were cast by a faint light that seeped around the edges of some boards used to cover what looked like a small opening in the wall. He tried to focus on how he had been captured and by whom, but every time he tried to tap into his memory his thoughts just slipped away. Anger threatened to swamp him again but Declan was not prepared to increase his vulnerability by being emotional, so he deliberately pushed it away.

He decided to turn his head back towards the girl that lay beside him. It was more a pleasant view, he thought, one that he could appreciate even more if this was going to be his last moments on earth. A loose, white robe covered the subtle curves of her body. He contemplated the odd idea of trying to figure out how long he had been there. For a split second, it seemed necessary, but he soon realised that there was no way he could figure that out. Abandoning what he decided was a useless pursuit, Declan watched the girl next to him, mesmerised by the rhythmic rise and fall of her breasts. It was much more fascinating and alluring in that instant than anything else. But it was not to last. As darkness filled the room, even that small pleasure was taken from him.

Light flared suddenly. It startled him, and turning towards its source and saw an elderly man slide into his line of sight. The man ignored Declan, who watched him closely, wondering who he was, and stepped around to the side of the bed that gave him access to the girl. A noise alerted Declan that someone else had come into the room. Movement at the end of the bed confirmed that there were at least two others.

The next thing Declan knew was that he was lying on his side in damp grass. He wasn't sure how it had been done, but there he was. Realising he was no longer paralysed, he immediately pushed himself up into a sitting position and scanned his surroundings. He was in the middle of what looked like a small clearing in a woodland. The old man, malevolence written all over his face was there, and standing next to him, her gaze penetrating and cold, was an exotic looking woman. She looked past them towards the trees where Declan could see shadows that told him that there were others watching.

Before he could even begin to formulate any idea of escape, he heard a noise behind him. Swivelling quickly around, he expected Jean. Instead Declan saw the dark haired girl, sitting up, leaning against a large squared piece of stone. She was naked and quite beautiful, despite the empty, glazed look of her eyes. Blue swirling markings on her limbs and across her breasts seemed oddly familiar to him.

As Declan turned back towards the others, he felt someone coming up behind him. Rough hands pinned his arms, while other hands grasped his head. The old man moved to the front of him, forcing a cup of some kind against Declan's lips and a bitter tasting liquid filled his mouth. The lethargy that had been hampering his movements up to this point instantly disappeared. He was just about to jump to his feet when, whatever control he had of his body, disappeared.

Declan could hear the old man say something about the long wait, and his inability to fulfil his mission. He was obviously pissed off about it. He was deferential to the woman, whom he called Mistress, and he seemed to be following her instructions.

The shadows in the trees had now moved out into the starlight, becoming defined. A group of men and women were dressed in grey robes. Their faces were painted in blue patterns similar to the designs on the face of the unconscious woman. Silently they picked her up and laid her on top of the stone, her legs spread.

He felt rather than heard, some words he didn't understand, and found himself walking around to the end of the stone slab. It was then, just as he looked up the length of her lovely legs, that he felt a rush of lust surge through him. He staggered, his cock suddenly hard, urgent and throbbing with the need to take the girl in front of him. He became instantly aware that he was watching what his body was doing from somewhere deep inside his mind.

Another set of words, that he recognised must be a spell, almost wiped away this sense of himself as he felt compelled to climb up onto the stone. On his knees, looking down at the empty eyes, the part of him that was still aware briefly wondered who she was, but his need to take her, took over everything. Urgently pushing the long shapely legs up to expose her sex, lust took over the last remnant of rationality. As he entered her, he felt her move to meet him.

The instant he moved inside of her, he felt her wake up, her body fitting itself under him, moving rhythmically to the sound of a drum that was coming from somewhere behind him. Looking down at her face as he thrust himself inside her, he saw what looked like two faces in one. The beautiful face of the girl he had seen before, with another sharper, harder face, that seemed to shimmer within the girl's features. Arms grasped him and pulled him harder and faster, nails digging into his arse, demanding and all consuming.

Declan was desperate to come, but he couldn't. Something was stopping him. Seeking to override the compulsion to keep thrusting and pumping himself into the girl, he tried to extend what was left of himself outwards into his mind, to take more control. But instead he encountered another. He had somehow penetrated into the consciousness of the girl he was fucking. Fear almost compelled him to withdraw, but curiosity held him there just long enough for him to realise there were two separate people in that mind. One of them was locked inside her brain, hiding in a corner, it was the owner of the body watching what was happening to her.

The sound of a horn pierced the night, and as the last note drifted away, he felt the body under him arching in ecstasy and he was finally released. Declan thought he might die right there and then from the sheer joy of that moment. As the waves of pleasure slowly faded, he looked down at the woman beneath him. The rage in the eyes that looked back into his, was utterly terrifying.

He landed on the ground hard, having been unceremoniously thrown off the top of the stone. Laying there trying to gulp air into his burning lungs, he became aware that some sort of celebration was taking up the attention of his captors. Thinking to escape, he looked surreptitiously around him, seeking a way into the dark of the trees. Rolling over onto his knees, he almost fainted from the pain. Before he could recover, he felt rough hands dragging him up onto his feet and he was forcibly turned around.

Seeing the flash of a large blade sweeping towards him, Declan knew he was dead. It was so fast he didn't even have time to cower, but just as it touched his neck, it was stilled. A woman's voice said something in a language he didn't recognise and it was gone. He turned his head, looking for whoever had spoken. He found himself staring into the eyes of the woman he had just fucked. She smiled, if that is what you could call it, but said nothing else.

As Declan was dragged away, he dropped his eyes, trying to avoid her gaze. As he did so, he encountered her breasts, gleaming in the starlight, nipples puckered in the chill of the air. Lust flared again, in spite of his fear and fatigue. His cock suddenly sprang up, hard and insistent. Appalled, he listened to the laughter of those around him. She moved so quickly; it was almost a blur. She had her hand on his cock, stroking it, and she moved against him, brushing his chest with her breasts. The laughter immediately ceased. Saying something over her shoulder, she released him, then patted his cheek.

As he was led away, he felt bereft, as if he had been cut off from something that was necessary. Something he had to have. He staggered and would have fallen if he hadn't been held up by a man on either side of him. He was bundled into the back of a van, a smelly old blanket thrown over him. Gradually the lust and desire fading and exhaustion taking over, Declan drifted into unconsciousness.

69

Gavin was exhausted. It had been three days since the sounding of the horn and there had already been reports of several incursions into this realm from the other dimensions. It was a disaster! They had failed to stop Scáthach, and in the process lost Kiera and her Amulet. Now this latest bit of news from Finn! He had no idea what it might mean.

Aware that Brian and Stewart had just arrived, he took a deep breath and muttered a small spell of rejuvenation. He had to be careful not to over do it. Even Immortals could damage themselves by failing to give their physical bodies enough rest. As a wave of energy infused him, he moved away from the window where he had been standing, moodily gazing at the Banach's garden.

Turning at the sound of the others approaching, he noted that Brian was tired. That attack on him had been vicious. Thankfully, Connell has been able to restore most of his energy. He was going to need it now the dimensional barrier was breached. With only two Amulets in their possession, all they could hope for was to put a temporary patch in place.

"So what did you find?" Rouan asked, as they all settled into the living room. It was Brian who answered. "Well Morgan is positive that it's not Jean. The farmhouse was completely obliterated, and although the body is male, she is certain that it isn't him. We will have to wait for the DNA but, there is a possibility it could be Declan".

"Why do you think that?" Connell asked, his voice controlled and precise. Gavin looked at him closely. The Banach men were starting to piece together some disparate events of the last few years. They had all been speaking about it with Erik earlier, trying to determine the timeline. Brian's voice broke through his thoughts.

"Inspector Riley contacted me. They have found the car that was seen at the cabin in Knott's Wood. He thinks it was Declan's car despite its registration details, and it doesn't look like he chose to leave it willingly. It was abandoned on the side of the road with the lights on, and the engine running".

As they all digested this, Gavin saw Brian and Stewart exchange a silent message in a glance, then Brian started speaking again, directing his gaze at the Banach men.

"You know that Stewart and I work for an Intelligence and Security Firm, but what you don't know is that it is aligned with Government Security".

Gavin had suspected as much but was a little confused about why this was important. Brian continued in a hesitant voice.

"Well we can't say too much, but it means that we have access to information and that our access is monitored." He stopped for a minute and looked at Stewart, who, with a subtle move of his head seemed to give him consent to continue. "We were called into a meeting with our superiors. They sent us to a particular department, and well, we are now working within a rather special area of the agency. One that is apparently aware of your existence and the existence of magic."

Gavin was shocked. "So what does this mean?" He asked, trying to keep his voice even.

It was Stewart who answered. "That we have been directed to help you and the council in any way that we can. Apparently there is an understanding within the department that this needs to be dealt with outside of the normal channels".

Suddenly, Finn's strange message started to make sense. Connell's voice, harsh with fear, intruded.

"So there is an agency within the government that knows that magic exists".

Gavin could relate to the dread he heard in Connell's voice.

"Well, um, yes," Brian replied. "As you can imagine both Stewart and I are a little stunned by this. In fact, I have to say, I am still trying to get my head around it". Brian replied.

"But how did they know that you know?" Rouan almost stuttered, his eyes wide with shock.

Again, Brian hesitated, and Gavin was suddenly reminded that these two men were already committed to their prior allegiance to the Government. Stewart answered Rouan, his voice quiet but firm. "We had an obligation to alert our superiors of the threat".

Sitting back, he grinned in a boyish manner. "Honestly, we were expecting to be sent for psych testing, but they took it seriously".

The two Banach men looked at him, disbelief written all over their faces. They had all been so careful. Century after century keeping their activities as quiet as possible. How did they not know that they were being monitored by the government! But someone had known, that was now very clear from the message Gavin had received from Finn. Turning it over in his mind, he was unsure about whether to tell the others. Looking at Brian and Stewart, he found himself reluctant to share this piece of news with them, sure that it would end up in a report to their faceless superiors. Making his decision, he focused his attention on the immediate danger.

They were just trying to work out what this new information might mean, when he heard Erik's voice booming a greeting to Neve, Connell's wife. Glad he was back, Gavin looked towards the hall in anticipation, and sure enough the look on Erik's face confirmed for him that they had been right. After greeting the others, he launched straight into his report. He had been to Skye, the ancient home of both Scáthach and Gavin. All the signs had pointed to this being the location of Scáthach's return.

"We found the site of the ceremony. It was in the old grove. They used the ancient alter." He stopped and looked at Stewart, a softening of his expression alerted Gavin to what would probably come next.

"I am sorry, Stewart, I know that you are fond of Keira. She was obviously used as the vessel. I could pick up remnants of the rite from the surrounding area, because it was still so fresh."

Stewart simply nodded his head. His expression was neutral as he asked Erik what that meant exactly. Gavin could tell that Erik was a little reluctant to be too explicit but there was no point in protecting peoples feelings at this point. Taking the lead he encouraged Erik to continue. "Go ahead, Erik. It's important we all understand what has happened".

Erik continued explaining that he and Morgan had explored the whole area and that they had found traces of Keira, the woman who had attacked Brian, and someone that Morgan had identified as most probably Declan. There had been no sign of Jean. As Erik explained that it looked like both Declan and Keira had been the centre of the ceremony, Gavin felt a cold chill up his back. Who was behind this?

Stewart's tight angry voice asking Erik to clarify what exactly had happened to Keira reminded him that neither of these men knew the history of Scáthach's banishment. He wasn't sure that the Banachs were aware of all of the facts either. It was time for a history lesson. They needed to understand what they were up against. Stewart's next question came to the very heart of the matter. Gavin forestalled Erik's answer by responding himself.

"We can't be sure if Keira has survived Scáthach's invasion of her body and mind". He said as gently as he could. "She is very strong, but untrained. I can't give you any reassurance that even if we manage to banish Scáthach again, we will get Keira back".

As Stewart digested this, Brian's brow furrowed. Gavin sensed a vibration and then Brian was digging into his pocket to retrieve his phone. He looked closely at the screen, then a smile curved his mouth. "It's Rhonwen!" He announced as he put the phone to his ear.

Letting her know he was with the others, he put her on speaker. She had been at her mother's for almost a week and had used her time well. Gavin was surprised at how well she had recovered. Having found her talent, she had found a sense of confidence that was new to her. He was happy that his fears for her sanity had been groundless. All Rhonwen had needed was to be opened up to her inheritance. And now she had found the family spell room, and information that confirmed a lot of what they had suspected.

"So, according to the letter from Sophie, the Grimoire and a whole set of notebooks with instructions, were left hidden at the cabin. There is a second set of diaries and notebooks here, and a box of objects that I think are magical, but I will need some help sorting through it all". Rhonwen told them in a voice full of suppressed excitement.

As they made plans for Rhonwen to be collected from her mothers and join them here at Whitehaven, Gavin noted that Rouan was very quiet. He was watching Brian thoughtfully, his lips pressed in a thin line. This business with the boys working for some hitherto unknown government department had undermined the cohesion of the group. Because he felt uneasy about it, Gavin was listening very carefully to what Brian was saying to Rhonwen. She worked with them after all, and they had their own secrets.

He didn't think the others had picked up on it, but Gavin was certain that the way Brian used several words was some sort of message just for Rhonwen's ears. It was smooth, as was Rhonwen's response. He wasn't happy about Brian having another master, especially one that was of the mundane world. This would need to be addressed. He needed to know that all of them would follow his lead unquestioningly or they would fail.

As Brian finished speaking with Rhonwen, Gavin refocused their attention on what Erik and Morgan had discovered on the island. "What about the rift?" He asked. "I've had a couple of reports about incursions from up on the far coast". Erik nodded as he responded. "Morgan has put a sort of patch on it that she thinks will hold until you get there. Also, she's following the trail of a couple of demons that slipped through and may need help with them."

"Well that's our next step then." Gavin replied turning to Brian. "You, Connell and I will need to go to Skye and see if we can close the rift down. It would be easier if we had even one more Amulet, but we don't, so we will have to do our best with the two we do have. And Erik, you and Rouan can help Morgan".

70

Brian found himself more than a little uneasy. Gavin had decided that it was more important for him to have some understanding of his power, and how to tap into it, than for them to rush off to Skye ill prepared. As they worked through some exercises, designed to help him open himself up to his innate magic, he was keenly aware of a coolness in Gavin's demeanour.

Connell, too, had become wary of him. He had feared that his disclosure about the agency would undermine the fledgling trust that had been growing over the last few weeks, but Stewart had been right. They had an obligation to their government and nation. They"d had no option.

Suddenly sparks flared from his fingers and he almost set one of Connell's trees on fire. Gavin growled a warning at him to focus, bringing him back to the task at hand. Putting himself back into training mode came easily after his many years in the defence forces. Brian called on his considerable intellect and emotional control and followed through with the instructions he was given. Over and over again, he dug deep into the well of his being, to find that core of magic that he needed to learn how to control and use.

It was late in the afternoon, and he was bone tired. He was also jubilant. He had managed to learn how to deliberately call up the magic that had erupted accidentally, in the foyer of his apartment building. The experience of being able to control and aim this new weapon of his was exhilarating. But he also recognised the addictiveness of this power. As the three men walked back up to the house, he felt that there had been some healing in the rift between them, but Gavin's watchfulness was still very evident.

Climbing up the back steps he heard Stewart's voice, and his heart quickened. That meant that Rhonwen was here. Walking through the kitchen door he was stunned at the change in her. She was standing in the light of the window, her burnished red hair glowing from the last rays of the late spring sun. Her green eyes were flashing with excitement, and her cheeks flushed with pleasure as she saw him. He had never seen her look so relaxed and confident before, and a wave of desire almost halted him in his tracks.

Later, sitting in the living room, Rhonwen nestled at his side as he accepted a cup of tea from Neve and relaxed back in his seat. He felt like he could nod off right there and then and was drifting a bit listening to Stew chatting to Neve in his usual easy going manner. Enjoying the warmth of Rhonwen's thigh alongside his, Brian casually surveyed the room and was suddenly alerted by a seriousness in Gavin's expression.

"Its time we spoke about why Scáthach was banished in the first place". Gavin said gravely. "Connell and Neve know the story, but there are details that you all need to know, and that have not been discussed for many centuries". He continued looking directly at Brian and Rhonwen.

It was Neve's nervous glance in their direction that confirmed for Brian that the story behind his nightmare was about to be revealed. He carefully put his cup down on the table and collected his thoughts. His dreams had given him an inkling of his ancestors' relationship to Scáthach and the sacrifice of Rhonwen's ancestor, and he was apprehensive about the story's effect on Rhonwen.

The details were lurid to say the least. His ancestor Bryn's betrayal of his betrothed Aine was shocking. That he had been magically seduced, and was not in control of his actions did little to lessen the impact of the story. Rhonwen had been appalled, her own ancestor, sacrificed by Scáthach, cruelly and barbarically. Her throat slit, and her blood drained to be used as paint, to adorn Scáthach's warriors as they rampaged through the countryside, destroying first the people of Skye, and then those on the mainland.

"But why did she want Aine's blood?" Rhonwen asked Gavin in a puzzled voice.

"Don't forget that she was your ancestor. The magic that runs through you also belonged to her. By mixing her blood with the woad that Scáthach's warriors used, they increased their strength and resilience. Many kept fighting after being wounded when normally they would have fallen. It made Scáthach's war band almost invincible. Only magic could defeat them in the end".

As the story unfolded, scwraps of memory, like flashbacks intruded on Brian's mind. He kept seeing that same scene over and over. The procession, the torches lighting the path through the grass. He could almost feel the anguish his ancestor felt, and yet Bryn did nothing to stop it. He had allowed himself to be distracted by lust for the very woman who was orchestrating the death of his love.

As Gavin continued the story of how the families were brought together to save their people, and banish Scáthach from this realm, Brian became increasingly convinced that there was something important in this memory. Taking advantage of a pause in the story as Connell clarified some details about a particular battle, Brian took Rhonwen's hand and squeezed it. She looked at him inquiringly, and he spoke quietly to her.

"I have to tell Gavin something that I have been dreaming about, and its pretty awful. Please remember that it isn't about us. It was our ancestors."

Rhonwen's brow furrowed. "That's right! You told me you had been dreaming too". She shuddered. "If it's like mine then You're right, its ghastly".

Looking up, Brian realised that everyone else in the room was looking at them. Seeing the look in Gavin's eyes, Brian knew that there was no backing out now. Keeping hold of Rhonwen's hand he cleared his throat and began. "I have been dreaming about Bryn at the time of Aine's sacrifice. By that I mean, the very instance of it".

Stewart gave him a startled look and Connell's eyes narrowed. But it was Neve who immediately understood that this was going to be very difficult for him. She got up from her chair and came over to the lounge, where he and Rhonwen were sitting. "I sense what you will tell us is painful and will hurt you both, but I also know that it is about the past. It is not about you, but those that came before you." She smiled reassuringly as she spoke, and then taking up a position next to Rhonwen she took her other hand and stroked it slowly with her thumb.

Emboldened by her support Brian began, careful to tell them exactly what he saw in his nightmare. He felt Rhonwen tense, but she stayed with him, her hand remaining tucked within his own as he described Bryn's experience on the night of the sacrifice. Having finished his story he waited for the reaction. Gavin's face was thoughtful, while Connell just looked thunderstruck. The silence was starting to seem a bit too long when Gavin finally spoke.

"This sounds like Bryn was still aware in some part of his mind. Obviously unable to affect his actions, but able to watch himself and Scáthach."

It was Neve, her voice soft as she looked up at her husband. "That could explain our families' stories about Bryn Cuinn. It would make sense if he had been enthralled". Connell looked back at her, his eyes filled with love, and he nodded his head, a smile slowly breaking up the lines of tiredness and grief around his eyes.

"Yes, it does". He turned to the others and continued.

"The Banach family story of the last battle tells the story of Bryn Cuinn going Berserk and leaping off the cliff".

"What do you mean berserk?" Stewart's voice interjected from the other side of the room.

Connell answered him, his voice moving into a lyrical pattern that suggested he was recalling oral history.

"At the last great battle when the Shadowy One was sent from this land, from this realm. As the sky was rent and the earth was set on fire, Bryn Cuinn, Scáthach's general gave out a cry of lament. Taking up his great sword he went forth and slew all who had fought with him. Berserk, he killed all within his sight and as the War Band died, he laughed. At last, when all who had stood for Scáthach were dead, he leapt from the high cliff to the sea below, crying out her name, the name of his dead love, Aine."

Neve, looking first at Gavin and then at Brian said in quiet, proud voice. "I am related to you, Brian. I come from another branch of the Cuinn family. We have always held that Bryn was enthralled."

Brian just stared at this lovely, calm woman. That he had no idea she was his relative was mind-blowing. That she knew about Bryn, and the story of Scáthach's banishment, while he had never had any idea about his family inheritance, was equally stunning.

Gavin's and Connell's voices brought him out of his shock. "So when you and Morgan stripped away all of Scáthach's magic spells, Bryn must have regained his own identity. He only killed his own War band." Connell said in a contemplative voice.

"And himself!" Responded Neve.

It was Stewart's voice that brought them back to the here and now. "So, it's possible that if Keira is enthralled she could come back to herself?" He asked in a hopeful voice.

Turning to him, Gavin gave a slight shake of his head. "It's different with Keira, Scáthach has taken over her body and mind. She has been replaced so to speak. On the other hand if Declan was used as I suspect, then like Bryn he is probably enthralled."

Stewart's disappointment was palpable as he sat back in his chair. Brian felt sorry for him, and Keira of course, but it was the reference to Declan that had his attention. *What if he had been enthralled the whole time?* As he worked his way around that idea, he realised that it didn't change the fact that Declan had been a criminal before he had broken into Rhonwen's flat.

Feeling a squeeze of his hand he glanced at Rhonwen. The others were still tossing ideas around, but like him, she was basically waiting for direction. Leaning in she spoke very quietly, but with a determination that he knew would be hard to shake. "I want to come to Skye with you. I know I don't have my Amulet, but I think I should be there." Before he had time to answer, Gavin interrupted his conversation with Stewart and spoke authoritatively.

"Yes, Rhonwen. You are right, you should be there." And then turning to Neve, he informed her that she should also join them.

"Both of you have innate magic that can bolster the magic of your partners. It will be necessary for us to use all the resources we have."

Brian had felt Rhonwen stiffen at this, but when he turned to look at her, it wasn't irritation he saw on her face. Their eyes met, and a recognition that had gone unacknowledged for so long passed between them. He knew in that instant that the last three years of dancing around their attraction to each other was over.

The sound of the door bell startled them all. Connell left the room to answer it, and the rest of them waited for him to return. Hearing the sound of Connell's voice raised in a warm greeting seemed to release some of the tension in the room. Gavin rose from his seat, a smile loosening the grimness of his mouth, and started towards the door as Connell returned with their visitor in tow. Introducing them all, Gavin explained that Mac was the skipper of his yacht, now anchored off Whitehaven waiting to take them across to Skye. As Brian shook Mac's hand he looked into his eyes and found himself almost mesmerised. Large and dark, they seemed to move like liquid picking up the light in the strangest fashion.

Stepping back to let Stewart greet this new member of the team, he noted that Mac was small and slender, with that compact strength you see in men who work physically. His long silky dark hair, captured in a band at the back of his head flowed down his back. Out of the corner of his eye Brian caught sight of Rhonwen, her eyes wide with fascination. A stab of jealousy wrenched his gut, but as he watched her, he recognised that it was her intellect that was in overdrive.

As Gavin and Mac discussed the arrangements for the following day's departure he was struck by the lilting quality of his voice. It seemed an odd contrast to the way he moved. His walk and the roll of his hips were that of a seaman, but there seemed to be an awkwardness as well. It seemed strange to Brian, but then what wasn't strange about any of the last few weeks? Rubbing his eyes, he suddenly felt very tired. All he really wanted right now was some sleep.

71

Michael Riley wasn't used to being so frustrated and he didn't like it. Sitting in his office at Scotland Yard, staring at the whiteboard he was using to map his case, his head hurt. Yet another fragment of information that didn't seem to fit anywhere. But he knew it meant something. The sound of Stapleton humming under his breath was starting to irritate him. His off sider was sitting at the side of the desk engrossed in his laptop, chasing down a lead to some property that was apparently owned by the mysterious Margarite Bran.

His attention was caught by a CCTV photo of Brian Poole's apartment building. It was grainy and indistinct except for the flash of blue that lit up the foyer. Taken almost a week ago, from a camera that faced east down the street, all he could see was vague shadows that seemed to be men in some sort of fight. But as usual, by the time he got the photo, there was no evidence that anything had happened. No complaints of disturbance, nothing.

"Sir!" Stapleton's voice broke into his reverie. "I have just been blocked again. Every time I try to chase down anything to do with property in the name Bran, I come up against a blank".

"What do you mean a blank?" The Inspector grumbled back.

"Its like I am trying to access privileged information. You know when you go to a site you're cleared for. Its the same thing."

"Not cleared for! That's ridiculous. You're just doing a property search. And anyway, we didn't have this problem last week when we found the Bran place in Cornwall."

"I know sir, thats just it. Something has changed and I'm blocked".

Before he could respond, Constable Grey knocked on the frame of the open door. He had called her off the surveillance of the Antique Shop, after being harassed about the expense by the Division Head. He had to admit that nothing useful had come out of it, but it still irked him that the accountants could decide what he could do. He gestured her to come into the office, noting the sideways glance she gave Stapleton.

"What can I do for you, Constable?" He asked, trying not to be irritated by the interruption.

"Well, Sir, I had an idea, and well, I know you didn't ask me to, but I did a little search on reports of blue lights and, well you know, blue flashes like in that photo." She said hesitantly as she pointed to the white board.

His attention caught; he focussed on her face.

"And did you find anything about blue flashes?" He asked quietly.

Her pretty face broke into a grin, and she said in a much more confident voice. "Yes, Sir. There have been increasing reports of blue and green lights in remote locations all over the north of England, and on the Isle of Skye. And there was a major incidence of these blue flashes reported in the Yorkshire Dales, that the local police followed up on".

"And what did they find?"

"A completely burnt-out farmhouse, and the charred remains of a man they have yet to identify". The constable answered looking down at the paperwork in her hand.

His interest piqued, he held his hand out for the report. As he read through the documents it emerged that the farm was owned by some city-based hobby farmer that none of the locals knew. There had been no car found on the property, and the local police had not been able to locate the owner. Their thinking was that the dead body would turn out to be the owner, but, and this is what really got Riley's attention. The local police had not been able to trace the name of who actually did own the property. "Stapleton, I want you to put the address of that farmhouse into the same search parameters you were using for Margarite Bran's property."

Could there be a connection? He had no idea what blue flashes might be, but a dead body in a remote farmhouse was something he did understand. He watched as Stapleton put the information into the programme he already had on his screen. The look on the young constable’s face told him what he suspected. "I am getting blocked in the same way as I did before. I don't understand".

Riley sat back in his chair, watching his young colleagues trying to work out why they couldn't access the information he wanted. He left them to it, pretty sure that they would fail. His mind working overtime, he started connecting bits and pieces of information. There was something big going on here. It was apparent, given Poole's history and current role in intelligence. He had suspected that the Agency Poole worked for was related to Government security, and now he was sure of it.

Before he could take that thought any further, his phone rang. Looking at the caller ID, he didn't immediately recognise the name, but it turned out to be the Cumbrian Police Department. He had asked them to keep an eye on Rhonwen Tierney. He didn't really suspect her of being involved in the Bran woman's death, but his instincts had told him she was somehow pivotal. Sure enough, she had left her mothers earlier in the day, picked up by Stewart Eggleston. Ending the call, he looked up at his board, and the names he had listed there, wondering where they all were at this moment. Cutting costs had meant no more surveillance, but there were other avenues. Rhonwen Tierney's inability to account for her whereabouts and injuries suggested that the Whitehaven Police had not closed that missing person case when she was found. They had been happy to keep an eye on the Banach place and share any information that came their way.

Putting a call through to the constable in charge of the case, he wasn't surprised to find out that Rhonwen Tierney had arrived there in the last few hours, or that both Poole and Eggleston were also visiting. Apparently, several other people had come and gone over the course of the previous twenty-four hours. Everything seemed quiet and normal to the local police, who held the Banach family in high regard as one of the old families of the area. They were hesitant to be seen to be harassing them.

The constable reported that this was a low priority for them, as they were too busy with other business and understaffed. So, after listening to the usual complaints about too few resources, Michael Riley tried not to slam the phone down too hard.

Looking over at the other desk where the two young police, heads close together, were talking quietly, he became aware that the Division Head was at the office door. She was a plain woman in her middle years, and they were not great friends. She looked disdainfully around his messy office and sniffed, curling her thin lips at the sight of boxes of files littering the floor. Riley knew his hold on his office was tenuous. He wasn't senior enough in her book.

Without any preamble, she got to the point. "The Commissioner wants to see you".

Without a further word, she spun on her heel and walked back through the open plan room, where most of the other detectives worked. Where he may well end up, he thought moodily to himself, as he hefted his bulk out of his chair. The other two, having gone silent the moment they had become aware of her, looked at him with blank faces.

He knew what they were thinking. It was never good to get called to see the Commissioner. His long friendship with the man aside, it was not usual for them to meet at work. He couldn't help but feel a bit of apprehension as he made his way into the hall. He was also puzzled. Waiting for lift to arrive, he worried about what Gerald wanted to see him about. *Was it to do with the case or something entirely different?*

Less than an hour later he walked back into his office to find it empty. The two constables had been re-assigned, and there had been no sign of them in the outer office. Feeling like he was on automatic pilot, he started to take down the photos from the whiteboard, stacking them on his desk, before retrieving a file box to put them in. He was still stunned. He had never had a case closed before. A sound at the office door interrupted his thoughts, and turning, he found Gerald's secretary standing there.

"I've come for the case file," he said quietly, obviously trying not to meet Riley's eyes, his own shifting to the side towards the whiteboard. Riley just grunted and efficiently cleared his desk into the box. As he handed it to him, the man nodded at the whiteboard and, using the same quiet tone, said, "You better wipe all of that off as well before you leave."

Riley felt a surge of rage. The thought of what the departmental gossips would make of this twisted his gut. All of Gerald's reassurances about "the bigger picture" didn't change the fact that everyone else would think he had been disciplined. *Twit!* He muttered as the other man retreated out of the door. It took less than ten minutes for all sign of the case to be erased from his office. Grabbing his coat, he walked past the curious gazes of the other detectives and headed out of the building.

On his mobile was an address. His orders had been very explicit. He was to report to the secretary on the third floor of a Ministry building that he had not known existed until just over an hour ago. He had been given a choice. He could be redeployed, or he could go on leave. He knew he could have chosen to walk away and just go on leave, but something about this case had gotten under his skin. If he went on leave, he would lose all hope of chasing down any more leads, and it would give the gossips more to talk about.

Getting through the traffic didn't take as long as he thought. As the lift doors opened into the third floor's silent carpeted world, he looked into the eyes of a smartly dressed middle-aged woman. She rose and greeted him politely, then, without any preamble, asked him to accompany her. As she punched a code into the security pad at the door behind her, he was startled to note that she carried a gun. Neatly tucked under her jacket to be sure, but she was armed.

72

Brian watched Connell intently as he took Rhonwen's hand and guided it over what appeared to be a simple gap between two small standing stones. He thought he saw a shimmer, but it was the way Rhonwen reacted that confirmed it for him. The look of awe on her face as she turned towards him said it all. Standing with Brian and Neve a few feet behind them, Gavin rewarded her with a beaming smile and said approvingly.

"You may not have your Amulet, Rhonwen, but you have a great deal of innate talent." Turning to Brian, he continued, "You both do. And from what I have seen of Keira and heard of Declan, they, too, seem to be as gifted. For some reason, your generation is strong."

Neve suddenly looked sad, and her eyes moistened as she quietly spoke. "Both Riona and Rouan matured into their talents early. She was especially strong."

Gavin looked at her closely and gently took her hand, squeezing it in compassion, saying nothing. But Brian noted that as the Immortal turned back towards the rift, his eyes darkened, a look of concentration shaping his ageless face into a hawkish appearance.

The journey across to the island on Gavin's yacht had been relaxing. The weather was unusually calm and pleasant, and Brian had used the time to recharge and ready himself for their task. He was entirely out of his depth and had no experience closing magical rifts. Feeling a bit apprehensive, he did a quick readiness check. The sort of audit that all soldiers do before battle, checking that they have everything they need and are prepared. But this time, his only weapon was his Amulet firmly clasped in his hand.

Stewart, as usual, had his back and was currently monitoring the surrounding area. He could feel him a couple of meters to his left and behind. He had always trusted Stewart completely, and they had survived some pretty hairy times together. Seeing his friend diving into the ghosts in the foyer of his apartment building reassured him that even magic would be no deterrent to Stewart's sense of mission.

Connell had moved back from the rift, bringing Rhonwen with him so that they could discuss their options.

"It's a worry that the rift is here and not in the grove." He said in a quiet voice.

Gavin nodded and looked keenly around him. "After we close this one, we will need to check the whole island in case there are more,". He said in an equally quiet voice.

Connell nodded. "That will be time-consuming. I wonder if that is their game - to keep us busy."

"Yes, I have been thinking that myself," Gavin growled. Calling them all over to his side, he continued. "Let's get this one sorted".

Brian listened as the men worked out what spell would work best and tried to keep his mind focused on how they used the wording to control the outcome. Gavin had warned him that the actual wording of a spell was as important as the intent behind it. Phrasing any incantation the wrong way could be catastrophic. That's why most practitioners used spell books and grimoires.

A familiar hiss from Stewart alerted him, and he turned quickly, just in time to see a black amorphous shape hurtling down the slope towards them. Goosebumps rose along his arms, and he could feel his Amulet as it instantly flared in warning. Out of the corner of his eye, he registered Connell's hand raised and open, his Amulet flashing a clear blue light directly at the creature. It was all over in seconds.

Stewart grinned and nodded in approval at Connell.

"Nicely done, old man". He quipped as he turned back to his task of watching over them.

"*Old man* indeed." Connell snorted as he tramped over the long grass to the black spot that had been their assailant. "I wonder how many of those are lurking around the island?" He said as he peered down at the burn marks.

"We will have to do a complete sweep of the area before we leave," Gavin responded, looking around the area with his penetrating gaze. "Fortunately, those imps can't cross water, so they will be easy enough to find. The question is, what else came through."

"Well, let's get this rift closed then so we can get on with the clean up". Connell said as he returned to the group.

Over the next hour, Gavin and Connell prepared the area, and the rest of them, for the task ahead. Rhonwen would stay with Brian and Neve with Connell. Each of them would channel their power into their partner, augmenting the magic of the Amulets. Brian found the intimacy of Rhonwen's touch distracting at first. Her hand resting on the back of his neck, her body close behind him. So close he could feel the heat of her through his clothes. He knew she was feeling it too.

But as they worked, practising over and over, the sheer strength of their combined power took his total attention, and he found himself able to focus entirely. Finally satisfied that they all knew what to do, Gavin signalled to Stewart to join them, and as he jogged down from his vantage point, the rest of them took their positions.

"Stewart, I need you here right behind us". Gavin said as he dug a strange-looking wand-like object out of his coat. Giving it to Stewart, he smiled lopsidedly. "Just point it at anything that comes our way. It will automatically switch on if it senses danger. It's my version of a gun."

Brian watched as Stewart hefted the silver rod, turning it in his hand to get the measure of it. There was an apparent difference between the ends, one of which had indentations that indicated the handle. Gavin showed him how to hold it, using the pressure of his thumb as a stabiliser. Looking up at Gavin, Stewart nodded. Having quickly grasped the function of this new weapon, he moved into position, his back to theirs.

As they started the incantation, the slight shimmer that had been the only indication of something there became increasingly bright and active. At first, it seemed to grow, becoming a sizeable jagged fissure of light in the air between the two stones. For just a few moments, Brian thought he could see beyond it and into it, but as they worked the spell, all five of them in unison, the flickering at the edges became wilder. A strange sucking noise emanated from the middle, and a moaning sound came from behind them.

Knowing not to turn, trusting Stewart, he followed Gavin's instructions. As they said the last phrase of the spell, he pointed his hand at the heart of the fissure. Then he channeled every ounce of magic through his Amulet into the rift. Buffeted by a sudden change in air pressure, he saw the rift start to collapse, and just as it closed, a black shadow sped into its heart.

Exhaustion wanted to claim him, but there was no time. He was immediately aware that there was a battle going on behind him. As he grasped hold of Rhonwen and shoved her to his side, he saw Gavin move with dazzling speed into position next to Stewart. Stewart was hard pressed by half a dozen of the black amorphous things that Gavin had called Imps. He was holding them off, having already dispatched one with the wand. Gavin stretched out both his arms, and with a sweeping movement, he gathered them together. Knowing what was expected, Stewart used the wand to finish them.

"Poor things!" Neve said tiredly. “They just wanted to go home".

"Yes". Gavin replied quietly. "There will be more casualties from both dimensions before this is finished".

Looking around him, Brian was surprised at the ordinariness of the little hollow where they stood. A couple of small stones amongst the bracken and grass and now a few blackened patches that gave no clue to their origins. Rhonwen's hand slid into his, bringing him back to himself. Turning, he smiled at her seeing his tiredness mirrored in her eyes. "What next?" He asked Gavin, who was still peering up the slope towards a corpse of trees.

Turning toward them, Gavin seemed to take in their exhaustion in a glance. "I think that you all need a rest and some food,” he said as he intently looked at the hills around the hollow. "It's getting late, and we would be better indoors before the light changes". The thought of food made Brian suddenly very aware that he was starving. As the six of them made their way back to the car, he realised that he hadn't even thanked Stewart for protecting them. Turning to his friend, who was just behind him as usual, he caught his eye. He didn't need to speak. His look told Stewart how he felt. He dropped back slightly so they were in step, and the two friends walked behind the others.

It was a short drive to Gavin's home, which turned out to be an ancient sprawling farmhouse located in a shallow depression above a sandy beach. Mac met them at the door and ushered them into a large welcoming dining room with a massive stone fireplace. The fire was low and gave off just the right amount of heat to banish the slight chill of the evening. Gavin poured them all a whiskey, and they settled into the comfortable chairs arranged around a large table.

It was only a matter of minutes before Mac was back with a tray of food that he busily arranged before them. Feeling tired, Brian sipped his drink slowly. He had come to realise that working magic drained you in a way that he hadn't expected. Stewart caught his eye, using a well-rehearsed set of small movements with his fingers, and drew Brian's attention to Gavin and Mac. Their voices were low, they were conferring about something, which wasn't remarkable, but the look of concern on Gavin's face suggested something was going on. Connell's voice broke his concentration. "What's the problem?" He demanded his voice almost a growl as he ground the words out through a clenched jaw.

Turning towards them, Gavin's eyes narrowed as he nodded to Mac. Surprisingly, it was Mac who answered. "I have noted several indications that there are some uninvited guests in the valley behind the house. These ones are human, but not islanders. I have secured the perimeter. However, the signs suggest that at least one is very powerful."

Looking back at Gavin, Brian thought he saw something wolfish about his face. A vague outline around his features that was gone before he could be sure it was there in the first place. Connell had started grilling Mac about the property's defences when Rhonwen and Neve entered the room. Neve immediately reacted to the tone of her husband's voice, and her eyes widened with alarm. Rhonwen, picking up on the tension in the room, hurried over to Brian's side.

He had just started to tell her what was going on when Gavin made a quiet, almost musical sound that cut through the room. It stopped Connell dead in his tracks, and as they all looked at Gavin, he gestured for them to come closer to him. His eyes were dark and penetrating as he gathered them into a circle and quietly informed them that the house was being watched. He weaved a symbol with his hands, and the air pressure changed abruptly as he spoke.

"Christ, it's a cone of silence," Stewart muttered, the first to realise that they were surrounded by utter silence and a strange sort of stillness. Gavin stared at him; his expression unreadable. Then, turning back to the group and speaking quietly, he explained what he wanted them to do.

"We are all going to move into the hall that leads to the kitchen. Mac, will you take the lead?"

Brian took Rhonwen's hand wanting to keep her close, and they all followed Mac, Gavin at the rear of the group. The moment they were all in the short corridor, the door to the drawing room closed, and a panel in the wall opened revealing a hidden passage.

Following Mac into the passage, Brian was immediately aware of the magic all around him. He heard Rhonwen gasp, and realised that she, too, had sensed it. The stone surfaces were clear of webs and dust, and although there were no obvious sources of light, they had no trouble finding their way down the winding stairs and into a large room below the house. A spell room! He knew it immediately for what it was, despite not having actually been in one before.

As Gavin closed the door, the tension in him softened slightly. "You are safe here. No one can listen in to what we say, and no one can get into this room". He gave Connell a penetrating look, and then turning to Brian and Stewart, beckoned them both over to a large table in the middle of the room. "We have to deal with this now. I managed to get bearings on those that watch us, and there are at least five of them".

"What's your plan?" Connell said in a wary voice.

"I want to capture at least one of them. We need to find out who is involved in this scheme, and if possible, where they are based."

Brian watched quietly as Connell digested this, realising that unlike Stewart and himself, Connell had no experience of battle. Neve's voice broke the silence.

"But Gavin, Connell and Brian are already tired. How are they going to manage?" Her voice filled with worry.

Gavin looked at her kindly, gentleness softening his features as he replied. "I am hoping that we can manage with a restorative, at least for a short while, until Mac gathers his family."

"It won't take me long!" Mac said from the other side of the room.

That's when Brian noticed that Mac was stripped down to swimmers and was working a mechanism in the wall behind them. The sound of stone sliding against stone, alerted him to the opening that was becoming visible in the wall. Beyond it was a cavernous black hole, and as a blast of salt air entered the room, he recognised that it was a cave that connected to the ocean.

"You're not going to swim without a wetsuit surely?" Stewart sputtered as he looked through into the cave, and the dark waters in its depths. Mac gave him a grin but said nothing as he nodded to Gavin and headed into the dark. It was Rhonwen, her voice filled with wonder, who answered Stewart. "I don't think the cold will be a problem for him, Stew." She turned to Gavin, her gaze questioning as she continued. "I am right, aren'tI?

Gavin smiled at her in approval and nodded his head, but before he could reply, Brian heard Stewart's indrawn breath and the sound of a splash. He turned to the cave just in time to see a sleek dark head bob back up to the surface before it disappeared again under the waves, the flick of a tail breaking the surface.

Looking at Stewart, he saw his shock mirrored in his friend's face. "What the...!" Stewart said as he turned to the others. But it was Rhonwen's question to Gavin, that had just registered with Brian. "How did you know?" He breathed in awe. Rhonwen's face was lit with joy, her eyes filled with excitement as she rushed over to him. Taking his hand and turning back to Gavin, she told them about the story of the Selkie that her grandmother used to tell her when she was a little girl. She had loved the tale of friendship between the "people of the sea" and her family in the olden days.

"My mother hated that story. She used to tell my grandmother she was evil for telling me about them. I never understood how you could hate something as wonderful, as being able to swim like a seal, but still dance like a person." Rhonwen finished.

"But how did you know about Mac?" Stewart asked.

"I am not completely sure, but I just sort of recognised him. His silky hair, the, um, I don't know how to explain it. There is a sort of fluidity about him, the way he moves. It just came to me that if all the other things my grandmother told me are true, then Selkies could be too."

The sound of the wall closing against the chill of the cave brought them back to the immediate threat that had forced them away from their dinner. Gavin nodded at Rhonwen, his smile warm as he responded to her story.

"I will tell you more about all of this at another time, but now we must deal with those that wish us harm."

Turning to Neve, he continued pointing to the other end of the large room. "I should have all of the ingredients you need to make a potion for Brian and Connell, to help restore their energy". Neve, turning to Rhonwen, beckoned. "Come, I will teach you the recipe".

Rhonwen immediately joined her, and the two women started to gather what they needed. Gavin asked the men to join him at the other end of the room, where he said a brief spell and made a small gesture. The usual musical note, like a small bell sounded and the wall slid to the left, exposing another room just as big as the one they were in. This one however was filled with weapons.

"Now this is something I do understand". Stewart said as they followed Gavin into the centre of the room, where another table stood.

Looking around him, Brian was stunned to see ancient spears, all in perfect order, without a speck of rust, leaning against the wall with cross bows, battle axes and maces. Along another wall were guns from the seventeenth and eighteenth centuries, carefully stored on shelves in their original cases, lids open so that they could be identified, but unbelievably there was no sign of corrosion. Wandering over to look more closely, he found himself entranced by a beautiful pair of duelling pistols. Stewart had headed in the other direction, and he suddenly whistled, his in drawn breath catching Brian" attention.

Joining his friend, Brian found himself looking at a collection of modern weapons that would do any armoury proud. Realising that Gavin and Connell were focused on something on the table he nudged Stewart in the ribs, and cocking his head towards the others went to Gavin's side.

They were looking at a topographic map of the immediate area, and Gavin was pointing out where he had sensed their adversaries were hiding. "They are all together amongst that small corpse of trees. Once we're ready, I'll get up here and herd them out into the open". Then looking up at Stewart he motioned to his collection of modern weapons. "Stewart, would you arm yourself from my stores? Warlocks and witches are as vulnerable to bullets as the rest of you".

Connell, rubbing his chin in a way that Brian had come to understand signalled that he was worried, broke in. "Mac said one of them is very powerful. They may well be able to deflect an attack".

"Absolutely!" Gavin answered. I can sense a strength in one of them that will need all three of us to focus on. So I am going to work at separating her out of the group. Mac and his brothers can deal with the others, and Stewart is our backup." As he said this, he lowered his voice, and looking straight into Stewart's clear blue eyes, he said quietly, “I need you to make sure that Rhonwen and Neve are safe."

Brian immediately sensed Stewart's conflict. He was Brian's wingman. He never left his side in battle. But before Stewart could object, Gavin continued, understanding what he was asking of Brian's protector. "I know. But Brian will be safe. I make my pledge to you that even if it means we retreat, I will keep him safe." Stewart was obviously finding this hard to accept, but before he could retort there was the sound of a commotion in the other room and they all turned to see a dripping wet Mac emerge from the cave. "We're in place." He said, as he tracked water across the stone floor, his gleaming torso rippling with finely carved muscles.

Brian couldn't help staring, wanting to find the clues to Mac's alternate shape. Now that he knew, he could sense something, and without thinking he opened his mind to the magic. Suddenly he caught sight of the outline of a different being, shifting gently under Mac's skin. Mesmerised, it was a sharp pain in his ribs that brought his focus back. Stewart was watching him, his eyebrow raised. Suddenly embarrassed, Brian started to stutter out an apology, but Mac just grinned.

Leaving the house through another passage, the four of them moved quietly into position. Mac took Connell and Brian with him to join his family, who turned out to be a half a dozen fit young men, all of whom looked strikingly similar to Mac. Crouching down behind some rocks, they waited for Gavin's signal. The potion the girls had brewed had cleared Brian's head and sharpened his focus. He felt incredibly alert, energy now coursing through his body, his magic barely contained. It felt like it wanted to jump out through his skin.

There was a shout, and then movement as several shapes emerged from the trees above them. Blue flashes lit up the brush and the battle began. Brian picked his target, the blue fire all but leaping from his fingertips as it arced across the grass to pierce the man's chest. A cry of agony cut off abruptly as he fell. Moving fast, surrounded by Mac and his brothers, Brian and Connell continued the attack. He counted three down in the first couple of minutes, then from behind a tree to the right, an arc of blue shot past Brian, and he heard a grunt behind him.

Without hesitation he traced the trajectory back to its source and let go of another stream of energy, taking out the fourth intruder. Before he could turn to see who was hit, a massive boom erupted further up the hill, where Gavin should have been. The shock wave hit, and he was on his back, stunned by its force. Battle hardened he was first to recover, the others still stunned around him. Quickly scrambling up to get some cover, he grabbed his Amulet and willed himself to see beyond the barrier of the trees.

Gavin was illuminated by a orange glow, hard pressed as he fought off an attack. Instantly recognising her, Brian leapt to his feet. It was the same tall slender women that had attacked him in London. His instincts were to join Gavin, but as he started to move, he heard a groan and recognised that it was Connell. Turning back for a minute he was reassured to see Mac attending to the older warlock. As he turned back towards Gavin there was another flash, accompanied by a screeching sound and darkness descended over the small valley.

73

Gavin was gone. All that was left was a crater. Confident that he was alive, both Mac and Connell tried to reassure Brian. "It will take more than that to kill him," Connell said. But his voice was tired and filled with pain. A burn snaked its way down the side of his arm, now bound in a makeshift dressing made of his shirt.

"Gavin will join us when he can," Mac said prosaically. "There is no point hanging around here. We have to get back."

One of Mac's brothers was also wounded, and they needed to get him back to the sea so he could be healed. Carrying Jeb between them, the Selkie men made straight for the beach, while Connell and Brian headed for the house. Brian felt vulnerable. Not knowing where Gavin was, or if their enemy was still haunting the hills behind them made him uneasy. Not having Stewart at his back intensified the feeling, and he didn't like it.

Connell led them towards the side door. He muttered a spell that he explained was a signal he and Neve used that would alert her to his approach. Just before they started up the few steps to the small porch, Stewart appeared at his side, Gavin's magical gun in his hand. "Neve knows You're hurt." He said quietly to Connell as he unlocked the door and ushered them into the kitchen. The women were waiting, an extensive first aid kit open on the table. Their eyes were wide with fear, both wired with tense energy.

Neve took one look at Connell and visibly relaxed, taking him by the arm, and leading him to a chair obviously set up for him. Stewart pulled another chair out from the table, and almost pushed Brian down into it, as Rhonwen exclaimed. "You look awful!"

He felt awful. He wasn't just exhausted, he felt empty, hollowed out.

"Give him a cup of the herbal tea we brewed." Neve said without raising her head from her husband's wound. As a warm cup was placed in his hand, he looked up into Rhonwen's anxious eyes. "It's OK! The potion's worn off, that's all. I'm not hurt."

He sipped the brew, trying to calm his own anxiety. *Where could Gavin have gone?* In any other battle he had been in, a crater like that meant death. Feeling the tea working, a sense of calm returned, and as he took a deep breath, it occurred to him that the others hadn't asked after Gavin. Startled he looked up at Stewart who was watching him. "Gavin!" But before he could go on Stewart held up his hand. "He's fine. Neve got a sort of telepathic message not to worry, and to wait here for him."

"Told you". Connell said from the other side of the table. "You can't knock off one of the twelve. Not unless your one of them".

"So we wait". Neve said calmly. "And in the meantime, you two need to have something to eat and then go to bed".

Brian had no confidence that he would be able to eat, let alone sleep, but as he sat amongst the others, old friends and new, he felt his strength return with each sip of the slightly bitter tea. Rhonwen having refilled his cup, had beckoned to Stewart and they had left to retrieve their dinner, still laid out in the dinning room.

The aromas of the warming food stirred his appetite. The others busily set the table and left him and Connell to recover. Sitting companionably at the kitchen table, a familiar chiming of a musical bell alerted him to Gavin's return. He strode into the kitchen, his face set in a neutral expression, but his eyes were penetrating as he looked closely at both Connell and Brian. After a few seconds his face relaxed and he nodded in approval.

"You too look much better than I had hoped". He said as he turned to Neve. "That recipe of yours is a marvel".

It was Rhonwen who thought to ask after the injured Selkie. "Jeb is also expected to recover". Gavin replied warmly to her question, relief obvious in his voice. It occurred to Brian that they knew nothing of Gavin's life. His close association with these magical creatures was a clue to this man. Or maybe he should think of him as also being a magical creature. After all who were these Immortals, the council of twelve? Stashing these ideas away in for later reflection, Brian allowed himself to relax. They were safe and he was hungry.

As if reading his thoughts, Gavin looked at the now laden table and grinned. "Food! Come, we will wash these evenings work off ourselves before we eat." With that he ushered the three men through a door at the end of the room. Once they were out of earshot of the two women, his expression changed to one that was altogether far more somber and confided that they would have little time to rest. He had heard from Erik. Their help was needed. "Details can wait until after we have eaten."

Later, as he prepared to get some sleep, Brian turned everything over in his mind, trying to grasp the full implications of what Gavin had told them. The woman he had fought was unknown to him. This in itself was of great concern to Gavin. She was immensely talented, and she should have been known to the council. At this point, Gavin was entirely in the dark about her; he didn't even know her name.

Connell and Neve had questioned Gavin, digging for more information. Listening carefully, Brian had come to realise that there were protocols and rules, that should have prevented an unknown witch of such power emerging, suddenly into view. He had also recognised that Gavin was holding something back. Brian's gut told him it was something important.

Another problem was that she had eluded Gavin when he had followed her as she fled. Connell's difficulty in understanding how an Immortal could lose, even a highly skilled witch, had led to a very interesting discussion. One that had given him an insight into the politics of the Council of Twelve, and the fact that there was some resentment harboured by ordinary magic users about the controls that the council tried to exert over them.

However, putting all of that aside, they had to move swiftly to help the others. Having lost his quarry, Gavin had instead gone looking for Morgan, who, along with Erik and Rouan, had been on Scáthach's trail. The Warrior Goddess, and those that had orchestrated her return, had been busy collecting magical items of power from all over the country. Having two of the Amulets in their possession, it looked like their plan was to augment that power with other artefacts. They had broken into several museums, and at least two Ducal seats, stealing items of great historical, as well as magical value. Apart from anything else, this was going to attract attention from the police and the media.

His and Stewart's new boss had already sent a demand for them to report in ASAP. Since it was now after midnight, he had made an executive decision to leave that until the morning. Rhonwen was already asleep, as was Stewart. It was time he followed their example and got some rest. Gavin had put them up in what looked like a small dormitory, with Connell and Neve in a private room across the corridor. Sipping his now cold herbal sleeping concoction, he recognised that there was some sort of spell at work in the brew. His senses were becoming more and more attuned to this new world. It struck him that it felt right, like it should have always been this way.

74

Still feeling somewhat dislocated from their strange journey, Rhonwen looked around her at the ruined castle. They were deep in the wilds of Scotland, amongst a pile of stone that had once been a Broch owned by Morgan. Far from the tourist trail, it was rarely visited. The land about it still empty, after the Highland Clearances of the eighteenth century.

Morgan and Gavin were deep in conversation, while the three reunited Banachs exchanged their news. Brian and Stewart had immediately joined Erik, ranging out over the heath, to check the defences that Erik had already established. Left to her own devices, and feeling a little lost, she wandered through the stones trying to make some sense of the place.

As her hand brushed over a particularly large piece of granite she felt a tingling in her fingertips. Having become more attuned to the magic around her, Rhonwen was intrigued. Placing both hands flat against the rock, she closed her eyes and tried to open her third eye, the way Neve had taught while they were on Skye. Nothing!

She was just lifting her hands away when she was suddenly assailed by sounds and colours. Startled she opened her eyes. The overgrown heap of stones looked the same as before. Her heart racing with a mix of excitement and fear, Rhonwen was just about to put her hands back on the stone when she heard a sound behind her. Jumping guiltily, as if caught out being naughty, she turned to see the woman Morgan looking at her speculatively. "So, you're the Tierney girl." She paused, her eyes narrowing. "It would seem that Gavin is right about you".

Rhonwen froze. All of her instincts told her that this woman was dangerous. The elegantly husky voice was infused with a timbre that seemed to reverberate, and she could feel Morgan's power slicing through her, peeling back the layers of her being and exposing her inner core. Then just as suddenly as it had begun, it was over, and she felt as if she"d been released from something.

Standing there, shaken, watching the Immortal's retreating, she heard Brian call her name. Turning to the sound, she felt a massive rush of relief and almost ran into his arms. As if sensing her distress, Brian quickly came to her side and took her hand; looking down into her face, his eyes full of concern, he asked. "What's wrong? I could feel your fear."

His voice was as much tinged with wonder as it was with anxiety. Rhonwen marvelled as she looked into his lovely blue eyes. Yes, she felt afraid. Of that woman, and what was going on with Scáthach and Kiera, but she was no longer afraid of her feelings for Brian. In fact, she wanted to grab his face and pull his mouth to hers and never let go. As if he could read her mind, he gently squeezed her hand, and leaning down close to her, his lips brushing her mouth, he murmured: "I really want some time alone with you."

The noise of the others intruded into their moment, and they pulled apart regretfully. Stewart's voice was the closest, off course. He was never far from Brian's side. Making far more noise than necessary, Stewart emerged from behind some small bushes that had grown over the remnants of the old building. Looking meaningfully at them both, he nodded his head towards the other side further out of earshot of their companions. Taking his cue, they quietly moved to form a small circle. Checking that they were alone, Stewart pulled his phone out of his pack and quickly turned it on.

Rejoining the others, Rhonwen felt significantly better about this whole adventure. Yes, she was excited about being magically talented. It felt right, and she felt whole for the first time in her life. But knowing that the familiar world of an Intelligence Agency was there in the background was reassuring, despite the fact that they were basically on their own. As they entered the clearing, Gavin looked at them, his eyes piercing, drilling into them as if to seek out their secrets. At least, that's how it felt to her. She knew that these were the good guys, but there was so much that she didn't know about them. She remained uneasy about their casual use of immense power and the fact that most people had no idea that this whole other world was inside their reality. Then again, in the past, when people were more aware, they hunted and killed these people. *My people! Me!* Her inner voice reminded her.

A sudden shout startled her. Automatically turning towards the sound, she saw movement out of the corner of her eye and realised that Gavin was no longer standing where he had been only seconds before. Feeling the pull of Brian's hand, she turned back. He was staring at his Amulet, already retrieved from beneath his shirt. It lay quiescent in his hand, no red glow of danger. Obviously puzzled, he muttered. "That's strange! Do you think it's still working"?

Stewart, alert, his new magical gun ready in his hand, was looking across at Connell. He too was looking at his Amulet, and it showed no sign of alarm. "No. I think that we are safe." He replied. Although she noted he did not relax his vigilance, his body placed half in front of Brian's.

The Banach family moved closer to them, and the men bowed their heads close together to confer while Neve smiled reassuringly, coming over to her side. Looking around the clearing she noted that both the Immortals and Erik were gone. Not sure whether she should be afraid, Rhonwen listened intently to Brian and Connell. A flare of blue bathed the scrub and rocks to their left and both Amulets suddenly flared. A young man, his eyes filled with fear and hate crashed through into the clearing, but before he could get any further, he collapsed face down in the dirt, Erik on top of him. The giant Viking had him completely pinned. Looking up at the others, the men encircling the women, all of them ready to defend themselves, he grinned in triumph. "Got him!"

Dragging the now winded boy by the scruff of the neck, Erik propped him up against a rock and with a quick gesture bound him with some sort of magical tether. Rhonwen could just make out the pattern of the ties, but when Brian took her hand, suddenly they were as clear as if they were made of rope. "Can you see that"? She asked. Brian looked at her and nodded, his eyes filled with wonder. "Some of this stuff is really handy". He replied, his voice tinged with awe.

Having deposited his catch, Erik started back towards the edge of the clearing only to be met by Morgan and Gavin returning. Their faces grim, Morgan's eyes glittering with tiny lights that reminded Rhonwen of icicles. Or maybe white fire! She wasn't sure. Both immortals seemed to have a sort of orange glow like an aura, that faded almost as soon as she saw it. Some kind of communication passed between Gavin and Erik, and then Gavin focused his attention on the prisoner.

Morgan was so swift that her movement was a blur. She was standing over the young man, who was barely conscious, a snarl on her face. There was a shimmering outline around her features, hawklike and dangerous.

"Morgan!" Gavin's voice had so much power funnelled through it that Rhonwen could feel her whole body reverberate. She knew instinctively that if he had called her name, she would not have been able to move. Morgan stopped and looked back at him, the corner of her mouth curled.

"We need this one alive." Gavin continued, moving closer to her, obviously prepared to enforce his will if necessary.

"This one?" Connell almost spluttered. "There were others?"

Gavin and Morgan still locked in some sort of battle of wills, ignored him, but Erik, Connell's friend for so many years, quietly gathered them together to tell them what had happened. He was not apologetic, and there was no hint of remorse as he informed them that there had been three attackers and that two were dead. They had teleported in, weapons ready and plainly charged with not just spying on them but doing damage as well. Suppose Erik hadn't been watching. If they had relied on the perimeter defences, their enemies might have succeeded. Erik looked at Connell, and then deliberately let his gaze fall on Neve. "They tried to get past me. I wasn't their target".

Connell's face was suddenly suffused with fury as the import of Erik's words took hold, and Rhonwen felt herself being pulled closer to Brian, his jaw set and his eyes flashing with rage. "Who the hell are these people?" Rouan almost shouted, obviously as appalled as the rest of them.

"That is what we are going to find out". Erik replied.

Stewart's sharp intake of breath directed their attention back to the prisoner. He was currently floating about three feet off the ground, staring at the Immortals in horror, and screaming soundlessly at something Rhonwen couldn't see. Gavin and Morgan were circling him like predatory animals, then Morgan lifted her hand, and the magical bindings seemed to flare. A wave of heat hit Rhonwen despite them being a good twenty feet away from the terrified man.

As Rhonwen watched she felt sickened by the process, but then a picture of Keira's face came into her mind. She might not have liked that girl but what these people had done to her was horrendous. Gavin suddenly stopped his prowling and darted in, a flick of his hand cast aside the bindings, and the man dropped like a rock. "He's ready," was all he said, before he and Morgan both took an arm each, and then placed their other hands on the man's head. She could sense Brian's fascination. They were all transfixed, waiting. Finally, after what seemed like ages but was probably only a few minutes, both the Immortals let go of the man, letting him slump to the ground unconscious. Morgan spoke first, making a comment that was obviously targeted at Gavin, and which Rhonwen did not understand. Gavin's reply provided no further illumination to what seemed to be a private matter between them.

Then Gavin turned towards them, his eyes dark and haunted. Rhonwen suddenly understood that he had hated what he had done. "We need to move fast," was all he said as he beckoned Erik to his side. The three of them spoke quietly with each other for few minutes, before Morgan abruptly disappeared with the unconscious warlock, and Erik bounded off over the rise. Returning to their side, Gavin quietly informed them that they had a very short time frame in which to try and save Keira and return Scáthach to her own dimension.

"This position is compromised, and we need somewhere safe to make plans for our next move". He said in a tired voice.

75

Gavin had been preoccupied and distant while they waited for Morgan and Erik. He had told them very little about what he had learned from the young warlock he had tortured. Connell and Rouan were clearly shocked and dismayed by the level violence. Brian feared that the tenuous threads of trust that had pulled them together over the last few weeks, had started to unravel. Father and son were suspicious and angry, and Neve was struggling to prevent an open confrontation with Gavin.

Looking down at Rhonwen he wondered what she made of all of this. Stewart, always on guard, had his back turned to them as he watched the hills around the southern side of the Broch while Gavin had moved out of sight to keep watch on the northern side. Squeezing Rhonwen's hand, he flicked his head slightly and pulled her gently further away from the others. "Are you OK?" He asked quietly, watching her intently.

"Well, you know it's different being in the middle of it, isn't it?" She said, her beautiful face set in a serious and thoughtful expression. Before he could answer she continued. "After all, I am an analyst. I've never been in battle or anywhere near violence before all of this. But I feel safe with you and Stewart, and I think we can trust Erik."

He noted that as she spoke, she looked over at the Banachs. "There"re out of their depth," he said quietly". She nodded; “Yes, but I think Neve will pull them into line."

Brian was surprised by this comment but before he could ask her what she meant, the sound of a car broke through the silence of the afternoon.

Gavin was instantly back amongst them. He moved quickly out through the other side of the ruins to greet Morgan, who had retrieved what she had called her truck from a nearby village. It was big enough to carry all seven of them, and Brian had been given explicit instructions on how to get to a farm Morgan owned near Stirling. The two Immortal's would meet them there the next day, but for now they had business to attend to, while Erik had disappeared without a word. Gavin's refusal to tell them where He'd gone or what they were planning had infuriated Connell.

Brian had to admit the secretiveness of the Immortals was irritating, but he and Stewart had decided to wait it out. After all, it was common in their line of work for information to be compartmentalised. As Morgan gave him the keys, her lovely, elegant hand flirtatiously brushed his fingers. He knew it for what it was, but she was so seductive that he responded automatically. Pulling himself up, he saw the look of triumph glint in her eyes. As he clambered into the driver's seat, he looked across at Gavin who shook his head irritably.

Morgan's instructions were clear. By the time they arrived at her farm she would have dropped in and changed the magical locks to allow them entry. Turning the engine on, he glanced through the rear vision mirror to find Rhonwen looking at him. He didn't need to imagine what she was thinking. He could see it in her eyes. "How long did Morgan say the trip will take?" Stewart asked as he scanned the open heath, his brow furrowed. "About three hours." Brian replied, puzzled by an undertone he heard in his friend's voice. "What's on your mind, Stew"?

"Well, its just that since we are the soft targets, I would have thought that one of them would have moved us magically. You know, like Gavin did to bring us all here in the first place".

"Ah! Thats far more dangerous than us driving like normal people." Connell interjected from the back seat. "You see, magic makes a noise. The amount of magic needed to transport us would alert our enemies that we were on the move".

"Yes," added Rouan in a thoughtful tone. "But only another Immortal or someone really powerful would be able to track Gavin or Morgan."

"I think that may be the crux of matter." Connell replied in a grim tone. Whatever that poor bastard they tortured told them, had stirred them both up. "There is something very significant about what there"re not telling us."

Brian knew that Connell was right. But he also knew that foot soldiers rarely knew the whole story. He just wasn't used to being at the bottom of the command chain. Glancing across at Stewart who was riding shot gun, he caught his eye. An eyebrow raised and a look was all he needed to know that Stewart was on the same page. Whatever was going on, they needed to complete this task, which was to get the others to safety. They set off across country towards the greyish ribbon of the road that wound its way around the side of the valley.

Thankful for the long light evenings of the north, Brian finally manoeuvred the large four-wheel drive along a narrow lane that should end at Morgan's farm. It had been a tiring drive throughout which the Banach men had spent a good deal of time speculating about who might be behind the return of Scáthach. Trying to piece together the bits of information they had, and their knowledge of the politics of the ruling elite he had been stunned by the feudal ordering of the magical world. The level of discord and enmity that apparently existed between different groups meant that the Council of Twelve was a bit like the UN, and from what the Banachs were saying, it sounded like it was just as powerless and riven by its own politics and factions.

Abruptly, as he followed a curve in the road, he came to a set of gates. Just as he pulled up, they swung open, and he felt a slight warming of his amulet against his chest. But before he could become alarmed, it had cooled again, and he heard a familiar musical note. Morgan had told him that she had tuned her wards to both his and Connell's Amulets. All they had to do was basically turn up, and they would have access.

Driving through the gates, he looked out through the rear vision mirror as they swung shut. He thought he saw a shadow flit across the lane, but nothing came through the gates after them. Rouan had also been watching out the back window. "I think I saw something out there". He said in a tense voice. "Whatever it was it didn't come through the gates".

Stewart, swivelled around, looking back through the side window. "Those hedges are pretty high and, in this light, if someone was climbing over, we would see them pretty clearly".

"Knowing Morgan, they would probably be fried by the time they got halfway up". Connell muttered as he peered out his window. "I don't sense any danger," he continued, looking back into the car, his hand reaching for his Amulet, his eyes seeking Brian's through the rear vision mirror.

"Well, let's get up to the house. I have no doubt that it is safer than the grounds." Brian said firmly as he eased the car along the drive through a row of ancient-looking trees.

Jean watched as the car made its way up the drive of his mother's farm. His rage at his mother for changing her wards was now counterbalanced by his triumph. He was in, and with a simple ruse, he had avoided detection. He quietly moved through the undergrowth beneath the trees, following the car. He'd recognised all of its occupants. He had no idea what they were up to, but his mind was alight with curiosity. This could be fortuitous.

As the car followed the curve that led to the house, he angled through the trees in the opposite direction. He was headed to an old worker's cottage that he had played in as a child. It was hidden in a corpse of woods, almost half a kilometre from the main buildings. The slight breeze stirred the trees, and he caught a whiff of himself. He was filthy and tired.

Coming up to the clearing, Jean stopped under the low-hanging branches of a tree and carefully surveyed the area and cottage. He could sense his wards, still intact and with no sign of tampering. Impatient as he was, the last few days had taught him to be even more cautious than usual. Satisfied that he was alone and unobserved, Jean slipped out of the shadows and through the small narrow door. Flattening himself against the cold stone wall, he peered into the semi-dark of the one-roomed dwelling. There was an annex with a bathroom to the right, its door wide open, and a kitchen along the far wall. He could sense no presence but his own, and there was no trace of anyone else.

Breathing again, Jean realised that he was running on empty. Since the attack at his farm he had barely rested, let alone slept. Securing the shutters so that no light bled to the outside, he switched the power on. The noise of the hot water system ramping up sounded worryingly loud. Using only one light, he went about the room, lifting the dust covers off the furnishings, then retrieved his pack from beside the door.

Not knowing how long his mother's guests would be visiting or when she might arrive, he couldn't waste time. Quickly peeling off his clothes, he showered in the semi-dark. His stomach felt hollowed out, and food was a necessity, so he ate a tasteless sandwich he had purchased at a local fuel stop and planned his next move.

Jean had no answers about who or why, but he had been forced to accept that a more significant game was at play than his. Now, having managed to glean some information over the last few days, he needed to try and make sense of it. If Morgan had sent this bunch of fledgling magicians here for safety, they might know something that would help him figure out what was going on. And, of course, there were now two Amulets within his reach and no Immortals here to protect them.

One of the exceptional features of his little cottage was that it was close to the opening of an old hidden passage into the main house that would give him access to the ground floor and an opportunity to learn more information. He'd moved silently through the grounds and had made his way through the tunnels and into the space behind the panelling in the main living room. The bodyguard, Stewart, had just finished speaking to someone on his mobile and told the others that the police had identified the body at his farm. Jean now had a name to fit with the face. Marcus Neville. He knew that name. Neville had been an associate of Marguerite's, and she had been very keen for Jean to meet with him. *What had that bitch been up to?*

Preoccupied by his own thoughts, it was the sound of his own name that re-focused his attention. "So they could have sent Neville to steal Jean's amulet". Poole responded thoughtfully.

"Well, obviously, they either underestimated him and he got away, or they have him as well, which gives them three Amulets," the older of the Banach men countered.

Jean's mind went into overdrive. Keira's and Declan's were the only two other Amulets not currently in this house. That meant that they were captives of the mysterious *"they"*.

Someone else was after the Amulets!

He hadn't had time to extract information from his attackers, being forced to kill one, now identified as Neville, and wounding one of the other two. They had gotten away after torching his place, and he had been tracking them for the last week.

Then Rhonwen Tierney came into the room, and he was immediately aware of the shift in her. No longer the mousy little straight girl, he could feel her power. The only way that could have happened was if the barrier he had found in her mind had been dismantled. He wondered if she remembered the farm. Once he had realised her memories had already been tampered with, he knew that his spell might not be as secure as he had hoped. The sound of her voice, filled with rage as she spat out his name, gave him the answer. Oh well, at least he hadn't pursued his original plan to seduce her. He could probably talk his way out of the kidnapping.

Their discussion caught his attention. "What if Jean is in league with them? We know he was associated with Declan".

Jean noted that it was the junior Banach who responded first. "It's possible, but from what we know of Neville's activities, his plan had been at least twenty years in the making. Jean would have been too young to be part of it.

"But we don't know for sure that Neville was in league with whoever has brought Scáthach back. He could have had his own plan." Rhonwen countered.

Scáthach! Pieces of information suddenly coalesced in Jean's mind. The fearful whispers among the northern covens about a dimensional breach, the way his quarry had managed to elude him. He had felt a shift in the magic on Beltane and wondered at the power of it. He knew about Scáthach, of course. Morgan had been instrumental in ensuring her banishment. Despite his mother's careful censuring of that piece of history, Margarite had given him access to all the details of the time.

Jean's mind went into overdrive. His adoptive mother's involvement with Gavin now made sense. Their alliance had puzzled him, but protecting the Amulets and their bearers would have forced them to put aside their differences. They had no evidence that he was involved, and there was no link to him that they could follow. He could come out of this as being yet another victim of whoever Neville was working with. Gleaning a reasonable picture of what had been happening from their conversation, he felt a pang of honest regret about Keira. Declan's fate, however, had almost made him laugh out loud. Enthralled and enslaved!

As the others turned to more immediate matters of settling in for the night, Jean decided he had enough information. Slowly moving around the cramped space of the priest's hole, he manoeuvred himself back into the narrow passage that would lead him out of the house. He was stunned by what he had heard, but it all made sense. As he turned it over in his mind, he found himself dwelling on the type of ceremony that would have been used. As he imagined Keira as the vessel, he remembered her dark hair fanned out over the pillow, her lovely face suffused with lust. While his physical response to that vision was immediate and urgent, his mind was focused on finding an opportunity to turn this new set of circumstances to his advantage.

76

The clash of weapons reverberated through the cavernous stone lined vaults beneath the fortress. He could smell blood and sweat, and the stench of the men who worked at their training in the rooms above him. His blood sang with the desire to join them but that was not his task. This was not his time. He had not yet been born when Scáthach had ruled here.

Crouching to fit into the smaller tunnel that would take him past the kitchens, he noiselessly passed through the lower levels of Dun Scaith. Gavin had shown him the layout of the place, so he knew where he was headed. They had timed his arrival for Samhain the year before Scáthach had met Bryn. A year before, she had become obsessed and allowed passion to lead to her destruction.

Gavin knew she would be away from the Fort of Shadows this day because she and Gavin had been away from Skye for most of that year dealing with the Romans in Dacia. This was an opportunity too good to be missed. Unknown to all in this time, and this place, there was less chance that Erik would inadvertently affect the future.

Finding the circular stairs that led to the upper levels, he paused to listen. There was no where to hide once he started up, and they were far too narrow for two persons to pass. A slight scuffing of leather on stone alerted him to someone on their way down the stairs, a couple of floors above him. If his timing was right, the kitchen staff who mostly used these stairs, should all be cleaning up after the midday meal. Listening intently, he waited, hidden in a dark corner of the passage.

A slightly built boy of about fifteen emerged from the bottom of the stair well, hurrying towards the kitchen, the remnants of a meal on the tray in his hands. Erik sent a seeking spell up the stairs, and satisfied that they were empty, he quickly climbed up to the third floor. He was headed for Scáthach's own quarters. Secreted somewhere amongst her possessions was a talisman that could help them defeat her.

The Warrior Queen's apartments took up the whole floor of this section of the fortress. Once on the landing Erik paused, sending a small questing spell beyond the door in front of him. He couldn't sense anyone in the room, so moving quickly Erik let himself in, and quietly closing the door behind him surveyed the room. Surprised by the luxuriousness of the furnishings, he hesitated and looked around. Something felt wrong.

Noting that there was a disparity in the size of the room and the dimensions of the tower, he realised that this room took up only half of the space it should. Cautiously moving further into the room, his attention was caught by a large ornate chest at the end of the bed. He was contemplating its lock when he felt the stirring of the air behind him and to his left. Turning quickly, he had just enough time to fling himself out of the way of a blade that had been aimed at his back.

Rolling across the skins that covered the floor, he landed on his feet, crouched low, his own dagger in his hand. His eyes met a pair of black orbs that glittered with malice. His attacker was small and compact, his skin dark and wrinkled with age, and his face tattooed in an intricate pattern. Needing to forestall any alarm being raised, Erik had little choice. His own dagger had already left his hand, headed towards his assailant's throat, cutting off any opportunity for him to call out.

Irritated that he would now have to dispose of the body, and concerned about the effect this death might have, Erik retrieved his dagger, his attention caught by the door that was now exposed by a gap in the tapestries. Stepping over his attacker, Erik peered cautiously into the other room. Reassured that no one else lurked there, he took a hesitant step across the threshold, watchful of any twraps that may be waiting.

This room was much more like what he would have expected of Scáthach. Its furnishings were plain but beautifully made from local timber, with the motives of battle carved deeply into the wood. It was light and airy, the shutters of the large window flung back against the wall. One of the walls was covered by a beautiful tapestry showing a battle scene, while another held a rack of weapons.

About to move further into the room, he felt, rather than heard a sound. He froze, and turning back to look behind him, Erik felt his hackles rise. Sensing the magic at work around him, he watched the eyes of his assailant slowly open into narrow slits. Realising he had been the victim of a clever ruse, Erik reacted quickly. Instead of brute force he reached out with magic and cut off the other man's breath before he could raise an alarm, or worse utter a spell.

Turning his dagger over in his hand he realised it was clean. It had never really penetrated flesh. Despite a grudging respect for the skill of this magician, Erik needed to silence him. For now, he resorted to smashing his skull in with the first heavy object that came to hand. A large bronze bowl. Knowing this might not be enough, he then bound and gagged him with magical ties.

Erik assessed his new situation by sitting on the floor, watching his unconscious companion. He would have to be creative. Dead or alive, this magician was a problem, now and maybe in the future. He would be missed, and then Scáthach would be alerted to the theft. But what if he took everything valuable? Made the theft obvious. He made it look like an inside job.

First things first. He had to find the talisman Gavin had sent him here for. Then he needed to find a way to get a body and a pile of goods out of the fortress. If he was really lucky, Scáthach might actually believe that her little Pictish magician had betrayed her. Looking around he spied an ornate silver box. Whether it held the object he was looking for or not, it would be the first thing a thief would take.

Less than an hour later, Erik was ready to leave. He had found the talisman in a simple wooden box in plain sight, on a shelf in the hidden room. Having gathered every portable item of value in the apartments, he had filled a wooden storage box with it all. Looking out of the window on the western wall he had found that it was on the outer wall of the fortress, close to the forrest. A length of rope coiled on the floor beneath it had given him his escape.

He looked at his prisoner with more interest. Perhaps he had just interrupted a theft that was already set to occur. Once the box and its human passenger were on the ground, he followed. It took little effort for him to lug the whole lot into the cover of the trees, leaving the rope as evidence.

An hour later, he had found the cottage Gavin had told him about. Small and neat, it was secured against intruders by a simple spell. Standing amongst the brush at the edge of the clearing, Erik checked that no one was around, then, satisfied that he was alone, he made a small gesture and let himself in.

The magician remained unconscious, but Erik could sense a vital spark of life force. Having turned the problem over in his mind, Erik was disposed to giving the little Pict an opportunity to live. It would be tricky, and he might still have to kill him, but Erik had already interfered too much with history. Who knew what this little man might be meant to do?

Settling the Pict on the rushes before the hearth, he removed the gag and tended the head wound. Using some healing herbs, he found in the cottage he made a restorative and slid a few drops into the man's mouth. It didn't take long. The Pict's heart beat deepened and his colour returned. Erik was prepared for him to come back suddenly and go immediately on the attack, but he didn't. The dark eyes opened. Instead of malice, they were curious. The magician turned his head slowly to look around him, and a small smile twitched at the corners of his mouth.

He spoke, but it was unintelligible to Erik, who just shook his head and lifted his shoulders to indicate he didn't understand. The little Pict looked closely at him for a moment and then spoke again—this time in Latin.

"So, you are not one of her champions?" He spoke. He kept his voice low and his body very still, obviously trying not to startle Erik into impulsive actions.

Erik grinned. "No. And I suspect that you are not a great friend of hers, either. Am I right?" Erik replied in halting Latin. It had been a long time he had spoken this ancient tongue.

Over the next hour, they played cat and mouse around their respective identities and plans, but gradually they came to a detente. Erik's suspicions had been correct. A theft had already been planned, the target of which was a ritual cup stolen by Scáthach. As the clan Shaman, it had been his responsibility, and like Erik, he had taken the opportunity of Scáthach's absence to retrieve this critical object.

Luckily for the Pict, Erik had recognised its value, and it was amongst the objects he had taken from Dun Scaith. Neither wanted anything but what they came for, the Pict sensibly knowing that it would put his village at risk if any of Scáthach's treasure were ever found there. Having decided it would be prudent to be nowhere near the Dun when the theft was discovered, Erik chose to accompany the wily little magician through the forest towards the coast. Irrespective of what happened, Gavin's time spell had only a twenty-four-hour window. Erik would instantly return to Gavin's side at the appointed hour, no matter where he was.

Burying the treasure in the forrest near the cottage took very little time. The Pict used a masking spell to ensure it would not be easily found. Erik suspected that he also added a location spell so that at a later time he, or his people could recover it.

Moving silently through the trees, Erik breathed deeply. He had forgotten how clean it smelt. The scent of newly harvested grains and the hint of woodsmoke awoke in him a longing for the simplicity of his early life. No matter where he went in the twenty-first century, he could smell petrol. Even on the moors and in the deserts of North Africa, cars left their mark in the air.

77

Gavin tried to keep his emotions in check, but the sight of his dearest friend, bloodied, almost dead, fed the rage the had been growing since Scáthach had re-appeared. Erik had returned as planned, but not in the condition he had expected. He had known that the task he had set his friend on was dangerous, but Gavin was so used to Erik's indestructibility, he had never really believed in the risk. Now, helpless he watched Neve working on his companion, coaxing his life force back.

He couldn't believe the state of him. He was covered with gaping sword wounds. Great gashes that still oozed blood even now, after he himself had staunched the bleeding, cauterising the jagged and torn edges magically. Erik's left arm had been almost severed above the elbow, his face swollen and bruised beyond recognition. There were several arrow holes in his back, that had only just missed his spine, but had pierced his lungs and one had nicked his heart.

How could Erik look so small? He was a massive man. A Viking! It didn't matter that Gavin had several thousand years of experiencing death. When it came to those he loved it was the same as it was for everyone. Immortality did not change that reality. Morgan looked at him from the other side of Erik's body, their eyes locked, and he took a deep breath. She was one of the best healers amongst the Immortals, and Neve was one of the best amongst the mortals.

Aware that the others were fearful, but holding onto each other, and that even Jean, not one of them, was lending his own magical strength to the healing, Gavin focused. Gradually, together they brought Erik back. His life force strengthened and held firm. The power of the two Immortals was bolstered by the power of the trained and untrained magicians. They all directed their love and power to Erik, stabilising him.

"He will recover!" Morgan finally pronounced.

Standing next to the bed as the other's started to move away, it was Brian who turned to him, Stewart only a few steps behind him. Fully aware that the relationship between Gavin and Erik mirrored his own with Stewart, Brian spoke quietly with conviction. "We will all do whatever it takes to help Erik recover so he will be at your side again."

Looking over Brian's shoulder into Stewarts eyes, he experienced a sense of continuity. Over the many centuries of his life, the various incarnations of Bryn and his companion, had always been a solid and predictable presence. Clasping Brian's hand, he allowed himself to believe that he had not killed his dearest ally, by sending him on such a dangerous mission. *He will recover!*

❧ ❧

Erik slipped through the underbrush of the semi-dark forest like a brown dragon brushed with shades of blues and greens. He was pleased with himself as he had managed to stalk the tall lean man for the past several days without being detected. At least that was what Erik hoped for. Both had made their way through the thick forest, one the predator, the other the prey. He knew that time alone would reveal who was who, but for the moment Erik chose to think of himself as the predator and it was, he had decided, time to take what he had come for.

This would take much work as Erik knew the man was an excellent wizard with magical powers that surpassed his own. It wasn't magic, however, that would decide this encounter, he thought. Stealth and speed with the blade would be Erik's weapon, not the whimsey of a supernatural mind. The strength of the body was to be the ultimate decider in any battle. At least, that was what he had been taught from the time he could walk.

He refocused his attention on the man who was walking casually along the narrow path that was almost entirely covered by the forest's undergrowth. He never missed his step, walking across the uneven surface as if gliding across an ice-covered lake. Erik had to marvel at the man's agility and balance. He may not have had the bearing of a warrior, but he moved with the grace and balance of an elf, and that, in Erik's mind, made him even more dangerous.

The man suddenly stopped, forcing Erik to freeze in a precarious posture amidst the ferns and thistles. An eerie silence settled across the patch of forest where neither birds nor animals could be heard.

The man, his face shaded under a green hood that was part of a long flowing mantle, cocked his head, intently listening into the silence. Time passed and Erik watched the still figure that now appeared fixed in time and space.

Well, trained in the art of stealth, Erik had enough practice in the art of concealment that he was able to remain in the same position for as long as it took. So, the solidly muscled warrior stilled his breath and quietened the beat of his heart and waited.

Slowly, ever so slowly, the tall man in green turned, and when he finally stopped, he appeared to look directly towards Erik. In that instant, Erik knew that there was no longer any need for stealth or concealment. The wizard knew precisely where he was. For a moment, he wondered how long the man had known he was being followed, for the place he had chosen to stop was the least promising for any combat. The path was narrow at this point and edged by tall solid trees, limiting a warrior's reach and swing with the sword.

Erik however chose to stay concealed behind the thick trunk of a tree and the surrounding forest growth. The wizard could make the first move, he decided. He waited to watch the still figure of the man. Well over six feet tall, possibly closer to seven, Erik judged the man to be possibly half elven, but with the man's head concealed underneath the hood it was difficult to tell.

Erik didn't have to wait long to discover the nature of the stranger on the path. The man suddenly flicked the hood from his head revealing the distinctly rounded ears of a human.

"Why do you still hide when you know that you have been discovered?"

Erik slowly stepped from the thicket. His left hand rested casually on the pommel of his still sheathed sword. A man of few words Erik came straight to the point.

"What will it take for you to surrender the amulet, wizard?"

The tall man was silent for a minute while a broad smile spread across his face. There was no anger, no maliciousness in the smile, only a warmth that Erik did not quite understand. Did the man not know he was about to die?

"The amulet is not for you, my ambitious friend." The man paused and then turned to walk on.

Erik disliked being ignored and he felt dismissed like a small child. He aggressively stalked after his foe and demanded he acknowledge him.

"You should know that it is rude to ignore someone's simple question, wizard. I asked you politely and I expect a polite answer." Erik hissed belligerently.

The man stood quietly looking casually at Erik. He smiled again.

"If I thought you wanted an answer, I would have replied to your question." The wizard casually raised his arm. "I do, however, ask politely that you let me go in peace so that no harm shall befall you."

Erik, shocked by the man's gall to threaten him and his apparent indifference to his own impending death, held his position. "You are, are you not, aware that I am about to kill you if you do not give me the trinket?"

"You see? There you have it. You have no interest at all in an answer from me, as you have already made up your mind that you will kill me and then relieve me of my treasure."

The man suddenly spread open his cloak. Startled, Erik instantly jumped back while his sword appeared from the scabbard as if by its own volition. Firmly gripped in Erik's hand the weapon cut the air in an aggressive arc. Undeterred the man continued to speak calmly. "Unlike you," the man continued, "I am unarmed, so what glory can be had from defeating an unarmed man? Surely you have been bound to honour your code."

Erik had to admit killing an unarmed man held little glory and would certainly do nothing to enhance his reputation. In fact, if any of his teachers were to discover this he would be forever barred from the company of heroes past, present and in the future. He would be an outcast, a rogue swordsman left to fend for himself as best as he could, while having to accept a fate where anyone would be free to kill him without retribution.

"Surely a clever wizard like yourself would not travel unarmed," Erik suggested.

The man smiled, something that was beginning to irritate Erik. "A clever wizard such as I is in no need of weapons," he paused for a moment, "and neither are you."

As his right hand completed an almost imperceptible gesture Erik found himself standing in front of the wizard stripped of all his weapons and armour. Disarmed and furious Erik screamed, "Are you insane, wizard?" and then, as he took a further threatening step towards the man, he appeared to bounce off an invisible wall.

"Hmm, that, my friend, is possibly open for debate. In the meantime, you have a choice. To behave and perhaps join me on my journey or quietly leave in peace, and I will make sure that you will get all your weapons back in due course."

"So you have now taken on the role of a father for me?" taunted Erik.

"It appears to me that you are in need of one," the wizard smiled wryly.

Erik had to concede that the tables had turned and that at least for the moment he was the prey. Although Erik liked to promote the idea that brawn was better than brains, he was a very quick and curious student. That trick with the hand was new to him, and so was the invisible barrier. An idea started to take form as he mulled over the options He'd been given. Perhaps knowledge would be a greater treasure.

"Well, wizard, you do have me at a disadvantage." Erik paused for a second and, scratching his head said, "but it appears that I could do with some more training in magic, and it seems that you want for a companion."

Erik paused then decision made continued. "I guess we could do worse than travelling together."

Erik then tapped the invisible wall in front of him. "If you would be so kind and remove this obstacle, we could perhaps get to know each other better."

"Well chosen, my friend," said the wizard and took a step towards Erik.

"I am known as Gavin of Skye," the man smiled again disarmingly, "so who might you be?"

"They called me Eiríkr back in my homeland, here they call me Erik."

The man in green stretched his hand out. "Then be welcome, Erik, and let us travel in peace."

Erik grinned broadly and firmly gripped the outstretched hand.

"Well, then, wizard. Let the brawn and the brain travel together."

78

It had only been a few hours, but the change in Erik's condition had been almost miraculous. Gavin's sense of relief was profound. He felt an incredible amount of gratitude to all those who had given their strength to the healing process. Looking at the sleeping form of his companion of so many centuries, his fear gone as he now knew Erik would be back at his side. He also knew that there was no point making wild assertions that he would never put him in danger again. But he wanted to.

Staring out of the lounge room window, trying to formulate a plan, Gavin became aware of Morgan's approach. Sliding tiredly into a chair nearby, she looked at him with a determined expression.

"It was fortunate that Jean arrived just when we needed him the most. The combined strength of the three Amulets turned the tide. Erik will make it because of their power." She said quietly.

"So, what you are saying is that Jean was instrumental in Erik's recovery". Gavin said tentatively, aware that despite all of her reservations, Morgan wanted her adopted son to be on the right side of this battle.

"I don't know for sure". She admitted. "But his strength and skill seem to have turned the tide".

"And your previous concerns about his activities? Are you convinced by his explanation"? Gavin countered.

"There is no doubt in my mind that his Amulet was also targeted. A lesser adept may not have survived the attack on his farm". Morgan responded firmly.

Gavin had to admit that Jean's version of events, was plausible. His farm had been destroyed, and he had freely admitted to working with Declan. His story that he had sent Declan to watch Lydia after he had become aware that she was stalking him, fitted with what Brian knew from the Inspector. Gavin was not convinced by his vehement denial of having orchestrated Declan's theft of the Tierney Amulet, but it could be true.

Even his story of having tracked Declan to the cabin and finding Rhonwen unconscious, fit with the facts. As to his reasoning for using magic on Rhonwen, to find out what she knew, and whether she was working with Declan, that also made sense. As to his abandoning her on the side of the road, there had been a call put through to the Ambulance, alerting them to her whereabouts, which could have been him, as he claimed.

It all hung together, but Gavin had little doubt that Jean had left out an extraordinary amount of important detail, all of which would cast his role in a very different light. The others were understandably reluctant to believe him, and irrespective of the truth of Jean's claims, he was dangerous. But his presence meant that they now had the power of three Amulets, as well as the Talisman that Erik had retrieved. Combined and directed properly, this force gave them a very real advantage in the coming conflict.

Turning to Morgan, he gave her the acceptance she needed. "Jean's training saved his own life and now it has helped save Erik's. Having him with us should strengthen our group, if he is prepared to let go of control, and allow his talent to be guided".

"Given it is in his own best interests to help us, I think he will be able to do so. However, the others will have to stop treating him like a leaper for this to work." Morgan replied, an edge to her voice as she gazed across the room.

Heaving himself out of the chair, Gavin nodded in agreement and headed through the door to the dining room to speak with Jean. He looked at the young man about whom he felt so much ambivalence. "Thank you for your help tonight, Jean". He said quietly before joining the three younger men in the kitchen. Rhonwen and Connell had taken Neve up stairs to bed, as she was drained and needed sleep.

Stewart looked at him closely, and then past him towards Jean. "So do you believe his story"? He asked quietly as he busied himself making a pot of tea.

"I don't think we have the entire story, no. But I do think that at this point he knows he is safer aligned with us. On his own, well, he is vulnerable."

"We need him, don't we"? Brian muttered.

"We certainly need his Amulet on our side and not in the hands of our enemy," Gavin replied.

"And exactly who is our enemy?" Jean asked as he entered the kitchen.

Yes, thought Gavin. This was the very heart of the matter. Who was their real enemy? He looked at the men, all waiting for the answer he didn't have. Morgan had followed Jean into the kitchen, and it was Morgan who offered the bare bones of what they now knew.

"We know that the return of Scáthach has been the work of a Coven based here in Stirling, but who is actually behind this plan remains unknown to us".

"So that poor bastard you tortured didn't know who he was working for?" Connell growled, having just come downstairs and overheard the conversation.

"He thought he did". Gavin replied. "The whole coven has been seduced into this task over a generation ago. Both Neville and Margarite Bran were part of the plot to acquire the Amulets, so that Scáthach's return could be permanent".

Jean was the first to react. "Who is Margarite Bran"? He asked, his eyes narrowed and fixed on his mother.

"Apparently that was Lydia Chambers real identity". Morgan answered, holding her son's gaze and continuing before he could comment. "I had no idea she existed".

Recognising that it was time to fill everyone in on what he and Morgan had discovered, Gavin forestalled any further discussion. This was Morgan's house, so he deferred to her, but he made it very clear that all of them needed to be present. Morgan being in agreement on this, set about organising them all and allocating sleeping quarters. Even Jean fell into line and cooperated with her, agreeing to return from his cottage the following morning. They would gather when Erik and Neve were able to join them.

Slipping away from the rest of them so he could order his thoughts, Gavin returned to Erik, still sound asleep on a makeshift bed in the living room. He automatically did a quick assessment of his injuries and, relieved that Erik's immortality provided him with rapid healing powers, he sat at his side and let himself relax.

Breathing rhythmically, he turned his focus inward and started sifting through all the information he now had about the events of the last few weeks. Erik had completed his task. They had the blade that had once almost ended Scáthach's life. Originally belonging to the only warrior who had ever bested Scáthach, it was a powerful talisman, magically forged, and in the right hands potentially lethal to the Warrior Queen.

79

Both Immortals were almost glowing with rage. To say that Erik's report had stunned them was an immense understatement. Erik had told them about his encounter with the Pictish Shaman. His decision to escort the wounded man back to his waiting compatriots, had brought the immortal Viking to the brink of death. Both were skilled magicians, yet they had nearly walked straight into an encampment that had been so well secreted within the forest, that it was only at the last minute that Erik had sensed it.

It wasn't just good magic that had hidden this group from view. It was modern camouflage technology. Erik had managed to avoid being detected, and to get a good look at the weapons, which were like nothing he had seen before. Some sort of composite bows that were cleverly disguised but definitely made of modern materials. Brian and Stewart had both closely inspected those arrows as they were removed from their new friend. They were state of the art twenty first century technology.

It was while they were doubling back to get around the camp that Erik and the Pict encountered a band of warriors armed with identical bows. The Shaman had died quickly, leaving Erik to battle twenty warriors. Riddled with arrows, his last memory was of his consciousness fading, his blood loss too massive even for him to sustain. It was the automatic return feature of Gavin's spell that had saved him.

Brian was still trying to get his head around the whole-time travel concept. That Erik had gone back to 200BCE to retrieve a particular weapon that had power over Scáthach was still unbelievable. Despite Gavin's explanations that to achieve this he had needed Morgan's power to augment his. Both the Immortals had been very clear about this being a desperate act. Not only was it prohibited by the council, but it had also weakened them, and with the added energy they had needed to use to help heal Erik, they would need several days to recover.

So, if he was to accept that Erik had, in fact, been two thousand years in the past, then he had to accept that the modern weaponry that almost killed him had somehow been transported there as well. That, of course, was the real issue. Both immortals were keeping their own council about this information, but they were obviously horrified.

He was still trying to figure out what that could mean when Gavin's voice pulled him out of his reverie. They had driven for about an hour, into the hills to the west of Morgan's estate to train for the coming battle. As they climbed down into a gully, Brian kept a close eye on Jean and deliberately manoeuvred Rhonwen towards the other side of the clearing away from him. None of them really believed Jean to be the innocent victim he claimed to be, but his talent and training was needed if they were to succeed. *But would banishing Scáthach back to another dimension really be the end of this?*

They were lined up, Rhonwen behind him, Connell and Neve next to him, Jean and Rouan on the other side. Stewart as usual, was at his back, his gaze turned towards the hills, scanning them for danger. Rouan had reluctantly agreed to be paired with Jean, knowing that he would be of more use that way. As Gavin drilled them, repeatedly, Brian lost himself in the task. Summoning his power, scooping up the tendrils of Rhonwen's magic, as it snaked into his arm from her hand on his shoulder. He propelled it as hard and fast as he could onto the target set up by Gavin.

It had been well over four hours of hell and all of them were exhausted. Sitting amongst some boulders out of the wind, he took a swig of water and passed the bottle to Rhonwen before turning to speak with Stewart. Instantly alert, fatigue put aside he signalled to the others, pointing to a shimmer in the middle of the clearing. Morgan was there immediately, Jean at her side, his arm outstretched. Brian could feel him powering up and his own power ignited in response. "Wait". He heard Gavin's voice call out. "It's Finn".

The shimmer seemed to gain a level of density and then, the deeper blue in the middle expanded, and a familiar figure emerged, accompanied by a small, dark-haired woman. Brian was too far away to hear what was said, but Jean turned and walked back towards them, a scowl on his face. Gavin having joined Morgan, spoke for several minutes with their two visitors. The body language said it all. This was not a friendly visit.

“They're in trouble, aren't they?" Stewart muttered quietly. “Yep,” Connell replied, "Erik's little trip to the past, I'd say."

Jean, having joined them nodded in agreement. He offered no comment, but watched the tableau keenly, his body taut and tense.

"What will happen to them?" Rhonwen asked tentatively.

It was Jean who replied, a sardonic expression on his face. "Finn is a great friend of Gavin's, but there will still be consequences. Given the circumstances, and the fact that they have given the council important information they wouldn't have had otherwise, might help."

Brian wondered, not for the first time, how they were ever going to make this work. He couldn't warm to Jean, and Rouan had put plenty of distance between himself and Jean the moment he was no longer needed to partner him—a look of wariness in his eyes when ever he looked at Morgan's adopted son.

They all watched, waiting to see what would happen. Finally, Finn and his companion seemed to have finished their business with Gavin and Morgan. The tall, elegant man lifted his gaze towards them. He might as well have been standing in their midst; his voice was clear and authoritative.

"Your Amulets and power come with a price. Your obligations and your heritage are gifts to be used for the good of all. We are watching and we will stop any misuse of your power."

Brian felt, rather than saw Jean's reaction, knowing, as they all did, that he was the target of this warning. His rage was palpable as Finn continued, his gaze focused on Morgan and Gavin. "Put aside your rivalries or all will be lost. We all must adjust to these new alliances".

With that, the shimmering vortex reappeared, and the two Immortals stepped out of the glen and disappeared. "What on earth did he mean by that?" Rouan asked his father, as they watched Morgan stride up the hill towards them. Her face was a mask of fury, her eyes intense and very dark focused on Brian and her mouth twisted into a snarl. She beckoned Jean to join her, and they both walked quickly out of ear shot, across a small stream that ran down into the gully.

None of them spoke. Glancing at Stewart he could see his own assessment of the situation mirrored on his face. Gavin, his mouth set, also made his way out of the gully. He watched the other two for a moment, then with a slight shake of his head he turned his gaze towards them all, still clustered on the side of the slope.

"Finn has confirmed what I suspected. The sheer amount of noise that has been generated by the return of Scáthach points to this being a distraction".

"A feint". Stewart said thoughtfully.

"Yes. But there is more to this. The Amulets have all been found and gathered for the first time in centuries. Bringing Scáthach back was a guarantee of this". Gavin replied.

"So, what are the Council going to do about it? They now know who is involved. Surely they are going to put a stop to it"? Neve asked in a worried voice.

"They were planning to until they heard the news about the encampment that Erik found and the transference of modern technology to the past. Now, it is apparently important that we work with the national security services". Gavin said sardonically turning his attention directly onto Brian.

"What does that mean?" Rouan asked.

Ignoring the question, Gavin stared at Brian, his eyes feeling like they were boring holes in his head.

"You are expected to call in to your agency daily, are you not"? The Immortal said, in a icy voice that made the hairs on the back of his neck stand up. Answering him in the affirmative, Brian waited.

"Apparently they have found the Stirling coven's location. Finn has informed me that there is a “liaison officer” assigned to “our case". He will be in Stirling this evening and you are to meet with him".

The distaste Gavin managed to infuse into this pronouncement matched the slight curling of his lips.

They were all still staring at him in shock when Morgan and Jean returned from their little tete a tete. Noting the looks on their faces, Morgan snorted. "So, you have told them about the council doing the bidding of the government. Dictating to us. "And you!" She almost spat out the words as she looked at Brian and Stewart. "You can't straddle two worlds. You will have to choose. You mark my words."

❧ ❧

It was close to nine in the evening, and the light shimmering red from the surrounding city illuminated their waiting at the appointed place deep within the castle.

"I don't understand". Rhonwen spoke very quietly so only Brian and Stewart could hear her. Since the confrontation with Gavin and Morgan over their loyalty to their agency, they had been keenly aware of the gulf between them and the others. Now standing apart they had a chance to talk privately.

"Why couldn't they find the coven magically? I mean they can time travel, for heavens sake!" Rhonwen continued.

"It's to do with magic. If the coven doesn't use any magic, they can't be traced that way." Brian replied.

"That's what they mean by magic being noisy, isn't it"? Stewart muttered, his back to them as he watched the area. Before Brian could respond, he heard Stewart mutter an expletive. Turning swiftly, he found himself looking at Inspector Riley heading across the lawn. Shock was a mild word to describe it. "What is he doing here"? Rhonwen exclaimed.

The Inspector must have heard her after all the place was extremely quiet and empty at this time of day. However, a twist of his lips into an ironic smile was the only acknowledgment he provided. Brian noted that although he looked tired, there was something different about the Inspector.

"There's a spring in that man's step". Stewart noted quietly.

As Inspector Riley came to a stop in front of them, Brian saw a twinkle in the man's eyes that had never been there before. Riley had always seemed cynical, and a little burnt out, but no longer. In fact, he looked younger.

"Good evening Ms. Tierney, gentleman." He said as he looked past them to the shadows where Gavin stood watching like a hawk. "Mr Skye, I have been informed that you will be able to hear us". He said in acknowledgement of the Immortal.

"Good evening, Inspector". Brian responded startled by the mans equanimity about being observed.

The Inspector looked at them all for a moment before he spoke. "Apparently like me, you have all recently become acquainted with some unexpected aspects of our reality. More importantly, you are now in it up to your necks"!

Brian was about to answer but the Inspector held up his hand to forestall him. "My briefing has been thorough, so I am aware that you were ignorant of all of this prior to the incident at Ms. Tierney's flat".

"What exactly is your role in all of this?" Stewart interjected.

"To tell you the truth, I am not completely sure about the extent of it all, but I am basically the liaison between you and the police."

"So, somehow the Police have been able to locate the Stirling coven's hiding place, and your here to tell us where that is". Stewart continued.

"Yes. From a policing perspective, there is no proof that they have kidnapped Ms. Blair and Declan Tierney. In fact there has been no complaint made about Ms. Blair being missing. Declan Tierney is a wanted felon, but the circumstances of his disappearance have left no clues that police can follow."

"So how do you know where they are?" Rhonwen asked, her voice tight with repressed anger. The Inspector turned to look at her straight on. "Ms. Tierney, please understand that I am a policeman. This has not changed. Until I was brought up to speed, so to speak, the murder in your flat was such a confusing picture, I needed to be sure you were not involved. As to how my new boss knows the information, I am here to give you, that is also a police matter. My instructions are to give you the location of the members of the coven who are involved in this particular affair."

Brian decided he needed to step in at this point. The Inspector had never been anything but fair. He would love to know how he had ended up standing here in Scotland, but this was not the time.

"So what can you tell us, Inspector"? He asked calmly, taking hold of Rhonwen's hand and squeezing it, hoping she would back down.

"That six members of the coven that are involved in this plot are holed up in a farmhouse 15kms out of Stirling. I have sent you a text with the address. They have been there for the last few days, and there is no doubt that both Ms. Blair and Mr Tierney are with them. Our source does not know how long they plan to be there".

Before any of them could respond, the Inspector lifted his eyes to stare at the darkness where Gavin stood, concealed in the shadows. "I have been directed to ask you to keep this as quiet as you can. Apparently, there is at least one news agency sniffing around. The army will claim responsibility for any, lets say, unusual disturbances, but it needs to look credible".

With that the Inspector stepped back. He looked at the three of them for a moment and then spoke again, his voice was quiet but firm. "We have all found ourselves in a very unexpected and somewhat unbelievable situation. I am here to be of help to you, but unlike you, I remain a simple policeman. I have no jurisdiction here. At this point all I can do is relay information".

"Thank you, Inspector". Gavin said quietly as he joined them. "What sort of time frame do we have if we are to make use of the Army as our cover?"

"They will be here in the area for twenty-four hours as part of a routine exercise". The Inspector answered, staring with undisguised fascination at the Immortal standing in front of him. After a what seemed like ages but was only seconds, he dragged his eyes away and turned to Brian. "Good hunting." And with a slight nod to them all, the Inspector turned and walked back across the square towards the castle gate.

80

“They've chosen this place well". Stewart muttered as they watched the farmhouse from a ridge on the western side of the property. Set in a valley surrounded by open fields, there was little cover for their approach. A movement at the door of one of the sheds caught Rhonwen's eye. Turning to Brian she saw that he had seen it. He was focusing his binoculars on the young woman standing at the door, her attention held by something inside and out of their line of sight.

They were ready. All of them in place waiting for Gavin's signal. Looking towards the hills, it seemed incongruous somehow that it was such a lovely evening. The sun backlit the clouds that were strung across the sky like cotton wool with a soft reddish glow. As a gentle breeze played around her face, Rhonwen found it almost impossible to grasp the reality that they were about to enter into battle. But here they were, waiting to begin the assault.

She knew that both Brian and Stewart had automatically moved into a well trained and rehearsed mental state. But she and the others had no experience at this. She was scared out of her wits and trying desperately to quell the fear that was turning her legs to jelly. Glancing over her shoulder at Neve, she saw her own anxiety mirrored in the older woman's eyes. Catching her eye Neve took a big breath and then smiled at her reassuringly.

Brian took her hand and squeezed it, nodding towards the other side of the farmhouse. She could just make out a slight shimmering in the air, its bluish tinge muted, and pale compared to what she had become used to seeing.

"It's starting". He said giving her a tight smile. "Lets get moving".

They had all gone over the plan many times, and each knew their role. As Morgan and her team appeared simultaneously on the eastern side of the house, Gavin appeared just to the side of the barn. The young woman, suddenly alert jumped back, but it was too late. A flare of blue snaked towards her and she disintegrated without a sound.

At the same time, Brian led them through the sparse cover of some low-lying brush towards the other end of the house. Gavin had scouted out the location of the coven members and their prisoner. Much as she hated it, Rhonwen had been forced to accept that she must help to rescue Declan. Morgan, Jean, Erik and Rouan were tasked with securing Keira/Scáthach. But all of the Amulets needed to be within close proximity to her, in order for their magic to banish Scáthach back to her own dimension.

Suddenly flares of magic erupted from the house on three sides. The noise was deafening, and there was an acrid smell in the smoke that was starting to fill up the hollow where the house stood. Getting a glimpse of Jean and Rouan, Rhonwen saw them grappling with several attackers, but as she watched, Jean let go of a massive bolt of magic and half of them were destroyed.

Brian, who had not let go of her hand, dragged her down to the ground just as something she couldn't even identify passed over their heads. The Banachs were crouching down behind a small shed and Stewart had disappeared. Before she could even begin to worry about where he was, she was startled by the sound of several gun shots and Stewart's face appeared briefly at the window of the room that Declan was being held in.

Signalling to Connell with his hand, Brian looked into her eyes, formed his mouth into a shush, and nodded towards the house. And they were on the move again, straight across the yard to the window that was now open. Stewart met them, and helping her over the window ledge, she found herself confronted by the glazed and vacant eyes of her cousin. As they all crowded into the small room, she almost tripped over the body of a man who was slumped face down on the floor, a pool of blood seeping out from beneath him.

She could hear the fight in the other part of the house. Explosions and yelling emanating from where Morgan and Jean were attacking. Stewart, standing close to the door suddenly jumped back. "Incoming" he yelled as he dove for the floor. Rhonwen found herself crushed behind Brian with the corner of the narrow bed rammed into her back. The door splintered as a bolt of blue light smashed through it. She could feel both Connell and Brian powering up their Amulets. "Are you okay with him?" Brian asked Stewart nodding towards Declan. "No problem". Stewart answered.

"We have to be ready for when Gavin calls us." Brian said quietly. I'll go through the door first, Rhonwen you stay behind me, and Connell and Neve follow. Both of you girls need to stay as close to our backs as you can without us all tripping over each other. OK?"

A massive explosion shook the whole house and smoke filled the room. As it started to clear, Rhonwen looked through the broken door to find that the house was rapidly turning into a pile of rubble. She could see Erik on the other side of what used to be the other end of the house, wrestling with a tall dark-haired man who seemed to match his considerable size. It obviously took a lot of effort, but she watched Erik subdue his opponent. A quick twist of his head by Erik's massive hands, and he dropped like a stone.

Before she had time to even register her shock, Gavin's voice boomed, its timbre low like a growl. This was quickly followed by a scream filled with agony, and then a sort of stillness settled across the rubble. But it didn't last. A stream of blue narrowly missed Erik who had ducked out of its path with only a second to spare. Another scream, this time one of pure rage filled the air. Rhonwen saw Gavin jump across what was probably the remains of a sofa and then he was gone from her line of sight.

Moving cautiously, Brian led their small group further into the house towards the battle. Finding shelter behind some fallen roof timbers, he silently told them to settle behind him, mouthing the injunction to be quiet and still. Her stomach still roiling from the fear, Rhonwen found herself getting increasingly nauseated, and by the look of pallor in Neve's face, she was pretty sure she wasn't the only one. Shifting her body slightly so she could reach the other woman, she grasped her hand and smiled as confidently as she could.

It had felt like they had been crouched down still and silent for hours, but it was only minutes before the noise stopped, and Gavin called Brian and Connell to his side. The four of them stepped carefully over the debris and several dead bodies, making there way to where the other's stood. Keira/Scáthach was standing between Morgan and Jean chained up in some sort of web, only it was made of electricity. Or at least that's what is it looked like to Rhonwen.

She was snarling and straining at her bonds, her eyes filled with rage and her lips curled in derision.

"So, you think that you have won, don't you"! She spat at Gavin who seemed to be the focus of her hatred. Her gaze slid to the side, and a wicked, knowing smile formed on Keira's beautiful mouth. But although it was Keira's voice that spoke the curses she proceeded to scream at Morgan, there was something quite different about it. It was more guttural and there was a strange inflection in her tone.

Having finished with Morgan, she turned once more to Gavin, but as her eyes moved, she spotted something behind them. Instantly stilled, she sneered. Turning to look behind her, Rhonwen saw Stewart emerge from what was left of the house, Declan in toe. The expression of horror on Stewart's face as he looked at Keira, possessed by evil and captive to magic, bared her friend's soul, and Rhonwen's heart went out to him. She felt Brian stiffen, as he too had witnessed his friend's pain.

It was Connell's voice that called her back to the scene in front of them. "Where's Rouan?" His voice thick with fear, Connell was turning, searching, his wife clinging to his arm, a terrified expression contorting her face. It was only then that Rhonwen realised that both Erik and Rouan were not among them. Gavin quickly moved to the Banachs side his expression reassuring and his voice gentle. "He has been wounded, but he will recover. Erik is with him now and will guard him while we finish our task".

Keira/Scáthach opened her mouth to speak, but before she could utter a sound, Morgan made a gesture with her hand. The mouth worked but no sound came out. "That is enough from you"! Morgan snapped angrily. Then turning to Gavin, she raised her still perfectly arched brow, her expression questioning. "Are we ready to do this?

If you could come over and retrieve Keira's Amulet while we hold her, we can get this over with."

A fleeting look of irritation crossed his face, but he nodded in assent and quickly moved over to Morgan's side. Keira/Scáthach continued to twist frantically in her bonds but Gavin had no problem pulling the Amulet on its chain over her head. The moment he did she went limp, no longer able to resist the magical bonds.

Turning back to the still shocked and distressed parents" he asked them gently if they were ready. "The sooner we do this the faster we can get Rouan into his mother's care". Gavin added.

Taking a huge breath, Connell visibly calmed himself, and putting his arm around Neve held her close to him in a tight embrace. A strangled sob escaped as Neve pulled herself up, straightening her back, she nodded at her husband. "We are ready." Connell said in a firm voice.

Gavin quickly moved over to where Stewart stood and taking hold of Declan's limp hand he looked into his eyes searchingly. "He remains enthralled". He looked up at the hills behind them and swept his gaze across the vicinity. "He should have been released when the magic user responsible died. We might yet have more company. Stewart would you please tie him up to something, so he doesn't wander off. I will need you to keep watch."

Stewart quickly organised Declan into a safe spot within the rubble and tied him up with what looked like an old curtain cord. Then, taking a few minutes to check the weapons he had slung around his body, he nodded at them and was gone, ranging out around the back of what was left of the building.

Within a minute, the Immortals had organised them all into a circle around Keira/Scáthach, the guardians of the Amulets in front of their supports. Without Rouan, Jean had to go it alone. Both Morgan and Gavin were needed to add the weight of their power to the spell, but they now had four of the Amulets as well as the only blade that ever came close to killing the Goddess.

"I know your tired and this will take everything you have, but we can do this if we focus all of our attention right here and right now". Gavin said as he took his position to the side of Brian and Rhonwen, while Morgan moved up next to Jean to complete the circle, a small venomous smile playing around her mouth. "Back to hell for you, my dear." She snarled as she started to weave the spell.

Rhonwen could feel Brian open his mind, focusing on the conduits that channelled his innate magic. As it filled him up with it's strangely arousing energy, her own body started to tingle. It was like little sparks of electricity collecting all through her cells. As the energy began to swirl around her chest, gathering into a focus, the palm of her hand, resting on Brian's shoulder seemed to fuse to him. It was as if there was no barrier between them, and, more powerfully than ever before during practice, she felt the pull. Her own magic was being sucked out of her.

Too fast, she thought, startled and fearful, every instinct wanting to snatch her hand away. Brian must have sensed her terror. She felt a hesitation and the flow of power slowed. Her sense of the very essence of her life being dragged out of her disappeared, and her terror subsided. The rhythm they had established through hours of training took over and leaning her forehead on Brian's back, Rhonwen gave herself to the bond.

The sound of Jean's voice shouting at Connell jerked her out of the symbiosis. Looking over Brian's shoulder, Rhonwen became aware of several things at once. A large dangerous looking man was almost on top of Connell and Neve, hotly pursued by Stewart. The couple's stream of magical energy was wavering and losing its form as they were startled out of their focus. As she looked closely at Keira, Rhonwen realised that she was collapsed on the ground, a smoky shadow of something other than Keira straining to cling to the unconscious girl.

As the Banachs went down under the onslaught of their attacker, the circle broke. Gavin had turned to lend his aid to Stewart to protect the Banachs just as a tall blond woman darted out of nowhere into the circle through the gap, her hand extended to the ephemeral Scáthach.

Morgan shifted her focus to deal with this new intruder, but within a blink of an eye, Scáthach had let go of Keira, and as her ghostly hand touched the other woman, she seemed to merge with her.

Morgan's cry of outrage just added to the noise of the battle going on over the Banachs bodies. Before Scáthach's new vessel could evade her Morgan struck. A stream of power rushing from her fingertips, the Immortal blasted the woman into ash, the shadow of Scáthach disappearing as she disintegrated.

Almost immediately, she heard a scream of rage, and a bolt of blue fire came from somewhere behind them. Rhonwen was abruptly disconnected from Brian as he jostled past her, his face twisted with a mix of fear and rage. Stewart was down, smoke curling up from his body. Everything was chaotic. Gavin had just dispatched the Banachs attacker when a blast from somewhere outside the ruins barely missed him. Tracing it back to its source she saw Jean racing through the rubble, his gaze fixed on something she couldn't see.

Within moments all was calm again. The traces of smoke quickly dissipating in the light breeze, and the semi dark of the early night descending on them. Looking around her Rhonwen was surprised to find Morgan cradling Keira in her arms, a genuine look of concern on her face. Brian had reached Stewart, his hand shaking as he turned his friend over. She rushed to join him, noting as she ran past them that Gavin was looking after the Banachs.

As she knelt next to Stewart's body, she felt a rush of tears filling her eyes. Then he groaned, and looking closely she realised that his clothes had been burned away along his side, and that although there was an ugly wound, he was whole. She looked up into Brian's eyes and saw a look of such profound relief, that she felt a small twist in her guts. A pang of jealousy that she was immediately ashamed of.

They were all preoccupied tending to the injured when Jean returned. He reported that he had found another member of the coven further up the hill, sneering a little as he commented that their initial surveillance had obviously been flawed as there had been a portal in the shed. Without waiting for a response, he joined his mother and Keira, who was starting to stir out of her unconscious state.

Gavin's frown was the only recognition he gave to Jean's comment. Turning back to the Banachs he helped them to their feet telling them all that Erik would be along any minute with some transport, and then he came over to check on Stewart. "It looks like he will be OK he said after looking over the wound. Very sore for a while, and it will scar but he is alive. You all are."

Brian was not surprised to hear the relief in the Immortal's voice. He had been all too aware of the risks that they had taken, but they had won. Scáthach was gone.

Before he could continue, Morgan's called to them. Keira was sitting up, her eyes were clear but the expression in them vague and unfocused. Gavin fished the Ninian Amulet out of his pocket where he had hastily shoved it during the fight. Handing it to Morgan, she gently hung it back around Keira's neck. "This will help her to return to us. But we still need to find the Tierney stone."

"Safe with me." Erik's voice came out of the dark.

None of them had heard his approach. "I found it on the body of the guy who attacked Rouan". He continued as he joined them, making a beeline for Gavin and pressing something into the Immortals's hand. He immediately turned to the Banachs, his voice soft and reassuring. "Rouan is in hospital. He needed surgery as I could not stop the bleeding." "But how did you explain his injuries?" Neve asked, her voice filled with anxiety. Eriks face split into a lopsided grin. "The advantage of having a "Police Liaison" person. Inspector Riley has sorted out the cover story. A car accident, apparently."

Pleased as she was that Rouan was safe, Rhonwen found herself focused on the Amulet in Gavin's hand. She felt drawn to it; an impulse to get up from where she was kneeling and go to it was getting stronger and harder to resist. As if suddenly aware of her need, Gavin turned to her, his expression puzzled. He stared at her intently, and she stared back just as intently but at his hand. The tug of the Amulet becoming painful to resist.

"The Amulet is linked to Declan. You shouldn't be feeling this attraction, unless;" Gavin suddenly turned and looked back into the ruins of the farmhouse. Moving quickly, he made his way to the safe little hollow in the debris where they had secreted the unconscious man. He returned with Declan's body in his arms. Laying him carefully on the ground, they could all see the gaping hole in his chest.

She looked at her cousin, trying to feel some sort of regret or sadness, but nothing would come. All she could think about was the Amulet. A part of her was horrified at her callousness, but, down deep in her heart, she knew that she was glad he was gone. Looking up at Gavin, her eyes dry and clear, she held out her hand. As he looked back at her, she felt like he was drilling down into her soul, stripping away all the layers, all of her defences.

He beckoned silently, without a word, and she found herself standing. Pushing her errant hair back off her face, she walked to his side. "Rhonwen Tierney. Do you accept the obligations and consequences of your family's inheritance? Do you choose to be the guardian of this Amulet?" He said in a powerful and sonorous voice as he held the stone out to her on the palm of his hand.

Standing there, keenly aware of the others watching her, Rhonwen resisted the impulse to grab the Amulet from his outstretched hand. Raising her head proudly, her heart beating so loudly she was sure the world could hear it, she replied using as much gravity as possible. "I choose to take my place as the guardian of my family's Amulet".

Gavin held it out to her, the smooth stone encased in its golden setting and dangling from a silken cord. As she took it in her hand, it flared a clear blue, with touches of green flashing through its centre. Rhonwen marvelled at the beauty of it, and as she nestled it against her chest, she felt a sense of completeness.

EPILOGUE

Accompanying Erik on one last sweep of the property, Brian looked back down the hill towards what was left of the farmhouse. The shed at the back where they had found the portal was still standing. However, he would never have recognised the portal for what it was. There was no outward sign of anything unusual about the back wall to him, but Erik had immediately recognised the sliver of a mirror hanging from a nail on one of the uprights. This was obviously how the last of their attackers had slipped in behind them.

With Scáthach banished once more, Gavin and Morgan quickly seized the opportunity to return to Morgan's farm, where they knew they would be well-warded. Shifting Stewart and the still dazed Keira out of the ruined farmhouse had been a priority, but the Banachs' need to reassure themselves that Rouan was safe had lent an urgency to the move.

Now, with the rest of the group safely gone, Erik was teaching him how to remove the more obvious traces of magic from the surrounding area and dismantle the traps set by the Stirling coven. In many ways, it was no different from any mopping-up operation that followed a battle.

The sound of several cars behind the trees to their right startled him. Peering through the branches, he saw a police car and a military all-terrain vehicle driving slowly towards the property gate. "Time for us to leave", Erik said quietly, and they slipped quickly down the hill towards the shed. As he moved into the darkened building, he glanced back towards the rubble where they had left Declan as the police car swung past the door. Brian was not surprised to see the Inspector's face at one of the windows, a look of incredulity on his features as the pulsing blue of the portal caught his gaze. Lifting his hand in a quick gesture of acknowledgment, Brian turned away and stepped through the portal with Erik close behind him.

The reports about the significant disturbances around the Scottish city of Stirling took the lead in most news outlets throughout Britain for several days. Witnesses to the astounding sounds and the blue flashes in the sky posted their photos on Facebook and enjoyed their few minutes of fame. However, interest in the Defence Department's "scheduled weapon test" at an old abandoned and derelict farm was quickly superseded as an item of interest by Britain's unexpected loss in Rugby.

www.ingramcontent.com/pod-product-compliance
Lightning Source LLC
Chambersburg PA
CBHW030541310726
48979CB00010B/1988/J

* 9 7 8 0 9 9 9 2 6 6 8 6 1 *